JASON AND THE ANGEL

BY HAL DICKENS

Please visit the Youtube channel: Hal Dickens Songwriter and go to the "Jason And The Angel - novel" playlist for added emotional impact to this story. There you will find music and songs written specifically for certain scenes from this book.

CHAPTER ONE

The searing pain in his wrists told him his suicide attempt had failed. Jason Wilkes opened his eyes and anger filled him. *I should be dead*, he thought as he looked around the darkened room. *Where the hell am I? Why am I alive?*

There was a machine with flashing lights beeping to the right of him and he traced the line running from it down to his arm. He saw his arms were bound to the railings of the bed at the elbows and his wrists were heavily wrapped in bandages. *Fuck!* his head screamed and he grit his teeth. He remembered slashing his wrists with the long kitchen knife and lying down in the bathtub which was followed by a feeling of peace as his life poured out of him.

He looked again at the flashing lights on the machine and tried to relax. *It figures*, he thought. *I can't do anything right.*

Why?! he thought again. *Why am I alive?!*

He opened his eyes and was startled to see someone sitting in a chair to his left by his bedside. "Shit! You scared me!"

He could barely make out the shape of a woman but couldn't see her features. She sat motionless and didn't say anything.

"They sent you to spy on me?" he asked and chuckled. "It's not like I can hurt myself tied to the bed like this."

She stayed silent and he got angry.

"Nurse, tell me how I got here!" he said and winced from the searing pain when he clenched his fists.

"Why?" she asked, her voice gentle and non-threatening in her British accent.

"Why what?"

"Why did you do it? Why did you try to kill yourself?"

He stared at where he thought her eyes were and didn't care what she thought of him.

"Because I don't have a reason to live anymore. There's no point to my life. I have no purpose. Does that answer your question?"

She didn't answer and he got angry. "You know I'll just try again when they let me go."

Her hand reached out of the darkness and gently touched his.

"You're wrong," she softly said. "You do have a purpose."

Jason's eyes filled with tears and he looked away from her and stared up at the ceiling.

"My wife is dead and my daughter's too busy to talk to me anymore. I have no one. What's the point of living anymore? They should have left me to die."

The woman's fingers closed around his hand and a sweet warmth ebbed into his arm.

"No, Jason," she said in that gentle voice of hers. "There's a reason why you're alive."

He laughed. "Well if there is I don't know what it is!"

There was silence between them again and he looked at her. "Why do you care anyway? You're just a nurse assigned to watch over a pathetic man who tried to kill himself."

The warmth from her hand moved into his chest now and he shivered at how suddenly safe he felt.

"I care because…."

He tried to focus on her face again. "You care because why? I don't understand."

"Just know that I'm here for you now, Jason," she answered in that soft soothing voice of hers. "I won't let you hurt yourself again. Your life *has* a purpose. I'm here to help you find it."

He burst out laughing and her hand left his. Closing his eyes tightly, he tried to block out the pain from his torn wrists. When he opened them again, she was gone. He sighed and tears rolled down his cheeks. A nurse suddenly walked into the room and opened the blinds so Jake could see the snow falling outside.

"Well, look who's finally awake!" she said cheerily. Her face was round and pretty and her short blonde hair curled out from under her nurse's cap. Jason knew this wasn't the same woman because she didn't have the lovely British accent the other nurse had.

"It's hard to believe it's only a month until Christmas, isn't it?" she said happily.

"Would you send the other nurse back in? I need to ask her something."

"What other nurse?" she asked as she checked the beeping machine by his bed. "I'm the only nurse on duty tonight."

He grit his teeth. "I want the other nurse! I need to talk to her!"

She frowned at him. "I *told* you there is no other nurse. Do I need to get the doctor?"

His eyes blinked rapidly in frustration. "No! No! Just forget it!"

"I'll check in again later," she said with a look of pity on her face.

"Whatever," he said disgusted and she left the room while the tears flowed down his cheeks again.

I must be losing my mind, he thought. *I know I didn't imagine her.*

He lay there and thought about what she'd said. "My life has a purpose," he chuckled sadly. Closing his eyes, he fell into a deep sleep.

A beautiful woman with wings appeared in his mind. "I'll help you," she whispered. "I'll be here for you and help you find your purpose."

His eyes flashed open. "Oh please! Oh please let it be true!"

Soft lips touched his and the kiss was so gentle that he moaned loudly.

"It *is* true," she whispered. "I'll show you what life can be like when it has meaning."

A warmth flowed through him then and he felt again that wonderful feeling of being safe. "Oh God," he whispered. "Please let it be true."

CHAPTER TWO

Over the next few days, they sent professionals to talk with him. Jason forced himself to answer their questions about whether he'd try to hurt himself again. He must have convinced them he wouldn't because on the third day, they unbound his arms from the bed. A few hours before he was to be released, a mental health specialist sat by his bed and looked at him. Her eyes were warm and kind as she asked, "Are you sure you're ok? You're not depressed in any way?"

Jason was just happy he could get out of the bed and away from the bedpans and crappy food. "The only thing I'm depressed about is having to pay to have my door fixed."

The pretty blonde woman frowned. "What are you talking about? What door?"

"The door the police had to break down to get to me."

"Oh, you don't know, do you?" she said, surprised.

"Know what?"

She smiled. "They didn't have to break your door down. A woman brought you here."

"What?!" he said, shocked. "What woman?"

The specialist stared at him, surprised that he didn't know who had brought him to the hospital. "She wheeled you into the emergency room. She must have had nursing experience because she'd packed your wounds well and bandaged them up before coming here."

"Are you serious?" he asked, his eyes opening wide.

"You wouldn't be alive if it weren't for her. You'd lost a lot of blood."

"Oh my God," Jason whispered.

"It's too bad she didn't stay. They wanted to get information about you but she disappeared."

Jason frowned. "Disappeared? What do you mean?"

"Before the nurse could ask her any questions, she left you there and walked out the exit."

"What did she look like?" he asked, his heart beating fast.

The specialist looked at him like he was crazy. "Don't *you* know who she is?"

Jason lifted his head from the pillow and shook it back and forth. "No, I don't. Please tell me what she looked like. I need to know."

The woman stared at him and after a moment of silence said, "I was told she was very beautiful. That's all I know."

His head sank back down onto the pillow and he looked up at the ceiling. "I wonder who she was."

The specialist lightly touched his arm and softly said, "Maybe it was your guardian angel."

Jason looked at her and shivered. "Maybe it was."

CHAPTER THREE

The police dropped him off at his place and he slowly walked up the flight of stairs to his apartment. He stared at the door for a moment before taking his key out to open it.

It was dark inside. Cautiously, he walked towards the bathroom and hesitated. He took a deep breath and switched on the light. "Oh my God!" he cried when he saw the blood. The trail led from the bathtub towards the living room. He fell to his knees at the ghastly sight and began to cry.

"Horrifying, isn't it?" a gentle voice said from behind him as a soft hand touched his shoulder.

Jason looked over his shoulder and saw a woman in a pure white dress standing behind him. "Is it you?" he asked, his voice quivering. "Are you the one who saved me?"

"Go into the living room and sit down," she said in a firm voice. "I'll clean this up and then we need to talk."

Jason stood up and she walked by him into the bathroom. She was shorter than him by a foot. He stepped into the darkness of the living room and sank down into a chair as he watched the woman get a bucket and some towels from the cabinets. He still hadn't seen her face and was curious. It took a few minutes as she removed all traces of his blood. Finally she was finished and walked slowly into the room and sat across from him.

"How are you feeling?" she asked.

"I'm a little shaky from seeing all the blood but I think I'll be alright."

He leaned over to a side table to turn on the lamp there but she said, "Leave it off."

"Alright," he said and waited.

"Are you going to try to hurt yourself again?"

"Maybe," he answered truthfully.

She sighed and softly said, "*Jason.*"

"You wanted the truth, didn't you?"

"What am I going to do with you?" she sighed.

He couldn't stand the suspense any longer. "Who the hell are you?! Why do you care?!"

She got up and moved to stand over him. "Turn on the light," she ordered.

His hand shook as he reached for the light. He hesitated. "I don't want to. I'm scared."

"Don't be scared, Jason," she said in that sweet gentle voice of hers. "Turn on the light."

He turned the lamp on and looked up at her face. "Oh my God," he whispered.

She looked down at him, her long golden hair curling softly about her shoulders. "Are you surprised?"

Her eyes were the kindest eyes he'd ever seen and their beauty took his breath away. "My god, you're beautiful, so beautiful," he whispered.

She smiled. "Thank you, Jason. You're not so bad yourself, you know."

He lowered his head and quietly said, "I'm old and useless."

Her face turned sad. "Don't say that. Don't *ever* say that. It's not true."

He looked up at her and wished he was twenty five years younger.

"Tomorrow is the first day of the rest of your life, Jason," she softly said. "You need to start again with a clean slate."

He stared at her intensely and her mouth opened into a wide smile.

"Who are you?" he asked.

She knelt in front of him and gently took his hands in hers. Looking deeply into his eyes, she quietly said, "I'm your guardian angel, Jason and I'm going to show you how important your life is."

CHAPTER FOUR

Jason sat silent for a while and felt very small in the angel's eyes. She studied his wavy brown hair and his handsome features and waited for him to speak.

"I don't know what to say," he finally said. "Is this some kind of a joke?"

"This is no joke, Jason," she answered.

"If you're an angel than where are your wings?"

She turned slowly and he noticed two small feathery nubs sticking out of the edges of her upper back. "They're retracted now," she said and turned around to face him again.

Jason felt a small shiver run up his spine. Was this really happening?

"I don't know what to say," he said again. "You're an angel but you're not invisible. How can that be? I must be dreaming."

She smiled. "Believe me, Jason, you're not dreaming. I can take a physical form whenever I wish. Now why don't you start at the beginning and tell me why you tried to kill yourself?"

He looked down at his bandaged wrists and whispered, "I'm nothing. No one cares if I live or die."

The angel gently touched his chin and made him look at her. "Please don't say that, Jason."

"But it's true," he said, his eyes sad. "They demoted me at work and my wife died years ago. My daughter's too busy for me now and I can't get a date. That's the whole pathetic story. I'm all alone."

She felt an ache in her heart. "I know you are. I wish I could have done something about it earlier."

"You've been watching me?" he asked, surprised.

She smiled. "I've watched over you since you were a baby, Jason. I was there when your dog died and I was there when your wife passed away. Didn't you feel my presence?"

His eyes opened wide. "I did in a way. I never knew what it was but I felt like someone was watching me."

He was curious. "Can you read my mind?"

She laughed lightly. "No, no, I can't read your mind!"

"Do you know *everything* about me?"

"No," Rebecca replied. "That's why I'm here now. Before I can help you I need to know why you did what you did. There's got to be more than what you already told me."

"Can we talk about this tomorrow? I'm very tired."

"Of course," the angel answered. "Take your time. I have all the time in the world."

"I never asked you what your name was," he said.

She smiled sweetly at him. "My name's Rebecca, Jason."

"That's a pretty name," he said as he gazed over her perfect form.

"Like what you see?" she asked, a sly smile on her face.

He looked away, embarrassed and the angel laughed lightly.

"Hey, it's ok if you look! I don't mind. In fact, I find it flattering!"

"You really don't mind?" he asked, looking back at her.

Her eyes twinkled. "Not at all. Take a good look."

She stood up and slowly turned in a circle so he could admire her figure until she was facing him again. The look on his face said it all and she smiled. "Ok, did you get that out of your system? Can we move on?"

He just stared at her and she said, "Look Jason, most people I watch over consider me to be some kind of holy figure and don't treat me like the woman I was. I appreciate your obvious admiration but now you're making me feel uncomfortable."

Jason quickly looked down. "I'm sorry but I can't help it. You're so beautiful, Rebecca."

She felt a twinge in her heart and changed the subject. "Have you had dinner?"

"They fed me before releasing me. But what about you?"

Rebecca laughed. "Seriously? Don't you know that angels don't need to eat?!"

"Oh," he said glumly.

"Oh, don't get me wrong," she said quickly. "I love a good meal but I can go a long time without one."

"Oh," he said again, his eyes dead.

She watched him closely as he stood up and began to start a fire in the small fireplace. There was a large artificial Christmas tree in the corner and he switched the lights on so the tinsel glittered brightly. He sat down in the large leather chair facing the fire and stared blankly into the crackling flames.

Rebecca went to him and knelt by the chair. Jason looked at her and she reached for his hand. His eyes searched hers for understanding and her fingers wrapped around his. "I'm not going anywhere, Jason," she whispered. "I'll stay here all night long if you want me to."

Tears filled his eyes and she got up and sat on the edge of the chair so she could pull him towards her. Her warm body was comforting and he pressed his head against her side as she ran her fingers through his hair.

"Thank you," he said softly and they sat like that for a long time until the fire began to die out.

When the last of the embers still glowed, Jason looked into the angel's eyes and saw only kindness there. She quietly said, "It's time I put you to bed. You need your rest so you can heal."

He let her lead him to his bedroom and she watched as he went into his small bathroom and brushed his teeth. She had found his pajamas hanging on the back of the bathroom door and handed them to him.

"I don't usually wear those," he said and immediately regretted his words.

She smiled. "I know. I thought you might want to put them on though because *I'm* here."

"You know?" he asked, alarmed. "You've seen me naked?"

She giggled. "Of course, silly! I'm your guardian angel!"

"But...." he meekly said.

"Look, you don't have to wear them if you don't want to. I won't mind," she said, hanging them back on the hook.

Jason went back to the bedroom and began to slowly undress. The angel didn't look away and he felt very embarrassed when he got to his underwear.

"Go ahead," she encouraged. "I said that I don't mind."

"Could you look away?" he asked, pleading.

"Would it make you feel less nervous if I did?"

"Yes," he whispered.

She looked away and he quickly pulled his underwear off and climbed into bed. He pulled the covers up to his neck and said, "Ok, you can look now."

She sat down by the edge of the bed and noticed him shivering.

"Everything's going to be alright, Jason," she said softly. "Trust me."

"Will you stay in here with me tonight?" he asked quietly.

The angel's hand was as light as a feather when it touched his cheek. "Of course I will," she whispered.

He closed his eyes but suddenly opened them. Rebecca saw they were filled with fear.

"What's wrong, Jason?"

"Do you think God hates me?" he asked quietly.

"Why would you ask that? Of course he doesn't hate you," she replied.

"But I tried to kill myself. I know that's a sin."

The angel squeezed his hand to reassure him. "No, Jason. God doesn't hate you. You just went a little astray. All you need is guidance."

"Do *you* hate me for what I did?" he softly said.

The angel's eyes twinkled with kindness. "No, I don't hate you, Jason although over time you and I will have to talk about what made you do it. Before you can go forward we have to fix what's wrong."

"What if it can't be fixed?" he asked, his eyes sad.

She was quiet for a moment and finally said, "I'm going to do my best to help you. Please trust me."

His eyes looked into hers with hope and she switched off the light on the nightstand by the bed.

"Thank you, God for sending me this angel," he whispered.

"Jason, God didn't send me," her soft voice said. "I heard your call and answered it."

He was surprised. "My call?"

"Yes, your heart called out to me."

"Thank you, Rebecca," he whispered.

"Sleep well and dream of nice things, Jason. You're safe with me."

He let her words sink into his head and his eyes slowly closed. The warmth of her hand holding his gave him comfort and he fell into a peaceful sleep.

CHAPTER FIVE

He awoke to the wonderful smell of bacon in the air. Sitting up in bed, he looked down at his bandaged wrists and frowned. *I guess it really happened*, he thought. *I was hoping it was all a bad dream.*

Jason got his pajamas and put them on. Then he brushed his teeth and combed his hair. The smell of bacon was stronger now and his stomach growled.

"There you are," Rebecca said happily when he entered the kitchen. "I hope you're hungry. I made you bacon and eggs."

"It smells wonderful. Thank you," he said and sat down at the table. She'd already set it and soon loaded his plate with the most perfectly cooked bacon and eggs he'd ever seen.

"I always burn mine a little," he said as his mouth watered. "This looks perfect."

She sat down across from him and watched him begin to eat. His wrists ached badly and he had trouble holding the fork.

"Here, let me do it," she said and took the fork from him.

"You're going to feed me?" he asked, surprised.

"Yes, if you don't mind."

He gazed at her beautiful face and opened his mouth. Rebecca smiled and scooped up some eggs with the fork.

"I'll bet no one's done this for you since you were little," she said, amused.

"You're right. It's been a very long time."

The angel began to feed him and every now and then he closed his eyes and moaned happily. "This is the best bacon I've ever had."

She smiled. "I'm glad."

Jason finished every morsel on his plate and smiled at her. "That was amazing. Thank you, Rebecca."

She looked him in the eyes. "It's time we talked more but first I'm guessing that you probably have some questions for me."

He thought about the night he tried to kill himself and asked, "How did I get to the hospital? My door wasn't broken down and they told me a woman brought me there."

The angel quietly said, "I saw what you'd done, Jason so I took care of your wrists and carried you there."

"You carried me there?!" he asked, incredulous.

She smiled. "Actually, I flew you there. I'm a lot stronger than I look."

"Thank you. You saved my life."

"What else would you like to ask me?"

Jason remembered something he'd always wondered about and asked, "How big is the universe? Does it go on forever? I've always wanted to know."

Rebecca frowned. "Yes, it goes on forever as far as I know. I have no idea how and I don't ask why. It just *does*."

He sat still and she grew impatient. "Seriously? That's all you want to ask me? How big the universe is?! You must have something better than that to ask me."

"Ok," he said softly. "Why me? Why did you save *me*?"

"I already told you I heard you calling," she answered.

"But I thought you were always around. Why would you need to hear me calling?"

"I'm *not* always around, Jason. I do watch over others, you know."

"Are they as pathetic as I am?" he asked, his eyes sad.

Rebecca reached for his hand and held it. "You're not pathetic, Jason."

"But why me?" he asked, still not understanding. "People kill themselves all the time. Why don't you save all of them?"

The angel lowered her head. "They can't all be saved, Jason. Unfortunately, some must die so they can live again and advance."

"Advance? Advance to what?"

Rebecca lifted her head and looked at him. "Advance so they can become better people. Sometimes it takes many lifetimes."

"But why *me*?" he asked again. "What makes *me* so special?"

Her eyes seemed to twinkle and she softly said, "That's why I'm here, Jason. I'm going to help you find out."

He suddenly thought of the recent vicious killings of two women in the neighborhood and a rage filled him.

He stood up. "What about people who are raped and murdered?! Why doesn't God help them?!" He pounded his fist on the table and winced from the pain in his wrist. "Why not them?!"

"Please sit down," she said quietly. "Calm down and I'll tell you."

Jason felt his heart pounding in his chest and sat down. Rebecca waited for his heartrate to slow before continuing.

"That's what I like about you, Jason. There's a passion and intensity in you that's unusual. We can use that."

The angel could tell that he didn't understand what she meant.

"Never mind that for now. To answer your question, God created all of us but what we do here on earth is of our own doing. We make our own decisions, good or bad and those decisions decide how we advance spiritually. He doesn't interfere even when bad things happen."

"Then why are *you* here? Aren't you interfering?"

"I'm not interfering. You see, Jason, you're here for a specific reason. You just haven't found out what it is yet."

"And how do I do that?" he asked angrily.

"With my help," she answered softly. "I'm going to help guide you."

Jason frowned. "I don't understand why some people turn evil. What makes them do bad things?"

Rebecca thought for a moment and quietly said, "I've been asked that question before and the only thing I can say with certainty is that they lost what most of us have."

"What's that?" Jason asked.

The angel smiled and lightly touched his chest. "They lost what you have inside of you, Jason. Empathy for others. It's one of the things that make you special."

"I'm special?" he asked, surprised.

"Yes, you are."

"I wish I could find someone who felt that way about me," he said quietly. "I've always wanted to feel cherished for who I am."

"Didn't your wife feel that way about you, Jason?"

"No," he said sadly, shaking his head. "I realized over time that she wasn't into me. I thought she was the one but I was wrong."

"What do you mean, Jason? Didn't you both love each other?"

He stared into the angel's eyes and she saw the intense loneliness in them. "Have you ever been in a crowd but felt incredibly alone?" he asked.

"Yes," she answered. "Unfortunately, I have."

"That's how I felt with her. For a long time it didn't dawn on me what was wrong until one night when we were done making love. She looked at me and there was no passion in her eyes. All those years we had sex it wasn't intimate if that makes sense. We were like two strangers going through the motions. Oh, it felt great but there was no closeness."

Rebecca stayed silent and Jason continued. "A few days before she died we were lying in bed and she suddenly grabbed my hand and looked at me sadly. I asked her what was wrong and she said, "I'm sorry I'm not your soulmate, Jason."

Rebecca felt her throat tighten in grief. "And what did you say?"

He lowered his head and she saw his shoulders sag. "I didn't say anything because I knew she was right. Neither one of us was the other's soulmate. We were just two lonely people who had a few things in common and that's all. Don't get me wrong. I cared very much for her as she did for me but the intense love I'd always wanted with a woman wasn't there."

"Do you regret marrying her?" Rebecca asked.

Jason looked at the angel and smiled. "Oh no. Not for an instant because we had a beautiful daughter together."

"Tell me about her, Jason."

His face turned sad again. "Susanna doesn't talk to me much anymore. She's busy with her job and her boyfriend. She doesn't have time for me. I don't know what happened but whenever I call her she has to get off the phone after a minute or so. We used to be close. I was a good father to her. I just don't understand what happened."

The angel lightly touched his arm. "I'm sorry, Jason. I truly am."

Tears filled his eyes and he suddenly stood up. "I don't want to talk anymore."

The angel smiled. "I have an idea. Would you walk with me?"

"Where?"

"Somewhere special," she answered and stood up.

"Maybe I should go back to bed. I still feel weak."

"No. We're going for a walk," she said firmly.

Jason didn't want to argue with her so he found his winter coat and Rebecca helped him put it on.

"Ready?" she asked.

"Won't you be cold?" he asked. "You could wear one of my coats if you'd like."

Rebecca smiled. "I'm an angel, remember? The weather doesn't affect me."

He frowned. "Oh, sorry. I only thought…."

"Look, if it makes you feel better then I'll wear one," she said.

He led her to the closet and she picked out a warm coat. Her long hair spilled over the collar and Jason couldn't stop staring at her. She was the most beautiful woman he'd ever seen.

"What's wrong?" she asked. "Why are you looking at me like that?"

He quickly looked away and opened the door. "I'm sorry," he said and stepped into the hallway. She closed the door behind her and followed him down the stairs. Rebecca seemed to float as she walked and her bare feet hitting the steps made no sound compared to Jason's heavy footsteps. They stepped outside into the chilly winter air and Rebecca noticed Jason stumble a bit on the ice. She grabbed him around the waist and looked up at his face. "I've got you," she said. "Hold on to me."

Jason hesitated for a moment but slowly placed his arm around the angel's shoulder. "Ready?" she asked.

He nodded and as they walked by people she quietly said, "Everyone has a story, Jason. How your story ends is up to you."

After a few blocks, Jason felt a rush of weakness overtake him. Rebecca sensed it and quietly said, "We're almost there. Lean into me."

Jason leaned against the woman and she took his weight easily. She felt him shiver again and hugged him tighter around the waist. "Don't worry," she whispered. "I won't let you fall."

Jason saw the church on the corner and he suddenly knew she was taking him there. They made it to the front door and he felt very faint. She wrenched open the big wooden door and helped him inside. Jason staggered a few feet and Rebecca gently lowered him into a back pew. She sat down next to him and looked very concerned. He sagged against the hard back of the pew and closed his eyes so his head would stop going around in circles.

"I'm sorry I made you walk," the angel said. "I thought you'd be stronger."

His eyes felt weary when he reopened them. He gazed at the lovely woman sitting next to him. "I guess the whole experience has been a little too much for me," he said quietly. "Waking up in the hospital after trying to kill myself and then finding out an angel saved me. Yeah, it's just a little bit overwhelming."

Rebecca held his hand. "Breathe deeply and look around. Tell me what you see.”

Jason looked towards the front of the church and saw the large Christmas trees on either side of the altar. They were adorned with glowing blue lights and round gold ornaments. The sweet smell of pine was in the air and he breathed in the scent. There was a feeling of great peace in this place and he looked at the angel and smiled.

“It’s beautiful, isn’t it?” she asked. “The perfect place to speak to God in.”

Jason looked at the altar again. A great cross with Jesus crucified to it hung on the wall behind it. There were large green wreaths on both sides of it and for a moment he saw nothing else but Jesus’s face.

“He died for our sins,” the angel said. “You need to live again, Jason so your life’s not a waste. You owe him that.”

Tears blurred his eyes then and she asked, “What do you hear?”

He closed his eyes and listened intently to the silence of the church.

“Nothing,” he said. “I hear nothing.”

“Open your eyes, Jason.”

He opened his eyes and the angel pulled him close so his head rested on her shoulder. Her arm went around his waist and she whispered, “Listen closely, Jason and tell me what you hear.”

He felt the swell of the angel’s breasts against his arm and a wonderful feeling of being secure flooded his senses. Listening intensely for any sound, he closed his eyes again and she waited patiently. Jason sank against her and it was if his ears had always been blocked but now were suddenly open.

“I can hear you breathing,” he whispered. “I’m not alone. You’re here with me and you care.”

The warmth from the angel’s body seeped through his coat and she lightly kissed his forehead. “Yes, Jason,” she whispered. “I care and so does God. Trust in him and I’ll help you find out what kind of man you truly are. Will you put your faith in me to help you do that?”

He softly said, "Yes" and she felt him drifting off.

"Sleep Jason," she whispered. "God and I will watch over you until you wake."

He opened his eyes and stared up at her face. "I wish I'd known you when you were alive, Rebecca."

She smiled and he closed his eyes again and snuggled against her. After a few minutes, she knew he'd fallen into a deep sleep. She felt a tear slide down her face and whispered, "So do I, Jason. So do I."

CHAPTER SIX

When he woke, he felt as if he was in a soft cocoon. His eyes opened and he felt like a small child being held in his mother's arms.

Rebecca's eyes twinkled as she watched him yawn. "You've been asleep the entire morning. I guess you needed that."

Jason snuggled against her as he tried to burrow closer. She hugged him tightly and he looked up at her face. She was smiling at him. "Are you feeling better?"

His eyes looked into hers and the intensity of what he was feeling made him shiver. "I feel so safe right now, Rebecca. I've never felt like this before. I wish we could stay like this forever."

"I'm glad," she said, smiling.

He closed his eyes again and smiled. "My angel's here with me," he whispered.

The silence of the church relaxed him so she let him sleep for a few more minutes but finally woke him. "Jason, you need to eat so you can get stronger. Let's go back home."

His eyes fluttered open and he yawned again. "I don't think I've slept that deeply in my entire life."

"I watched you the entire time. Did you know you had a smile on your face while you slept?"

He rubbed his face against her. "I couldn't help it. I feel so protected right now."

"Let's go home," she said.

He was weaker than before but the angel held him steady as they walked back home. People passing by stared strangely at them, wondering how the small woman who wore no shoes could so easily hold up the man who had trouble walking.

It was an effort to get up the stairs but the angel was there to support him. She got him inside the apartment and helped him into his favorite chair in front of the fireplace. He sagged into it and she frowned. "We need to get you stronger before we progress. You're still too weak."

She left him there and went to the kitchen to cook him a meal. The smell of spices was soon in the air and Jason got up and went into the kitchen. "What are you making?" he asked. "It smells really good."

Rebecca turned away from the stove and smiled. She was stirring something in a pot. "Chicken with dumplings smothered in my special gravy. You had everything I needed right here."

Jason smiled sadly. "At least I can do something right."

Rebecca put the spoon down and went to him. The top of her head came to his chin and she looked up at his face. "I want you to stop beating yourself up, Jason. Will you please do that for me?"

He felt so small in the angel's eyes but he quietly said, "I'll try."

She smiled. "That's all I ask."

Jason sat down and she returned to the stove. "I need to change the dressing on your wrists today," she said, looking over her shoulder at him. "We need them fully healed before we can go on."

"Go on with what?"

"Your story," she replied. "You need to write the next chapter."

He watched as she loaded a plate with the chicken and dumplings. She poured some of the gravy over it all and brought it to him.

"For you," she said, smiling.

Jason picked up a fork and winced. Rebecca frowned and sat by him. "Would you like me to feed you again? Would that be alright?"

"Yes," he whispered, feeling helpless. "*Please.*"

She scooped up a piece of chicken with a dumpling and lifted it to his lips. Jason took it in his mouth and closed his eyes. "Oh wow, this is delicious," he said as he chewed.

He opened his eyes again and Rebecca's smile was even bigger than before. "I'm so glad you like it. It's my own recipe."

He was curious. "Were you a chef when you were alive?"

She laughed lightly and nodded no. "I wish! No....I studied musical theater at Colton. I was a performer."

Jason's eyes lit up. "Really?! A performer?! Did you sing?!"

"Yes. I was pretty good at it too."

"Rebecca?" he said as he thought about what she said. "You know I write songs, don't you?"

"Yes," she answered.

"Would you sing one of them for me sometime?" he asked, his eyes hopeful.

The angel thought of her time on the stage many years before and smiled. "I'd love to, Jason. I'll sing one of your songs."

His face brightened and he felt a little better about himself. "Thank you! Thank you so much!"

Her face turned sad suddenly and she stared down at her lap. She knew she was starting to cross a line She'd let herself get too close.

"Is something wrong?" he asked.

She lifted her head and looked at him. Her eyes were full of pain. "I don't know if I should be here, Jason. I could ask another angel to help you instead of me."

Jason felt anguish in his heart. "Oh no! Please, Rebecca! Don't leave me! Was it something I said or did?!"

She reached for his hands and gently held them. "No, Jason, you did nothing wrong. It's me. I'm the problem."

"What do you mean?!" he said, anxious. "Please, Rebecca, don't leave me! I need you to guide me!"

"We'll see," she said and lowered her head again.

Jason's mind was filled with questions and he had to ask. "Rebecca, what happened to you?"

She looked at him again and her eyes were hard. "You mean how did I die?"

"Yes," he answered quietly.

"Why do you want to know?" she asked, her eyes turning softer.

"Because I care," he replied softly.

"This is why this might not work between us," she said. "No one's ever asked me this before. It's always been about them, never me."

Jason's lower lip quivered. "I don't understand. What am I doing wrong, Rebecca? Am I not allowed to care about you?"

The angel smiled sadly and gently touched his face. "You're doing nothing wrong, Jason."

"Then what?!" he yelled, standing up. "Tell me what's wrong! I don't understand!"

She stood up and looked up into his face. "Usually when I help someone it's one sided. I give them direction and they move on with their lives. You're different."

"How am I different?" he asked, frustrated.

Her eyes twinkled at him. "You care. That's what's wrong. No one's cared about *me* before."

His mouth dropped. "Of course I care! Why wouldn't I?!"

Rebecca gazed deeply into his eyes as she studied them. "You're so kind," she whispered. "Over the years I've watched how you treat your workers and others with respect and dignity. You're the kindest man I've ever met."

Her eyes stirred something deep inside his heart that he'd never felt before. "Rebecca…." he said softly.

The angel moved into his arms and she clung tightly to him as he held her. "Please don't hurt me, Jason. I couldn't bear it."

He didn't understand what she was talking about but whispered, "I'd never hurt you, Rebecca. You're my angel from heaven."

She began to sob against his chest and he held her closer. "Don't cry, my angel. I'm here," he whispered.

CHAPTER SEVEN

After a few minutes, Rebecca pulled away from him and wiped her tears away. They both sat down again and she resumed feeding him. Jason noticed there was something different about her eyes now. She looked at him differently and there was a deeper warmth in them that wasn't there before.

When he was done eating, she looked down at the empty plate. "I guess you like my cooking."

"I loved it," he said and licked his lips. "You're wonderful."

Her lower lip quivered slightly as she looked at him. She got up and took the dish away. Jason watched her take it to the sink and begin to wash it. He stood up and went to her. She gasped as his arms went around her waist. "Thank you, Rebecca," he whispered into her ear.

She leaned back into him and closed her eyes so she could savor the feeling of his arms about her. His nose nuzzled her hair and she turned around to face him. His arms were still around her waist and she lightly pushed back against his chest. "Please, Jason, stop. We mustn't."

"Why, Rebecca? Tell me one good reason why we shouldn't."

Her eyes flooded with tears. "Because I'm an angel, Jason. I'm dead and you're alive."

She walked away from him and went to sit in the chair by the fireplace. Jason followed her and knelt in front of her. "I don't care what you are, Rebecca," he said softly. "I just know what I'm feeling."

She looked down at him and her eyes turned hard. "Don't you understand? It won't work. It's forbidden. Please leave me alone."

Jason stood up then and his face turned red. "I wish I understood," he said angrily. "I care about you and I know you care about me. Why is that so wrong?"

"Because it's forbidden," she said again, her face set in stone.

"Why? What would happen?"

"I don't know," she said, her voice weak.

Jason's eyes looked as if they were on fire and Rebecca could see a hint of what he could be. She smiled and said, "Yes, Jason. That's what I need. Let the passion out."

He felt anger rush through him then and tightly clenched his fists. "Please, Rebecca, don't change the subject. If you don't know what would happen than why not take a chance and find out?"

He reached for her hands and held them. "Please," he whispered. "Give me a chance."

She looked up at him with questioning eyes. "If only I could be sure."

He went to his knees again in front of her. "What do I need to do to show you that I care, Rebecca?"

She stared into his eyes and said, "Be the man I know you can be, Jason."

His eyes brightened. "I'll do anything! Anything at all!"

His fists were clenched tight and Theresa saw blood oozing through the gauze on his wrists. Her eyes opened wide and she stood up quickly. "You fool! Look what you've done!"

Jason looked down at his wrists and said, "I couldn't help it. I'm sorry."

Rebecca led him into the kitchen and made him sit down. She sat down in front of him and had him hold his arms out. "I need to see how bad these are. I don't understand why they're bleeding."

She unwrapped the gauze from his wrists and Jason winced when he saw the angry looking cuts in them. Blood oozed around the sutures and Rebecca looked into his eyes. "Please, Jason. Please stop hurting yourself."

"I didn't mean to," he said, frustrated. "All I did was clench my fists."

"I know," she said, her eyes narrowing as she stared intensely at the wounds.

She went and got a damp washcloth and sat down again. Jason watched as she gently wiped the blood away and rewrapped his wrists. "There, all better." Her face was stern. "Don't clench your fists again, alright?"

"What happens if I do? What will you do?" he asked, amused.

"Just don't do it," she said firmly. "You wouldn't like it if I got angry," she said and lightly touched his face.

"I would think an angel doesn't get angry," he said, surprised.

Her eyes narrowed. "Believe me, even angels get angry."

The phone suddenly rang and Jason went to answer it. "Yes, yes, alright. I'll be there on Monday. See you then."

Rebecca saw that his face was pale when he came back to sit down. "What's wrong?" she asked. "Who was that?"

His eyes were so sad when he looked at her. "It was the library," he said glumly. "They want me back at work on Monday or else I'll be forced to take a leave of absence."

Rebecca felt the rush of anger surge through her. "Don't they know what happened? Why would they ask you to come back before you're ready?"

"They didn't even ask if I was ok," he said glumly, not answering her question.

"Please, Jason, quit that place. It's not good for you. You can find another job."

She felt the energy seep out of him and his shoulders slumped. "I'm too old, Rebecca. Where will I find another job that pays me what I'm making there? I'm fifty five years old, for Christ's sake."

The angel looked sternly at him. "It's not about the money at all, is it? It's your stupid pride."

Jason bit his lower lip and growled, "I can't let them win. Don't you see, Rebecca? That would kill me!"

"But Jason," she said and gently stroked his cheek. "You're not happy there. I can tell."

"I used to be," he said softly and lowered his head in shame.

"Tell me what happened there."

He took a deep breath before starting. "I was the supervisor of shelvers there for over thirty years. I had everything running smoothly until they decided to reorganize the place. They called it a realignment but I say it was a misalignment."

"Go on," she said when he paused.

"I never guessed they'd take my job away from me. Oh, they were clever about it so it'd look legal on paper. They added some minor duties to my job that I could have easily learned but they didn't give me that chance."

"So what happened?"

"The director didn't even have the decency of talking to me herself so she had her assistant call me in one day to tell me that they were posting my job because of the additional duties but I was welcome to interview for it or any of the part time positions they created."

"Oh no," Rebecca whispered. "I think I know where this is going."

"I knew right away that by encouraging me to apply for part time was their way of telling me I wasn't wanted anymore. Well, I interviewed for the position and the new head of the department they hired gave it to my assistant."

"What?! After all the years of experience you had?!"

Jason's eyes were haunted. "It didn't matter to them. Everything I'd ever accomplished was gone overnight. They changed everything I did just for the sake of change and made it worse."

"What happened then?"

He wiped away a tear and said, "They gave me an assistant job under my new boss. I'm basically stuck with menial tasks now and half of the day I sit by a machine that sorts materials. I have to bend up and down a lot of the time now which hurts my back. They're sending me a message. They want me to quit. Now do you understand why I can't let them win?"

Rebecca gently touched his arm. "But it's killing you, Jason. It's not worth it to stay."

He stared into her eyes and she added, "Besides, I know what you're not telling me. You hurt all over, don't you? I can see it in your eyes. The job only makes it worse."

Jason's eyes flooded with tears and he lowered his head again. Rebecca gently touched his chin and made him look at her. "Tell me how badly you're hurting, Jason. I want to know."

He started to cry and she felt her heart ache for him. "I hurt all over! My body's falling apart! My shoulders, my back, my hips! I'm a fucking mess!"

"Don't the pills I see you take help a little with the pain?"

"No," he answered, his voice miserable. "I had to get off of them a few weeks ago because the doctor said they'd eventually destroy my kidneys."

"I see," she said quietly.

"Now do you understand why I tried to kill myself?! I can't stand the constant pain and the humiliation and being alone! I'm sick of living!"

"I do understand," she replied calmly. She stood up and started to walk away.

"Where are you going?"

She stopped and looked at him. "I'm going to fill the bathtub so you can kill yourself, Jason. Isn't that what you want?"

"No!" he screamed, an anguished look on his face.

She came back to him and knelt in front of him. "Then tell me what you want, Jason. I need to hear it from your lips."

He looked down at the angel's beautiful face and her kind eyes melted into his. "I want to live again, Rebecca but I can't stand the pain. Please, please help me!"

He lunged into her arms and she held him tightly as he sobbed against her. "It's alright, Jason," she whispered. "Let it all out. I'm not going anywhere. I'm going to help you get through this."

He pulled away from her and her eyes burned into his with a warmth that soaked his soul. "Oh Rebecca, I wish I felt like a man again."

She smiled. "You *are* a man, Jason. You just need a little relief from the pain, that's all. Let's see if this helps."

Her face leaned into his and her eyes half closed. As his heart beat wildly in his chest, Jason suddenly felt her warm full lips press against his and his head exploded. He saw stars and gripped her tighter as their tongues met. "Uuuhhmm," Rebecca moaned. Jason felt the tears rolling down his cheeks as a great surge of energy raced through his system. The pain in his joints ebbed away and he felt more alive than at any other time in his life. He pulled his mouth away from hers and stared at her in amazement.

"Rebecca!" he gasped at how wonderful he felt.

She grabbed his head and pulled him back to her. Her eyes were glazed and their tongues met again in a sensuous embrace. Jason felt as if he was melting into the angel and he moaned loudly from the intensity of the moment. She finally released him and smiled as he stared stupidly at her.

"Oh my God," he whispered. "What did you do to me? What *was* that?"

Rebecca pulled him to her and he lay his head against her chest. "That was an angel's kiss, Jason," she whispered. "I took away your pain if only for a little while."

Tears filled his eyes as he gazed into her lovely eyes. "Thank you."

"Don't thank me just yet, Jason," she said. "The power of my kiss only lasts for a short time and then you'll be in pain again."

"Just to feel like this right now is worth it. I feel like I'm Superman."

She smiled and touched his face. "That's the idea, Jason. You're Superman."

CHAPTER EIGHT

They went for another walk only this time Jason felt strong and steady on his feet. In addition to his newfound energy, he also found it strange that he didn't even break a sweat. He beamed brightly from ear to ear and looked at Rebecca with adoration. "I wish I could feel like this always, Rebecca. I feel so alive!" he cried happily.

They stopped at an Italian restaurant and Jason asked for a quiet little table in the back. It was quite cozy and obviously meant for lovers because it was secluded from the rest of the dining area. Jason pulled the chair out for Rebecca and she smiled before sitting down in it. "Thank you, Jason. You're quite the gentleman."

"Only for a beautiful woman like you," he replied. He saw the look on her face and immediately regretted his words. They sat in silence as the waiter handed them their menus. Rebecca stared into space and Jason quietly said, "I'm sorry I said that, Rebecca. I didn't mean to make you feel uncomfortable. Please forgive me. It won't happen again."

She looked at him and her face was flushed. "Don't apologize, Jason. In all my years of watching over someone, no one has talked to me like you do. I told you already that I'm usually looked at as a holy figure of some kind."

Jason reached for her hand and squeezed it lightly. "Is it wrong for me to treat you like the woman you are? I don't see an angel when I look at you, Rebecca. I see a friend and...."

"And what?"

He lowered his head, embarrassed. "I must be crazy thinking someone like you would even think of me in the way I wish you would," he softly said.

Her fingers wrapped tightly around his and her eyes looked at him with sweet tenderness. "You're not crazy, Jason," she whispered.

"You mean?" he asked, hopeful.

"I'm sorry, Jason but if I cross the line there might not be any way back for me. I told you already that it's forbidden."

"Oh," he said sadly. "I understand."

"Do you? Do you really?"

His face turned red. "No, I'm lying. I *don't* understand. I have so many feelings for you. Why is that so wrong?"

"Jason," she said quietly. "Maybe you're just infatuated with me because I saved your life and took your pain away. Did you ever think of that?"

His face was grim. "No….it's not infatuation. I know what I feel."

She let go of his hand then and looked closely at the menu. "I haven't had chicken cacciatore in years. I think I'll have that. What'll you have?"

Jason fought back the anger he felt and said, "I love mostacciolli with meat sauce."

The waiter came back and they gave him their order. Rebecca sank back in her chair and looked around the small area they were in. "I've always loved places like this. They're so romantic. The perfect place to really get to know someone, don't you think?"

She could tell that he was hopefully smitten with her and didn't want to lead him on. *Shut up!* her mind screamed. *Don't make him think there's a chance!*

Jason gazed at her with thoughtful eyes and she suddenly felt uncomfortable. "Please stop looking at me like that. It makes me nervous."

He looked away and she felt badly. "I'm sorry. I'm just not used to it."

He looked at her again, surprised. "I don't believe you. How could a man not look at you the way I'm looking at you now?"

Her lower lip quivered and she shivered at the memory in her past. "I never had the chance to know anyone the way I wanted to," she said quietly.

He was surprised. "Why not? Weren't you ever in love with someone?"

The angel lowered her head and whispered, "He took that away from me."

"What do you mean, Rebecca? Who took what away from you?"

Her eyes were haunted and full of pain when she looked again into his. "I went to a small school for young women, Jason. Back then at Concord, it was difficult meeting boys. One night as I lay dreaming, a man broke into the dorm and came into my room. He tortured me for a long time. I was too terrified to cry out."

"What?!" Jason cried, aghast.

The angel's eyes filled with tears. "I used to dream romantic thoughts of a man who would sweep me off my feet but he robbed me of that, Jason. I remember begging him with my eyes as he squeezed my neck. I didn't want to die. I was so scared and alone."

Jason felt his own eyes fill with tears and he moved closer to the angel. "Oh my God, Rebecca! I'm so terribly sorry!"

She looked at him with her doe like eyes and he wanted to grab her and hold her forever. "I died a virgin, Jason," she whispered. "I never had the chance to love a boy."

He got up and pulled her into his arms. She sobbed against him and wrapped her arms around his back. The waiter came with their meals but quietly put them down on the table and left them there so they could be alone. Rebecca looked up into Jason's face and said, "I don't know why I told you that. I never get personal with anyone I watch over but you're different. You really seem to care about me."

"I *do* care about you," he said softly and wiped her tears away with his thumb. "I already told you I did. How could I not?"

She buried her head against his chest again and that's when he felt his newfound strength begin to ebb. He dreaded what was happening to him but tried to ignore it. They sat and ate their food with delight then but after a few minutes the angel saw the pain reappear in his eyes.

"Oh no," she whispered. "I'm so sorry, Jason."

"Could I have another kiss for the pain?" he asked, hopeful.

"I wish I could. But I don't think it's a wise idea."

"Why not?"

The angel held his hands and gently squeezed them. "Because it might be too much."

He didn't know what to say or do and they finished their meal in silence. Jason paid the bill and they left the restaurant and began the long walk home. Rebecca had to hold him up halfway there as the pain and weakness came back full force.

They got back to the apartment and she helped him undress to his underwear. "I think you've had enough for today. We'll do a little more tomorrow, alright?" she said, concerned.

He nodded and she helped him into bed. She pulled the covers over him and knelt by the side of the bed. "I care deeply for you, Jason," she whispered. "I truly wish I could help you with the pain. I can hold your hand if you want me to."

He nodded again and she got up and lightly kissed his forehead. Jason looked into her eyes and whispered, "I wish I could take your pain away like you took mine away, Rebecca."

She brushed away a tear. "I wish that too, Jason. Now go to sleep and rest."

Rebecca sat by the side of the bed and held his hand until he closed his eyes. Within minutes he was fast asleep and lightly snoring.

She watched his face for a long time as he slept and was relieved that there wasn't any pain there. Eventually, she let go of his hand and went into the living room. She looked out the window and saw that the stars were out and sat down to gaze at them.

The silence of the night was music to her ears and she smiled when it began to snow. Rebecca sat like that for hours until she heard the groans from Jason's bedroom. She quietly walked to his room, cracked open the door and peeked inside. Her eyes opened wide when she saw his hand moving under the blanket. He was stroking his penis with his eyes tightly shut. "Oh Rebecca," he moaned. "Oh God….Rebecca."

She slowly closed the door and stood there for a moment breathing heavily. Behind the door she heard him moan louder as he came. She couldn't believe what she'd seen and heard. This had never happened before with anyone she'd watched over and it should have worried her but didn't. Instead, she was strangely excited. *He said my name*, she thought. *He was thinking of me while he was doing it.*

She went back to the living room and did something she hadn't done in a very long time. She lay down in front of the fireplace and lifted her dress. Hesitant, she lowered her hand and gently touched her sex. A delicious shiver shot through her and she touched her clit with a finger. To her surprise, it was swollen and extremely sensitive. She smiled and pinched it between two fingers and came immediately. "Oh! Oh! Yes, Jason! I'm here!" she cried.

She worked furiously at her clit and came again with his face in her mind. He was smiling and holding her close and she shook with pleasure in his arms until he pulled away from her. "No!" she cried. "Please don't leave me!"

He disappeared from her mind then and she lay there panting and felt intensely alone. "Oh Jason," she whispered sadly. "Oh how I wish I were alive."

She rolled over then on her side and curled up in a ball and began to sob. "Why God?! All I ever wanted was to be loved!"

The angel joined Jason in sleep then and they both lay unhappily in their loneliness.

CHAPTER NINE

The morning sun woke Jason up and his eyes fluttered open. Rebecca was sitting by the side of the bed. He felt ashamed when he saw her eyes as he remembered masturbating the night before while saying her name. She just stared at him and he looked away.

"Jason," her sweet voice said. He looked back at her and she was smiling shyly. "I saw what you were doing last night."

His face turned red. "You did?! You saw it all?!"

"Not all of it. I turned away before you finished," she softly said.

He was terribly embarrassed. "I'm so sorry, Rebecca. I promise I'll lock the door next time."

"I heard you too, you know."

His eyes got huge. "You *heard* what I said?!"

"Yes," she replied, smiling. "You were masturbating while thinking of me."

"Oh God," he groaned. "I-I don't know what to say."

Her hand reached out and lightly touched his face. "I thought about it a lot last night and wanted to ask you something."

"What?"

She lowered her eyes but then looked directly into his. "Will you let me stay and watch next time?"

"What?!" He sat up, the covers falling from his body, exposing his muscled chest. "You want to watch me? Why?"

Rebecca felt her heart skip a beat as she looked over his body. "Wouldn't it be easier for you if I was right here in front of you instead of you imagining me?"

Jason's jaw dropped. He couldn't believe what he was hearing. "But you're an angel. You're *my* angel. It wouldn't be right."

"Jason," she said softly and sat on the edge of the bed. His sweet words had affected her greatly. "Yes, I'm an angel but I'm also a woman. I'm flattered that you think of me in that way. I told you no one else ever has. They've all been intimidated by me because I'm an angel. Why haven't you? Why are you so different?"

Jason stared into her eyes. "Because I have a feeling about you. I can't put it into words but I feel very close to you."

Rebecca moved closer to him. "I have that same feeling, Jason but I'm scared."

"I won't hurt you, Rebecca," he whispered. "Please know that."

She looked away and he lightly touched her arm. "Please know that," he repeated.

She looked back at him and a big smile crossed her face. "So does that mean I can watch next time?"

Jason blushed a brighter shade of red than the last time and nodded. "If you want to," he whispered.

"I want to," she said and suddenly stood up. It was time to get him moving. "You need to eat and then I have an idea how to get you going. Your recovery is taking too long."

Rebecca left the room and Jason went to take a shower. As the warm water rushed over him, he hummed a melody he'd had in his head for a while. He was drying off when Rebecca came into the bathroom.

"What was that you were humming? It was beautiful."

"You heard me?" he asked, surprised.

"Yes, I heard you from the kitchen. Remember, I'm an angel. My hearing's exceptional."

Jason smiled. "The melody's been in my head for a while now. I'm glad you liked it."

Rebecca moved close and put her hands against his chest. "Will you write lyrics for it, Jason? Then I could sing it for you. It could be my song to you."

"Of course," he said, delighted. He wrapped the towel around his waist and she stared down at his groin and then back at his face.

Her eyes were glazed. "Your food's ready," she whispered.

"I'll be right back," he said and left her to get dressed.

Fluffy pancakes with maple syrup awaited him accompanied by perfectly poached eggs and a tall glass of cold tomato juice with Tabasco sauce added. It was just like he liked it. He had to remember that the angel had watched over him through the years and knew his habits. Jason licked his lips and sat down at the table. "I feel like a king," he said happily as he waited for her to sit down.

She sat down across from him and said, "No, if I was dreaming you wouldn't be a king."

"Then what would I be?"

The angel blushed. "You'd be my prince and I'd be your princess."

Jason stared at her with his mouth hanging open.

"Are you alright?" she asked, laughing softly.

He snapped himself out of his daze. "That's a beautiful dream, Rebecca. I wish it could come true."

She lowered her head and whispered, "I fantasize too much. I'm sorry."

Jason got up and went to kneel by her side. He took her hands in his and looked up into her face. "Rebecca," he whispered. "I'll be your prince if you'll let me."

The angel's eyes welled with tears and she lunged at him and hugged him close. "Oh Jason! "I didn't want to die! I wanted someone to love me!"

He held her and stroked her long hair as she sobbed against him. "I'm always here for you," he whispered in her ear. "Please give me a chance, sweet angel."

Rebecca's eyes were dreamy as she gazed into his with hope but also caution.

"We need to start the next chapter of your story, Jason. You must remember, that's why I'm here," she said softly.

Jason looked sad and she said, "Hold out your arms. I have an idea how to get your wrists to heal faster. I'm not sure if it'll work but I'm going to try."

She went and found the sharpest knife she could and returned to him. "What are you going to do with that?" he asked, worried.

She put it down on the table and slowly unwrapped his wrists. "Let's see how these are healing."

His wrists were red and the angry looking cuts oozed pus. "Fuck, they're infected. I have no choice now. I'm going to try it."

"Try what?" he asked, worried.

She picked up the knife and held her slender right arm out. Her wrist looked so soft and feminine and Jason stifled a scream when she slowly sliced across it with the knife. Blood welled out of the cut and she put the knife down. "Let's see if this works," she said softly and pressed her bleeding wrist against his.

At first Jason felt like his wrist was on fire and he wanted to pull away but after a few moments a strange tingling sensation ran up his arm. Rebecca pulled her wrist away and Jason gasped in shock. The cruel cuts on his wrist were sealing up before his eyes. "How?" he whispered. "How is this happening?"

Rebecca smiled brightly and held her wrist against his other arm. "I had a feeling this would work," she said triumphantly.

After a minute she removed her arm and Jason gasped at the sight. Again his wrist sealed up before his eyes and he stared at the angel. "It's a miracle. I can't believe this is happening," he said in awe.

The angel stood up and looked down at him. "Now you're ready."

She extended her arm out to him and he saw her wrist had healed as well. "Come, Jason and begin your new journey. Follow the path you were destined for."

He took her hand and let her lead him to the hallway where they put on their winter coats. She wrapped a scarf around his neck and touched his face with her hand. "Are you ready?"

"Yes," he quietly answered.

They left the apartment, headed down the stairs and went outside to face the cold. Jason shivered and his bones ached badly. "Are you sure about this? I hurt all over. What do you have planned?"

"Follow me and you'll see," she said.

He wasn't feeling as weak now and she didn't have to support him as they walked. "Where are we going?" he asked.

"Just keep walking," the angel said and he walked with her for blocks until they heard a firetruck in the distance.

She turned to face him. "It's time, Jason."

"Time for what," he said, not understanding.

"We're close," she said as she turned her back to him and began to walk faster down a side street. Jason followed and his legs hurt. He began to lag behind her when he saw the house in the distance on the corner. Black smoke was pouring out of an upstairs window and Rebecca looked back at him.

"Hurry" she yelled and grabbed his hand tighter. She started to run and he followed breathlessly.

"What are we doing?!" he screamed, his legs aching.

"They won't be able to save them in time!" Rebecca yelled back at him.

Jason was out of breath and felt faint as they stood in front of the burning house. The firetrucks sounded far away and Rebecca's voice was urgent. "You have to do it, Jason. Only you can do it!"

Jason felt like he was going to throw up. He was thoroughly exhausted. "Me?! What can I do?!" he gasped as he tried to suck a breath into his tired lungs. "Look at me! I'm a wreck!"

Rebecca grabbed his face in her hands and looked into his eyes.

"Listen, Jason, this is why you're here. This is your purpose."

"But I'll die!"

"No, you won't. Be the man I know you can be."

"How? I'm old and broken down. I can't do this."

"I'll help you," she said and in that moment he was lost in her beautiful eyes.

"A kiss for good luck," she said softly and kissed him on the lips.

Jason felt the rush of warmth race through his body and a tingling sensation buzzed in his head. "Oh wow, that feels amazing," he said, surprised again by the power of her kiss. There was something different about this one though.

Rebecca smiled and waited as Jason felt the pain in his body ebb away. The pain was replaced by a feeling of power. Pure raw power. He felt young and full of life.

"Could I have another?" he asked, hopeful.

Rebecca leaned in close again and her warm breath smelled like hot cocoa. "You're a naughty boy, Jason," she whispered and kissed him again.

His eyes opened wide as he felt the energy surge through his body. His muscles rippled and he clenched his fists.

Rebecca pulled away from him. "Go now. You know what to do."

Jason smiled and took off in a run towards the house. A firetruck pulled up just as he got to the front door.

"Hey you!" a fireman yelled. "What do you think you're doing?! Get away from there!"

Jason ignored the man and grabbed the door handle. It was locked and he felt the angel's power surge through him as he ripped it away with a twist.

The door opened and he rushed inside.

"Help us!" a woman's voice screamed from somewhere upstairs.

Jason dodged a falling chunk of ceiling and raced up the stairs to where he thought he'd heard the woman's cries.

"Where are you?!" he yelled, looking from one closed door to the next.

"In here! We're in the far bedroom!" the voice answered. "Please hurry!"

Jason raced to the door and tried to open it but the doorknob burned his hand. He swore and backing away, he kicked out with his foot. The door caved in slightly but stayed on its hinges. Jason grabbed the edges with his fingers and violently tore it free. He flung it to the side and entered the room. The woman was on the floor. A large bookcase lay across her legs and her young son sat crying by her side. "Help me!" she screamed. "I tried to move it in front of the door and it fell on me!"

Jason grabbed the bookcase in his arms and his back muscles bunched up as he lifted it with ease. The woman looked in awe as he lifted it above his head and tossed it aside where it crashed against the wall.

"How?" she gasped as he helped her to her feet.

"Can you stand?" he asked.

She winced in pain as she touched the floor with her foot. "I don't think so. I think my leg's broken."

"Hold on to me," Jason said and before she could say anything he'd lifted her in his arm like she was a bale of hay.

"How are you doing this?!" she cried.

Jason ignored her and grabbed her small son with his other arm. Entering the hallway, he saw there wasn't much time as a far room belched a massive blast of fire towards him. He raced down the stairs with the woman and her son in his arms and dodged another piece of falling ceiling on his way out of the house.

When they emerged from the house, the firemen had just gotten the hydrant working and were spraying the top floor of the house. They stared at Jason with their mouths hanging open as he put the woman and her son down. A fireman helped support her and she leaned in close to Jason. "Thank you," she said and kissed him on the cheek. "I don't know how you did that but you're a good man."

"You're welcome," Jason said and smiled, knowing he'd done a good thing.

Rebecca was waiting for him by the sidewalk and opened her arms out to him. He ran to her and she hugged him close.

"I did it!" he cried. "I really did it!"

He began to sob and she whispered, "This is only the beginning, Jason. You've found your purpose."

CHAPTER TEN

Jason felt giddy with joy and had an urge to skip all the way home. His happiness made the angels heart soar and she laughed when he suddenly took off running. She followed and Jason did indeed feel as if he was Superman. His legs felt strong and he wasn't even out of breath by the time they reached the front door of his building. Rebecca gently touched his cheek and said, "I'm so proud of you, Jason."

He was beaming at her and fought against the urge to crush her in his arms and kiss her all over. "I couldn't have done it without you," he said happily. He pulled her close and she wrapped her arms around his waist as she looked up into his face. "Rebecca, I…." he whispered and she saw the blood trickle out of his nose.

Jason saw the look on her face and asked, "What's wrong?"

She was very worried. "You're bleeding. There's blood coming from your nose."

Jason felt the sudden nausea and touched his forehead with his palm. "I don't feel good."

"Let's get you upstairs," she said quickly and by the time they entered the apartment she had to practically carry him inside. She helped him to his bed and he flopped down weakly onto it.

"Oohhh," he moaned and broke out into a sweat. Rebecca quickly undressed him and when she was finished she covered him with a blanket. "Help me," he groaned. "Something's wrong."

She knelt by the bed and held his hand. "Jason," she whispered. "I think you may be having a reaction to my blood. It's too pure and your body can't handle it."

"What?!" he asked, alarmed. "Haven't you healed anyone before?"

"No," she answered, her forehead creased with worry. "Never."

"Am I going to die?"

She gripped his hand tighter. "No, you're not going to die. It's not your time yet."

"Then what's wrong with me?" he asked, his voice getting weaker.

"I wish I knew," she answered truthfully. "We'll have to wait and see."

Jason's face turned a deep shade of red and his eyes closed. He feel into a deep sleep and Rebecca watched over him through the late afternoon and long into the night. At three in the morning, his eyes opened and he looked at her, exhausted. "Am I dead?" he asked.

The angel's eyes twinkled in amusement. "No, you're not dead. Far from it."

"Then what happened?"

"I'm guessing you had a bad reaction to my blood and got very sick from it. How are you feeling now?"

His eyes closed and after a moment they reopened. "I'm exhausted but ok, I guess."

Rebecca smiled. "I'm glad, Jason. I'm sorry this happened."

"Don't be," he said. "How many other men can say an angel healed them?"

Rebecca felt proud but worried anyway. She stood up and looked down at him. "I hope I never have to heal you again."

Jason nodded and fell back asleep. The angel watched over him until morning when she started breakfast for him.

Jason awoke to that incredible smell of bacon in the air again. Rebecca stood in the doorway and asked, "Ready for breakfast?"

He remembered his heroics from the day before and smiled. "Yes, I'm ready."

He got out of bed and the blanket slid past his hips when he tried to grab it. Rebecca looked down at his penis and back at his face. "Please put that away. I don't want to see it," she said and went back into the kitchen.

Jason slipped on some boxers and a T shirt and went into the kitchen. Rebecca put a plate of food in front of him and sat looking down at her clasped hands. Jason started to eat and after a moment asked, "Rebecca, are you alright? Are you mad at me?"

The sight of his penis had stirred something in her and she didn't like the feeling because she knew it was wrong.

"No, I'm not mad at you. I'm mad at myself."

She saw the look of confusion on his face. "I don't want to talk about it now."

He went back to eating and they sat in an awkward silence. When he was finished, she got up and took his empty plate to the sink. "Thank you," he said unenthusiastically.

She nodded without looking back at him and he got up and said, "Now that my wrists are healed I better get back to work. I've got no reason to stay away now."

She nodded again and he went to take a shower and get dressed. He was surprised when she handed him a paper bag before he left for work. "What's this?"

"I made lunch for you," she said quietly.

Jason wanted to touch her so badly but resisted. "Thank you, Rebecca. Will you be here when I get home?"

"Yes," she said and he nodded.

"I just have one question," he asked before leaving.

"What?"

His eyes turned soft. "If you weren't an angel would you feel differently about me?"

She didn't want to encourage him and decided to lie. "No, Jason. I wouldn't."

She saw the hurt in his eyes and had to look away. "Oh," he said and turned away from her as he brushed tears from his eyes. She reached her hand out to touch his shoulder but he stepped out the door before she could.

"Jason, I'm sorry," she whispered as the door closed. "I'm so terribly sorry."

CHAPTER ELEVEN

Jason felt strange as he drove to work. He had that sick feeling in his stomach he'd had lately before going to work and it bothered him greatly. *I remember when I used to like going to work*, he thought sadly.

He sat in the parking lot for a few minutes before going in. The library had always felt like home to him but ever since he'd been demoted it was more like hell now. He was greeted by fake smiles and pats on the back when he walked into the sorting area. His supervisor, Peter approached him and looked at him, curious. "So what happened? Where have you been?"

"It's personal," Jason answered as he stared at the man who used to be his assistant but was now his boss. The man's blonde hair looked extra greasy today and his breath smelled of garlic. Jason resisted the urge to push him away but didn't.

"I was told you weren't sick so what happened?" the man persisted in asking.

Jason pushed back his anger. "It's nobody's business."

The man leaned in close and Jason felt like puking from the stink of his breath. "C'mon man, tell me where you've been," he whispered.

Jason felt his face turn red and he angrily said, "I don't want to talk about it!"

Peter smiled knowingly and nodded. "That's alright, Jason. Human Resources wouldn't tell me everything but I'll bet you were out looking for another job. I'm right, aren't I?"

Jason walked to the door to the basement where old magazines were stored and opened it. He looked back at the man and beckoned him to follow. They headed downstairs and walked into the large room together. "Why did you say that?" Jason asked angrily.

Peter smiled nervously. "C'mon, man. I know you're unhappy here. It's obvious to everyone."

Jason stared hard at the clean shaven man. He was shorter than he was and his little pot belly stuck out slightly making it look like he was pregnant. Jason smiled at the thought and said, "You're right, Pete. I'm *not* happy. I don't like what they did to me."

Pete stared at him and quietly said, "I know, Jason and I'm sorry. If you find another job, go for it. Get out of this place."

"Thanks, man," Jason said and they shook hands.

"I'll give you a few minutes alone but then you'd better get back upstairs. Boss lady is coming down to review our new sorting procedures soon."

"Ok," Jason said and watched his old assistant head upstairs. He sat down in a chair and looked around the room. Old magazines filled the shelves of metal ranges and there was a musty smell in the air because of their age. *I'm old too*, he thought. *Just like them.*

He thought back to the day the announcement came that Peter had gotten his old job. The man had walked around whistling that day which only made Jason angrier. "Hey man!" he'd said. "How you doin' today?"

"How the hell do you think I'm doing?!" he'd answered.

"Hey, don't be angry," Peter had said.

That same afternoon the humiliation continued when one of the women who worked in the back with them came into the office. Pete was sitting in Jason's old chair and the woman walked right past him and stopped in front of Pete. "Congratulations, Pete! I think it's great you got the job!"

"Thanks, Myrna!" he said and they hugged. The woman looked at Jason and his face was burning. *You bitch*, he thought. *You had to congratulate him in front of me?*

Jason wiped away tears as he shook the memory of that day out of his head and headed upstairs to take his place by the sorting machine. He sighed as he sat down and the treadmill continued to feed books and DVD's into the large bins they'd been assigned to.

Jason admired the intelligence behind the technology but hated it just the same. It was backbreaking work as he had to unload each bin. By the time he'd gotten to the children's books his back was breaking and his legs ached.

"Hey guys," Margo, the department's head said as she entered the room. Jason looked over at the woman who'd made the decision to hire Pete over him. Lately, she'd been critical about everything he'd ever stood for and had even made a comment during a recent meeting that fun and games were over with for the shelvers and now things were going to get serious under her watch. She was implying that he'd never done his job well and it humiliated him. He also remembered during his interview that she was critical of his hiring people who were older. "But they're more reliable than high schoolers. They give us stability," he'd told her.

The woman stared at him and he added, "Besides, we don't discriminate based on age, right?"

She didn't answer and the interview continued. He talked a lot about how he supervised and his ideas regarding shelving methods. By the end of it, Jason had a good feeling that he'd kept his old job. But he was wrong.

He snapped himself out of it and stared at her. She was talking to everyone else and deliberately ignoring him again. Some of the questions she asked about procedures he could have answered but she acted as if his thirty plus years of experience didn't matter. He was dead to her and he knew it.

There was a moment when just before lunch he was the only one left in the back room. He sat there and stared at nothing as tears clouded his eyes. *This is my existence,* he thought bitterly. *Everything I've ever done here meant nothing.*

Lunchtime came and he headed up to the lunchroom. He opened the bag Rebecca had given him and saw there was an apple inside and a delicious looking smoked ham sandwich. A fudge brownie was for dessert and he smiled at the angel's kindness. *She knows just what I like,* he thought.

There was a folded piece of paper at the bottom of the bag. He unfolded it and saw it was a note from her. *Dear Jason,* it read. *Though I can't be to you what you want me to be please know that I care deeply for you. You are a special man. With much love-Rebecca.*

He smiled and felt an ache in his heart. *If only....* he thought.

After eating alone in the lunch room, he sat and looked out the window at the snow covered trees. *I have to get through this,* he thought grimly. *I must get through this. I can't let them win.*

After lunch, he returned to the sorting machine and sat like a zombie and did his job. A few mind-numbing hours later, he headed upstairs to the committee he'd been signed to as a token gesture of respect. He knew it didn't really matter whether he attended it or not but he did anyway. One of the department heads under the director had already written the usual words on the blackboard.

"Ok," she said when everyone was settled with their coffee. "Let's start again."

Jason stifled a laugh when she said, "Where are we going?"

It was the same old crap from the stupid Think Tank Institute the library was following the doctrine of. There were never any answers as each week the same idiotic questions were asked.

Jason raised his hand. He'd had enough.

"Yes, Jason," the lead speaker asked warily. She knew the circumstances of Jason's demotion and was afraid of him. He was clearly angry these past few months and knew the library had backed him into a corner as they piled humiliation upon humiliation upon him.

He stared at her and asked, "With all due respect, what's the point of this? You asked the same question last week and the weeks before and each time we have answers for you."

In response, she read from the same tired script that the institute had given the library to follow.

"We must always reassess what we're doing and where we're going, Jason. You know that."

"This is bullshit," he said quietly. "What's the point if our answers aren't heard by the higher ups?"

She sighed because she knew he was right but she was forced to defend the library so she said, "Jason, you can leave this committee if you don't like how it's conducted. I need to follow the instructions here."

He knew there was no use in arguing so he stayed quiet and listened for the rest of the meeting as the pointless questions were asked and answers that would never be used were given.

Thoroughly depressed, he headed back to the work room when the director of the library suddenly appeared from the children's room. She saw him and tried to walk by but he stepped in front of her. "Mrs. Walton, may I talk to you sometime about my job?"

She stared at him and he saw kindness in her eyes which surprised him. "Of course, Jason. I have time right now. Let's talk."

He had a good feeling about the way she had looked at him and followed her upstairs to her office. She closed the door behind him and motioned for him to sit down across from her. "Ok, what's on your mind?" she asked, smiling.

He let it all out, baring his soul to her. "I was very hurt at having my job taken away. I'm wondering why it happened."

The long blonde haired woman's eyes seemed to change in a second and she suddenly seemed amused. Settling back in her chair, she looked at him as if he were a bug. "I was wondering when you'd come talk to me."

He wanted to ask why she didn't tell him herself months before that his job was being taken away but didn't.

She leaned forward in her chair and smiled. "Why did you hire older people?"

Jason couldn't believe his ears. "I hired them because they brought stability to our workforce. Teenagers don't last long and older workers have a greater sense of dedication to the job."

"They're slow," she said, her face stuck in that weird doll-like smile.

He sat frozen and she said, "Do you remember me telling you I wanted averages for shelving times?"

He thought back and remembered the argument they'd had years before. "Yes, but I said then and I still believe you can't have averages. Sometimes the shelves are full and the shelver has to shift the books around. Shelving times vary from day to day. That's why averages don't work."

She stared at him and didn't respond. He sat uncomfortably and felt the ache in his tired muscles. This wasn't going well at all.

"I still believe you have value here. You can still contribute something to this organization." Her eyes turned cruel. "Of course, you can always go to part time."

There it was again. *She wants me to leave*, he thought.

"You had your time," she said. "Maybe you should just relax and do the job you've been assigned to."

His eyes filled with tears and he was angry with himself. *Don't show weakness!* his mind screamed. "But I feel like I'm being ignored," he said quietly, hoping for sympathy of some kind. "Myrna doesn't ask me anything about the job. She only criticizes me. Why, just the other day she said I had hired too many shelvers which is ridiculous."

The director's eyes took on a lizard like appearance and narrowed. "I always say if you can't stand the heat then get out of the kitchen."

Jason couldn't believe she'd said that to him. He wanted to launch himself at the bitch but felt a soft gentle pressure on his shoulder. Something stopped him and he knew he had to get away from her. His heart was pounding in his chest and she continued to smile at him like he was inferior. She was enjoying his suffering and didn't bother hiding her satisfaction. He stood up and knew his hands were shaking. "Thanks for your time," he said quietly and she ushered him out.

She smirked at him and he felt like a bug. "Anytime, Jason. I'm glad I could help."

Jason stood outside her door and felt crushed beyond repair. He walked slowly past the director's secretary with his head down and headed to the basement.

Rebecca had watched the whole thing in her invisible state and quickly made herself visible. The director had her back turned to her and was still gloating over the poor man's suffering. She turned and Rebecca was standing a few feet in front of her desk. "What the hell?!" the woman cried. "You startled me!"

Rebecca stared at her, still not fully believing what she'd heard and moved closer.

"Who are you? How did you get in here?!" the director asked, her eyes blazing.

"I'm Jason's girlfriend," Rebecca answered quietly.

"So what?!" the woman said. "Get out of my office!"

Rebecca's eyes seemed to glow and the woman backed against the wall in fright. "What the hell!" she gasped.

Rebecca came closer. "You're a cruel woman. I can't believe you talked to him that way. You've undone everything I tried to help him with."

"What the hell are you talking about?!" the woman cried in her fright.

Rebecca felt like crying and shook her head sadly. "That poor man….I'll never understand how people can be so cruel to each other."

The director became brave and took a step towards Rebecca.

"Don't," the angel said, lifting her hand. "I swear I'll hurt you."

The woman frowned and Rebecca gave her a cruel smile of her own. "You'll live many lives. I'm sure of it because that's what it'll take to pay for your sins."

"Get out of my office!" the woman yelled.

Rebecca turned away but before she stepped out she looked back at the director and said, "Jason is so much better than you'll ever be."

With that, she left the director's office and headed invisibly to the basement. She found Jason sitting in a far corner in the dark. He was sobbing and she knelt in front of him. "Jason," she whispered.

He looked at her and saw her soft glow. "Rebecca. How?"

She touched his face and the warmth from it made him tremble. "I saw the whole thing, Jason. I've been here all day with you."

"You saw the whole thing?" he asked, ashamed.

"Yes. She was very cruel."

His eyes were haunted. "I'm nothing, Rebecca. I don't matter to anyone."

Her hand caressed his cheek and she leaned close and pulled his head to her breasts. "You matter to *me,* Jason. Don't ever forget that."

He sobbed against her and she held his shaking body against hers. "It's alright, Jason," she whispered. "You're going to be alright. Your angel will make sure of it."

CHAPTER TWELVE

"You need to go back to work now," she said when he'd stopped crying.

"I don't know if I can," he replied sadly.

Rebecca gently held his face between her hands and looked into his eyes. "Jason, I *know* you can. Be strong. Do it for *me*."

He nodded and stood up. "I'll be waiting for you in your car when you're done," she said.

Jason watched her glowing form fade away and he forced himself to return to work. The sorting machine was relentless and his entire body ached by the time his shift was over.

Rebecca was waiting in his car as promised. "You did it," she said, smiling. "I knew you could."

He nodded and drove them home. Rebecca made a delicious pasta dinner for him and he quietly ate it with his head down. When he was finished, he thanked her and went to the bathroom. He was holding something by his side but she couldn't tell what it was.

She stood outside the bathroom door and waited patiently but after a few minutes of silence she asked, "Jason, are you alright?"

He didn't answer and she had a bad feeling. She tried to open the door but he'd locked it. "Jason! Let me in!" she said.

She got no answer so she effortlessly tore the door handle away and pushed open the door. Jason was curled up by the side of the toilet with a steak knife in his hand. He'd made light cuts on his wrists and was just about to slice deeper.

"No!" she cried and lunged at him. She knocked the knife out of his hand and he stared at her with sad eyes.

"Why?" she said and knelt by him.

He began to sob and she pulled him into her warm body. "I thought we were past this, Jason," she said calmly. "Why were you about to hurt yourself again?"

He looked at her and felt ashamed in her eyes. "I'm nothing," he cried. "What's the point of life? You won't let me be close to you so I have no one."

She sighed. "I'm sorry, Jason. Let's go into the other room and talk, ok?"

They sat down in the kitchen and he waited a moment as she collected her thoughts. "Maybe I was too harsh. I won't let myself get close to you because I'm afraid of what might happen, Jason."

He was confused. "Afraid of what?"

Her lovely eyes searched his. "I'm afraid I might fall in love with you."

"You could fall in love with me? Really?"

She lowered her head and then looked intensely at him. "I lied about something. It's not forbidden. There's no rule about it."

"I don't understand, Rebecca. What's wrong with being close to me then?"

She lowered her head again and whispered, "I'm afraid of being alone, Jason. I won't always be here, you know and it'll hurt too much when I need to leave you."

"You won't always be here?" he said, his lower lip trembling. "You'd leave me? Why?"

She reached for his hand and held it. "I don't want to leave you but once my job is done here I must, Jason. There are always other people I need to help."

He felt as if the world was collapsing around him. "But I thought you were *my* angel," he said sadly.

She smiled. "There aren't as many of us around as you may think. Not everyone who goes to heaven becomes an angel."

"Oh," he said glumly.

She squeezed his hand and gently said, "Promise me you won't try to hurt yourself again. *Please*, Jason….I'd hate to lose you."

"I promise," he said and got up. He went into the living room and turned on the TV. Rebecca sat down next to him as he mindlessly flipped through the channels until he got to the news. He settled back into the chair and closed his eyes. She watched as his breathing slowed and she knew he was falling asleep. Something on the screen caught her eye and she watched it closely.

"Who is the man who saved this woman and her child?" the reporter said as the camera showed the burning house. The woman Jason had saved appeared on screen and she was smiling.

"I never got to ask his name," she said. "He smashed the door in and lifted a bookcase off of me like it was nothing. My son and I wouldn't be here if it wasn't for him."

The reporter came into view again and said, "Whoever you are, thank you. You're a true hero."

The camera moved to show the firemen. One of them breathlessly said, "He smashed the door in and ran into the house. He came out carrying them like they weighed nothing. Amazing! That's all I'll say!"

Rebecca shook Jason's shoulder. "Jason, wake up! They're talking about you!"

He jolted awake and opened his eyes as the report went on to say that the fire department wanted to give him an award for heroism. It ended with the little boy looking into the camera and waving. "Thanks for saving us, mister!" he said.

Jason looked at Rebecca and she was smiling from ear to ear. "You see, Jason. You *do* matter."

He allowed himself to smile and then rushed to the phone. "I've got to tell my daughter!"

He started to dial but then put the phone down. "What's wrong?" Rebecca asked and came to stand by him. "Why did you stop?"

His eyes were sad. "What's the use?" he said. "She'll just get off the phone as fast as the last time. She doesn't want to talk to me."

"You have to try, Jason. Give her another chance," the angel said.

He hesitated and then picked up the phone again. He dialed the number and waited. A woman answered the phone and Jason excitedly said, "Hi baby! It's Dad! Guess what? I'm on the news!"

The woman mumbled a few things Rebecca couldn't hear and Jason's face turned sad. "Yeah, yeah, I guess I'll call another time. No, no, it's ok. I understand," he said.

Rebecca leaned in close so she could hear the conversation. "Daddy, I'm sorry," a young woman's voice said. "I have to get off the phone. He's coming."

She hung up before he could say goodbye and Jason stood for a long time with the phone in his hand. Slowly, he put it back in the receiver and walked past Rebecca to sit in his recliner again. His shoulders slumped and she went to him. "See?" he said glumly. "She doesn't care about anything having to do with me. Where did I go wrong?"

Rebecca looked down at him and said, "Jason, something's wrong. I can sense it."

"What do you mean?" he asked, alarmed.

"Her voice….she sounded scared. Couldn't you tell?"

"No. That's how she always sounds on the phone."

"She said *he* was coming. Was she talking about her boyfriend, Jason?"

He thought for a second and said, "I guess so. He's in construction or something. That's all I know. Maybe it was him she was talking about."

The angel gripped his shoulder. "Something's wrong, Jason. She needs you."

He laughed. "She doesn't need me! She hasn't needed me in years! Besides, I'm no good to anyone."

Rebecca knelt by his chair and grabbed his chin. "Now listen! I've had enough of this! Stop feeling sorry for yourself and get your ass in gear! Your daughter needs you!"

Jason's eyes were scared because he had the feeling she could easily crush his skull if she wanted to. "Ok, I'll call her and tell her I'm coming to see her."

"No," she said firmly. "You need to surprise her. If you tell her you're coming she'll just say no."

"But I've already been away from work for a while. I'd have to use more sick time. They won't like it."

Her face turned red with anger. "I don't give a shit what they like! You're going to see your daughter and that's final!"

Jason's face turned pale. He was surprised by the angel's anger.

"We'll leave first thing in the morning," she said.

"I'll need to call work before we go."

"Fine," she said, her face grim.

"Rebecca," he said softly.

"What, Jason?"

His eyes looked at her with admiration. "You're *my* hero."

She almost lost it then and turned away from him. "Get a good night's sleep, Jason. I have a feeling you're going to need it."

He got ready for bed and before he got under the covers he knelt by the side of his bed. Rebecca looked down and smiled as he folded his hands in prayer. "God, I know that Rebecca came here of her own free will but I want to thank you anyway for making her an angel," he said quietly.

She rested her hand gently on his shoulder and he smiled up at her. His eyes were twinkling. "You're an amazing woman."

Rebecca knelt by him and folded her hands in prayer. She stayed silent and Jason waited a few minutes and finally asked, "What are *you* talking to God about?"

She looked at him and smiled. "It's between him and me, Jason. Just know that's it's about you."

"Me?" he said, surprised. "What are you saying to him about me? I want to know."

She gently touched his face with her soft hand and said, "It's just a wish, Jason. A secret wish."

He didn't know what she was talking about and she leaned her head against his shoulder. "A very special wish," she whispered. "A wish for you and I."

CHAPTER THIRTEEN

Jason was about to go to bed when Rebecca heard a voice cry out in her head. Her eyes narrowed in anger and she said, "Get dressed and pack a bag with some extra clothes. We can't wait. Susanna needs you *now*."

Jason knew better than to argue with her and jumped out of bed to get dressed. He had a bag packed in five minutes with clothes and toiletries. Rebecca stood impatiently in the kitchen and was tapping her foot when he walked in. He opened the drawer to get his car keys and she grabbed his hand. "You won't be needing those," she said.

"What?" he said, surprised. "How are we supposed to get there then? She's two hundred miles away."

"Put a heavy coat on and follow me." He put on his heaviest winter coat and they left the apartment. He followed her to a small grassy area behind the building where she suddenly stopped.

"What are we doing back here, Rebecca?" he asked, not understanding.

"You wanted to see my wings," she said as she turned her back to him and lowered her white dress over her shoulders.

Jason gasped as the feathery nubs slowly pushed out and expanded from her upper back. Within a minute her great wings opened wide and his eyes bugged out of his head at the wondrous sight. The angel turned around and faced him. Smiling, she flapped them a few times making his hair blow around and he laughed with joy. He came closer and ran his hands lightly over them. "My God, Rebecca! They're as beautiful as you are!"

The angel smiled wider as he gazed at her wings. They were as white as newly fallen snow. He stopped smiling when he suddenly realized what her intentions were. "Oh no," he said weakly, backing away from her. "We're not going to fly there, are we?!"

Her eyes narrowed. "Hold on to me and don't let go."

Jason latched his bag onto his belt and came close to her. She opened her arms to him and he moved into her body. He wrapped his arms around her waist and shivered. "I'm afraid," he whispered.

Rebecca kissed his forehead and said, "There's nothing to fear, Jason. I promise I won't let you fall. Ready?"

He nodded and Rebecca bent slightly at the knees and with a powerful push of her legs launched high into the sky. Jason felt the whoosh of air around them and clung tightly to her as they rose higher. Just as he thought they were about to fall back to the ground, her great wings began to flap. "Oh my God!" he cried as they began flying through the air. They went higher and higher until the lights of the city were small.

Jason was amazed at how fast they were going and asked, "Don't you want me to tell you where she lives?"

The angel smiled at him. "Jason, I'm an angel, remember? I already know."

He nodded and pressed his face against the space between her neck and shoulder. Rebecca had the softest skin he'd ever felt and he breathed deeply as he inhaled her sweet scent.

"Don't get any ideas, Jason," she suddenly said. "Don't try to take advantage of me while I'm flying."

He couldn't help himself and nuzzled against her neck and kissed it lightly. Rebecca moaned and he kissed her again in the same spot. "Stop that, you naughty man," she scolded, breathless.

His mouth moved lower and settled above her covered breasts where his hot breath made her swoon. "I said stop that!" she yelled and dove towards the ground. She twirled round and round and Jason thought he was going to lose his grip on her waist.

"Rebecca! Please stop! I'm going to fall!"

A tall building loomed in front of them and she headed straight for it.

"Please! Please! I promise I'll stop!" he screamed in terror.

She pulled up just in time and he rested his head against her shoulder. Rebecca could feel him trembling so she wrapped her arms around him and said, "Would you mind if I went faster?"

Jason clenched his teeth and nodded. Rebecca smiled and the wind blew through his hair as she flew faster. The wild rush of what was happening finally pushed him over the edge and he started screaming. Rebecca slowed and softly said, "Jason….breathe….breathe for me. Everything's going to be alright. Don't be scared."

He stopped screaming and his wide eyes stared into hers. "This is incredible! I can't believe this is happening!"

"Believe it," the angel said as they flew on into the night. "Close your eyes now and try to sleep. I'll hold you so you don't fall. We still have a long way to go."

He closed his eyes and she wrapped her warm arms tighter around him. He snuggled against her and was soon asleep.

Hours went by and Jason woke as the sun was rising in the distance. "It's so beautiful!" he cried and she hugged him tighter.

"Yes, it is!" She began to slow. "We're almost there."

A minute later she flew lower and then they were suddenly vertical. The angel's great wings flapped wildly as they gently landed in front of a small house. Rebecca let go of Jason but still he clung to her. "Jason, we're here now. You can let go of me," she said, amused.

He reluctantly let go and she could see his lips were blue. "Come here," she said as she opened her arms.

Jason's teeth chattered as he moved closer. The angel hugged him to her body and he was amazed at how warm she was. He could feel the swell of her breasts press against him and she let him nuzzle against her neck again. "Jason," she whispered.

"What?" he asked and pulled his head away to look at her.

She was smiling and her eyes had a glint in them. "Why were you kissing my neck?"

"I couldn't help it," he said, not wanting to make her angry. "Your skin is so soft and you smell so good. I'm sorry."

"I see," she said, still smiling. "What am I going to do with you when you're so naughty?"

He lowered his head and whispered, "I didn't mean anything by it. I said I was sorry."

The angel touched his chin with her hand and made him raise his head to look at her. "Jason," she said softly. "I have a confession to make."

"What?"

Her soft lips brushed against his ear. "I *liked* it," she whispered.

CHAPTER FOURTEEN

Jason stood for a minute in front of his daughter's house and hesitated.

"What's wrong, Jason?" Rebecca asked.

"Isn't it a little early to be here? What if she's still asleep?"

The angel frowned. "You're not getting out of this, Jason. We'll just have to take that chance."

He sighed and rang the doorbell. A minute went by and no answer. Rebecca reached past him and tapped on the door with her fist. A few seconds later, it opened a crack and a voice said, "Who is it? What do you want?"

Jason smiled. "Susanna, it's me. Dad."

The door opened wide and his daughter stood in shock staring at him. "Daddy!" she yelled and flung open the door. "Oh God!" she cried as she lunged into his arms. He felt her tremble against him and she pulled back to look at him. That's when he saw her swollen eye. "Why didn't you tell me you were coming?!" she said.

His smile faded as he stared at her bare upper arm. There was a bruise by her elbow. She saw him looking at it and quickly covered it with her other hand. "Come in," she said and Jason and Rebecca stepped inside. The angel looked at the lovely girl who seemed nervous. Her long blonde hair fell below her shoulders and her light blue pajamas barely hid her curves.

There was a noise upstairs and a voice shouted, "Susanna, who's at the door?!"

They saw the fear in her eyes then and she yelled, "It's my Dad!"

"Matt likes to sleep late," she said and looked nervously around as if searching for a way out.

"Susanna, are you alright?" Jason asked.

"Yes, why do you ask?" she answered, her eyes sad and tired.

"Just a feeling," Rebecca said and stepped forward.

"Who are you?" Susanna asked.

Without hesitation, Rebecca answered, "I'm a friend of Jason's. He asked me to come with him."

"How'd you come?" Susanna asked. "Did you drive or fly?"

Jason looked quickly at Rebecca and said, "We flew."

The angel cracked a smile and Susanna asked, "Did you have a smooth flight?"

Jason nodded. "Yes. It was the smoothest flight I've ever had."

Rebecca grabbed his arm lightly and smiled even bigger. "I'm glad you thought so, Jason."

Susanna looked at her strangely and froze when the clomping started at the top of the stairs. Jason looked up to see a very large man in blue jeans coming down the stairs. He was barrel chested and wore no shirt. He grabbed Jason's hand in his. "Hey, nice to meet you!"

"Nice to meet you too," Jason said. The man was huge and well over six feet tall. He towered over Jason and made him feel small. His eyes were a cool light blue and his rugged features were handsome.

"And who's this?" Matt said as his eyes quickly scanned Rebecca. She saw the leer in them for a split second and smiled.

"I'm Jason's friend, Rebecca."

The big man looked at Susanna and his face hardened a bit. "You didn't tell me your dad was coming."

They saw the panic in her eyes and she quickly said, "I didn't know he was coming. It was a surprise."

The big man's eyes darkened. "Oh."

"Is that a problem?" Jason asked.

Matt looked at him as if he were sizing him up. "No, I guess not."

They stood staring at each other until Matt finally turned away and pointed at Susanna. "Make me some breakfast. I've gotta be at work by 9."

Rebecca bit her tongue. *Make it yourself, you prick!* her mind screamed.

Jason bit his tongue too and Susanna hurried to the kitchen. They followed as Matt clomped back up the stairs to finish getting dressed.

"Susanna, is everything alright?" Jason asked as she grabbed a pot and filled it with water.

She turned to him. "Yes, everything's fine, dad."

Her face betrayed her fear and he quietly asked, "How'd you get those bruises, Susanna?"

His daughter raised her hand to her face and smiled. "Oh, you mean this? It was an accident."

Rebecca moved closer. "That was no accident. He hit you, didn't he?"

Jason watched his daughter's lower lip quiver and he felt anger rush into his mind like a runaway buffalo. "That sonofabitch," he mumbled.

Susanna grabbed his arm. "No dad! You've got it wrong! He said he was sorry afterwards."

"Why did he hit you, Susanna," he asked, his face grim.

She lowered her head and whispered, "I made him mad."

"What did you do?" Rebecca asked.

"It doesn't matter. He cried afterwards and said he'd never do it again."

Jason and Rebecca looked at each other. A second later Matt came clomping down the stairs dressed in a plaid shirt and jeans. "Is my breakfast ready?" he asked.

Susanna's eyes got huge and she quickly turned back to the stove. "It'll be ready in a few minutes."

Matt's eyes turned cold and Rebecca couldn't hold her tongue any longer. "Is that a problem?" she asked.

He smiled the smile of a snake. "No....no, it's not a problem. I just expect stuff done on time when I ask."

"We were talking, Matt," Jason said. "That's why your breakfast's not done."

The big man laughed and settled down in a chair at the kitchen table. "Hey, it's ok!"

They sat across from him and he looked directly at Jason and asked, "So, is she your girlfriend or what?"

Rebecca answered. "I'm his friend."

"I asked him," the big man said, a hint of anger in his voice.

"And *I* answered you," the angel said, smiling sweetly.

His eyes turned hard. "You need to learn your place, lady and only speak when spoken to."

She continued smiling at him. "And who's going to teach me that? You?"

"If you were my girl, then yes, me."

She glared across the table at him. "Seriously? You're joking, right?"

His face went blank for a moment and then he laughed. "Of course I'm joking!"

Jason grabbed the angel's hand under the table and squeezed it lightly. She lowered her head and decided to play the part of a submissive woman to draw Matt out into the light.

"Forgive me. I'm sorry I snapped at you like that, Matt. I'm just tired. It was a long flight."

The big man relaxed more and the tension left the room. He flashed a big smile at Rebecca. "I understand. I get grumpy too sometimes. I guess being a woman makes it worse."

"What do you mean?" she asked and raised her head to look at him. She kept her eyes even so they wouldn't show the rising anger she felt.

He laughed again. "Oh, you *know*! You girls have those messy periods which make you crazy!"

Rebecca's hand squeezed Jason's tightly and he knew he had to diffuse the situation somehow. "Yeah, Matt, you're right. Hey, so Susanna hasn't told me much about you. What do you do?"

Matt leaned back in his chair and proudly puffed his chest out. Rebecca thought he looked like a fucking peacock. "I work at the old mill in town hauling logs," he said, smiling.

"That must be how you got so big," Rebecca said and smiled. She had a feeling the big ass loved to have his ego stroked. She guessed right. His entire mood changed and he seemed even happier than before.

Susanna brought a plate of eggs to him and he dug in as if he'd never eaten. She then quickly placed a tall glass of milk and a few buttered pieces of toast in front of him and he was as happy as a pig in mud. "Thanks, babe!" he said and patted her on the buttocks.

She blushed and scolded, "Not in front of my dad, Matt."

His hand did something then and a few seconds later her face turned bright red. She tried to squirm away and Rebecca could tell whatever it was he was doing to Jason's daughter was sexual because the woman's eyes glazed over and her lips parted.

"Matt....stop...." she groaned and his hand pulled away and he smiled lecherously at Rebecca. She could see the glistening fluid on his fingers and kept her face emotionless.

Susanna quickly moved away from Matt and Rebecca saw the young woman's pajama bottoms were lower than when they'd met.

"So what are your plans?" Matt asked.

Jason looked at Rebecca and shrugged his shoulders. "I hadn't really thought about it. I thought maybe I'd just visit with my daughter for the day."

Matt finished and stood up. "Well, it's been nice meeting you."

He turned to Susanna and she came to him and kissed him. "See you later, babe," he said and a minute later he'd grabbed his coat and left the house. They noticed that Susanna seemed relieved and her eyes brightened suddenly.

"I'll be right back," she said. "I have to make sure sweet Chelsea's alright."

"Who's Chelsea?" Jason asked.

"She's my golden retriever. I keep her in the garage because Matt won't let her in the house."

Rebecca looked at Jason as his daughter rushed off and said, "This guy's a real prick, you know that?"

Jason laughed softly and she asked, "What's so funny?"

He smiled at her. "I'm laughing because you're an angel. I kind of expected you not to use crude words but you're right. He is a prick."

Her eyes became intense. "Look Jason. I may be an angel but I was a human being once. I can't help it if I get angry."

"I understand," he said, amused.

Just then Susanna came back and her shoulders slumped as she sat down. She grimaced in pain and lifted off the chair for a moment before slowly sitting back down. Rebecca noticed her pain and filed it away in her mind. The young woman looked at her and it appeared as if her spirit was gone. She was thoroughly exhausted.

"She's ok, just lonely," Susanna said sadly.

"Has she always lived in the garage, Susanna?" Jason asked.

His daughter's eyes looked so sad. "No, Matt was ok with her when we first met but after a few months she growled at him and he banned her to the garage."

"Asshole," Rebecca muttered under her breath.

"What did you say?" Susanna asked.

"Nothing," Rebecca quietly answered, fuming.

"Susanna, is Matt the reason you always get off the phone so fast with me?" Jason asked.

His daughter's eyes welled with tears and she slowly nodded yes. "I'm sorry, daddy. He-he doesn't like it when I'm on the phone."

"But I'm your father," he said gently. "Surely he understands that, doesn't he?"

She lowered her head and looked at the bruise on her arm. "He wasn't always like this," she said quietly.

Rebecca had seen enough. "He's been beating you, hasn't he?" she asked, her face grim.

Susanna looked at her but didn't answer.

"Why do you stay with him?" the angel asked.

Susanna smiled then. "You don't understand. Matt's really a sweet guy. He cares about me. I just need to not make him mad."

The angel looked at Jason and saw tears forming in his eyes.

"You need to leave him, baby," he said and reached for her hand. She took it in hers and he added, "He's no good for you."

A tear fell from one eye and she whispered, "I can't."

He fought against the frustration he felt. "Why not?"

She looked at Rebecca then and the angel saw the fear in her eyes. "I just can't," she whispered.

They sat in silence until Rebecca leaned towards Jason. "I need some time alone with her," she whispered in his ear. He nodded and stood up.

"I need to use the washroom," he said. "My stomach's a little upset."

"It's down the hall that way, daddy," Susanna said and pointed him in the right direction.

"Thanks. I may be a little while."

She looked at him and her eyes were warm and loving. "Dad?"

"Yes, baby?"

"Thanks for coming. I'm really glad you're here."

"I'm glad too, baby," he said.

Susanna got up and moved to the sink to wash the dishes.

Rebecca grabbed Jason's arm and quietly hissed, "Do you know what that asshole was doing in front of us?! He was fingering her!"

"What?!" he gasped. "How do you know that?!"

Rebecca's face turned red. "Because I know, Jason. Her face told me everything. The asshole was deliberately humiliating her in front of us! It's a power thing, don't you see?!"

His face turned deep red and his hands clenched into fists. He wanted to kill the bastard! "That motherfucker," he growled. "I didn't realize it."

"I'll get to the bottom of this," she said. "Stay in the bathroom until I give the signal its ok to come out, alright?"

"Sure," he said and she saw the concern on his face.

"Everything will be alright, Jason," she whispered and lightly grabbed his hand. "Trust me."

He nodded and Susanna turned just then to see the tender look they gave each other. Jason headed to the bathroom and Susanna dried her hands before gingerly sitting down again.

Rebecca saw her wince again and asked, "Susanna, are you alright? You seem to be in pain. What's wrong?"

Jason's daughter ignored the question and stared hard at the angel. "Are you and my father in a relationship?"

Rebecca was taken aback by the direct question and sat back in her chair.

"What makes you say that?"

Susanna's eyes narrowed. "I saw the way you looked at each other just now. Something's going on between the two of you, isn't it?"

Rebecca smiled and chuckled. "No, no, nothing's going on between us. We're just good friends, that's all."

Susanna's face turned serious. "I'm sorry to be blunt but I know you're lying. I can tell you're more than just friends."

The angel sighed and quietly said, "I care deeply for your father, Susanna but believe me there's nothing going on between us."

She knew the young woman didn't believe her and watched her wince again as she shifted in her seat.

"Susanna, why are you wincing? Why are you in pain?"

The woman looked at her in fear. "I'm not."

"Yes, you *are*," Rebecca said and reached across the table to gently hold the girl's hands. They were cold and she knew Jason's daughter was scared. "Please tell me," she said softly. "You can trust me, Susanna."

"I can't," the young woman said, tears welling in her eyes.

"You don't have to be embarrassed, Susanna," the angel said. "Your father's not here. It's just us girls. You only have to show *me*."

"Show you?" Susanna said in a voice so quiet that most people wouldn't hear her.

Rebecca squeezed the woman's hands lightly. "I need to see, Susanna. Show me what he did to you."

"You can't be serious," Susanna said, smirking. "I just met you and you expect me to show you my ass? That's never gonna happen."

Rebecca let go of Susanna's hands and had a thought. "What if I show you mine first? Will you do it then?"

Susanna grinned. "You're fucking with me. I just know it. You won't do it."

Rebecca stood up and turned her back to the girl. Glancing back at her, she slowly lifted her white dress over her hips to her stomach and held it there. Susanna's jaw dropped as she stared at Rebecca's naked buttocks. "You're not wearing panties," she said quietly.

"You're right, I'm not. I never do," Rebecca said and lowered her dress. She turned around again and sat down.

Susanna stared in astonishment at her and whispered, "I can't believe you just did that."

Rebecca smiled a reassuring smile. "Now it's your turn."

Susanna slowly stood up. She glanced towards the bathroom and Rebecca reassured her. "Your father will be a while. Please show me. No one else is here."

Susanna nodded and slowly turned around. She hooked her thumbs into her pajama bottoms and looked back at Rebecca. "I can't," she whispered.

"You *can*," the angel said, her smile kind. "Please trust me."

Susanna slowly pulled the pajamas down past her buttocks and Rebecca gasped. The poor girl's bottom was covered with black and blue bruises. Some of the bruises were older and turning yellow.

"He did that to you?" Rebecca asked and Susanna quickly pulled the pajamas back up. She turned, looked at Rebecca and blushed a deep red.

"Yes," she quietly said. "I get a spanking once a week. Matt says he does it to keep me in line."

Rebecca fought the urge to break the table in two and kept her composure. "I'm sorry, Susanna."

The girl sat back down again and tears ran down her cheeks. "I know I make him mad sometimes. I don't mean to."

Rebecca's head swirled with violent thoughts but she kept smiling. "Susanna, you need to get out of this relationship. It's no good for you."

The young woman's eyes became terrified. "I can't," she whispered. "He'd kill me."

Rebecca grit her teeth. "No one's going to hurt you, Susanna. *I'm* here now."

"Who *are* you?" Jason's daughter asked. "Why do you care?"

Rebecca reached for the girl's hand and gently held it. "I care because your Jason's daughter and besides, no woman should ever be treated the way Matt treats you."

"But what can *you* do," Susanna asked as she wiped away tears. "You're smaller than I am. Do you know karate or something?"

Rebecca laughed lightly. "*No,* I don't know karate. Just believe in me. That's all I ask."

Susanna stared into the angel's eyes. "I don't understand this. I don't know you but you make me feel so safe. I almost want to believe you."

Rebecca smiled. "You can believe me, Susanna. I *can* keep you safe."

"I see now why my father likes you. There's something different about you. Something comforting."

Rebecca blushed and Susanna asked, "Do you love him?"

The angel lowered her head and then looked straight into Susanna's eyes. "I'm not sure yet," she answered truthfully. "I'm feeling things for your father I've never felt before."

"I knew it," Susanna said, smiling. "Does Dad know? Have you told him yet?"

"No. I need to be sure."

Susanna squeezed Rebecca's hand and said, "I like you. I really do."

"Thank you, Susanna. I like you to," Rebecca replied.

"Ok, I'm done!" Jason suddenly yelled from the bathroom.

Rebecca and Susanna laughed together. "Ok, you can come back! We're done in here!" Rebecca yelled.

Susanna stood up and greeted her father with a kiss. "I really like her," she whispered in his ear.

He smiled and she looked back at Rebecca. "I need to take a shower and get dressed. Would you like a tour of the town when I'm done?"

"Sure! That'd be great!" Jason said.

His daughter glanced at Rebecca again and felt a warm tingle run through her. "I'm really glad you're here," she said and turned and left the room.

Rebecca waited until she heard the water running in the shower upstairs before she turned to Jason.

"Well?!" he asked. "What did you find out?!"

The angel's face turned red. "He's a total asshole, Jason. Don't say anything but I made her show me her backside. Her poor bottom is beaten black and blue."

"What?!" he cried, enraged.

"She gets a spanking once a week. That's in addition to the other bruises we saw. She's scared of him, Jason."

"That motherfucker! I'll kill him!"

"No," she said quietly and touched his arm. "I've watched over women before who are in abusive relationships. If we push her too hard, she'll just stay with him. We have to do this the right way."

"How?!" he asked, frustrated. "We can't just let him beat her. I won't allow it!"

"Let me work on her, Jason. She trusts me now."

"Alright," he said, defeated.

Rebecca pulled him close. "Jason, I know you want to stop him but please listen to me. I know what I'm doing. I need to convince her that she'd be safe if she left him."

He pushed the hair away from her cheek and gazed into her eyes. "Alright, my angel, I'll trust you," he whispered.

Rebecca grabbed his hand and held it to her face. "I like when you call me that, Jason. I like being your angel."

His eyes changed and for the first time in her life Rebecca felt a warm tingling run through her. The feeling was intense and for a moment she forgot she was an angel. "Oh Jason," she whispered and pressed her head against his chest. "Please hold me and don't let go."

"I'll always be here for you," he whispered as he kissed the top of her head. "You know I will."

A shiver ran through her. Her eyes were filled with fear as they gazed into his. "I don't understand what's happening between us," she whispered.

"Rebecca….I…."

She pressed her fingers against his lips. "Don't say it, Jason. Don't say it until you're absolutely sure."

He nodded and she took her hand away. Jason held her tightly. "Thank you for being here. Thank you for helping Susanna."

"Was your wife like her?"

Jason shook his head sadly. "No. Susanna's different. There's a tenderness inside her. Kind of like you."

Rebecca smiled. "Like me?"

"Yes. You both have a special warmth about you."

"We do?"

"Yes," Jason replied. "That's what I love about both of you."

Rebecca's eyes opened wide in surprise. "What did you say?"

Jason blushed and stared hard at her. "I said that's what I love about both of you."

The angel touched his face with her hand and stared into his eyes. She didn't say anything but her eyes said it all. There was a tenderness there and he felt them becoming closer than before.

Susanna finished getting ready and came back down to find them hugging each other. She stood in the doorway watching and smiled. Rebecca suddenly realized they were being watched and pulled away from Jason.

"You were going to show us the town," she said, her face flushed.

"Yes, of course!" Susanna said. "Let's go!"

They put on their winter coats and stepped outside.

Susanna said, "We can walk to town. It's not too far from here."

"Ok," Jason said and they began their journey.

They could see their breath in the air as they walked. After a while, Jason shivered and Rebecca pulled him close. Susanna smiled at the gesture of kindness. *I really like her,* she thought. *She's good for Dad.*

The trees were covered with a light dusting of snow as they headed down a gravel path. "The town only has a few hundred residents," Susanna said. "There's a big barn we have where activities take place like bingo and tractor pulls. Lots of people from the surrounding area come here for those."

"Sounds like fun," Jason said.

"It is," Susanna said. She pointed at a large wooden building a few hundred feet away. "There it is. See? I told you it wasn't far."

The barn was indeed big. Jason could see how tractors and a large group of people could fit in it. The large door was ajar and Susanna looked puzzled. Rebecca saw the look on her face and asked, "Susanna, is something wrong?"

"That's strange," she answered. "It's usually locked when there's nothing going on inside."

Jason grabbed the door and with a little effort pulled it open a bit. "Can we look inside?"

"Sure, why not?" his daughter replied.

They stepped inside and a tingle tickled the angel's nose. *Oh no*, she thought. *I know what that smell is.*

She sniffed the air and frowned. Jason looked at her and said, "What's wrong? Is it too musty in here for you?"

"Yes, a little," she lied.

They looked around and saw bales of hay everywhere plus some old farm equipment. There were long tables lying against the sides of the barn and Susanna said, "Those are for bingo night."

Rebecca stepped forward and sniffed the air again. There it was again. That rusty smell she feared.

"What's going on?" Jason asked. "What do you smell?"

"There's something here," Rebecca said quietly and moved slowly towards the center of the large barn. There was a coating of fresh sand on the floor and she moved it around with her foot.

"What is it? Tell me," Jason said, worried.

Rebecca got on her hands and knees and moved the sand away. A large dark red spot appeared and she leaned down and sniffed it. Her face scrunched then and she stood up to face Susanna. "What did you say happens in here?" she asked.

"Bingo, tractor pulls and other stuff. I don't come here for everything so I'm not sure. Why do you ask?"

The angel shivered. "Because that's blood on the floor."

"What?! Are you sure?!" Jason cried.

"I wish I was wrong but I'm not," she said.

Susanna looked frightened. "Blood?! How? I don't understand?"

"I don't either," Rebecca lied. She knew exactly what had happened here and didn't like it.

"I'll get to the bottom of this," Susanna said. "I'll ask Matt. He comes here a lot. Maybe he knows."

"No!" Rebecca cried and grabbed the woman's arm. "Don't ask him!"

Susanna was shocked by Rebecca's sudden reaction. "Why not? I told you he comes here a lot. Why shouldn't I ask him?"

"Please just listen to me and don't ask him."

"Alright," Susanna said softly and the angel let go of her arm.

Just then they heard a sound outside like a car door closing. Rebecca kicked the sand back over the spot and grabbed Jason and Sus-anna's hands. She pulled them towards a far wall and whispered, "Don't say a word about the blood, understand?!"

They nodded just as the barn door opened wide. "Hey!" a man yelled. "What are you doing in here?!"

They turned and saw three men standing in the entrance. They were dressed like lumberjacks and holding shotguns.

"Hey, Ike," Susanna said, smiling.

The men moved closer. "Susanna?! What are you doing in here?" the biggest man asked.

"The door was unlocked so we came inside."

Jason extended his hand and said, "Hi, I'm Susanna's father. She was just showing us around town."

The man ignored him and stared intensely at Susanna. "Does Matt know you're here?"

Rebecca saw the sudden fear in Susanna's eyes as she answered, "No, he doesn't. I told you the door was unlocked so we came in."

"Who's she?" the second largest man asked with a sneer on his face as he stared at Rebecca.

"I'm her father's friend. Nice to meet you," she said and extended her hand.

He stared at it like it was poison and then glared at her. "You shouldn't be in here. It's off limits."

"But I thought this place was for bingo and tractor pulls. At least that's what Susanna told us. Why should it be off limits?"

The man's eyes were cold and unfeeling and she sensed his anger. "Because I said so," he said quietly though his voice was threatening.

Rebecca laughed then and said, "It's a public place. Do you own it?"

He moved closer and gripped his gun tightly. "You've got a real mouth on you, don't you, little girl?"

Susanna didn't like the way the conversation was heading so she stepped in front of Rebecca and said, "C'mon, Jerry. She didn't mean 'nothin. She's not from around here. We'll leave, ok?"

The man glared at Rebecca who stood her ground and smiled brightly at him. "What's so funny?" he asked menacingly.

"You are," she answered.

His face turned red and he took another step towards her but the man named Ike grabbed his arm. "Ok, Jerry. Enough."

He looked at Susanna and said, "You know we'll have to tell Matt about this, don't you?"

Rebecca had had enough. "Why?" she asked loudly. "She can do what she wants without his permission, can't she?!"

Jerry leered at her then. "I wish Matt was *your* boyfriend. He'd set you straight real fast!"

Rebecca looked at him and laughed. "There isn't a man alive who can set me straight!"

His face turned a brighter shade of red and Susanna grabbed Rebecca's arm. "C'mon, let's go," she said.

The men moved out of the way and the three of them slowly walked towards the entrance. The man named Jerry yelled, "I hope we meet again! Just you and me, lady!"

Rebecca stopped and turned to look at him. "I hope so too," she said and smiled. "I really hope so."

She turned back around then and followed Jason and his daughter out of the barn. They walked a couple hundred yards and Rebecca knew Susanna's heart was pounding like a jackhammer. "What the hell were you thinking?!" the woman suddenly yelled and grabbed her arm.

Rebecca looked at Susanna and said, "Let go of me. I only allow people to touch me when I want them to."

Susanna's nostrils flared but she sensed something dangerous in Rebecca and let go of her arm. "That was stupid!" she said. "Jerry's a bad man and you just pissed him off!"

"Do I look worried?" Rebecca laughed.

Susanna looked at her father. "Is she crazy? Where'd you find her anyway? Wacko Village?"

Jason smiled. "No, Susanna. She's not crazy, just confidant."

She looked at Rebecca and said, "I don't know what the deal is with you but around here women need to respect men."

Rebecca laughed. "You mean be a good little girl and do everything they ask, is that it, Susanna? Be their good little sex slave and make their breakfast, lunch and dinner for them? Is that what you mean? Well, fuck that! I'm not that kind of woman, are you?!"

She suddenly realized she'd gone too far and Susanna's head lowered in shame. "It wasn't like that at first," Susanna whispered. "Matt was kind and decent to me."

"Then what the hell happened, Susanna?" her father asked. "What made him change?"

She looked sadly at her father. "I don't know for sure, daddy. He changed when I let him move in with me after I bought the house. At first, we had disagreements about what furniture to buy and then what colors the walls should be. Eventually I just let him make all the decisions. It's better that way."

"How'd you meet him?" Rebecca asked.

Susanna smiled. "I work at the hardware store in the tool department. One day he walked in and we started talking. He's so handsome and I couldn't help liking him. We just hit it off."

"Susanna," Jason said. "I know we haven't talked much since your mother died but when you moved out of the house why'd you pick this place to live? It seems so….remote."

She looked around and sniffed the air. "Because it's fairly quiet, dad and peaceful. Most of the people that live around here are nice. Life moves slower here too and I like that….a lot."

"I understand," he said. "I just miss you, baby. We used to talk a lot, remember?"

"I remember," she said softly. "I'm sorry dad, but I was angry with you."

"Angry at me? For what?!"

She sighed. "When mom died you became different. I needed you then but you withdrew from me. Don't you remember?"

"I'm sorry," he said quietly. "I was so lonely and in a lot of pain. My body's falling apart and I don't know what to do."

Susanna looked at him like he was a stranger. "What the hell are you talking about, dad? What do you mean you're falling apart?"

He felt like a fool and said, "My job, Susanna. They demoted me and I work much harder now. It's more physical than it used to be."

"Then quit," she said matter of factly.

He looked at Rebecca and back at his daughter. "I can't," he whispered.

Susanna glared at him. "Why, dad? Is this about your stupid male pride?"

Rebecca smiled. "You're very perceptive, Susanna. I think the same thing."

Jason changed the subject. "You never asked me why I was on the news, Susanna."

Her eyes got big and she felt badly about that.

"I'm sorry, dad. I was preoccupied with my own problems when you called. Will you tell me about it now?"

"I saved a woman and her son in a fire!" he said proudly.

"What?! Really?!" she exclaimed.

"Yes!" he said and she looked at him in a new light.

"My father's a hero?" she asked and looked at Rebecca.

The angel smiled. "You should have seen him, Susanna. He ran into that house and carried them both out."

Her jaw dropped. "How? I thought you said you were falling apart. How did you do what you did then?"

Jason looked at Rebecca and his eyes twinkled. "I had help from someone special."

"You?" Susanna asked as she stared intensely at Rebecca.

The angel nodded and Susanna smiled. "There's obviously more to this than what you're both telling me. I'm very curious what it is."

Just then, the three men from the barn drove slowly past them. The nasty one who'd threatened Rebecca stuck his head out the window and said, "You still here?"

Rebecca smiled at him and said, "Yeah and I'm not going anywhere."

He sneered at her and they drove on. "Jesus, Rebecca, I wish you wouldn't goad him," Susanna said, worried. "I've heard things about that man."

"Like what?"

Susanna's face turned pale. "Oh, just rumors about how he hates women."

Rebecca laughed and put her hands on her hips. "Don't worry about me, Susanna! I can take care of myself."

Susanna looked at her father and said, "Yep! She's crazy alright!"

They started walking again and Susanna pointed out the town's small gas station and country store. Every building seemed to be frozen in time and unchanged for years. Jason began to see why his daughter loved this area. It was very intimate in a way. The perfect place to settle down in.

They came to the small diner and Jason said, "Good, I'm hungry. How about you, Susanna?"

She nodded. "Yeah, I could use a bite to eat. They have great burgers here."

Jason opened the door which had a bell attached at the top. It rang and they entered. There were about ten booths and tables inside but only a few were occupied. The man named Jerry sat alone in one of them with his shoulders slumped while drinking a cup of coffee.

"Maybe we should go somewhere else," Susanna whispered.

"No," Rebecca said as she stared at the man. "I like it here."

A young waitress approached them and smiled. "Hi Susanna! You want your usual booth?"

"Sure, Nancy. That would be great," she replied.

Jerry turned and saw them as they were shown to a booth a few feet away from him. The cute waitress handed them menus and then walked over to Jerry. They sat down and Jason looked around. "I really like this," he said. "It reminds me of my childhood. Walgreens used to have a small dining area that looked like this. My mother used to take me there."

"You never told me that, dad," Susanna said.

"Yeah, they had good food. It was also one of the few places a kid could get chocolate milk at."

He looked over the menu and his eyes got wide. "Hey, they've got chocolate phosphates!"

Just then, Jerry's voice could be heard loud and clear. "Hey Nancy, why do you allow people like them in here?"

"C'mon, Jerry, please lower your voice," the waitress said, worried. "They'll hear you."

He laughed and said, "Who? That bitch?!"

Jason's face turned red and he was about to get up but Rebecca grabbed his arm to stop him. "No, Jason, let me deal with him."

Susanna started to protest but Rebecca shot her a look that shut her up. "Wait here," she said and walked over to where Jerry was sitting.

"Mind if I sit down?" she asked.

"What the fuck do you want?!" he asked nastily. His face was etched in anger but his eyes showed something different which she recognized. He was hurting. Badly.

"I just want to talk, that's all," she said softly.

He motioned to the seat opposite him. "Go ahead. Nobody's stopping you."

She sat and stared at him and he squirmed uncomfortably in his seat. His face was rugged and it looked like he hadn't shaved in days. Rebecca guessed he was in his fifties but he seemed much older.

"Well, what do you want?" he asked and gripped his shotgun tightly.

Rebecca quietly said, "Tell me why you're so unhappy, Jerry."

The man's eyes opened in surprise and he looked quickly around the room to see if anyone was listening.

"No one else can hear us, Jerry," she said. "You can tell me. I know you're not really a bad man."

"Oh really?!" he laughed. "And how do you know that?!"

"I can tell," she said. "You were just being mean earlier to show off for your friends, weren't you?"

His eyes turned hard. "No, you're wrong. You're just another bitch as far as I can tell. Now fuck off and leave me alone."

Rebecca didn't flinch. "Jerry, were you ever married?" she asked.

His right eye twitched. "Yeah, I was married once. What's it to you?"

"Did you talk to your wife the way you talk to me?"

He stared at her and wiped a tear from one eye. "Leave me alone," he whispered. "Please go away."

Rebecca slowly reached out and touched the hand that wasn't holding the shotgun. He stared down at it like he'd been stung by a bee. "It's ok, Jerry….you're ok. Please tell me about her."

He looked into her eyes and she saw the terrible hurt in them. "Her hands were soft like yours," he said quietly.

Rebecca wrapped her fingers around his and she felt him shiver. He leaned the shotgun against the side of the booth and she reached for his hand. "Please leave me alone," he whispered.

Rebecca ignored him and said, "Give me your hand, Jerry and show me what happened."

His eyes filled with fear but he let her hold his other hand. They faced each other in silence for a moment until Rebecca said, "Let me in, Jerry. Please let me in."

He nodded and she gripped his hands tighter. Her mind was suddenly flooded with images of a beautiful auburn haired woman with bright blue eyes and a kind smile. "She's lovely, Jerry," she said, thinking there was something in this sour man that his wife had loved.

His mood changed then and he growled, "She was a bitch like all women!"

Rebecca looked deeper into his eyes and he softened. "I hate her," he said quietly. He wasn't very convincing and she smiled.

"No you don't," Rebecca said. "You loved her very much. I can sense it."

Suddenly she saw his wife lying in a hospital bed. The beautiful woman was now frail and sickly looking. Jerry was standing over her holding her hand. His face was hardened by strain and he said, "I hate you, Amy. I hate you for leaving me."

The dying woman was terribly hurt by his words and he felt ashamed. She closed her eyes then and took her last breath.

Rebecca felt a tear slip down her cheek and she gasped. Jerry tried to pull his hands away from hers but she wouldn't let him. "Let go of me," he growled.

She let go of his hands and said, "You didn't mean to say that to her, Jerry. You don't hate her. In fact, you loved her very much."

"How do you know what I said?" he asked, shocked.

"I saw it," she said. "I saw her final moment."

He lowered his head and began to cry. "She left me!" he whispered. "She left me all alone."

"She didn't mean to, Jerry. She had cancer. It wasn't her fault."

He lifted his head and tears streamed down his cheeks.

"I know you're angry but you don't have to take it out on others, Jerry," Rebecca said quietly. "Amy loved you very much. She wouldn't want you to be like this."

"I could kill myself for telling her I hated her," he said. "When she needed me most I wasn't there for her. I only thought of myself."

"You're only human, Jerry," Rebecca said when she saw the wispy shape take form by the man's side. "You have to forgive yourself. *Amy* does."

"She does?" he asked, his eyes opening wide with hope. "How do you know that?"

Rebecca smiled and looked at the dim form of his wife sitting next to him. A tingling warmth surged through Jerry and he gasped.

"I know because she's sitting right next to you," Rebecca softly said.

Jerry looked to his right and a shiver ran through him. "She is?!"

Rebecca released his hands and said, "Yes, Jerry. She's reaching for your hand."

The man looked down at his right hand and something invisible pressed against his palm. A sweet warmth made him gasp and he felt soft fingers close around his. Startled, he looked at Rebecca. "How? This can't be happening!"

"Tell her how much you love her, Jerry," she said. "This is your chance."

He trembled as he stared at his hand. "I love you, Amy. I'm so sorry I said I hated you. I didn't mean it. Oh God, I miss you so much!"

He leaned to the side and began to sob. Invisible arms wrapped around him then and soft lips kissed his cheek. His heart leaped in his chest. "Oh my God! You're here. You're really here!"

The voice was barely audible but he heard it anyway. "I love you, Jerry," it said.

His eyes opened wide and the grip on his hand loosened. "No! Don't go, Amy!" he cried. "Please don't go!"

He felt the sudden void next to him and he looked at Rebecca with pleading eyes. "She's gone, isn't she?" he asked.

Rebecca nodded yes. "It took a lot of effort for her to be here with you, Jerry but she needed to see you to tell you that she loved you."

"Will she come back?" he asked, hopeful.

Rebecca reached for his hands and he quickly took hold of them.

"I'm sorry, Jerry but you won't see her again until you cross over to the other side."

His eyes lit up. "I can't wait! I'll just kill myself!"

"No!" Rebecca said quickly. "If you do that then you'll *never* see her. The only way is to lead a good life. That's what Amy wants."

"*How?*" he said, his eyes blurring with tears. "I don't know how."

"Just live your life, Jerry and be a good man."

He nodded and looked deeply into her eyes. "How do you know so much?" he asked. "Who are you?"

She smiled a smile so kind it made his heart surge with new life. "I'm your friend, Jerry."

He shivered and said, "I never asked you your name."

The angel smiled and quietly said, "Rebecca....my name's Rebecca."

"Thank you, Rebecca," he whispered. "Thank you so much."

She let go of his hands then and got out of the booth, her eyes penetrating his. "Goodbye, Jerry and remember. Live a good life."

"I will," he said, his eyes beaming with gratitude.

"I know you will," she said and turned away to rejoin Jason and Susanna.

They stared at her dumbfounded and she wiped tears from her eyes. Jerry got up to pay his bill but stopped by their table first. "You folks have a good day now," he said, smiling.

"Thanks, we will," Jason said. The man looked at Rebecca then and his eyes became softer.

"Goodbye Rebecca. I enjoyed our talk."

She reached for his hand and squeezed it lightly. "I did too," she said.

She let go of his hand and he paid his bill and left. Susanna looked at Rebecca in awe.

"What the hell just happened? That man hated your guts a few minutes ago and now you act like you're best friends! What did you say to him anyway?"

Rebecca smiled. "Jerry's not a bad man. He was acting out, that's all. I just talked to him and he listened."

Susanna stared at her in amazement and then looked at her father. "Dad, this friend of yours is creeping me out. She's not normal."

He smiled and his eyes twinkled as he gazed at his angel. "You're right. She's *not* normal. In fact, she's the most wonderful woman I've ever known."

Rebecca blushed. "I just did what was right. Sometimes what we see on the outside is not a reflection of what's on the inside."

The waitress, Nancy came over then and said, "Sorry I left you alone for so long but I was watching from the back. I thought there was gonna be a fight for sure."

Jason smiled. "No, everything's fine. We'd like to order now because I'm starving!"

He ordered the chocolate phosphate he'd been excited about and a hamburger with extra onions. Susanna asked for the mostacciolli with meat sauce and an iced tea while Rebecca asked for a small bowl of peppermint ice cream with hot fudge on top.

Nancy walked away to fill their order and Susanna looked strangely at Rebecca. "Aren't you hungry? Don't you need more than just ice cream?"

The angel smiled. "When I was a little girl my dad would take me to a little candy shop in town that served ice cream. This was my favorite."

"Oh really? Where was that?" Susanna asked.

Rebecca stared at her and said, "It's not there anymore."

"What do you mean?" Susanna asked.

Rebecca's entire demeanor changed and she seemed tense. "I don't want to talk about it."

By the look on the woman's face, Susanna knew not to push the issue so she stayed silent. Jason closed his eyes and smiled. "Do you smell that?" he asked. "It smells just like Walgreens did when I was a kid."

Susanna grabbed her father's arm and squeezed it. "I'm glad you're happy, dad."

"I am," he said. "How could I not be happy sitting here with my two favorite girls?"

Nancy came out with their food and drinks then and set it down in front of them. "There you go. Can I get you anything else?"

"No, this is perfect! Thank you!" Jason said and immediately grabbed the juicy looking burger. He took a bite of it and closed his eyes while moaning happily.

"You're funny, mister!" Nancy said. "I wish everyone who came in here liked our food as much as you do!"

Jason stared at the food like a man who'd gone days without eating and Susanna laughed.

Nancy walked away then and they started to eat. Rebecca licked her lips and moaned herself after taking a taste of the hot fudge. "Oh wow. It's been so long."

"You two are hilarious," Susanna said and smiled. "You act like you've never eaten before."

She took a few bites of the mostacciolli and moaned herself. Jason and Rebecca stopped eating and looked at her. "Hey!" she said. "If you can do it then so can I!"

They burst out laughing and heard the bell over the door ring. Jason turned around and saw four large men enter the diner. "Yeah, there they are," one of them said. He had red bushy hair and his face was weathered from the sun.

Jason looked away and whispered, "Oh shit."

The four men approached and stood at the side of the booth looking down at them.

"I heard you were snooping around at the barn," another man said, looking at Jason. He was even bigger than the redhead and had broad shoulders and huge forearms. "Find anything interesting?"

Susanna said, "I told Ike earlier that the door was unlocked. I was just showing my dad and his friend around town."

His eyes flashed angrily at her. "Shut up, Susanna. I was talking to him, not you."

Jason's jaw dropped. "Who the hell do you think you are?! That's my daughter you're talking to!"

The man leaned close to Jason and smiled an evil smile. "I don't give a fuck who she is, mister. Women around here don't talk unless we tell them to."

Jason surprised himself and lashed out with his fist. It caught the man in the belly and his eyes bugged out. Gasping for breath, he fell into the arms of another man. The burly redhead grabbed Jason by the shirt collar and yanked him out of the booth. "You son of a bitch!" he snarled.

Rebecca tried to get out of the booth but one of the men slammed his fist on the table. "You stay here!" he said threateningly.

The redhead drove his fist into Jason's stomach and he fell to his knees. "Get him up!" he ordered a man.

Jason was lifted to his feet and his arms were pulled behind his back. Rebecca looked up at the man blocking her and sneered. "Real tough guys, aren't you? Why don't you fight him fair?"

"Yeah, I figured it was you. I heard you've got a real mouth on you, girlie. How 'bout I shut it for you?!"

"Leave her alone!" Jason yelled and he lashed out with his leg and caught the redhead in the groin with his foot. The man groaned and collapsed to the floor. With a surge of strength he didn't know he had, Jason wrenched free of the man holding him and lunged at the one threatening Rebecca. "Asshole!" he yelled.

The man quickly turned around and hit Jason in the jaw with a stunning right cross that made his knees weak. He fell as if in slow motion and Susanna screamed, "Daddy!"

"Yeah, just as I thought," the man who hit him said. "You're a pussy just like this bitch with the big mouth is, ain't you, tough guy?"

His back was turned to Rebecca who'd gotten out of the booth. He suddenly felt fingers on the side of his neck pinch something there. Immediately, his lower leg jerked and he was frozen and helpless. "Got you, asshole," she whispered in his ear. "Isn't it amazing how a pinch in the right spot can turn your legs to jelly?"

He let out a squeak and the other three men stared at her amazed. The redhead gasped, "Let him go, bitch or you'll be sorry."

He took a step towards her and she said, "Stop right there or I'll hurt him real bad."

The men hesitated and looked at each other. "Take your friend here and get out now while you can," she said calmly.

One of the men laughed. "Fuck you! You can't take us all on no matter how much karate crap you know!"

Her eyes narrowed. "Try me."

Just then, a giant of a man came out of the kitchen. His bald head was sweaty and his big belly pushed out the front of his cooking apron. "Ok, Alan, enough," he said calmly. "Leave these people alone."

"But Jeff, they attacked us!" the redhead wailed.

The cook's eyes glared at him. "No they didn't. You started the whole thing. I think it's time you left."

"But, Jeff!"

The man lifted his big hands and made fists. "You heard what I said. Get out."

The men backed away and Jeff looked at Rebecca. "Let him go," he said.

"Aren't you going to call the police?"

"No," he said. "Look lady, I don't want no trouble. Just let him go."

"But they'll be waiting outside for us," she said.

He clenched his fists tighter and stared blankly at the men. "No, they won't. They know better than to mess with me. Now let him go."

She released the grip on the man's neck and he fell into another booth like a store dummy. His legs felt like jelly and he was numb all over. He managed to push himself up and stared at Rebecca with hate in his eyes. "You'll be sorry for this," he gasped as he rubbed the back of his neck.

Jeff lumbered forward and glared at him. "Threaten her again and you'll be in the hospital for a week!"

The man sneered at the cook and stumbled out of the diner behind the other men.

Jeff looked at Rebecca and Jason and said, "If I was you I'd get out of town real quick."

"But we didn't do anything wrong, Jeff!" Jason protested. "We just came here to see Susanna!"

"I'm sorry," the cook said. "Whatever you did pissed them off. I know them. They won't back off."

"I used to like this town. Now I'm not so sure anymore," Susanna said sadly.

Jeff towered over her but he seemed very kind and not threatening. "Susanna," he said in as tender a voice as he could muster. "You don't belong here. You're a nice girl but these people are different. Some of them aren't so nice."

"But I have a job and own a house here," she said. "I can't just leave."

He lightly gripped her shoulders. "You have to, Susanna. Find another job somewhere else and sell your house."

"But what about Matt? I can't just leave him."

Rebecca had heard enough. "Yes, you can," she interjected. "You have to for your own well being. He's no good for you, Susanna."

"But what about my things and Chealsea? I'd have to pack."

"We'll help you," Jason said. "Will you let us?"

A tear fell from one eye and she nodded yes. "Alright, dad," she whispered.

He smiled. "You can live with me for a while. Would you like that?"

"Really? You'd let me stay with you?" she asked, touched by her father's kindness.

"Of course," he answered. "You're my daughter and I love you."

"What about Chelsea?" she asked.

"My building accepts pets. She'll be fine there."

His daughter's face lit up and she seemed genuinely happy but then she looked scared.

"What's wrong?" Rebecca asked.

"How do I tell Matt I'm leaving? He's going to be mad. *Real* mad."

"We'll be there when you tell him, alright?" Rebecca said and lightly touched Susanna's arm. "Don't worry. Everything will be fine."

Susanna nodded and turned to Jeff. "I'm going to miss it here. You've always been so nice to me and I love your food."

He smiled and bent down to kiss her cheek. "We'll miss you too, Susanna. Take care of yourself."

Nancy appeared and went to hug Susanna. "I'm sorry it has to be like this. I'll miss you."

Susanna nodded again and Rebecca said, "We'd better get going."

They started to walk away but Jason suddenly turned and said, "Hey, we forgot to pay for our food."

Jeff laughed. "Forget it, man! It's on me!"

"Thanks," Jason said and followed the women out the door.

The air had turned chillier and Jason felt uneasy. "Let's get going," he said.

They walked slowly back to Susanna's house and she pointed out areas she had always loved to visit. They stopped here and there until she motioned them to follow her down a grassy path. "Where are we going?" Jason asked.

"This is where I come to think," she said and walked on.

It wasn't far and Jason gasped when they stopped in front of a small pond surrounded by large evergreen trees. The scene was like something out of a Christmas card. "Susanna, this is beautiful," he said. "I can see why you like it so much."

She smiled and looked out at the glistening water. "It's so peaceful here," she whispered.

Rebecca came close and stood next to her. "Yes, it is," she said. "There aren't many places like this left."

Susanna stared intensely at her and asked, "Rebecca, how did you know there was blood on the floor back at the barn?"

The angel hesitated before answering and looked at Jason.

"I have a good sense of smell," she said finally.

"Oh," Susanna said and glanced back at the water. "You're not from around here, are you?" she said quietly.

"What do you mean?" the angel asked.

"I *mean*….you're not from *here*. Am I right?"

Rebecca smiled. "You're very perceptive, Susanna. Where do you think I'm from?"

The girl gazed into the angel's eyes with a curious look. "I haven't decided yet," she said.

Jason rubbed his sore chin and Rebecca reached out to touch it. "How bad are you hurt?"

"It's just real sore but I think I'll live. It's my stomach that hurts. That guy's fist almost broke me in half. I was careless. I should have expected him to do that."

Rebecca put her arm around his and looked at him with admiration. "You stuck up for me. No one's ever done that before."

He smiled but said glumly, "Yeah, I did great, didn't I?"

"Under the circumstances, you did the best you could, Jason," she said. "You're *my* hero."

"You still insist you're just friends, huh?!" Susanna laughed. "Look at the two of you. Who do you think you're fooling anyway?!"

Jason blushed and Rebecca let go of his arm. Susanna looked around one last time. "I need to pack some things before Matt comes home from work so I'll be ready to go," she said quietly.

"We can help if you'd like," Rebecca said.

Jason looked at her strangely. "Can I talk to you alone for a moment?"

They walked to a corner of the pond where Susanna wouldn't hear them and he seemed concerned.

"What is it?" Rebecca asked.

"How are we going back? You can't fly me, Susanna, her dog and her things back, can you?"

She burst out laughing and said, "Of course not, silly! You'll have to rent a car!"

He nodded and they walked back to where Susanna was standing with her eyes closed. The young woman was breathing in the crisp fresh air and said, "I wish there was someplace else like this."

Rebecca touched her hand and said, "There is, Susanna."

"What? Where?" she asked, surprised and stared at Rebecca.

The angel closed her own eyes and whispered, "Where we go when we die."

Susanna's jaw dropped open and she slowly backed away from Rebecca. "Who are you?" she whispered, her eyes wide with fear.

Rebecca opened her eyes and smiled at her. "Susanna, you have nothing to fear from me. I already told you that I'm your friend."

Jason's daughter stared intensely at her and she turned to walk back the way they'd come. "Let's go," she said.

They walked in silence the rest of the way until they stood in front of Susanna's house.

"Can we help you pack in a little while?" Jason asked. "I've got to go rent a car."

Susanna looked around. "Where's the rental car you drove in from the airport?" she asked.

Jason thought fast and answered, "A taxi dropped us off."

"Oh," his daughter said. "Well, don't worry about it. We can take my car. It's big enough."

"Ok, great!" he said.

They entered the house and Susanna said, "Make yourselves at home. I'll go see if I have any boxes I can use. If not, I can pick some up from the hardware store."

Being winter, it was starting to get dark outside early and the shadows crept into the house. The sun went behind the clouds and it looked like it was going to snow. Rebecca and Jason waited patiently and looked around the living room. She picked up a small snowglobe with a Christmas scene and shook it gently. "I'm sorry Susanna has to leave this place," she said. "It *is* nice here."

They heard yelling and suddenly Susanna appeared in the doorway. Her face was ashen.

"What's wrong, Susanna?!" Jason asked, worried and rushed to her side.

"He's taken her," she whispered. "He's taken Chelsea."

CHAPTER FIFTEEN

"Who's taken Chelsea? Matt?" Jason asked.

"Yes," she whispered, worry etched on her face.

"How do you know it was him?" Rebecca asked.

"I just know," she said and her shoulders slumped.

"But you said he's at work. It can't be him."

Susanna handed her the note she'd found. There was one word on it. It read simply, "Bitch."

Rebecca looked at Jason and handed him the note. His face scrunched up in anger. "Why? Why would he do this?"

"Those men at the diner," Susanna said. "I'll bet they told him what happened. He probably did it to punish me."

She began to cry and Rebecca put her arm around her shoulders. "Susanna," she said gently. "Maybe he didn't take her anywhere. Maybe he just let her out and she's running around out here."

"Really?" the girl asked, her eyes hopeful. "She might come back then, right?"

"Yes," the angel reassured her. "Why don't you wait here in case she comes back while your father and I look around outside for her, ok?"

"Thank you," she said and pulled out a photo of the dog from her wallet and showed it to her. "Please, Rebecca, find her for me. I love her so much!"

"Let's go," Rebecca said to Jason and they stepped outside.

"Where do we start looking?" he asked. "She could be anywhere."

Her face was grim when she answered. "I think I know. We have to hurry."

Jason followed her until they got past a small clump of trees where no one could see them. Rebecca grabbed him then and before he knew it her wings had popped out and they were flying again. "Where are we going?!" he yelled as the cold air brushed his face.

"To the barn!" she answered.

It took only a minute or so and they gently landed a few feet in front of the barn. There were a lot of cars parked in the lot now and Jason was curious. "I wonder if they're having bingo now. It's a little early for that, isn't it?"

Rebecca stared at him. "No Jason, they're not here for bingo."

"What then? Why are we here?"

"You'll see. Prepare yourself. You're not going to like this."

They heard the faint sound of yelping inside and Rebecca looked at the locked front door.

"There must be another way to get in," Jason said. "We have to find it."

"We don't have time," she said as she grabbed the lock in her hands and twisted it until it broke into two pieces. Jason watched amazed and Rebecca pulled the big wooden door open with ease. She let Jake enter first and he gasped when he saw the carnage. A pile of dogs, some not quite dead lay in a heap by the corner closest to them. A large group of men stood in a circle in the middle of the barn cheering at something. Rebecca moved quickly forward and Jake followed. One of the men heard them and looked back. His eyes widened in surprise and he tapped the shoulder of the man standing next to him. They moved aside and Jason and Rebecca entered the circle. Jason's jaw dropped when he saw his daughter's golden retriever, Chelsea struggling on the ground as a big pitbull shook her back and forth. She whined pitifully as the strong jaws of the dog clamped tighter around her neck.

"You assholes!" he yelled as he lunged at the pitbull. He grabbed the dog's head in his hands and tried to pull it off Chelsea. It wouldn't let go and Rebecca moved in. She bent down and lightly touched the dog's head. Its eyes rolled back in its head and its jaws loosened their grip. She gently pried them open and the dog rolled onto its side and fell asleep.

"What the fuck!" one of the men yelled, surprised at the sight.

Rebecca knelt by Chelsea and gently lifted her head. Blood pulsed steadily from the puncture wounds in her neck and Jason whispered, "Oh God, Chelsea. Oh no."

The poor animal tried to wag its tail and whined. Rebecca looked out at the group of men who surrounded them. "You make me sick," she said, her eyes blazing in anger. "It never ceases to amaze me how cruel men can be."

Jason sensed the rage in her and whispered, "Rebecca, kiss me. Let me deal with them."

She looked at him grimly. "No, they're mine."

She petted the golden retriever's head and its eyes glazed over.

"She's dead," she said and a tear fell from one of her eyes.

Standing up, she clenched her fists and looked from one man's face to the other.

"You're going to pay for this," she hissed.

"Get her!" one of the men yelled as he released his dogs. The two large animals charged at her but she showed no fear. Drool flew from their mouths as they ran and the angel went to her knees and held her arms out to them. She lowered her head and they stopped a few inches from her and sniffed her fingers and began to wag their tails.

"What the fuck!" a man said, amazed and watched as Rebecca patted the dog's heads. She recognized him as the redhead who'd attacked Jason at the diner. He ran at her and she stood up.

"Bitch!" he yelled as he swung his fist at her. She made no effort to get out of the way and her head jolted violently to the side from the punch. She wiped the blood from her split lip and her attacker saw it seal up in an instant. His eyes widened in fear and he gasped. "What the hell!"

Rebecca smiled. "So you like to hit girls, huh?"

The man began to back away from her and she stepped towards him. "Well, this girl hits back."

Two of the men pulled guns from their jackets and aimed them at Rebecca. She smirked. "Cowards. You're nothing but cowards."

She advanced towards them and one said, "Take one more step and you're dead, lady."

A sound from the barn entrance made them turn. "Drop your guns!" a familiar voice yelled.

Jeff from the diner stood with fists clenched next to Jerry who had his shotgun raised and ready to fire. "Put your guns down now," he said. "I won't ask you again."

"But Jerry," one of the men said. "We can't let her go. She knows too much."

Jeff walked towards the group. "Real tough guys, aren't you? She's just a little woman. Why don't you fight her without the guns? That would be more of a fair fight then, I think, don't you?"

They laughed and dropped their guns to the ground where he bent and picked them up. He looked at Rebecca and smiled. "They're all yours now."

"Thanks, Jerry."

He looked at her with warmth in his eyes. "You're welcome, Rebecca."

The group of men looked uncertainly at each other and back at Rebecca. She tapped her foot impatiently and held her arms out. "Who's first, tough guys or should I take you all on at once?"

The redhead, Alan smiled sadistically. "I'll go first. This bitch is no match for me."

He stepped towards her and she shivered. "Oh please, Alan, don't hurt me!" she cried while smiling.

He stopped and stared at her. "You're crazy, you know that, cunt?"

Her face turned grim and she growled, "Men who torture dogs for fun. Men who think women are their slaves. Well, that all ends now. I'm going to teach you a lesson you'll never forget!"

Her eyes were furious looking but Alan ran at her anyway. Rebecca thrust her arms out faster than anyone could blink and hit the man in the chest with a blow that caved two ribs in. He staggered and blood dribbled out of his mouth before he fell face first to the ground. The other men stared at her in shock and came at her from all sides. Jeff and Jerry listened to their grunts of pain as one by one they fell by the angel's feet. Soon, only one remained standing and Rebecca smiled evilly.

"Well, well," she snickered. "It's down to just you and I."

The man began to blubber and back away but she flew at him and grabbed him in her arms, crushing him to her in a bearhug.

"Don't kill me," he gasped. "Please don't kill me."

Her eyes turned kind. "Oh you poor man, you have nothing to worry about. I follow the ten commandments."

"What does that mean?" he asked as she squeezed him harder.

She smiled, her face an inch away from his. "It means I won't kill you but…."

"But what?" he asked as he trembled in her arms.

She grinned. "I won't kill you but I sure can hurt you."

"No…." he groaned.

"Yes," she whispered and instantly broke three of his ribs as she gripped him tighter.

"Uugghh!" he cried and she released him. He tottered for a moment and then fell to the floor amongst the other men.

Rebecca looked at Jeff and Jerry whose mouths were hanging open in shock and said, "You better call an ambulance. In fact, you may need more than one. And get some help for the dogs that are still alive."

One of the men had crawled to her and grabbed her ankle. He looked up at her with pain filled eyes and whispered, "You'll die for this, bitch."

Rebecca smiled and bent down to gently pry his hand from her leg.

Smiling, she used her other hand to bend back three of his fingers until they broke loudly. He shrieked in agony and she let him go. "Let that be a lesson to you," she whispered. "Don't ever threaten a woman again."

He began to cry and held his broken hand against his chest. "I'm sorry!" he screamed. "I'm sorry! Please don't hurt me again!"

Her eyes were kind and she gently stroked the man's cheek. "You'll be alright. I'm sorry I had to do that to you."

The warmth from her hand calmed him and she gently took his broken hand in hers. A strange tingling sensation flooded into him and he smiled when the pain lessened. "Thank you," he said and Rebecca released his hand.

Rebecca looked at the mass of groaning bodies on the floor and frowned. The realization suddenly hit her that Susanna's boyfriend wasn't among them. "Oh no," she whispered and looked at Jason. "Where's Matt? He isn't here!"

"Oh shit!" he cried and they raced out of the barn. Rebecca quickly scooped him up in her arms and her wings sprouted out. Leaping high into the air, she flew towards Susanna's house.

A few minutes later they landed and rushed towards the front door. It was open and Jason peeked inside. "Susanna!" he yelled.

"Oooooooohhh," the low moan came from the back of the house. They rushed towards the sound and Jason gasped when he saw his daughter crumpled in a ball by a large bookcase. Her eyes were puffy and swelling and blood trickled from her split lip. Jason looked away when he realized she was practically naked, her long dress hanging in tatters around her.

"Susanna!" Jason yelled and lunged at her. "Ooowww!" she cried when he grabbed her.

"Let go!" Rebecca said. "She might have broken ribs!"

"I'm sorry!" he cried and backed away. "Oh God, Oh God…."

"How badly are you hurt, Susanna?" the angel asked, concerned.

"I need to talk to you alone," she whispered.

Rebecca turned to Jason and said, "Please give me a minute alone with her."

"What about an ambulance?" he said as his eyes blurred with tears.

"It'll just be a moment. Then we'll deal with that."

He nodded and left the room. Rebecca turned back to Susanna and lightly touched her shoulder. "Talk to me, Susanna," she said softly. "It's just you and I now."

The young woman tried to sit up and Rebecca helped her. She pulled her close and ran her fingers through Susanna's hair. "What happened, Susanna?" she asked.

The woman's eyes looked with sadness at Rebecca. "Chelsea's dead, isn't she?" she asked sadly.

"Yes," Rebecca answered. "I'm sorry. We didn't get there in time."

"Oh God! Poor Chelsea!" Susanna cried and leaned against Rebecca. "That bastard told me he gave her to the men to use as bait but I didn't believe him!"

"I'm sorry," Rebecca said.

Susanna looked at her and her eyes were filled with horror. "He'll be back! I know he will and then he'll finish what he started! He'll kill me!"

"No he won't," Rebecca said, her voice firm. "I promise I won't let him hurt you again. Why did he do this?"

Susanna tried to smile but winced as her lip split open even wider.

"He kept asking me what you and Dad found in the barn. I told him I didn't know anything about it but he didn't believe me. He beat me, Rebecca," she moaned. "And when he was done he raped me. Oh God, it hurt so badly. I thought he'd never finish!"

Rebecca looked quickly over Susanna's body and saw the bloody welts on the side of her backside. "Yes, he beat me there too," the poor girl whispered. She coughed then and blood spewed out of her mouth.

"Jason!" the angel yelled. "Get in here!"

He hurried back into the room. "Should I call the ambulance now? The hospital's a few miles from here at the edge of town. They could be here in a few minutes."

Rebecca was very worried. "No, there's no time. I'll get her to the hospital. Find a weapon in case he comes back and wait for me. I'll be back soon."

She looked into Susanna's eyes and quietly said, "I'm going to get you to the hospital. I'll try not to hurt you, alright?"

The young woman nodded and coughed up more blood. "Help me get her up," Rebecca said.

Jason came over and together they gently lifted his daughter to her feet. She groaned in pain and Rebecca moved her horizontally so she could hold her under her legs and back. Susanna moaned and stared at Rebecca, amazed as the woman carried her through the house and out the front door. She looked into the girl's eyes and asked, "Are you ready, Susanna?"

She nodded and wrapped her arms around the angel's neck. Rebecca's wings slowly extended from her back and Susanna gasped at the sight. "I knew you weren't from here," she whispered and closed her eyes as her head slumped against the angel's chest.

"She's unconscious," Rebecca said. "I have to hurry. She's busted up inside."

Looking at Jason, she said, "Be careful. I'll be back."

His lower lip quivered. "Thank you," he whispered.

She flew straight up into the air and headed to where the hospital was. She had never flown as fast as she did now and got there in a hurry. Dropping down lightly in the parking lot, she retracted her wings and carried Susanna through the emergency room doors to the front desk. "I need help," she told the astonished nurse who sat behind the desk.

"She's been beaten and raped and may have some broken ribs.

She's been coughing up blood."

"Quickly!" the nurse shouted. "Get a gurney over here! Now!"

Susanna was placed on the gurney and wheeled away. Rebecca turned to the nurse and said, "Take care of her. I'll be back with her father. I'll give you all the details then."

Before the nurse could say anything, Rebecca ran out the exit and took a few steps before flying back to Jason. She landed quietly by the front door and heard crashes coming from inside the house. "Asshole!" Jason's voice shouted.

She ran inside just in time to see Matt lift Jason high into the air and fling him into a wall. Jason hit hard and crumpled in a heap as he landed.

He moaned and tried to rise but couldn't. Matt grinned at her as she went to kneel by Jason. His eyes were filled with pain and he whispered, "I couldn't beat him. He's too strong."

She gently touched his cheek and said, "Look away, Jason. This won't be pretty."

Matt chuckled and pointed at her. "So you think you're tough, bitch?!"

Rebecca rose to her feet and her eyes blazed like fire at him. "You're an evil man," she whispered. "How could you do that to Susanna?"

He laughed. "She got nosy snooping around in my business. I was getting tired of her anyway!"

"And poor Chelsea. I *hate* dogfighting. I think I'm going to hurt you," she said as her eyes narrowed.

"Bring it, bitch!"

She launched herself at him and drove him into the china cabinet. His hands clawed at her face and she got him in a bearhug. Before she could break his ribs, he headbutted her and she let go of him. Backing away, she shook the stars from her head. Shocked that he'd actually hurt her, she became even more enraged and scowled at him.

Any other man would have fled in terror but he stood his ground and smiled. "Yeah, I heard you were tough but I'm tougher. You need a lesson in obedience, lady and I'm just the guy to teach you. When you're unconscious I think I'll fuck you in the ass. I bet you'd like it too. Maybe I can make you scream louder than Susanna did."

Rebecca clenched her fists. "You raped her there too?" she asked, not surprised at his cruelty.

"Oh yeah!" he answered, beaming with sick pride. "I used all her holes! That's all bitches like you are good for anyway!"

"You son of a bitch," Rebecca whispered. "I'm *really* going to enjoy this."

He waved her in and she flew at him again. He tried to put his hands up but she was too fast and her fist hit his jaw so hard his teeth broke. "Uunngg!" he cried and spit pieces of them out of his mouth.

Rebecca backed away and smiled. "You're not looking so handsome anymore," she said and laughed. "By the time I'm done with you no woman will ever look at you again."

He screamed in rage and jumped at her. She grabbed his arm in midflight and using her weight flipped him headfirst into a book case near where Jason lay. His head went through the glass doors and he hung there for a moment before pulling himself out. He turned to face her and picked bits of glass out of his face. His forehead was gashed open and he spit blood onto the floor. "No more karate tricks," he growled. "Fight me fair and square."

"Ok," she said gleefully and raised her fists in a boxing stance. "Are three minute rounds alright with you?"

"Yeah," he said and sneered.

Rebecca pulled on the imaginary rope to the bell. "Ding….ding."

Matt charged at her and she hit him with two left jabs which rocked his head back followed by a hard right to the pit of his stomach. He collapsed to the floor and vomited. She stepped over and stood looking down at him. "You're not very good at this, are you?" she said, disappointed. "I was looking forward to this lasting a lot longer."

He looked up at her and smiled evilly. "Don't worry, bitch. I'm not done yet."

She backed away and let him stand. He gripped his stomach in pain and she giggled. "What's the matter, Matty?" she laughed. "Does the wittle boy have a stomach ache? Want mommy to kiss it?"

"You fucking cunt," he whispered. "I'm gonna fuck that ass of yours for hours until you beg me to kill you."

The angel's face turned serious then as she said, "You know, this is getting tiring. Let's just finish it now, alright?"

He staggered towards her and swung his fist at her face but she bent low and thrust her leg out sideways into his chest, breaking three ribs with her foot. His eyes bulged out in pain and she grabbed his arm before he could fall. Gripping his hand, she took hold of his thumb and looked at him. "Let's play a game, shall we?"

"This little piggy went to the bank," she said in a little girl's voice as she bent the thumb back until it cracked loudly.

"Fuck!" Matt yelled in agony.

"And this little piggy went to school," she cooed and twisted his forefinger around until it fractured.

"Oh God, stop!" he shrieked.

The angel took hold of his middle finger then and wrenched it back and forth until it snapped loudly. "And this fucking piggy said, "I'm sorry, Susanna!"

Matt lost control because of the intense pain and pissed himself. Rebecca smelled his urine and smiled. "Oh, poor baby. It hurts that bad?" she said with fake sympathy. "Don't worry. We're almost done."

She grabbed the next finger and slowly bent it backwards. "Oh God, please stop!" Matt cried and his legs started to shake.

The angel quickly snapped the finger in half and wrenched it back and forth as Matt lost control again, leaving a growing puddle on the floor. "One more to go," she whispered.

She took hold of his little finger and wiggled it lightly before pulling it sideways until it broke with a light snap like dry kindling. Matt squealed in agony and his eyes rolled up in his head. Rebecca released his hand then and he slowly fell to the floor. She stood above him and he moaned and held his injured hand. "Shall I start on the other hand next or maybe your feet?" she asked.

He looked up at her, his eyes clouded with pain. "I'm gonna kill you," he whispered.

Rebecca's eyes blazed with anger and she squatted by him and grabbed by the hair, wrenching his head towards hers. "You'll do nothing!" she spat. "I decide whether you ever walk again! Understand?!"

She glanced down between his legs and smiled. "Oh my, I forgot the biggest piggy of all," she said softly.

She let go of his hair and his head hit the floor with a thud. He cried out in pain and she kicked his legs apart. She smiled and placed her foot on his groin.

The man's eyes bugged out of his head when she started to press down. "Oh God, no….oh please don't….I'm sorry! Oh God! I'm sorry!"

Rebecca was beyond thinking straight anymore and her eyes were clouded with anger. "I wonder if a penis can be broken," she said quietly and looked into his eyes. "Shall we find out?"

"No!!! Please no!!!!" he screamed and she grinned at him.

"You'll never hurt another woman with this ever again," she said.

"Rebecca! No! Don't!" Jason suddenly screamed and staggered quickly over to her. He grabbed her arm and she lashed out at him with her foot. It grazed his ankle and he cried out in pain.

"Don't fucking touch me! He's mine!" she shrieked.

Jason lightly touched her arm. "Please, Rebecca, don't do this.

You're an angel. You're *my* angel."

His words shook her and her eyes opened wide. She looked back at Matt and gasped at the sight of what she'd done. His eyes rolled up in his head and he passed out. She started to shake all over and stared at Jason with frightened eyes.

"Rebecca," he whispered. "Come back to me. Please come back to me."

"Oh Jason!" she cried and lunged at him. He hugged her tightly to him and she began to sob against his chest.

"Oh Jason! That wasn't me! Oh God! I went too far! I lost control!"

"It's alright," he whispered into her hair. "It's over. You made him pay."

"Oh God, what have I done?!" she cried and looked back at the broken man on the floor.

"You did what had to be done," Jason said grimly. "Remember, he hurt Susanna. I'm sorry but he deserved this."

Matt slowly regained consciousness and his eyes fluttered open. Jason and Rebecca stood over him, their faces impassive. "I'm calling the police now," Jason said and pulled out his phone.

As he talked to the police, the man's eyes opened wide in terror as Rebecca leaned over and lightly touched his chin. "If I ever see you again I'll break every bone in your body. Do you understand me?"

He nodded rapidly and said, "You won't see me again, I promise."

"Good," she said and stood up. "Now get up. We're going outside to wait for the police."

He managed to get to his feet and stared intensely at Rebecca. "Got something to say to me?" she asked.

He shook his head no and staggered to the front door. "I hope you become somebody's bitch in jail," Jason said.

He didn't look back at them and stepped outside. The cops were there in minutes and Jason explained that Matt had raped and beaten his daughter and put her in the hospital before coming back to the house and attacking him. He told them about the dogfighting that preceded it too. Strangely, they didn't seem fazed by any of what he was telling them except for one thing.

"How'd you do this to him?" one big burly cop asked Jason. "He's one of the toughest guys in town."

Jason laughed and pointed at Rebecca. "I didn't. She did."

The cop's eyes lit up in surprise and he stared intensely at Rebecca. "I guess he got what he deserved then," he said.

They hauled Matt away and Jason and Rebecca watched them shove him into the back seat of the squad car and shut the door. He stared back at them and moaned from the pain of his broken ribs and busted hand.

"Let's go see your daughter," Rebecca said as she turned to Jason.

They stepped outside and watched as the squad car pulled away. Rebecca pulled Jason close and asked, "Ready?"

"Yes," he whispered and her wings opened. With a powerful thrust of her legs she flew upwards and away towards the hospital.

Looking out the back window of the squad car, Matt watched in awe at the sight. He couldn't believe his eyes but a surge of anger ran through him. The woman wasn't human. *I'll be back*, he thought. *Human or not, I'll make her pay.*

CHAPTER SIXTEEN

Susanna was asleep when they got to her room. The doctor was still there looking at his clipboard as he checked her vitals.

"Doctor, how is she?" Jason asked.

He looked grimly at him and said, "Are you her father?"

"Yes, I am."

"Are you sure you want to hear this?"

"I want to know everything. Please don't leave anything out."

"Alright," the man said. "You'd better sit down. Whoever did this really must have hated her."

"Just tell us," Rebecca said.

The doctor quietly said, "To start with, she has numerous bruises but they can be dealt with. It's the other stuff that worries me."

Jason gripped the doctor's arm tightly. "What did the son of a bitch do to her? Tell me."

The man looked down at his arm and Jason let go. "Sorry," he said.

"That's alright. I can't even begin to imagine how upset you are by all of this."

He glanced at Susanna. "She went through hell. Four broken ribs and there's tearing in her vaginal area and anus."

"Oh God!" Jason cried.

"Will she be alright?" Rebecca asked.

"Yes, in time she'll heal but emotionally I'm afraid this experience may stay with her for a long time. She'll need your love and support."

"She'll have it," Jason said as he wiped tears from his eyes.

"I'll leave you now," the man said. "Visiting hours are over but you can stay. I think it would be good if you were here when she wakes up."

"Thank you, doctor," Jason said and shook the man's hand.

"I hope the bastard who did this pays dearly," he said.

Rebecca smiled. "Oh, he already has. Believe me."

The man looked at her, curious and she said, "We already took care of him. He's in police custody now."

"Oh….that's good," he said, surprised.

He left and they sat in chairs on either side of Susanna's bed. After an hour or so, Jason's shoulders slumped and he began to doze off. Rebecca moved her chair next to his and pulled him towards her so his head rested against her chest. He opened his eyes then and she smiled at him. "Go back to sleep, Jason," she whispered. "Your angel's here."

He smiled and closed his eyes. "My angel," he whispered and within seconds he was asleep again. Rebecca sat for hours holding him and watching Susanna. *I really like her,* she thought.

At some point she closed her eyes and Susanna opened hers for a moment and looked at her. There was something immensely comforting about the strange woman's presence. Who was she? *What was she?*

CHAPTER SEVENTEEN

Morning came and Susanna opened her eyes to see Rebecca sitting in a chair next to her bed with her father resting against her like a child. "I thought I was dreaming when I saw you there earlier. Have you both been here all night?" she weakly asked.

"Yes," Rebecca answered. She kissed Jason's head and Susanna smiled.

"I had a dream that I was flying and you were the one who brought me here."

Rebecca smiled at her.

"I *wasn't* dreaming, was I?" the girl asked then, her face serious.

"No, you weren't."

"I don't understand. What *are* you?"

Rebecca quietly said, "I think you know what I am."

Susanna's eyes opened wide. "Are you an angel?!"

"Yes, Susanna, I am."

"But *why*? Why are you here?"

Rebecca looked at Jason with affection. "Your father needed me. I *had* to come."

"What do you mean he needed you? Why?"

Rebecca hesitated before answering. "He…."

Susanna's eyes opened even wider. "Wait a minute. I know he's been very depressed for a long time. Did he try to…."

"Yes," Rebecca said. "I saved him. It wasn't his time yet."

"Oh my God!" Susanna cried. "Daddy!"

Jason woke then and opened his eyes. "Susanna!" he cried happily.

"Daddy," she said affectionately and reached for his hand. He took it in his and she squeezed it lightly. "Don't ever try that again. Promise me."

"What are you talking about?" he asked, confused.

"If you ever feel like killing yourself again I want you to talk to me about it first, alright?”

Jason's face turned pale and he looked at Rebecca. "You told her?"

"No," she said. "She figured it out on her own."

He looked at his daughter and said, "I promise I'll talk to you first but I don't think it'll happen again anyway."

"Why not?"

He smiled and looked at Rebecca. "Because I've found my purpose in life."

CHAPTER EIGHTEEN

Susanna wanted to know the details about what had happened back at the barn and they hesitated telling her. The pleading look on her face finally forced them to and she cried when they told her the details of her beloved dog's cruel death. She smiled though when Jason told her how Rebecca had taken on all the men. She seemed especially happy when told of the beating the woman had administered to Matt.

"Wow, that must have been some self-defense class you took!" she said, laughing.

Rebecca just smiled and nodded.

Word about what had transpired spread like wildfire across the town and Susanna was delighted when Jerry and Jeff came to visit her. Jerry handed her a big stuffed purple elephant and she was greatly touched.

"Thank you so much, Jerry! I love it!"

He sat down next to her bed and quietly said, "Susanna, I have Chelsea in my truck. What do you want me to do with her?"

Her eyes clouded with tears and she looked at her father. "Would you bury her for me, dad? In a box somewhere where she won't be found?"

"Of course I will."

"We'll help," Jeff said and the three men left the room.

Susanna stared at Rebecca. "Is Chelsea in heaven, Rebecca?"

The angel smiled. "Yes."

"So I'll see her again someday?"

"Of course you will."

"You're not lying to me, are you?"

"No, Susanna. I'm not lying. Chelsea will be waiting for you when you're ready."

Susanna closed her eyes and smiled. "My sweet Chelsea," she whispered.

She fell into a deep sleep again and the doctor came in.

"How's she doing?" he asked.

"She's doing ok," Rebecca said. "When do you think she can leave?"

"Maybe tomorrow."

"Good," she said. "We want to bring her home with us. She's leaving this town."

"That's a very good idea. There's too many bad memories here."

Susanna opened her eyes then and reached for Rebecca's hand.

"You aren't going, are you?!" she asked, panicked.

Rebecca took her hand and softly said, "Of course not. I'm not going anywhere."

"Thank you. I can see why my father loves you."

"What do you mean?!" Rebecca asked, alarmed. "How do you know that?!"

Susanna smiled. "Because I know my father. I've never seen him so happy and it's because of you. I just know it plus the way he looks at you tells me that I'm right."

Rebecca blushed and Susanna asked, "When are you going to tell him, Rebecca?"

"Tell him what?"

"Tell him that you love him too."

Rebecca wiped away a tear and her voice cracked when she quietly said, "I can't, Susanna. I'm his guardian angel. There's no future for us. How can there be?"

Susanna thought about that and sadly said, "That's too bad. You seem so perfect together."

Rebecca lowered her head and whispered, "I wish I could stay. I really do but I can't."

Susanna nodded. "I understand," she said softly.

Just then, her breakfast was wheeled in and Susanna was so weak that Rebecca decided to feed her herself just like she'd done for Jason.

When she was almost finished, she lifted the glass of orange juice to Susanna's lips and she took a sip. The girl looked at her afterwards and said, "Thank you for everything you did for me."

The angel leaned over and kissed Susanna's cheek. "I love you," the girl whispered.

Rebecca stared at her and fought the impulse to cry. She felt so emotional about what had happened and cared deeply for the girl. "I love you too, Susanna," she said.

"Will you watch over me like you've watched over my father?"

The angel touched the woman's cheek. "Always," she whispered.

CHAPTER NINETEEN

Jerry drove the men to the diner to get a big sturdy box and they came back to the house to do what Susanna had asked. They gently placed Chelsea inside and taped the lid shut. Jason found a spot underneath a big tree by the edge of the backyard where he thought she'd lay undisturbed. They took shovels from the garage and dug a hole. None of them said a word as they buried the dog and covered the grave with dirt. They stood there for long minutes until Jason finally said, "Rest well, Chelsea."

The men wiped away tears and walked back to the truck. Emotionally drained, they sat there for a while.

"I need to ask you something, Jason," Jeff said, breaking the silence.

Jason looked at the man and smiled. "I know what you're going to say."

"She's not human, is she?" the big cook asked.

"No, she's not."

The man smiled. "I didn't think so. What she did back at the barn is something I'll never forget. It was like something out of an action movie."

"Yes, she's something special alright. She's an angel. She's *my* angel," Jason said proudly.

"I knew she was," Jerry piped in. "She helped me see my wife."

Jeff stared intensely at Jason. "You're a lucky man, my friend. I don't know why your angel is here but you're damn lucky. I wish I had someone who cared that much about me."

"Yes, I am lucky," Jason said.

He suddenly realized that he needed some fresh clothes. "Will you give me a few minutes? I need to take a shower and change."

"Sure," Jerry said.

He ran into the house and slowly took his clothes off. Looking in the bathroom mirror, he grimaced at the sight. Big ugly bruises covered his chest. That asshole Matt had really done a number on him but he smiled when he remembered the punches he'd thrown in return. *I held my own for a while*, he thought proudly.

He took a quick shower and put on some fresh clothes before returning to the truck. They drove back to the hospital and found Rebecca in bed with Susanna. The girl was cuddled up against her and smiling in her sleep. Rebecca's arm was wrapped around her protectively and her eyes were closed.

"Well, I'll be!" Jerry whispered.

"Why are you surprised?" Jason said. "She's an angel."

CHAPTER TWENTY

Susanna slept for most of the day. Late that afternoon she saw her father wince and said, "Dad, you don't have to stay here with me tonight. I'll be alright."

He quickly said, "No, I'm not leaving you alone."

Jerry and Jeff looked at each other and then him. "Hey, Jason, you took a real beating from Matt. You don't look so good. Go home tonight and get some rest. We'll stay here tonight. Susanna will be fine."

Rebecca was worried. Jason did indeed look weary and in pain. "I think that's a good idea. C'mon, I'm taking you back to Susanna's house. We'll be back in the morning and hopefully with a good night's rest you'll feel better by then."

Jason looked at his daughter and she said, "Dad, go with Rebecca. I'll be fine."

He got up and kissed her lightly on the cheek. "I love you, baby," he whispered. "Call if you need me tonight."

Her eyes were bright with love for him. "I'll be fine, dad. Please let Rebecca take care of *you* tonight."

Rebecca took his hand and led him out of the room.

It was dark already. They'd been at the hospital for a long time. Rebecca wrapped her arms around him and they were in the air in no time. She felt him shiver and flew faster.

"Here we are," she said when they landed in front of the house.

Jason opened the door and let Rebecca walk in ahead of him. She immediately headed to the kitchen and found some pasta and sauce. "I'll make you some dinner and then you can relax a bit before going to bed. Alright?"

He nodded yes and sat down wearily in a big chair in the living room. The scent of spices permeated the air as the angel prepared his meal and Jason's mouth watered.

"Come and get it!" she said after a few minutes and he groaned getting out of the chair.

He sat down at the kitchen table and Rebecca put the plate of pasta in front of him. His eyes lit up. "Wow, that smells great! What's in the sauce?"

"Garlic, onion and a little oregano, that's all. Nothing special."

Jason's eyes sparkled. "Well, it's special to me because you made it. Thank you."

"You're welcome."

He ate in silence as she observed him. After a while she said, "You're really in a lot of pain, aren't you?"

"No, I'm fine," he lied but his eyes betrayed him.

Rebecca smiled. "No, Jason, you're not. This is me you're talking to. I can see the truth in your eyes."

"I can't hide anything from you, can I?" he asked quietly.

"Nope. Don't even try."

He sighed. "Ok, if you must know Matt battered me pretty good and I'm really feeling it now. My ribs are killing me."

"That's a start, Jason," she said. "It's no good trying to hide the truth from me. I know you too well."

"You do? If that's true then tell me what I'm thinking right now."

His eyes looked deeply into hers then and she felt her throat tighten and her heart beat a little faster. "I…."

"Well?" he asked.

She looked away then and blushed. "Why don't you relax on the couch while I do the dishes, alright?"

He smiled broadly and slowly got up. "Thanks again for dinner," he said.

She watched him leave the kitchen and realized her hands were shaking. *What's happening to me?* she thought, worried. *Why does he affect me that way?*

A few minutes later she went to join him in the living room. He was asleep on the couch. Looking down at him, she realized he looked like a little boy as he slept because his face was innocent and relaxed. She knelt by him and gently pushed the hair away from his eyes.

He slowly opened them and said, "I'm sorry. I'm just so tired."

"Let's get you to bed," she said and before he knew it she had lifted him in her arms and carried him to the stairs. He gazed at her in wonder as she ascended them. When they got to the spare bedroom, she sat him up in bed and looked away. He quickly removed his clothes and got under the covers. "All done," he said and she turned around again.

Leaning over, she kissed his forehead and whispered, "Goodnight, Jason. Sleep well."

"Goodnight, Rebecca."

She closed the door behind her and stepped into the hallway. It was as good a time as any so she began to explore the house. There was nothing truly interesting until she got to the basement and found an old shoebox filled with photos. There was a little boy in some of them and she realized they were of Jason. In most of them he smiled for the camera but as they progressed in age the smile was no longer there. There was a sadness in the boy's eyes and she sensed his loneliness.

Wiping away a tear, she put the box away and headed back upstairs. As she passed by Jason's bedroom, she heard him groan and lightly swear in frustration. Opening the door, she saw him lying under the covers like that other time with his hand working away beneath them. His eyes were closed and he looked angry.

He didn't hear her as she approached the bed. "Jason," she said softly.

His eyes flew open. "Oh shit."

His hand stopped moving and she sat down by the side of the bed and asked, "What were you doing just now, Jason?"

"Nothing!" he said and stopped moving his hand. "I wasn't doing anything!"

"Yes, you were. You were masturbating, weren't you? Remember the last time? You said I could watch."

His eyes were scared. "I thought you were joking. You were, weren't you?"

She glanced down to where his hand was beneath the covers and back to his face. "No Jason, I wasn't. Will you let me watch? *Please?*"

"No, it's too embarrassing."

"Embarrassing?" she said, surprised. "No it isn't. It's natural to masturbate. There's nothing to be ashamed of."

His eyes were frightened. "That's not it. I…I can't talk to you about it."

She knelt by the side of the bed and looked into his eyes. "What's wrong, Jason? What can't you tell me?"

"It won't work!" he cried, clearly frustrated. "It's been happening more lately. I hurt all over and can't concentrate!"

"What won't work, Jason? Your penis?"

"Yes," he whispered, thoroughly ashamed.

Her hand touched his face in a soft caress. "I'm sorry. Maybe I can help. Show me."

"What?" Jason asked, shocked. "No, I can't!"

She reached for the covers and looked into his eyes. "Please, Jason, let me look at you. I've seen glimpses of you naked over the years but now I *really* want to look at you."

"No," he whispered, frightened.

"Yes," she said softly and slowly pulled the blanket down until it rested by his ankles. She studied his body with loving eyes and reached out to lightly run her fingers over his muscled chest.

"You have a beautiful body, Jason," she said. "I like looking at it."

He held his breath as her hand moved lower to his stomach and rested there.

"Show me how you were doing it," she said.

He stared with fear at his hand covering his groin and she said, "It's ok, Jason. You have nothing to fear from me."

He slowly pulled his hand away and she saw his flaccid penis sitting in its nest of pubic hair. It looked red and inflamed. "What did you do to it? Why does it look like that?" she asked.

"It won't stay hard," he answered, embarrassed at being naked in front of her.

"Show me how you were doing it."

Jason blushed and took his penis in his hand. He gripped it tightly and began to furiously jerk at it. "Stop," she said quickly. "Just *stop*."

"Why?"

"You're being too rough. Have patience and maybe it will work."

"But it feels dead like always lately," he said, frustrated. "There's no feeling in it! God, I hate my body!"

The angel smiled and her kind eyes relaxed him. "Your body's pain is doing this. That's what pain does. Plus, over time men your age have problems down there."

"I hate my body," he groaned. "When I was younger I never had problems keeping it…."

He didn't finish because he felt totally humiliated admitting his erection problems to the angel.

Rebecca gazed deeply into his eyes. "Jason, will you let *me* do it? I've never done it before but I'd like to if you'll let me. Maybe it will work if I do it."

"What?! *You'd* do it for me?"

"Yes," she said softly. "Maybe all it needs is a woman's touch. But first I need something."

She reached behind her neck and gently pulled at something there. Wincing, she pulled a feather from her back and lowered it to his penis. Looking into his eyes, she softly asked, "Will you submit to my touch, Jason? Will you let me do this for you?"

He blushed bright red. "Yes," he whispered.

"Very good," she said and he jumped when the feather lightly touched the tip of his penis.

She gently touched his face. "Relax. I'm not going to hurt you."

"Oh Rebecca," he moaned when she ran the feather over his flaccid stalk. He suddenly felt a twinge in his member and his heart beat faster with joy. "Oh God, I feel something!"

His penis started to grow and the angel flicked the feather lightly over it in different spots until it was fully erect. "There now, that's more like it," she said softly. "I was beginning to wonder why being naked in front of me was having no effect on you."

Jason spread his legs wider and lifted his hips slightly as the feather flicked around his cockhead. Rebecca smiled and said, "*Yes*, Jason. It feels good, doesn't it?"

His thighs trembled and he gasped when she moved the feather between his buttocks where it lightly brushed against his anus. "Oh my God," he gasped. "Oh God, that feels....so intimate."

"Yes," she whispered and smiled. "It definitely is."

The feather moved back to his cock again and tickled under his frenulum. Jason gasped louder and Rebecca took the feather away. "Please....please finish me," he moaned as he thrust his hips towards her, his rigid penis close to bursting.

"Patience," she whispered. "You must have patience."

He gasped when her hand wrapped gently around his length and the warmth from it rushed into his body. His whole body tingled and her amazing fingers felt like feathers on him. "Rebecca," he gasped. "I feel....so much!"

"See, Jason," she whispered as her soft hand loved him. "All it needed was a woman's touch. I've never touched a man's penis before so you'll have to tell me if I'm doing it right or not."

Her hand began to slowly stroke up and down and Jason felt as if his head would explode. The angel's loving eyes gazed into his and his hips lurched upwards. She stroked him faster and he thought he was going to die from the pleasure. "Rebecca," he gasped. "Oh please, make me cum. It's been so long!"

She smiled brightly and leaned close to his face. "I love masturbating you, Jason. Thank you for letting me do this for you."

"Oh God!" he gasped as his cock pulsed in her hand. "It's happening! It's really happening!"

"Yes, Jason," she whispered. "Cum for me. Cum for your angel."

A great sound like a train rushing down tracks crashed into his brain and his whole body shook as his penis exploded in triumph. "Aarrgghh!!" he cried and she kissed him on the cheek.

Her eyes watched his as she stroked every drop from him and he gave himself completely over to her. He was hers and she could do whatever she wanted to at that moment. She could torture him, kill him; hell, she could do whatever she wanted as long as they could stay this close.

Her sweet hand slowed and he lay moaning. He shuddered as she milked out the last drop and finally took her hand away. She lay by him then and lay her head against his chest. "Did I do it the way you like it? Was it good?" she asked.

Jason was overcome with emotions and pulled her close. "Oh Rebecca! Thank you! My wife would never do that for me and it felt wonderful! I feel so loved!"

The angel looked at his face and gently touched his cheek. "I know I shouldn't have done that but I know you needed it."

Jason asked, "What about you? Will you let me touch *you* now?"

She smiled and whispered, "No, Jason. Tonight's about you."

They lay quietly for a while and Rebecca looked down at his shrunken penis.

"Do you like lying naked next to a fully dressed woman, Jason? Does it turn you on?" she whispered.

He shivered at the intimacy between them and nodded.

"Would you like me to touch you again?" she asked. "I sense that you're not quite done, are you?"

"Please…." he whispered.

She reached down and gently held his penis again. It began to grow again in her hand and she looked into his eyes. "*Oh my*, Jason. Is it growing because of the softness of my hand or is it because I'm looking into your eyes that's making it hard?"

"It's both," he whispered, trembling.

The corners of the angel's eyes crinkled in amusement.

"Please," he begged.

"Alright, but on one condition. I want to play a game," she said, her eyes twinkling. "Let's see how long you can last. It'll be fun. How does that sound?"

"Alright," he said quietly as his heart pumped wildly in his chest.

Rebecca smiled devilishly at him. "Remember now, hold out for as long as you can. Let's see if you can make it past ten. I'm going to really take my time with you now."

Jason nodded and sucked in a huge breath when she began to stroke up and down and started to count.

"One….two….three….don't cum yet….four….five…."

"Oh God," Jason gasped. "I don't know if I'll make it!"

Her hand stopped moving and she let his penis shrink a little. "You *better* make it, Jason," she scolded. "You wouldn't want me to punish you, would you?" she teased.

"Punish me?" he said, shocked. "How?"

She leaned close and whispered, "I'd take you over my knees and spank your bare bottom. How does that sound?"

The thought of the angel doing that to him had the desired effect she was hoping for and his cock swelled bigger in her hand and she smiled. "You'd like that, wouldn't you?!" she laughed. "You'd really let me spank you?"

Heart pounding, he nodded yes and yielded to the beautiful angel's hand again. Jason could hear her voice counting in the distance and felt the wave fast approaching.

"Eight…nine…ten," she finally whispered. He was on the verge of passing out when she suddenly stopped and looked into his eyes.

He stared at her as his cock was about to burst in her grip. "What's wrong?!" he asked, gasping for release. "I made it to ten. Why did you stop?!"

Her gorgeous eyes twinkled at him and she laughed lightly. "Nothing's wrong. I just want to try something."

His cock strained in her hand and she let go of him. "No!" he cried.

She scooted down by the foot of the bed and her head was between his legs, inches away from his bulging cockhead. "Now," she said and her finger lightly ran under the tip where it was most sensitive.

"Oh my God!" he yelled as cum shot out onto his stomach. Rebecca laughed and ran her fingernail lightly up his stalk and a great blast shot out again. "Oh shit! Oh shit!" he screamed.

"That's it! Cum for me, baby!" the angel cried happily. Jason's eyes rolled up into his head when suddenly her warm moist lips encircled him. Flashes of lightening burst in his head and he screamed and thrashed in ecstasy as she bobbed up and down on his straining member. Her tongue was like a feather as it caressed him and he gripped the bed with clawed hands as he came over and over again until consciousness left him. Rebecca took one last taste of his cock with her tongue and finally released him with a slurping sound. "God, you taste good," she whispered, smiling at him.

Jason didn't answer and Rebecca realized he was unconscious. She watched his chest rise and fall and a shiver ran through her. She lay next to him again and rested her head against his chest. "I think I could love you," she whispered. "I think you might be the one. We'll have to see."

CHAPTER TWENTY ONE

The morning sun woke him up and his eyes fluttered open. He'd never felt so at peace and didn't want to move. Rebecca was lying next to him with her head on his chest. Her eyes stared into his as her warm hand held his penis.

"My God," he whispered. "What did you do to me?"

Her eyes smiled at him. "I loved you like a man should be loved."

"Am I dead? Am I in heaven?"

Rebecca laughed. "No, you're not in heaven, silly! You're here lying naked with me with my hand holding your cock."

He stared intensely at the angel. "I wish I could be like this forever, Rebecca. I feel no pain right now. Only happiness."

She kissed his nose. "We can't stay like this all day. You need to eat."

She let go of his penis and got out of bed. Jason immediately felt empty inside and she looked down at him. "Please take a shower now and put that thing of yours away before I do something else to you. Your breakfast will be ready when you're done."

He whistled in the shower and Rebecca could hear him as she whipped up some eggs and bacon. She smiled and closed her eyes. *This is the life I would want if I were alive*, she thought. Her smile faded away then when she remembered the stark reality of her role here.

Jason came into the kitchen with a huge smile on his face. "Guess what?! I don't hurt as much and my bruises are fading away!"

She saw the bruises on his bare chest were much lighter now and smiled. "That's great, Jason. I'm glad I could help."

She turned her back to him to tend to the bacon and he came up behind her and wrapped his arms around her waist. "You heal me with your love, Rebecca," he whispered in her ear. "You heal me with your touch. There's nobody else like you."

She felt sadness overwhelm her then and whispered. "Please let go of me, Jason. What I did was a one time thing. It won't happen again."

"Oh," he said, disappointed and let go of her.

There was a loud banging on the door then and they both jolted. Jason quickly moved to the front window and peeked outside. Rebecca saw him turn pale. "What's wrong?" she asked.

He looked back at her and she could tell he was worried. "It's the cops."

"They probably want to talk to us about what happened at the barn or with Matt. Let them in."

"No. I have a bad feeling about this. Let me talk to them alone. Make yourself invisible."

Rebecca went to the door. "Stop worrying. We've done nothing wrong."

She opened the door and the big cop standing in the doorway stared down at her with no expression. "Are you, Rebecca?"

"Yes, I am. Why?"

She saw the twinkle in his eyes as he looked her up and down. "You need to come with us and answer some questions."

Jason stepped over. "She's not going anywhere. Ask your questions here."

The man put his hand on his holstered gun and his eyes turned beady. "You must be Susanna's father. This woman put a lot of men in the hospital. She's coming with us."

"I'll go with you," Jason said.

"No, you stay here," the man said.

"No," Jason said and grabbed the man's arm.

The cop standing with him was younger and stunk of cologne. "Hey!" he cried and pushed Jason away.

Rebecca grabbed the cop and quietly said, "Don't touch him."

The big cop smiled then and said, "Resisting arrest. Cuff her."

"What?!" she said, alarmed. "I wasn't resisting anything! Why am I under arrest?!"

The man sneered. "We're arresting you for the brutal beating of sixteen innocent men."

"They're not innocent! They were dogfighting!" she cried.

He ignored her and said, "Turn around and put your hands behind your back."

Jason looked worriedly at her but she seemed amused. "Why? Are you afraid of a little woman like me?"

The man grabbed her by the shoulders and spun her around. He was faster than he looked and had the handcuffs on her wrists in no time. He roughly turned her back around and grabbed her by the arm. "Let's go," he snarled.

"Don't worry," Rebecca said to Jason who stood wide eyed in disbelief over what was happening. "I'll be back soon."

The big cop smirked and looked at Jason. "I seriously doubt that."

She was placed in the back seat of the cruiser and the young cop got in beside her. They began to drive away and he stared at her long white dress. "You're pretty," he said.

She thought it was an odd comment to make under the circumstances. "Thank you."

As she looked out the window, he made his move. His hand rested on her thigh and she shuddered at the touch. It creeped upward and she stared at his face but he was looking at her chest. "Don't," she said but his hand moved over her right breast and squeezed it lightly.

His breathing became rapid and the big cop looked in the rear view mirror. "Red!" he yelled. "Stop that! Wait until we get to the station!"

"But Bob! I just want to touch her!"

"I said not now. Wait until she's in the cell," he growled.

The man pulled his hand away and Rebecca closed her eyes. *Jason was right*, she thought. *I should have made myself invisible.*

They were gentler with her when they arrived at the station. "This way," the big cop named Bob motioned as they entered. She was led down a narrow hallway to a cell which Red unlocked. "Get in," he said.

She stepped inside and he and Bob followed behind her. Red locked the cell door and Rebecca slowly backed up until she was touching the wall.

"I don't understand it," Bob said. "How could a little thing like you do what you did? We've got men with broken arms, legs and ribs. I just don't see it. You must know karate tricks. That's the only explanation I can think of."

Rebecca stayed silent and he smiled cruelly. "Well, it doesn't matter. You ain't getting' out of those cuffs. Turn around and face the   wall."

"What?" she asked, alarmed. "Why?"

He pulled a pair of latex gloves from his pocket. "It's routine. I'm going to perform a cavity search on you."

"Oh *no* you're not."

He looked at Red who unholstered his gun.

Red smiled and Bob said, "Turn around and bend over. Now."

Rebecca sighed. Was this really happening? What was wrong with the men in this town?

She smiled. "Are you going to finger me, officer? Are you going to make me moan until I beg you to stop?"

He laughed. "Yeah, you got it right, lady and when I'm done with both your holes we're gonna teach you a lesson you'll never forget."

Red pulled brass knuckles out of his pocket and smiled.

Rebecca felt the rage beginning inside her. "I bet you've done this before, haven't you? Preying on helpless women?"

"Yeah, we have. Now shut up and turn around."

She turned around and faced the wall.

"Put your hands against the wall," he said. "Then bend over and spread your legs wide."

She put her hands against the wall and hesitated before bending over. "Is this how you want me, officer?" she said, looking back at him with wide eyes. "Helpless and scared?"

Bob nodded and Red moved behind her. His hand suddenly rubbed her buttocks through her dress and she squealed.

"Yeah, bitch," he whispered in her ear. "We're gonna check you out real thorough like before we beat the crap out of you. Those men you hurt were friends of ours. You gotta pay. Now bend over."

Red backed away and Bob moved behind her. Rebecca gasped when his big stubby fingers began to lift her dress. She gave no warning and her foot lashed out and caught him in his big belly. "Oooofff!" he gasped and collapsed to the floor, holding his stomach.

Rebecca snapped the handcuffs in two, pulled her dress down and turned to face Red. He stared at her not comprehending and she wrenched each cuff off her wrists and threw them to the floor.

"Holy shit," he whispered. "How the fuck did you do that?!"

He tried to pull his gun but Rebecca was on him in an instant and had him in a bearhug. "So you like to fuck with your prisoners, huh?!" she said as she leered into his face. "How about I fuck you up instead?!"

He began to shake and suddenly pissed his pants. Rebecca smirked. "It seems like someone needs a diaper, officer," she whispered.

"Please don't hurt me," he said and stated to cry.

"You're pathetic," she said and let him go. "You're not a man! You and your fat friend here are disgusting cowards!"

She turned her back on him then and he quickly grabbed his keys so he could open the cell door. Rebecca looked back at him and smiled. "Oh no, you're not going anywhere," she said and glided towards him.

His eyes opened wide with fear and he took a swing at her but she grabbed his arm and quickly broke it in two places. He screamed and fell to his knees. "You bitch!" he yelled.

"Let's see now," she said. "Which hand was it that fondled me? Oh yes, it was the right one."

"Oh God, no!" he cried pitifully as she took his hand and slowly squeezed it. "Aaarrgghh!" he screamed as the bones ground together until they cracked loudly.

Rebecca let go of his hand and he stared at it in shocked disbelief. Bob started to rise from the floor behind her and she turned to face him. "You filth," she sneered and grabbed his hands. She pulled the plastic gloves off him and put them on. "How about I do a cavity search on *you*, asshole?!"

He backed up against the wall and his face turned white. "You wouldn't!" he said, terrified.

She slowly approached him. "I'll tell you what," she whispered. "I'll go in slow at first and then push deeper until my fist comes out your mouth. How does that sound?"

"Bitch!" he screamed and lunged at her. Faster than lightening, she drove her fist into his chest, breaking two of his ribs. He gasped in agony and she smiled. "What the fuck are you?" he said, every breath pure torture.

She grinned. "I'm your worst nightmare."

He snarled and she let him grab her neck in his big meaty hands. His eyes got wide as he squeezed with all his might. Rebecca smiled and his face went white. "What the hell?" he whispered.

"Is that the best you can do, officer?" she asked. "C'mon now, I'm just a helpless woman. You can do better than that. Squeeze harder."

He put everything he had into it then and tried to choke the life out of her but she just sighed.

"This is getting boring," she said and grabbed his wrists. With little effort, she easily pulled his hands off of her throat.

He tried to surprise her and swung a big fist at her head but she ducked and punched out with both fists into his groin. A low guttural moan escaped his lips and he fell to the floor and curled up in a fetal position. A second later, vomit spewed from his mouth and he shuddered violently. "I think you busted my balls," he gasped.

Rebecca squatted by him and said, "Now, before we continue any further I want you to promise me something."

"What?" he gasped, his face constricted in agony.

"You will never molest or harm another prisoner ever again. Do you understand me?"

He nodded yes and she said, "I'll know if you do because I'll be watching. You don't want me to come back, do you?"

"No! I promise!" he managed to croak out.

She stood up, went over to Red and stood above him. "Do you understand the same thing? If you make me come back, I'll hurt you worse. Do you want that?"

He shook his head violently from left to right. "No! No! I promise I'll be good! Please don't hurt me again!"

"Very good," she said. "Now gentlemen, I guess I'll be leaving. I trust you won't say a word about this to anyone because they wouldn't believe you."

Red lifted the keys to the cell door to her but she smiled. "Thanks but I don't need those," she said cheerily.

The men watched as she grabbed the iron bars with both hands and wrenched the entire door from its moorings. She carefully set it aside and looked back at them.

"Sorry," she said, smiling. "You need to get that fixed."

Astonished, they watched her leave the cell.

Outside the station, Rebecca closed her eyes and inhaled the chilly air.

The two cops had recovered enough to make it to the door. Rebecca stared back at them and their jaws dropped open as she extended her wings and flew away.

Jason was waiting for her outside the house when she got back and landed in front of him. She retracted her wings and moved into his arms.

"Was it bad?" he asked.

"Not really," she said against his chest.

"Want to talk about it?" he asked as he hugged her close.

"Not really. Just hold me."

They stood like that on the porch for a long time and Jason loved that he was giving comfort to his angel. He stroked her hair and she looked into his eyes. "I love you, Rebecca," he whispered.

Her eyes filled with tears and she slowly laid her head back against his chest. "Oh Jason," she whispered and her arms went around his back and squeezed lightly.

He waited for her to tell him she loved him too but she didn't. Disappointed, he said, "It doesn't matter if you don't love me back. I just needed to tell you finally how I felt."

She lifted her head again and gazed lovingly into his eyes. "That's ok. I understand. Just give me time. I *need* more time."

"Of course, my angel," he whispered. "Take all the time you need. I'll be here when you're ready."

CHAPTER TWENTY TWO

They heard the scream in the distance and saw a large man running towards them. "Rebecca! Help!" he yelled.

It was Jeff, the cook from the diner. Rebecca ran to him and saw his clothes were tattered and his face was covered with cuts and bruises. "What happened?!" she cried.

"Come quickly! They beat Jerry!" he gasped. "I fought them off but he's hurt bad!"

She and Jason followed him to Jerry's truck a half mile down the road. The tires had been slashed and the back was filled with empty boxes. "Susanna asked us to pack up her things and we were on the way here when they attacked us!"

Jason ran around the side of the truck and saw Jerry lying in the grass. He knelt by the man and saw the blood seeping out of his mouth.

"Oh my God!" Rebecca cried and knelt on the other side of him. "Oh Jerry! My poor Jerry!"

He moaned and Jeff angrily said, "He tried to help me fight them off but they pulled him away and smashed him in the chest with a baseball bat."

"Oh no," Rebecca gasped and lowered her head to the gasping man's chest. She looked at Jason and whispered, "His ribs are broken. He's bleeding internally."

"Rebecca," Jerry groaned and raised his arm to her.

She held his hand and smiled kindly at him. "I'm here, Jerry."

"We've got to get him to the hospital," Jason said but she nodded no.

"There's not enough time," she whispered sadly.

Jerry fought to keep his eyes open as he tried to focus on the angel's face. "Rebecca, is she here?"

Rebecca looked up and saw the faint outline of his wife in the distance. She looked at Jerry and blinked away tears. "Yes," she said. "Amy's coming."

Jerry tried to smile but more blood dribbled from the corner of his mouth. The faint figure knelt by him and touched his face. "Amy," he moaned when he felt the light touch on his cheek.

"She's here, Jerry," Rebecca said. "She's right beside you."

"I know. I can feel her touch."

Rebecca fought back tears. "Jerry, are you ready? You need to go with her now."

He managed to smile and whispered, "I'm ready, Amy. Take me home."

His wife's warm lips pressed against his and his eyes closed as he took his least breath.

"Jerry!" Rebecca screamed. "Jerry!"

She flung herself across his body and began to sob as she stared at Jason with anguished eyes. "It wasn't his time!" she screamed. "Oh God, it wasn't his time!"

Jeff gently touched her shoulder to comfort her and her eyes changed. They seemed darker now and intensely angry. "Where are they?" she asked.

He knew she was asking about the men who had attacked them. "There's a bar in town where they hang out. I'd bet they're there. Want me to go with you?"

Her face was like stone. "No."

She stood up and her eyes began to glow red. Jason had never seen her like this before. "Are you alright?" he asked.

Her face was emotionless. "I'm fine. I'll only be a little while."

She knelt by Jerry and kissed his cheek. "I'll see you in heaven, Jerry," she whispered.

A minute later, she was flying towards town.

CHAPTER TWENTY THREE

The men in the bar were gathered around the burly man who'd used the bat on Jerry. Their laughter was so loud it that they didn't hear Rebecca land softly on the roof. She bent down and pressed her ear against it so she could hear what they were saying.

"You should have heard the sound he made when I hit him!" the man laughed.

"Do it again, Dan! What'd he sound like?"

Dan sucked in a deep breath and waited until his face turned red before letting it out. "Aawwkkkkkk!" he squealed.

The men roared with laughter and one of them said, "The fucker got what he deserved. No one turns against us!"

Rebecca had heard enough. Enraged, she jumped high in the air and flew straight down. The wooden ceiling caved in and splintered into pieces. As the dust settled around her, the startled men stared in disbelief as she rose from the floor. "Hello boys," she said. "Mind if I join the party?"

"It's that fucking angel Alan told us about!" one of them yelled, pointing at her.

She smiled. "Believe me, I'm no angel."

Looking around the room with distain, she pointed at the man with the bat. "So tell me, did the fucker get what he deserved? Did you teach him good?"

The men gathered their courage and she seethed as they moved slowly towards her.

"Who wants to be first?" she asked as she walked forward to meet them.

Surprised, the men backed up and the one named Dan grabbed the baseball bat and raised it threateningly. "Stay away, you bitch or I'll smash your head in!" he yelled, his eyes wide with fright.

Two of the largest men rushed at her then and she bent low at the waist. When they were almost upon her, she smashed them with her wings and they flew into the bar. "Shit!" one screamed as his arm snapped in two from the impact. He lay on the floor and groaned in pain. The other man rose from the floor and ran at her again.

"I'll take your fucking head off!" he yelled and swung his big fist at her.

Rebecca stood her ground and swung from the hip. The uppercut broke his jaw and his eyes fluttered as he slumped to the floor in a heap.

"Get her!" a tall blonde-haired man yelled. A few of them rushed at her and she grabbed one around the neck and threw him into two others, taking them out. Another snuck up behind her holding a chair and smashed it against her back. She winced and lashed out with her foot. His mouth exploded in a mist of blood and several of his teeth flew into a wall like shrapnel.

Two more men rushed at her from the side and she was driven into the bar. A fist drove into her stomach and she gasped. "Look! I hurt her!" the man yelled.

The other man punched her hard in the side of the head and she went to her knees.

"That's it, Paul! You hurt her good that time!" a man cried.

He smiled and squatted in front of her. She tried to catch her breath and he grabbed her long hair and tugged her towards him. "You cunt," he growled. "You think you can just come into our town and beat *all* of us?!"

He slapped her across the face and a trickle of blood flowed from her cut lip down her chin. "I don't usually hit ladies but I'm making an exception for you," he said before rearing back and punching her in the nose. An explosion of blood clouded her eyes and she cried out from the crushing pain.

Two men recovered enough to rush over and grab her arms and legs. They pulled her to the floor and had to use every ounce of their strength as she thrashed about trying to break free.

"Yeah, hold her down," Paul said. "Let's see what we got here."

The man holding her arms knelt on her wings and crushed them to the floor. "Now you're gonna get it," he said as he leered down at her.

The man named Paul leaned over and smashed his fist into her face again after he saw her lip seal up and begin to heal. The wound reopened and he grabbed her by the throat. "So, angel, what you got under that white dress of yours?"

Rebecca grit her teeth and snarled, "You'll never know, asshole. I'm saving myself for one man and you're not him."

"Why you dirty bitch!" he screamed and moved his hands over her breasts. He leaned down to kiss her and her teeth closed around his lower lip. She clamped down hard and he shrieked in agony. He pulled away and looked down in horror at the part of his lip still between her teeth. "Get her up!" he cried as blood poured from the wound.

The two men holding her pulled her up and he reared back with his fist again. Rebecca lunged forward and drove her forehead into his face, smashing his cheekbone and knocking him unconscious. She pulled her arms free then but the man to her right drove his fist into her side and she fell forward to the floor. Rolling onto her back, she kicked upwards with her foot and snapped his head back with a powerful blow. He slumped to the floor unconscious and the other man backed away, shaking his head in disbelief. Rebecca got to her feet, smiled at him and he turned to run but she grabbed his arm and wrenched it violently to the side, dislocating his shoulder. He screamed and she pulled it back and forth in the socket until he pissed himself. "Please stop!" he screamed. "Oh God, it hurts!"

Rebecca laughed and tossed him aside. Dan was the only man left standing. He'd watched the whole fight and shivered in fright as she walked towards him.

"So, little man, you never answered my question. Did Jerry get what he deserved?" she asked.

He nodded. "He turned against us. We did what we had to do."

Rebecca's face turned sad. "Well, you got what you wanted. He's dead."

He turned white. "*What?*! No! You're lying!"

Rebecca shook her head slowly. "No, I'm not. He died right in front of me."

He started to blubber. "But I only hit him once! He can't be dead!"

Her eyes flashed red for an instant and the surrounding men crawled or limped away from her. "Once was all it took, Dan. Are you happy now? Jerry's gone."

He looked like he was going to collapse. "Oh my God," he gasped. "I didn't mean to kill him. Oh Jesus!"

"Jesus can't help you, Dan."

He stared at her and desperately tried to think of a way past her. "What are you going to do?"

She stared intensely at him for a moment but then her eyes turned soft. "I was planning on hurting you, Dan. I was going to break every bone in your body to make you pay for what you did."

She lowered her head and stared at her hands. "But I won't. I have a better idea," she said and looked at the group of injured men. The ones who'd been unconscious were awake now and moaning. "Get out. All of you," she said.

They looked at each other and one stared at her with a menacing look. He moved behind the bar and retrieved a long metal baseball bat.

Her eyes narrowed and she clenched her fists. "Really? Would you like to try again?"

The look in her eyes said it all and he slowly backed towards the door. The ones who could walk helped the more injured men to their feet and she stepped aside to let them leave. Dan tried to follow but she shoved him back with her hand. "No. *Not* you. *You* stay here with me."

"Oh God!" he cried and sank to his knees in front of her. "Please don't kill me!"

Her face was expressionless. "Don't worry. I won't kill you."

"Then let me go!" he sobbed.

"No," she said and put her hand on his forehead. "I want you to see the life you've taken."

"Oh God," he moaned as images of Jerry holding hands with his wife played in his mind. They kissed and seemed so happy. There were scenes of them sitting in front of a Christmas tree watching their children open presents and then it jumped to them having dinner in an intimate restaurant. They were holding hands and gazing into one another's eyes.

"Make it stop," Alan groaned pitifully. "*Please* make it stop."

The scenes went on and he began to sob harder. Jerry now stood by the side of a hospital bed and his dying wife lifted her arm to him. Alan wrenched his head away from Rebecca's hand and screamed, "Noooo!!"

She leaned over him as he curled into a ball on the floor. "That's the life you took, Alan. Now you have to live with what you've done for the rest of *your* life. You've cursed yourself with one violent unnecessary act."

He looked up at her with frightened eyes. "I didn't mean to! Please help me!"

Her eyes hardened. "I can't and I wouldn't even if I could."

She turned then and walked out the door, leaving him screaming behind her. The cold air bit into her face and she felt incredibly sad. *Why God?* she thought. *Why are people so cruel? Will they ever learn?*

Jason and Jeff were waiting for her by Jerry's car when she got back. An ambulance had just pulled away and Jeff said, "The police were already here. I told them what happened and they called to have

Jerry taken away. They're out looking for the men who did this. I gave them their names."

"What happened at the bar?" Jason asked.

She seemed physically drained and Jason reached out and lightly touched her arm. "I made them pay," she whispered against his chest.

Jeff shook his head in wonder. "You're a remarkable woman, Rebecca."

"Yes, she is," Jason agreed.

Rebecca looked up into his face and said, "Let's go get your daughter and leave this town forever."

He nodded and Rebecca picked him up and flew straight up into the air. She hovered there and yelled down to Jeff, "Please do what Susanna asked. Start packing up her things. We'll be back soon."

"I'll be glad to!" he shouted.

She turned then and flew away rapidly with Jason in her arms and they were at the hospital in no time at all.

Susanna was asleep when they entered her room. The doctor was standing by her bed and turned to them, a look of concern on his face.

"Is something wrong, doctor?" Jason asked. "Susanna's going home today, isn't she?"

The man nodded no. "I'm sorry but I still don't think she's ready. I don't like the sound of her breathing. She needs to stay at least one more day for observation."

"Is this because of her broken ribs?" Rebecca asked.

"Yes," he answered. "Every breath she takes is painful and it'll be quite a while until she's fully healed but it wouldn't be wise to release her just yet."

"I understand," Jason said. "Thank you, doctor."

They sat by Susanna's bed for the rest of the day and every now and then Jason took small breaks to eat. It was close to evening when he began to weaken. Rebecca heard him groan in pain as he shifted in his chair and she touched his face. "We need to get you home. You've been sitting too long."

As if on cue, Jeff walked into the room and said, "I'll stay the night and watch over her. You've done enough today. Go home and get some sleep."

"Thank you, Jeff," Rebecca said as she stood on tiptoes to kiss his cheek.

Blushing, he smiled and said, "You're welcome. Oh, most of what I thought was important is packed up back at the house. Just tell me what to do with it when you're ready. I can have it shipped to you or I'll be glad to drive it to wherever you want myself."

"You're a good man, Jeff," she said warmly. "I hope you live a long and happy life."

He smiled and Jason got out of the chair so the big man could take his place.

"Thanks," Jason said and they left.

Back at Susanna's, Rebecca went to the kitchen to make Jason dinner while he walked around and looked at all the boxes that Jeff had packed.

The smell of whatever she was making made him salivate and he headed to the kitchen. Sitting down, he stared at her as she stirred something in a pan. "You know, you're not my slave," he said. "I *can* cook for myself."

She turned around, surprised. "But I *like* doing this for you," she said. "Don't you want me to?"

"Yes, but I don't want to take advantage of you, Rebecca. This isn't the fifties anymore when women basically cooked and cleaned house while their husbands worked. I don't want you to think I'm some kind of chauvinistic pig."

Her eyes opened wide with amusement and she burst out laughing. Startled, he leaned back in his chair as she approached, smiling. She put her hands on his shoulders and gazed warmly into his eyes.

"Jason," she said softly. "I don't think you're chauvinistic at all. If I didn't like you I wouldn't cook for you. Don't you know that by now?"

He saw something on her then that suddenly made him shiver and she sensed his fear. She looked at him strangely and went back to her cooking.

"Thank you," he said as he ate. "It's delicious."

She came back and sat and watched him as a sadness washed over her. Reaching out with her hand, she felt him wince when she touched his wrist. She pulled her hand back and asked, "Jason, what's wrong?"

He stared at her with no expression but the look in his eyes gave him away. "Nothing's wrong."

"Yes, there is," she said, looking back into his face. "Don't lie. You're scared of me, aren't you?"

He stopped chewing but didn't answer.

She stood up then and looked down at him. "I'm going to leave you alone for a while. We'll talk later."

She walked out of the kitchen and he went back to eating. When he was finished, he cleaned his dish and fork and went upstairs to his room. He brushed his teeth and sat on the bed for what seemed like a long time. The moon was out and very bright and its light filled the room with a soft glow. He got up and gazed out the window.

"You know you don't have to be afraid of me," the soft voice came from behind him.

Jason turned quickly around and saw Rebecca standing in the doorway. She slowly moved towards him and he held his breath. "Please talk to me," she said softly and stopped a few feet from him. "Tell me why you're afraid."

Jason gulped and his voice croaked a bit when he asked, "It just suddenly dawned on me. The things I've seen you do….would you ever hurt me like you hurt them?"

"You mean those men at the bar? You weren't there. How would you know what I did to them?"

Jason pointed at the bottom of her dress and Rebecca looked down and saw the bloodstains. She ran her finger over one and said, "Jason, this is my blood."

"What?!" he cried. "They made you bleed? You mean you *can* be hurt?!"

She laughed. "Of course I can be hurt! I'm not superhuman, you know. I'm just a woman in angel form. A very strong woman but a woman just the same."

"Are all angels like you?"

The corners of her eyes crinkled in surprise. "What do you mean?"

He stared intensely at her. "I mean that you're supposedly an angel but you don't act like one."

Her eyes lit up. "Oh, *now* I understand. You're wondering how an angel can be so violent."

"Yes," he said. "I don't get it. You kick ass like a wild woman. How can you possibly be an angel?"

Rebecca sat on the edge of the bed and patted it. "Come sit by me," she said.

He hesitated but she said, "C'mon, Jason. I promise I won't hurt you."

He moved to sit down by her and she held his hand in hers. "Just because I'm an angel doesn't mean I still don't have human qualities, Jason," she said softly. "Angels aren't like what you read about in books. We get angry and sad just like you. We have feelings too."

"But those men at the barn….you hurt them badly. I've never seen anything like it. It's almost like you enjoyed it. I didn't know an angel could take pleasure in hurting others even though they deserved it."

She frowned. "I may be an angel, Jason but I'm not a saint. Those men did very bad things and needed to be punished."

"But isn't that God's job to decide?" he asked.

"Yes," she replied. "But he leaves it to us to decide whether we want to interfere in man's ways sometimes. The only thing we can't do is take a life."

Jason stared at her blankly and she said, "I know what you're thinking. Why you ask don't angels interfere everywhere when people are raped, tortured or murdered, am I correct?"

He nodded yes.

"It's a question I can't answer, Jason. We're all given a signal which directs us to help only certain people. It's God's will, I suppose."

"What kind of signal?"

She squeezed his hand lightly. "It's like a pulsing in my head. It led me to you as a baby and I have no idea why."

He was silent for a moment but then said, "I'm very lucky, aren't I?"

Her eyes were tender and warm as she stared into his. "Yes....you are, Jason. Don't try to understand what's happening. Just accept it. Will you do that for me?"

He looked down at her hand holding his and whispered, "Yes, I'll do that for you. I'll do anything for you."

He looked into her eyes then and felt weak in them. "I....I have so many feelings for you, Rebecca. I'm so confused. I don't know what to do," he said.

She leaned close and put her forehead against his. "I feel the same way, Jason," she said quietly. "I don't know what to do either. You're a man and I'm an angel. This isn't supposed to happen. We aren't meant to be together."

Her warm breath washed over his face and he felt intoxicated. "I don't care. Please, Rebecca, let me love you. Oh God, let me love you."

She touched him under the chin then and tenderly said, "I'm sorry but I can't yet. I need to talk to the others first."

"The other angels?" he asked.

"Yes. I need their advice."

"I understand," he said, his face sad.

She smiled and kissed his cheek. "Remember the old saying, Jason. Good things come to those who wait."

He brightened and she said, "Let's get you ready for bed."

Standing up, he began to take his clothes off as Rebecca watched. Blushing, he stood naked in front of her and she looked down and saw he was hard.

"Oh my," she whispered. "Is it hard because of me?"

"I can't help it. You're so beautiful and I want to touch you so badly."

She ignored what he'd said and asked, "I know I said it was a one-time thing but would you like me to take care of it? Will you sleep better if I do?"

"Yes….please."

She climbed onto the bed and sat against the headboard. "Come," she said and spread her legs wide. "Sit here between my legs."

Jason climbed into bed and sat down between her legs. "Lie against me," she said and he leaned back until he felt her breasts press into his back. "Now close your eyes and relax. I want to share a fantasy with you I've been having lately. I'm a little embarrassed by it but I think you'll like it."

"Alright," he whispered and closed his eyes.

Rebecca's hand was warm as her long fingers encircled his shaft. "Oh," he gasped as she began to slowly stroke him.

"I imagined I wasn't an angel, Jason. I dreamed instead that I was your girlfriend and you made me angry for some reason. Do you know what I'd have to do then?" she whispered in his ear as she held his head against hers with her other hand.

"What?" he gasped as her hand pleasured him.

"I'd have to punish you."

She felt him shiver and he quietly said, "How?"

"Well, first I'd tell you to pull your jammies down."

"But I don't wear pajamas."

Rebecca stopped moving her hand. "Be quiet, Jason and let me tell my story, alright?"

His hard cock pulsed in her hand and his breathing became more rapid. "Oh please don't stop. I promise I'll be quiet."

She went back to slowly stroking him. "Good, now where was I? Oh yes, I'd tell you to pull your jammies down and you'd stand in front of me with that thing of yours pointing in my face. I'd tell you you've been a bad boy and to lie over my knees."

Jason's felt his heart beat faster as she kept a steady rhythm with her hand. "And *then*...." she whispered in his ear. "I'd spank your bare bottom until it was nice and red. How does that sound?"

"Oh God," he moaned.

She giggled lightly when his penis swelled even more in her hand. "I'd say you like the sound of that by how hard your cock's getting, don't you?"

Jason moved his hips up so she'd stroke faster but she stopped her hand movement again. "Oh no, my friend. I'm going to do this at my own pace. You'll just have to hold out a little longer."

"But Rebecca," he groaned. "Please...I can't stand it."

She giggled again but louder. "Oh you silly boy! You have no choice! You must surrender completely to me or I won't make you cum."

He groaned again and sank back against her. "Alright....I surrender," he said, his voice jittery with the desire for release.

"Good boy," she whispered and resumed her torturously slow strokng of his rigid member. "After your spanking I'd have you lie on your back so I could tie your hands and feet to the bedposts with rope."

"What? Why?" he gasped as her hand began to pick up speed.

Rebecca smiled. "So I could torture you with my feather again. Remember how good it felt?”

“Oh God,” he moaned. “Yes….yes.”

She felt her face blush then at the thought of him lying helpless and begging for release.

“I’m almost done with the story, Jason,” she whispered as her hand moved faster.

He was literally panting like an animal now and his cockhead was dark red as Rebecca moved her hand higher so her thumb would hit the corona again and again.

“Oh Jesus!” he cried. “I’m going to cum soon!”

Rebecca blew lightly in his ear and whispered, “I’d take that feather and tickle your balls with it and you wouldn’t be able to stop me. You’d beg for release but I’d just laugh and run the feather up and down your shaft and watch it grow bigger.”

“Oh God!” Jason cried louder. “Oh God!”

Her hand stroked faster still and she knew he was close. “And when your cock was ready to blow like it is now I’d tickle your little pee hole with that soft feather.”

“Ooohhh,” Jason moaned and Rebecca felt his cock swell close to bursting in her hand.

“Yes, Jason,” she whispered. “Give into the pleasure. I want a great big cum from you now.”

“Oh shit!” he screamed and she licked his ear.

“And no matter how hard you begged me to stop, I wouldn’t,” she whispered. “I’d insert the feather into your tiny hole and wiggle it around and force every drop of cum from this handsome cock of yours.”

“Oh Rebecca!” he shrieked and cum shot out of the tip of his penis. It flew in the air and landed on top of her head and Rebecca laughed.

“Yes, Jason!” she cried. “Cum for me!”

Her forefinger tickled his frenulum then and his hips bucked wildly as more cum shot out of his cock and landed on her shoulder.

"Oh my God!" he screamed as he felt yet another wave coming.

Rebecca smiled and kissed the side of his neck. "Yes, one more time, Jason," she whispered. "I know you can do it, baby. Cum for me once more and I promise I'll hold you in my arms all night long."

Tears of joy rolled down his face and his neck muscles tensed and Rebecca aimed his penis back towards her face. She opened her mouth and gave him a few fast strokes.

"Rebecca!!" he shrieked and the blast flew straight back into her mouth. She swallowed it all and nuzzled against his neck as he shuddered in her arms.

He was covered in sweat and breathing heavily. "Oohhh," he groaned, his voice raw from screaming.

"I really enjoyed sharing my story with you, Jason," she said softly. "Now go to sleep and dream well."

She felt him relax against her and a smile crossed his face as he looked at her. "That fantasy of yours. Will you please do that to me in the future?" he said.

"You'd let me bind you to the bed, helpless?" she asked, surprised.

"Yes. I'd let you do anything you want to me."

"That could be fun," she said, smiling devilishly. "I may just surprise you one day and guess what?"

"What?"

She grinned. "There's more to the fantasy I didn't tell you about."

"Oh, please tell me!"

"No," she whispered. "It's time to sleep now. You'll just have to wait and be surprised."

He closed his eyes then and his breathing began to slow. "I feel so safe with you, Rebecca," he said so softly she could barely hear him. "I'm home in your arms."

Seconds later, he was snoring lightly and she kissed his neck again and whispered, "Yes, Jason, you're home in my arms."

CHAPTER TWENTY FOUR

Though it was rare for her to do, Rebecca felt herself doze off because Jason's body heat was warming her nicely. *He feels so good in my arms*, she thought. *I wish....*

Her eyes flew open and for a moment she didn't know where she was. She looked at the clock and was surprised she'd been asleep for hours. Jason was snoring in her arms and her ears suddenly perked up. There was a clinking sound far off in the distance but she couldn't quite figure out where. She gently pushed Jason aside and got out of bed. Standing silently in the dark, she listened again and heard a whoosh. She quickly covered Jason with a blanket and then heard a crashing noise like a window breaking.

"Shit!" she cried and rushed out of the room. Looking down the hallway, she saw a strange glow coming from downstairs. She ran to look and saw the living room was on fire. Flames were slowly crawling up the curtains and the smell of smoke hit her nose. "Oh no!" she gasped.

She ran downstairs and saw the flaming bottle lying on the floor by the television. Another one crashed through another window and rolled by her feet. She picked it up quickly and threw it back out the window before it could do any damage. Another loud crash in the kitchen and two more upstairs roused her to action. "Jason!" she screamed.

He appeared at the top of the stairs, rubbing his eyes. He was naked and yawned. "Rebecca, what's happening? I heard a noise," he mumbled.

Flames suddenly shot out of the far bedroom and raced along the walls towards him.

"Jason! Watch out!" she cried but he turned as if in slow motion and his eyes opened wide when he saw the fire hurtling towards him.

"Fuck!" she cried and raced up the stairs as Jason stood rigid with fear. The fire exploded towards him, scorching the carpeted floor along the way. Rebecca's wings shot out of her back and she grabbed him tightly.

"Get down!" she shouted. They knelt together on the floor and her wings wrapped around them both like a protective cocoon. Jason shuddered as the flames hit but she smiled and said reassuringly, "Don't worry, you're safe with me."

He saw the glow of the fire through her wings and then the air grew hot. "You can't save me!" he cried. "I'll be roasted alive!"

Rebecca grimaced. "Not if I can help it! It's not your time!"

Her wings suddenly flew back with a speed that a camera wouldn't catch and the fire was pushed back. She stood up then and Jason watched as she beat her wings with immense force. The fire was going out! She slowly walked it back into the room it started in until it fizzled out, leaving nothing but smoke.

An explosion downstairs rocked the house and she turned back and scooped Jason up in her arms. "Come on! We have to get out of here!" she screamed.

When they got downstairs, her eyes darted around as she quickly scanned the packed boxes. She ran to one and tore it open. Grabbing something inside, she put it inside her dress next to her breast. "Let's go!" she cried and Jason watched her beautiful wings open a path towards the front door. She lashed out with her foot and the door exploded outward. "Come on!" she screamed when another explosion from behind blew white hot fire towards them. She grabbed Jason and flew out the door, her wings smashing through the walls on both sides leaving a horizontal path of destruction.

They landed and rolled on the ground. Jason saw Rebecca's wings were smoking and he grabbed some snow and quickly rubbed it over the worst spots. She sat up and stared back at the burning house. Tears flowed down her face and Jason held her. "I couldn't save it," she cried. "I'm sorry, Jason."

Just then, he heard a shout from the side and a flaming bottle landed in front of them. "Look out!" he screamed as he shoved her away and jumped on top of it.

"Jason! No!" Rebecca shouted and it exploded beneath him.

"Oh God! No!" she screamed and lunged to turn him over.

Blood gushed out of the jagged hole in his stomach and his eyes were glazed with pain. "Rebecca…." he moaned. "Help me…."

"Oh Jason!" she cried and gently lifted him up in her arms. Gazing down into his face, she said, "Stay with me. I'm going to get you help."

A flaming bottle flew at her from the right and she lashed out just in time with her foot, sending it flying back at their assailant. There was an explosion of flames in the distance and a man began shrieking in agony.

"Burn, damn you!" she growled and flew up into the air. She looked back at the burning house one last time and then headed to the hospital.

Her wings retracted before she came through the emergency room doors. She saw the astonished looks on the nurse's faces and cried, "Please help him! He's dying!"

They rushed towards her and Jason was placed on a gurney to be wheeled away. Rebecca held his hand as he was wheeled towards the emergency room and stared intensely into his frightened eyes. "Don't leave me, Jason!" she wept. "Please don't leave me! I can't lose you!"

A doctor lightly touched her arm. "We'll do everything we can," he said.

She let go of Jason's hand then and they took him away. Her white dress was covered with soot and she smelled of smoke. A nurse approached her and asked, "Are you alright?"

She looked at the woman and felt like she was about to lose it. "No, I'm not. I finally realize I love that man. I can't lose him."

"He'll be alright. He's in good hands," the nurse said with confidence.

Rebecca slumped into a chair and felt a wave of exhaustion sweep over her. "He has to be. He sacrificed himself for me."

"He sounds like a very special man," the nurse said.

Rebecca looked into the woman's eyes and quietly said, "Yes, he is. He's a *good* man."

CHAPTER TWENTY FIVE

While Jason was in surgery, Rebecca visited Susanna in her room. The young woman was awake and her eyes opened wide at the sight of Rebecca's dress.

"Oh my God! Rebecca! What happened?!" she cried and sat up in bed.

The angel looked very tired and sat on the edge of the bed. "Susanna," she said quietly. "Your father….he's in surgery now. I hope he'll be alright."

"What?! Daddy?!"

"Yes. I'm sorry. We were attacked. Your house…."

Susanna's eyes filled with tears. "Oh my God," she moaned. "Why?! Why?!"

Rebecca's face turned grim. "When he's better we're leaving this town forever. I can't fight them all."

Susanna saw the strain on the angel's face and reached out and took her hand in hers. "You did what you could, Rebecca. Thank you."

The angel's eyes filled with tears and her lower lip quivered. "Your father….he tried to save me. He sacrificed himself for me, Susanna. Why would he do that?"

Susanna smiled. "Don't you know? How much more proof do you need? He loves you. He'd *die* for you."

The angel began to sob. "Oh God! I never told him I loved him!"

"I think he knows, Rebecca," Susanna said gently. "You've done so much for him….for both of us already. Believe me, he knows."

"Oh God, I hope so!" she said and Susanna pulled her close.

"Shhhhh, it's alright. I'm here for you," Susanna said as she held the sobbing angel.

They sat like that for hours until a doctor came into the room. "Oh, there you are," he said, looking at Rebecca. "I've been looking everywhere for you. He's out of surgery. Would you like to see him?"

"Can I come too?!" Susanna asked.

"Of course. I can only give you a few minutes though. He needs to rest."

Rebecca helped Susanna out of bed and they followed the doctor down hallways until they arrived at a small room in the intensive care unit.

Jason looked very peaceful lying in bed. His eyes were closed and there was a huge bandage covering his stomach. "We were lucky," the doctor said. "His muscles were torn up but none of his organs were affected."

"Thank God!" Susanna said and went to her father. She knelt by his side and took his hand. "Daddy," she whispered. "I'm here and so is Rebecca."

The angel walked slowly over and stood at the foot of the bed. Jason opened his eyes slightly and saw her. She smiled and he whispered, "My angel."

Rebecca went and knelt by the other side of his bed and moved a strand of hair out of his eyes with her hand. "I'm here, Jason."

"I'm alive?" he weakly said.

"Yes, you are," she answered. "But what you did was very foolish. Why did you do what you did? I would have survived."

"I had to protect you," he said and tried to smile. "You're my best friend."

Rebecca fought back tears and held his hand. "I'm your best friend? Really?"

"Yes, I trust you with my deepest secrets."

She leaned close to him and put her lips to his ear. "When you get out of here, I'm going to take good care of you and when you're all better I want *you* to touch *me*. Do you understand what I'm saying?"

His eyes suddenly filled with light and she pulled her head back. Susanna noticed the change in him and stared in astonishment at Rebecca.

"What did you say to him? It's like he's suddenly filled with energy."

"I gave him a little extra incentive to get through this," Rebecca answered. "Just a little something to look forward to."

"*Aaahhh*," Susanna said, smiling. "I think I understand. You're a wise woman."

The doctor motioned to them and Susanna kissed her father on the cheek. "Get better soon, dad."

Rebecca stroked his cheek and said, "I'll be waiting."

Jason nodded and closed his eyes. They left the room and when they were outside it, Susanna grabbed the angel's arm and said, "Why didn't you tell him you love him?!"

Rebecca stared at her with sad eyes. "Something's stopping me, Susanna. I need to talk to the others before I do something stupid with your father."

"You mean angels? You need to talk to other angels about love?"

"No....not about love but about whether it's permitted. I don't want to make God mad. I don't know what would happen if I did."

"Oh, I see," Susanna said. "I hope you get the ok."

Rebecca wiped a tear away. "Susanna, I've watched over many people over the years. I've helped them in many ways and they've always been grateful. But....they always saw me as an angel sent from God. Your father is the first one who's ever seen me as a woman."

Susanna gazed deeply into Rebecca's eyes. "You don't need to talk to the other angels, Rebecca."

"Why not?"

"Because I think I know what's going on here. You already showed my father his purpose in life, correct?"

"Yes, but...."

Susanna smiled and took the angel's hands in hers. "Hasn't it dawned on you that you've done enough and he doesn't need you anymore? Maybe it's *you* who needs him."

Rebecca's face felt her face flush and stared intensely at Susanna. The realization hit her then and she felt the hot tears roll down her cheeks.

"Rebecca," Susanna said, suddenly worried. "I didn't mean to upset you. Are you alright?"

She pulled the crying angel to her and embraced her. "Tell me what's wrong," she whispered.

Rebecca sobbed against her and said, "I've been so lonely. I guess I never realized it until I met your father and he treated me like a woman."

Susanna gently pushed her back so she could look into her eyes. "How could God be mad at you for loving someone?" she said softly. "Think about it, Rebecca. You don't need to talk to other angels about this. You already know in your heart whether it's right or wrong."

The angel brushed her tears away and smiled. "Susanna, how did you become so wise? Thank you. Thank you so much."

Susanna put her lips to the angel's ear and whispered, "Just go with how you feel, dear angel. If you truly love my father then show him."

Rebecca nodded and Susanna added one more thing. "You *both* need each other, Rebecca. You belong together. *That's* your purpose."

CHAPTER TWENTY SIX

Susanna was released from the hospital an hour later and told to take it easy for a few weeks. She asked Rebecca to take her back to the house to see what was left of it. As they flew, Susanna closed her eyes and smiled as the wind blew through her hair.

"I could get used to this!" she cried happily.

Rebecca didn't say anything because she was dreading the young woman's reaction to what they'd find.

"Oh my God," Susanna said when they landed in front of her smoking house. The firemen had already left and what was left was uninhabitable. "It's gone. It's all gone," she said sadly.

She felt faint and Rebecca held her so she wouldn't fall and said, "Do you want me to do something about this, Susanna? I will if you ask me to."

"No," she said in a small voice. "I just want to leave this town."

"Alright," the angel said.

A truck suddenly pulled up behind them and the women turned to look at it. A group of men got out and leaned against it.

"It's too bad about your house!" one of them shouted and smiled.

The men laughed and Rebecca's eyes narrowed in anger. Susanna tried to grab her arm but the angel was too fast. Before the men knew what was happening she was almost upon them. They jumped out of the way and she bent and grabbed the bottom of the side of the truck. She grunted and lifted it until it was almost sideways. Then with a great shrug of her shoulders, she flipped it and it went flying through the air and crashed upside down near a large willow tree.

"Hey, that's my truck!" a man angrily shouted.

Rebecca turned to face him and snarled, "That's what happens when you fuck with this family!"

He opened his mouth to say something but another man grabbed his arm and pulled him back. They all knew that the angel could destroy them without breaking a sweat.

Susanna spotted someone she knew in the group, a man who'd bought things at the hardware store she worked at. He'd always been nice to her which hurt her deeply. She stepped up to him and looked into his face.

"Dave," she said, wanting to cry. "How could you be a part of this? Why would you hurt me like this?"

Ashamed, he turned his back on her and she bitterly said, "I loved this town. I really did but you've made it impossible for me to stay."

He turned back around and his face was red. "I'm sorry, Susanna," he quietly said.

"Well *I'm* not!" a big beefy man said, his eyes full of fight. "We want you and this angel cunt out of our town!"

Susanna winced at his words and began to walk away with her head down. Rebecca sneered at the man and said, "If it was up to me I'd hurt you so badly you'd beg me to kill you."

He raised his arm as if to strike her and she smiled. "Give me a reason. I dare you," she whispered.

Fear entered his eyes and she grinned. "I didn't think so….you're a coward like everyone else who lives in this damn place. Now go away and leave us alone."

"We can't," a man said. "You turned our truck upside down!"

Proud of what she'd done, she smiled. "I sure did, didn't I? Well, I'll fix that."

She went to the truck, grabbed it by its base and wrenched it away from the tree with the sound of crunching metal. With a grunt, she flipped it back on its wheels and pointed at the men. "There! Now leave!" she shouted angrily.

Stunned, the men piled into the damaged truck. The roof was slightly caved in and the sides were banged up but otherwise it was driveable. They quickly drove off without looking back and Rebecca turned around and went back to join Susanna. They stared at the house and Susanna said, "I guess it wasn't meant to be. I thought this would be my home forever."

Rebecca put her arm around Susanna's shoulders and said, "Let's go. Let's leave this behind."

The girl nodded. "I'll call the insurance company later. Please take me back to my father now."

Rebecca gently lifted her and they flew back to the hospital. Susanna looked back at her house one last time and then buried her face against Rebecca's neck and began to sob. The angel knew words would be useless so she just held her tighter as they flew.

Jason was awake when they entered his room. Both women were surprised and the doctor came in and said, "I'm going to release him tomorrow. He should be ok to make the car ride home then."

Susanna's eyes lit up with joy. "But isn't it too soon? Won't his wound open up?"

"No, if he stays fairly still he should be alright. It isn't doing him any good being here."

He came close to Susanna then and whispered, "Does your father suffer from depression?"

Her eyes lit up with worry. "Why do you ask? Did he say something?"

The doctor looked back at Jason and then at her again. "While he was asleep he was moaning and asking what the point of life was."

"Oh no," Rebecca said. "That's not good. You're right. We need to get him out of here."

Susanna quickly said, "I'll call right now and get a rental car!"

"No you won't," said a low voice from the doorway. They turned and saw it was Jeff, the big cook from the diner.

He stepped into the room and said, "I'll drive you wherever you need to go. I'll shut the diner down for a few days."

"But you'll lose money!" Susanna said.

"It'll be fine," he answered. "It's the least I can do for my friends."

Rebecca's eyes twinkled. "I appreciate your kindness, Jeff. Someday God will reward you."

He looked like he was about to cry and she went to him. He lowered his head against her shoulder and began to sob. Rebecca held him and whispered, "Jerry's in a better place now, Jeff. I promise you he's happy."

He stood straighter and stared down at her. "If you ever create an army for God I want to enlist," he said softly.

"God's army here on earth. Now that's an idea," she said as she thought about it. "Yes….that's an excellent idea."

CHAPTER TWENTY SEVEN

Jeff was true to his word and when Jason was released he helped him to his truck while the women got in the back seat. Jason had a lot of room for his legs which made his stomach feel less painful. No words were spoken except when Rebecca needed to give Jeff directions. It was a long ride and Jason slept the whole way home.

"Here we are," Rebecca said when they pulled into a spot in front of Jason's building. She gently touched his shoulder and said, "We're here, Jason. We're home."

Hs eyes fluttered open and he looked around, dazed. "Oh," was all he said.

Jeff helped him out of the truck and Rebecca said, "Thanks, Jeff. I'll take it from here."

She handed him the keys to the apartment and lifted Jason in her arms. "It's on the second floor. Lead the way. I'll be right behind you."

Jeff stared in surprise at how easily she held Jason. "You don't need help?"

"Are you kidding?!" she laughed.

He shrugged his shoulders and entered the building. Susanna followed behind as Rebecca carried Jason. When the door to the apartment was unlocked, Jeff stepped aside and she went into Jason's bedroom and laid him down on the bed. "I'll be back soon," she whispered and went back to where Susanna and Jeff were sitting in the living room.

The big man got up suddenly and went to one knee and lowered his head. Rebecca stared down at him and said, "Jeff, what are you doing? Please don't bow to me. I'm not God."

He looked up at her face and his eyes were shining. "But you're one of his angels. I want to follow you."

"Follow me where, Jeff?" she asked. "I'm only here because of Jason."

"That's not true," Susanna interjected. "You say that but yet you've already affected my life and Jeff's life for the better. You even helped Jerry be a better man right before he died."

"What are you saying?" Rebecca asked.

"I'm saying that maybe you've found *your* true purpose, angel of God. Maybe you're here for more than one reason."

"And what would that be?" Rebecca asked, amused.

Jeff stared intensely at her. "To be God's weapon for good. You can spread his love if you try."

"But that's what priests are for," she argued. "I'm just an angel and nothing more."

Susanna stood up and embraced the woman. "Oh no, Rebecca. You're much more than that. You're also a woman who cares about people. You have it in you to help change the world."

"How?!" Rebecca laughed. "By breaking bones whenever people piss me off?!"

Susanna smiled. "Ok, you've got a point. Maybe you need to tone that down a bit but overall look at the positive things you've done. You can do so much more if you want to."

Rebecca almost smirked in response but didn't want to hurt their feelings so she didn't. "I really appreciate what you're both saying but you're wrong. I'm just here to help Jason. That's all."

Jeff ignored her and said, "When you create God's army I'll be ready. Please just think about it. That's all we ask."

"Count me in," Susanna said. "I'll do whatever's necessary."

The angel stared at them both like they were crazy and sighed. "Alright," she said quietly. "I'll think about it."

Jeff smiled and rose to his feet. "Well, I guess I'll be going now."

He stared deeply into the angel's eyes. "I'll be waiting for your call."

Before she could respond, he turned and walked out of the apartment. Susanna followed him out to his truck and grabbed him tightly around the waist. "Thank you, Jeff! I don't know what I'd do without you! If you ever need anything, just ask."

He stared at her for a moment and quietly said, "Well, Susanna, there is something but I'm ashamed to ask."

"What is it?" she asked, curious.

His face flushed. "Oh forget it. It's nothing," he said and got into the truck.

As he turned the ignition, Susanna touched his arm. "Tell me, Jeff. What were you about to say?"

He looked down and said, "I know I'm not much to look at, Susanna and I know you've been through a lot but…."

"What, Jeff? What are you trying to say?"

He looked at her then and softly said, "I just ask that you see beneath the surface to who I really am and give me a chance with you."

Susanna's face flushed and she pulled her hand away. "Jeff! I never knew you felt that way about me! You never showed it!"

"Well, now you know," he whispered and drove off.

She watched his truck turn around the corner and disappear. Standing silently in the cold night air, she shook her head in wonder and went back to the apartment. Rebecca was making hot tea in the kitchen and Susanna slumped down in a chair with her head down. The angel knew immediately something was wrong and came and sat by her. She didn't say anything and held Susanna's hands.

"He likes me. He asked me to give him a chance," Susanna quietly said to the angel.

"Is that a problem?"

"I never thought of him in that way. He's not the kind of man a girl…."

"He's not the kind of man a girl usually falls for? Because of his looks? Is that what you were going to say, Susanna?"

Ashamed, she whispered, "Yes."

Rebecca spoke softly. "What we all possess is just a shell, Susanna. It's the soul inside that really matters. Jeff is a very good man and because of that he's much more handsome than other men. Think of it in that way and you'll see him differently."

Susanna nodded. "You're right. I never thought of it before but you're right. Beauty is only skin deep. It's what's inside that really counts."

"Now you're getting it," the angel said.

"How's my dad?" Susanna asked, changing the subject.

"I'm going in there now to get him ready for bed. Would you like to say goodnight to him?"

"No, I think I'll sit here for a while. You say goodnight for me. I've got a lot of thinking to do."

"Alright," Rebecca said and picked up the hot cup of tea and went into Jason's bedroom. He was sitting up and she handed him the tea. "Here, drink some of this. It'll warm you."

"Thank you," he said and took a sip. "That's good."

"Are you hungry? I could make you something if you are."

"No," he answered, his eyes weary. "I think I'll go to bed now."

He tried to stand to undress but was slightly unsteady on his feet. Rebecca grabbed him and said, "I'll help you."

She gently removed his clothes piece by piece and when he was naked she tucked him into bed and made sure the blankets were pulled up to his chin. Kneeling by his bed, she touched his face and quietly asked, "Is there anything else I can do for you?"

His eyes suddenly filled with tears and she lay her head against his chest. "What's wrong, Jason?" she asked. "Why are you crying?"

"Because I wish I was dead!"

She lifted her head and angrily said, "Don't say that! Don't ever say that again!"

"I just want to die," he groaned miserably.

"What the hell's wrong with you?!" she shouted and slapped him lightly across the face. "Why am I wasting time with you if you say things like that?!"

"You should have let me die out there. That's what I wanted."

Her jaw dropped in shock. "But why, Jason? Why do you wish you were dead? I don't understand!"

He smiled sadly. "Because then we'd be together. I'd be in heaven and see you all the time then."

Her eyes opened wide in surprise and she began to laugh as tears rolled down her cheeks. "You fool! You silly fool! That wouldn't help! I wouldn't be around all the time even if what you say was true!"

"You wouldn't?" he said, his voice cracking. "But I thought that way you wouldn't leave me."

Her eyes turned tender and the anger left her face. "Jason, you don't need to die for me to be with you. I'll always be with you."

She pointed to his chest and head and softly said, "This is where I am. Always."

He just stared at her and she could tell he didn't believe her.

"Oh Jason," she said softly and gently stroked his cheek. "You are so special to me. I wish…."

"You wish what?"

She lowered her head and took her hand away. "You should sleep now."

"Goodnight, my angel," he whispered and closed his eyes.

"Goodnight, Jason," she said and stood watching him for a long while as he fell into a deep sleep. "I hope I'm in your dreams," she whispered.

CHAPTER TWENTY EIGHT

When Rebecca came out of the bedroom she found Susanna sitting in front of the fireplace. She'd made a fire and was staring intensely into the flames.

"It's funny how fire can be so calming to watch but also so destructive, isn't it?" Susanna asked.

Rebecca knelt by the woman's side and held her hand. Susanna turned and looked at her. "Is my father alright?"

"Yes, he's sleeping."

Susanna looked back at the fire and sadly said, "I lost everything....my clothes, my belongings....I feel so naked and helpless."

Rebecca squeezed her hand. "We'll get you some new clothes tomorrow."

"You'll go shopping with me?"

The angel smiled. "Yes, it sounds like fun. I haven't done that in years."

"How many?" Susanna asked.

Rebecca laughed. "Too many! It was before you were born!"

Susanna frowned. "I still can't believe you're an angel. You seem....so human."

"I was human, Susanna before I became an angel. I was a young woman just like you are now."

"What happened to you?"

Rebecca's lowered her head and Susanna felt bad. "Did I upset you? I'm sorry if I did. I've just been wondering why you're so young."

Rebecca had tears in her eyes when she lifted her head and looked at the girl. "I was this age when I was murdered, Susanna."

"Oh my God," Susanna whispered, shocked to her core. "I'm so sorry! Oh God, Rebecca! I'm sorry!"

The angel stood up and said, "It's alright. You didn't know."

The tears slid down her cheeks and she walked into the kitchen.

A few minutes later, Susanna followed her and made herself a sandwich. She ate quietly and Rebecca just sat in a chair with her shoulders slumped and her head down.

"Where will you sleep tonight?" Susanna asked. "I can sleep on the couch if you want the spare bedroom."

Rebecca looked at her, her face impassive. "Angels don't need sleep. I'll just sit in front of the fire until morning."

Susanna washed her dish and put it away before turning to the angel. "Rebecca?" she softly said. "If you ever need to talk, I'm here. I just want you to know that."

The angel nodded. "Thank you. I never had many friends, Susanna but I count you as one. You're very kind."

Susanna came and hugged her. "I'm so glad you came into *both* our lives, dear angel. We're very lucky."

Rebecca hugged her back and said, "*I'm* the lucky one, Susanna. I'm the lucky one."

CHAPTER TWENTY NINE

The next morning, Jason seemed a little perkier and has eyes had some life in them. He even joined the women in the kitchen for some breakfast.

"Did you sleep well, dad?" Susanna asked.

He looked at Rebecca. "Yes. I dreamed an angel was near me."

"Any particular one?"

He smiled. "I think you know."

Susanna saw the angel's face flush and smiled. "You two are so cute together," she said.

Rebecca wanted to change the subject and said, "Will you be alright if we leave you for a little while? Susanna and I are going shopping for some clothes and things."

"Of course! I'll be fine! I'll call work while you're gone."

Rebecca had cleaned the soot from her white dress during the night and Susanna put on one of her mother's dresses Jason had saved. It fit her perfectly and they left for the department store in Jason's car.

"I'll be glad to get my own clothes," Susanna said. "I feel weird wearing mom's dress."

"What was she like?" Rebecca asked.

Susanna brushed away a tear and said, "She was a good mother. I miss her so much."

They were almost at the store when Susanna turned to the angel and said, "They weren't happy. I could see that."

"How do you know that?" the angel asked.

Susanna smiled. "Because they didn't look at each other the way you and Dad do."

"And how do we look at each other?"

"There's a glint in your eyes and a warmth that's undeniable. You can't hide it," Susanna answered.

Rebecca half smiled. "I still don't understand how this happened. It wasn't supposed to be like this."

"What do you mean?"

"Usually I answer a call, give some advice and leave. This one is different."

"Have you asked yourself why?" Susanna asked, genuinely curious about what brought the angel and her father together.

Rebecca pulled the photo from her dress she'd saved from the fire and looked at it.

"Dad's photo from when he was little! You saved it!" Susanna cried.

"Yes, I had too and to answer your question this is why."

Susanna pulled into a spot and turned off the engine. "Tell me," she said. "What makes Dad different from the others?"

The angel stared intensely at the photo. "I remember when he was this age. I sensed he was different even then."

"In what way?"

The angel smiled and lightly touched the face in the photo. "Your father was and is the kindest soul I've ever met. Did he ever tell you about the time he rescued a girl from being bullied by a boy?"

"No, he didn't. He never told me about it," Susanna said, surprised.

"The other boy was much bigger than your father but he didn't care. He stepped in front of the girl like a knight in shining armor."

"What happened then?"

"The boy stopped harassing her and began to laugh. Jason stared him down and he eventually walked away. Your father could have been badly beaten that day but he didn't care about himself. All he could think of was helping that girl."

"What happened next?" Susanna asked, impatiently.

"Like the boy who'd been bothering her, she was much bigger than Jason. She looked down at him in surprise at what he'd done."

"Was she mad?"

Rebecca smiled as she remembered what happened next. "No, she wasn't mad. She leaned down and held him by the shoulders and kissed his cheek."

"I'll bet daddy blushed when she did that!"

"Yes….he did. It was so sweet. I think it was the first time a girl had ever kissed him. His face turned red and he tried to rub her kiss away. She laughed and then her face turned serious."

"Did she kiss him again?" Susanna asked.

"No. She knelt in front of him and told him he was special and that someday a lucky woman would fall in love with him because he'd be her hero."

"Oh….that's so sweet!" Susanna cried happily.

"Yes, it really was. I watched as she walked away and your father stood there and rubbed his cheek again. He suddenly looked so alone and sad then and I wanted to hug him to me but didn't."

"Why didn't you?"

Rebecca stared at the young woman and quietly said, "Because what he'd done had affected me greatly in a way no one else ever had. I wished that I was that girl. I wanted to be the one he'd saved. You see, Susanna, your father became my hero that day too."

"Oh Rebecca, that's so beautiful. You're going to make me cry."

The angel said, "That's why I had to help him. I had to bring out that special little boy in him again. Your father was meant to be a hero, Susanna."

"I don't know what to say. Have you talked to him about what happened that day?"

"No. He has no idea I saw that and so many other things that showed me how special he is," Rebecca answered. "I'm just here to give him little nudges in the right direction so he'll find his purpose again."

"Which you've already done," Susanna said and reached for the angel's hand. "So tell me honestly why you're still here then."

Rebecca gently squeezed the woman's hand and said, "Because I love that little boy. I've always loved him for the person he is."

"Then *tell* him, Rebecca. Why won't you tell him?"

The angel looked into Susanna's eyes. "Because I'm dead and he's alive. There's no getting past that and nothing I do will change it."

They sat in silence for a while and looked out at the half empty parking lot. "You know what your problem is?" Susanna suddenly said, "You think too much. Just go with the flow, Rebecca. Just go with the flow and see what happens next."

Rebecca didn't respond but absorbed the girl's wise words. "I don't know how," she finally said.

"I'll help you. Will you let me?"

"Yes," the angel replied.

They got out of the car then and entered the mall entrance. Susanna scanned the directory until she found what she was looking for. "This is the place," she said happily and Rebecca followed her as she headed towards her destination.

The small women's store wasn't busy and the saleswoman left them alone to shop. Rebecca sat on a stool as Susanna walked around and picked out jeans, shirts and dresses for herself. After grabbing a few bras and panties, she put them on the counter and asked the woman to save them for her. She looked back at Rebecca then and slowly approached her.

"And now you," she said softly.

"Me? What do you mean?"

"We're going to get you something new to wear for Christmas. It's only two weeks away and as much as I love what you're wearing you should have a little variety."

The angel was surprised and smiled as Susanna took her hand and pulled her away to shop for a new dress. After a while she found what she was looking for and handed it to Rebecca. "Here. Try this on. I think it should fit you."

Rebecca took the light blue dress and went into the fitting room. Susanna closed the door and stood on the other side and waited as the angel looked in the full length mirror and slowly pulled her white dress off. Standing naked, she gazed at her body and trembled as she reached for the new dress. She stared at it and said, "Could you help zip me up?"

"Of course," Susanna said and gasped when she opened the door. Rebecca turned and faced the girl. She held her arms across her breasts and waited for the stunned look to leave the woman's face.

"Why aren't you dressed?" Susanna asked after a long uncomfortable moment.

"I'm sorry I startled you, Susanna but I need to know something before I put it on and I'm trusting you to give me an honest answer."

"What do you want to know?" Susanna asked, swallowing hard.

Rebecca lowered her arms and stood totally exposed. "Do you think I'm beautiful?"

Susanna swallowed hard again as she gazed at the feminine perfection of the angel's body. "Why are you asking me that? Don't you know? Surely a man has told you already that you are."

"No. No man ever has," Rebecca whispered.

Susanna stared at her, uncomprehending. "Are you kidding me? You're drop dead gorgeous, Rebecca. How can you not see that?"

The angel shivered and said, "I don't know what a man would think, Susanna because I've never been naked in front of one before."

Susanna was shocked at her answer and stared at her. "Why don't you try this on and we'll talk about it later, alright?"

The angel nodded and Susanna helped her slip the dress on and zipped her up. Rebecca shyly turned all the way around until she was facing the girl again. "How do I look?"

Susanna smiled. "You want me to be honest?"

"Yes," Rebecca said, worried.

Susanna touched the angel's shoulder and said, "You look absolutely beautiful, Rebecca. Any man looking at you right now would need a bucket under his chin to catch the drool."

Susanna's words made Rebecca relax a bit and she burst out laughing. She spun around and lifted the bottom of the dress up in her excitement. Susanna blushed and said, "Oh no, that won't do. I know you're an angel but you can't walk around like that in this dress. You need to wear panties."

"Why?"

Susanna was surprised by the question and stammered, "Because….because you just do, that's all. Besides, a man likes to slowly undress a woman and there's nothing like the feeling of panties sliding down your hips as he removes them."

"Is that what Matt did to you?" Rebecca asked and immediately regretted her words when she saw the look on Susanna's face.

"No, he didn't. I wish he would've but he didn't take his time. He preferred to rip my clothes off instead and get right down to it."

"I'm sorry. I shouldn't have asked," Rebecca said.

"It's alright. Looking back, I don't know why I put up with his abuse for so long. I think I was so awed by his strength that I couldn't see his faults. He didn't know how to treat a lady."

"Do you think Jason does?" Rebecca asked, hopeful.

Susanna smiled. "There's only one way to find out, dear angel."

Rebecca blushed and looked in the mirror. "I don't know if I can do this."

Susanna lightly touched her arm. "Find the right moment and breathe deeply before taking off this dress. If my father is the kind of man you think he is then he'll know how to treat you."

Rebecca hugged her then and Susanna unzipped her so she could get out of the dress. She left the room then so the angel could get back into her white dress. Rebecca rejoined her as she was picking out some panties and a bra. She frowned and tried to take the bra off the counter but Susanna grabbed her hand to stop her.

"Sorry, Rebecca. We're getting this also because a man likes to remove this too. Undressing you is half the fun."

The saleswoman blushed and rang up their orders. They left the store, bags in hand and Susanna saw another shop she wanted to stop at.

"Wait right here," she said to the angel and went inside. A few minutes later, she came back out and Rebecca saw her face was flushed.

"What did you buy in there?" she asked.

"Oh, something personal," Susanna said and whistled as they walked back to the car.

"You must have bought something special," Rebecca said. "You seem very happy."

"Oh, I am. Believe me, I am."

"Thank you, Susanna," the angel said. "Thank you for being my friend."

Susanna was silent for a moment and turned to look at her. "Back there you said a man's never seen you naked. Why not?"

Rebecca sat silent and Susanna quietly said, "I'm sorry. I know I have no right to ask but I just don't understand. You're so beautiful, Rebecca. In fact, you're the most beautiful woman I've ever seen. Were all the men blind where you lived?"

Rebecca felt the hot tears roll down her cheeks and Susanna held her hand. "Oh God, I'm sorry. I didn't mean to make you cry. Forget I ever asked, alright?"

The angel looked at her, her face a mask of fury. "I went to an all girl's school if you must know! The few nice boys that were in town were already taken and the rest just wanted to cop a feel and get in my pants. I never met one like the one I…."

"Like the one what, Rebecca?" Susanna asked softly.

Rebecca wiped away her tears and whispered, "I used to lie awake at night and imagine I was a princess and a handsome man would find me and kiss me and hold me tight to keep me safe. Then one night a man came and made sure that would never happen, Susanna. He took my life away and I died a virgin. There. Now you know the whole sad story. Satisfied?"

Susanna sat with her mouth hanging open and felt her own eyes burn with tears. She lightly squeezed the angel's hand.

"I'm terribly sorry, Rebecca. Please, please forgive me."

"I just wanted someone to love me!" Rebecca cried and Susanna pulled her to her and hugged her close.

"And someone does," Susanna whispered.

CHAPTER THIRTY

Jason was asleep when they got back home and Rebecca sat by the bed and watched him while Susanna hung their purchases in the closet. When she was finished, she peeked back in and decided to leave them alone. She closed the door and went to sit in the living room.

Rebecca knelt by Jason's side and took his hand in hers. His eyes opened and slowly focused on her face. "Rebecca...." he whispered.

She took his hand and placed it against her chest. "I told you that I'd let you touch me. Would you like to now, Jason?"

His eyes brightened and he smiled. "You're really going to let me touch you?"

"Yes, but just a little," she replied. She stood up and slowly lifted her dress past her hips. "Touch me," she whispered. "I need to cum so badly."

She felt lightheaded when he lightly touched her thigh with his fingers. Impatient, she took his hand and moved it to her sex. Heat poured from it and Jason felt the moisture as she pressed him against her. He moved his fingers over her pubic hair and she stepped closer to the bed. "You know what to do," she whispered. "Find my clit....just my clit...."

Jason looked up at her face and her eyes were shut tight. Rebecca lifted the dress higher and Jason could see the gentle slope of her smooth belly. He moved his finger between the steaming lips of her pussy and found she was soaking wet. He traced his way up and found her clit. It throbbed beneath his finger and she moaned loudly. "Oh God....I'm so horny!" she groaned.

She thrust her hips towards him and her legs spread wider. Jason smiled and began masturbating her, his fingertip caressing the bulging nub. "Oh God!" she whispered. "Yes! Just like that! Just like that!"

Jason's finger felt like a feather and the wave rushed towards her as her pussy became even slicker. "Oh fuck! Jason!" she cried and the liquid gushed from her and ran down his wrist. He sat up in bed so he could get a better angle and she moaned as his finger pushed between her slick lips. He felt the obstruction and smiled. Rebecca opened her glazed eyes and quietly said, "You're the first man I ever let touch me like this."

"I'm honored," he whispered and she squealed in pleasure when he moved his finger back to her clit and ran circles around it.

Biting her lower lip, she braced for one last wave and it hit her like a thunderbolt. "Aaaaarrgghh!" she grunted in a low voice and clamped her thighs around his hand to keep it there. Her legs trembled as the orgasm made her swoon.

Jason watched and waited until she began to relax. Her eyes gazed into his and they were filled with love. "Thank you," she whispered as she opened her legs to release him. "That was fantastic."

He sniffed his fingers and smiled. "I love the smell of your pussy," he whispered and then his face turned serious. "I can hardly wait until you let me touch you again. But next time I want to experience *all* of you, Rebecca."

She felt all tingly inside and remembered what Susanna had said. "Soon," she whispered. "Very soon."

He lay back down and fell back to sleep and she felt a shiver run down her spine. *Oh God!* she thought. *I can hardly wait to give myself to him!*

Susanna was smiling when the angel came and sat beside her. Rebecca looked at her and was clearly shaken.

"I suppose you heard everything."

Susanna smiled and held the angel's hand. "Yes, I did."

"I can't stand it much longer, Susanna. I have to have him. I just don't know when the right time is."

Susanna gripped the angel's hand tighter. "You'll know when that time is. Just let your heart speak to you."

Rebecca thought of something then and smiled. "I think I know exactly when the right time will be."

CHAPTER THIRTY ONE

Over the next few days, Susanna and Rebecca waited patiently for Jason to recover. He grew stronger each day until finally he was able to go for short walks. On one of their walks they stopped and sat on a bench in a nearby park. Jason closed his eyes and smelled the crisp cool air. It was so peaceful here with the two women he cared so deeply for sitting on both sides of him.

"Dad," Susanna said softly. "I need to tell you something. I know I haven't done much with my life up to this point but I think I know now what I want to do."

He opened his eyes and looked at her in surprise. "Susanna, why are you saying that? I never said you were a disappointment."

She lowered her head and whispered, "Maybe not to you but to myself I am."

Rebecca quietly asked, "Why, Susanna?"

Jason's daughter lifted her head. "Because I got an art degree in college, Rebecca. I bet you didn't know this about me but I'm a damn good artist. Instead, I wasted my time and thought I was in love with a man who abused me. I went to work in a hardware store. That's not what I was meant to do."

"So you're going back to art?" Jason asked, hopeful.

His daughter smiled. "Yes but I also want to help people like you do, dad."

"What do you mean, sweetheart? I only saved two lives so far but that was with Rebecca's help."

She laughed. "No, no! I don't mean like that! I mean I'd like to do what you do at work, dad!"

"But I'm just a supervisor, Susanna. I don't help people. I tell them what to do."

Rebecca put her arm around his and smiled. "I think I know what Susanna means, Jason. Don't you realize you do much more than just supervise?"

"I don't understand," he said, confused.

"You also inspire, Jason and lead by example. Do you sit on your ass like some of the other supervisors in the building?"

"No….but…."

"But nothing, Jason," she said, her face serious. "You inspire the people who work for you and don't talk down to them. They respect you because you treat them decently and encourage them to be the best they can be. Of course, a few of them take advantage of your kind nature but they're the exception. Overall, you do much more then supervise, Jason. You make them feel good about themselves and that's important."

"Rebecca, you just explained it perfectly," Susanna said, her eyes filled with excitement. "I want to be like dad!"

"How are you going to be like me, Susanna?" he asked, blushing from the compliment she'd given him.

"I don't know yet," she said. "I have to find my purpose."

Jason shot a glance at Rebecca and she slowly smiled. "She's learning, Jason," she whispered. "Just like you have."

Just then, Susanna's phone rang and she picked it up and said hello. She listened for a bit and a slight smile crossed her face. "Yes, Jeff," she finally said. "We'll be there."

Jason watched as she put her phone away then and Rebecca asked, "That was Jeff? Is he alright?"

Susanna's face had a glow to it. "Yes, he's fine. I just found my purpose, dear angel and I want you to join me."

CHAPTER THIRTY TWO

Susanna talked fast and repeated Jeff's plan. Rebecca waited until she was finished and said, "No, I'm not going."

"But we need you, Rebecca! We can't do this without you!"

The angel's face was stern. "I said *no*. You *can* do it without me. I'm not going back to that hellhole you called home and you shouldn't either."

Jason looked at her and quietly said, "But aren't they God's children too, Rebecca? Won't you help them see the light?"

"But they're evil," she said, her voice tight. "They killed Jerry and hurt those dogs. Besides, they won't listen to anyone. All they know is hate."

"They're not *all* bad," Susanna said. "They're just lost and need guidance. Please help us show them *their* purpose."

The angel sighed and stared intensely at Jason's daughter. "You're a better person as a mortal than I am as an angel, Susanna. I feel ashamed. You're right. I'll help you."

"Yes!" Susanna shouted and raised her arms in victory. "We leave tomorrow morning. The meeting's at four right when the men get off work."

"I'm doing this just this one time, Susanna. Don't ask me again. Do you understand?" Rebecca asked.

"Yes," Susanna replied. "Thank you."

Jason's eyes gleamed and he smiled. "Tomorrow we change the world," he said.

"One day at a time," Susanna whispered.

Rebecca loved their enthusiasm and whispered, "Yes....one day at a time."

CHAPTER THIRTY THREE

The next morning they drove back to the town in silence. Jeff was waiting for them at the edge of town in his big truck and together they pulled into a parking lot. Susanna got out first and went to him.

"Hi Jeff," she said shyly as he got out of the truck. He seemed even bigger than the last time she'd seen him and Susanna realized she felt no fear despite his imposing height and size. There was something safe about the man and she was surprised at her reaction when he smiled warmly.

"Hi Susanna. I'm so glad you came."

He wasn't handsome in a conventional way but his kindness shone through and she began to see him in a new light. *Yes, there may be a future with this man,* she thought.

Rebecca and Jason got out of the car and Jeff's eyes became brighter. "I'm so glad you came!" he said.

"What did you tell the men?" Rebecca asked.

"I told them that someone very special was going to speak to them," he said, wary of the angel's response.

Rebecca slowly backed away. "Oh no! Susanna never said I had to speak!"

Jeff walked slowly towards her and she stopped backing up. "Please, Rebecca," he said and held his arms out to her. "You're just what this town needs. The men here….most of them are rough as you know but they're basically good. I just thought you could help them like you helped Jerry."

"How?" she said, smirking. "By beating the shit out of them again?"

"No," he said, disappointed. "You *know* what I mean. Just be yourself. These men aren't very religious and basically live for today.

They need to see that there's something to strive for beyond this life."

"If they already don't believe in God, Jeff then what difference does it make what I say?" she asked. "I'm just a woman."

"No, you're not just a woman, Rebecca," he said softly and took her hands and held them. "You're an angel."

CHAPTER THIRTY FOUR

They went back to Jeff's diner and he put the CLOSED FOR TODAY sign up in the window so they could be alone and talk. They sat down at the biggest round table and Jeff looked intensely at Rebecca.

"After you left, there was an uncertainty about everything that wasn't there before, Rebecca," he said. "The men started talking about how an angel came down from heaven and sought revenge for the bad things some of them had done. They're afraid."

"But that's not what should have happened!" she said, clearly agitated. "I wanted to teach them a lesson so they'd mend their ways!"

"I'm sorry," he said. "But we mortals are stupid, dear angel. What you did didn't teach any of them a lesson at all. Instead, they're scared and angry. They think God hates them and sent you to make them pay."

"What?!" That's ridiculous!" she cried and pounded her fist on the table. It cracked in two and she felt badly. "I'm sorry, Jeff. I didn't mean to do that," she softly said.

He laughed. "Don't worry about the table! I'm insured!"

"How do I fix this? I can't have them thinking God hates them."

His eyes were alight with passion. "Remember that idea I had?"

"That again?" she said, smirking. "Yes, I remember."

"I was serious about it. I believe you were sent here for a reason, Rebecca and this is it. You know what you have to do. It's time we mortals were shone the light. Recruit us. Become our leader."

She blushed and felt tears in her eyes. "Oh Jeff, I'm sorry to disappoint you but I wasn't sent here to lead anyone. I heard Jason calling and came to help *him*. That's it and nothing more. You're wrong about me."

He lowered his head in disappointment and Susanna reached out and touched the angel's hand. "What if he's not, Rebecca? What if *this* is your true purpose? What if you were sent here to save *us*?"

Rebecca stood up and stared in disbelief at them. "This is ridiculous. I'm nothing but an angel. You already have priests and a pope and countless religious people who have millions of followers. You don't need me."

Jeff stood up and placed his large hands on her shoulders. "You're wrong. What you're forgetting is they're all men. Just men, Rebecca. You however are an angel from heaven. *You* can be God's messenger."

She swallowed hard and stared into his eyes. "But what would I say to them?" she whispered. "I don't know what to say."

His eyes were kind and his smile comforted her. "Say what you believe, Rebecca. Tell them about heaven. Tell them what happens when they do good things. Tell them they're *loved*."

She reached up and touched his face with her hand. "Jeff," she said. "I'll do this just this once but after that *you* my friend will be the one to spread God's word."

He was surprised. "Me?"

"Yes," she said and smiled. "You have it in you to speak the truth. You will be God's messenger after today."

Susanna moved close to him and slipped her arm around his. He looked down at her and she smiled up at him. "And I'll be here to help you," she said.

"You will?" he whispered and she felt him shiver.

She moved closer and wrapped her arms around him. "Yes, Jeff," she said softly. "I'm staying here with you if you'll have me."

His eyes got huge and he looked at Rebecca. "Before you came I was just a cook. This is what I meant. You change lives, angel from God."

She saw the sweet look of adoration Susanna suddenly gave him and smiled. "So will you, Jeff. So will you."

CHAPTER THIRTY FIVE

As the big event slowly approached, Jeff filled everyone in on what had transpired the last few days. The men who'd participated in the dogfighting were out on bond and their trials were set for later in the year. Some of the men had to undergo orthopedic surgery for their broken bones which made Rebecca smile.

"I can't say I'm sorry about hurting them," she said. "Those poor dogs...."

Jeff continued and told them that the man who'd dealt the blow which eventually killed Jerry was in jail awaiting a future trial date. The other men who'd help beat him and Jeff had gotten off scot free.

"What?! You're fucking kidding me!" Rebecca yelled angrily.

Jeff winced at her use of words and she said, "Sorry....I know I don't talk like an angel should talk."

"They each had alibis for each other," Jeff said, his face red. "It didn't matter what I told the police. They ignored my account of what happened."

"But why?" Susanna asked.

The big man shook his head sadly. "The problem with folks around here is they're all related in some way or another. The sheriff is a cousin of one of the ones who jumped Jerry and me and the judge himself is best friends with some of the dogfighting boys. They'll probably end up getting off with no time."

Rebecca stared at him and he could tell she was fuming. "That's just wrong," she said quietly.

"I'm sorry, Rebecca, but that's the way things are around here. Good luck trying to get justice."

Susanna's face contorted then and she felt sudden fear. "What about Matt, Jeff? Have you heard anything about him?"

Jeff swallowed hard and lightly touched her face. "He was in the hospital for a few days, Susanna. Rebecca really did a number on him."

"And then he went to jail, right?" she asked and held her breath.

He lowered his eyes and softly said, "No. He was released."

"What?!" Rebecca screamed, her face a mask of rage. "Why?!"

Jeff looked at her and hoped she wouldn't destroy more of his tables. "Because the judge is *his* cousin, Rebecca. I told you everyone around here is either related in some way or good friends."

"But he raped Susanna!"

He winced and quietly said, "I know. Believe me, I know but he's free until his trial date."

Susanna's face turned ashen. "Does that mean I'll see him again? He's free to hurt me?"

He put his arm around her and said, "He'd have to go through me, Susanna. Besides, Rebecca gave him such a beating that from what I've heard he can barely move."

"Good!" the angel growled and Jason laughed.

Jeff headed back to the kitchen then to cook up some food for everyone and Rebecca saw how nervous Susanna was.

"I promise that asshole will never touch you again, Susanna," she whispered. "If he even looks your way, I swear I'll rip that cock of his right off."

Susanna smiled then and said, "I actually hope he tries. I'd love to see you do that."

The smells coming from the kitchen were making them hungry and they joined Jeff in the kitchen. From the looks of what he was doing, it was obvious the man wasn't just a cook. He was a real chef. "This looks fantastic, Jeff! What is it?" Jason asked as he saw the sauce the man was stirring. Three beautiful looking steaks were waiting to be cooked along with some mushrooms.

Jeff smiled. "I'm making us steak au poivre. It's a French dish."

"Seriously?!" Rebecca said excitedly. "I don't usually eat but that's something I'd like to try!"

Susanna came close to the stove and closed her eyes as she breathed in the wonderful scent. "Oh wow…that's exceptional, Jeff."

He smiled again and said, "I've always liked this dish. I love cream sauces."

"Are those peppercorns in it?" Jason asked.

"Yes," Jeff said proudly. "I *love* peppercorns."

Susanna leaned in close and gently touched his arm. "You surprise me, Jeff. Why are *you* here?"

"What do you mean?" he asked.

"I *mean*….why is a chef with your abilities working in a small diner like this?"

His face turned red and he looked away and went back to stirring. "I can't talk about it," he mumbled.

Susanna glanced at Rebecca and frowned. The angel's eyes narrowed and she gently touched Jeff's arm and closed her eyes. A moment later they shot open and she stared at him intensely.

"What's wrong?" Susanna asked but the angel shook her head and put her finger to her lips to silence her.

"Later," she whispered.

When the food was done and added to their plates, they all sat down and opened a bottle of Chardonnay that Jeff pulled out of a hidden compartment under the sink.

"To the army of God," he said proudly while holding up his glass of wine.

"May it grow large," Rebecca added and they all clinked their glasses together.

Jason turned to Rebecca then and lifted his glass. "To you, Rebecca for bringing light into our lives."

CHAPTER THIRTY SIX

To her surprise, Rebecca burped halfway through the meal as she sipped her wine. Her face flushed bright red and everyone laughed.

"I can honestly say that was the best thing I've eaten in the last twenty years," she said and everyone smiled. Moments later however, her mood visibly changed and she excused herself from the table. "I'm sorry. I need some air," she said.

They watched her step outside and stand by the side of the diner with her head down. Susanna looked at the men and said, "Stay here. I'll go talk to her."

Rebecca didn't lift her head when Susanna joined her. "Do you want to talk about it?" she asked the angel.

"No," Rebecca said so quietly that Susanna almost didn't hear her.

They stood for a while not talking and Susanna softly said, "Rebecca, when did you die?"

The angel lifted her head then and the tears rolled down her cheeks. She didn't say a word and Susanna felt her heart breaking for the angel. "Please talk to me, Rebecca," she said. "I'm your friend."

The angel looked away again and stared out at nothing. "I've been dead for sixty years, Susanna. That's when I finally became an angel."

"Finally?" Susanna said, curious.

The angel looked at her again. "Yes, I've had many lives but the last one when I was….murdered….that's when I became an angel. I suppose I'd paid enough for my sins by that time and God took pity on me."

"Is that how it works? You have to suffer for a while before you can become an angel?"

Rebecca chuckled. "I have no idea. I just know that when I woke up in heaven it wasn't a floating peace like all the other times I'd died. Instead, I felt alive again and realized I'd changed. I felt the wings on my back and knew I'd become an angel."

"That's amazing, Rebecca! So why are you crying? You should be happy you're an angel."

Rebecca stared deeply into Jason's daughter's eyes and her lower lip quivered, "Because I'm afraid, Susanna. Since coming here, I've done things an angel shouldn't do. I've become way too involved with your father and I've hurt people. I'm scared what God will do to me."

"Doesn't God love you, Rebecca? Why would he be angry? You're a good angel, an angel who cares passionately about people."

"That may be, Susanna but what happens if God doesn't see it that way?" she said. "I just feel like I've crossed too many lines and I'm afraid what will happen."

"Ok, I understand but why did eating Jeff's food make you cry?"

The angel trembled and felt strangely cold then. "I guess it made me realize how much I miss being alive."

"But you are alive," Susanna said. "You're standing here with me right now, aren't you?"

Rebecca shook her head no. "You don't understand. Being an angel isn't the same as being alive. It feels like I'm always in a fog of some kind that I can't escape. The only time the feeling goes away is when...."

"Is when what, Rebecca?" Susanna quietly asked.

The angel shivered. "That's what's scary, Susanna. The only time the feeling goes away is when I'm close to your father. The fog seems to lift and I feel like I did when I was alive. I don't know why and can't explain it."

"Then don't try to," Susanna said and gently took the angels hands in hers. "Let it happen. It was obviously meant to be. Isn't that what's really happening here?"

Rebecca's eyes twinkled then and she whispered, "Susanna, I fear I won't be able to stop myself from giving in to my urges regarding your father. I've just about reached my breaking point. I can't hold back much longer."

"What are you trying to say, Rebecca?"

"I'm finally going to tell your father that I love him."

After their talk, the women came back in and rejoined Jason and Jeff.

"Is everything alright?" Jason asked.

There was a new light in the angel's eyes that hadn't been there for days. "Yes, everything's fine," she answered and reached for his hand.

He took it in his and squeezed it lightly. "You're going to do great, you know," he said.

"I wish I felt that way," she said. "Strangely, I feel nervous about this. I've forgotten what it feels like to stand in front of people with all their eyes watching only you."

"You'll do fine and we'll be there with you," Susanna said.

They rested for a while after that until the late afternoon when Jeff stood up and yawned. "It's time," he said.

"Let's do this," Rebecca said.

CHAPTER THIRTY SEVEN

They didn't speak as they drove. Jeff parked in the far back lot and they got out and stretched their arms. "This way," he motioned. "We're going to the highest point. It's a hill that overlooks the yard."

It was a steep climb and Jeff led the way. When he got to the top, the men in the yard saw him and surged forward in one big mass.

"Hey, Jeff! What's going on? Why did you tell us to meet you here?" one of them yelled.

He raised his arms and looked down at them. For a moment, an image of Jesus doing the same entered his mind but he shook it away.

"Men!" he cried. "I'm here to tell you we've gone astray!"

"What the hell you talkin' about, Jeff?!" a big man yelled.

His voice became softer but still loud enough for them to hear.

"I mean we've gone *astray*," he repeated.

They looked around at each other, confused and started to grumble amongst themselves.

"I've brought someone who wants to speak to you. Some of you know her already. Please listen to what she has to say. That's all I ask."

He turned then and motioned for Rebecca to join him. When she appeared by his side, the men began to boo and yell, "Bitch!" and "Devil!"

Rebecca gently pushed Jeff away when they began to throw things.

"Get behind me," she said and then turned to face the men again. A rock hit her forehead and some of the men laughed. She touched the wound it made and stared at the blood on her fingers. The cut healed in seconds and some other men stared in disbelief. More rocks were thrown and she was struck in the side, legs and arms. She raised her hands and quietly said, "Stop….please stop."

The rocks stopped flying. One man, however picked a rock up and was about to throw it when someone grabbed his wrist from behind.

"Let her speak," they said. "Let's hear what she has to say."

The men became silent and Rebecca stared out at the vast expanse of the lumberyard. There had to be over one hundred men gathered in its center and they were all staring up at her. She felt strangely uncomfortable and closed her eyes. *Please lord, guide me*, she thought. *Help me show them the way.*

She opened her eyes again and smiled down upon them. "I'm here today to tell you about God," she said.

"Why?!" a man yelled angrily. "He hates us! He sent you here to punish us!"

She stared at the man and said, "Punish you? Is that what you think God does? You're wrong. It was *my* decision to punish you."

"Why?!" he cried and pumped his fist at her. "Go back where you came from and leave us alone!"

A haze of rage entered her eyes but she pushed it back. "How many of you knew Jerry, the man who died?"

A few men slowly raised their hands and she said, "Jerry was a good man and he died for what?"

"He turned against us!" a brave man yelled. "He deserved it!"

Rebecca's eyes narrowed and she sneered at him. "No! He didn't deserve it!"

A rock was thrown and she caught it in midair right before it could strike her head. The men's mouths gaped open as she crushed it to dust in her hand. "Don't do that again…" she warned.

A few men laughed and she lowered her head and slowly shook it back and forth.

"Why are you here?!" a man shouted. "What do you want from us?!"

She raised her head and looked at the group. "What do I want from you?" she asked. "I want you to be the men God wants you to be. The men you were *born* to be."

They looked at each other in confusion and Rebecca's eyes brimmed with tears. "Murder....rape....dogfighting....so much cruelty. It has to stop. Don't you see? It *has* to stop."

The men became quiet and she began to sob. Jeff moved towards her and put his arm around her shoulders. She smiled at him and gently pushed him away again. "I need to do this alone," she whispered. He nodded and moved back to stand with Jason and Susanna who watched from behind.

"It doesn't matter," she said and her voice became louder. "It doesn't matter if you go to church or your synagogue or wherever you pray! It only matters what you do in life! You must change for the sake of your souls! You must change for him!"

A rock flew at her but this time she didn't catch it. It struck her cheek and split it open. She looked sadly out at the crowd and said, "You're hopeless. I came here to tell you what you must do but you won't listen. I hope you're happy. Go back to your miserable lives. I'm through with you."

She turned her back on them and walked over to Jeff. "I give up. They won't listen," she said. Her cheek sealed up and he nodded.

Just then, a voice from the crowd yelled, "No! Don't give up on us! Tell us what to do!"

Surprised, she turned back around and went back to the spot she'd spoken from. "Who said that?" she asked.

"I did!" a tall skinny man answered.

"What's your name?" she asked, pointing at him.

"Robert Klein," he replied.

A smile crossed her face. "Robert, do you believe in God? Do you believe in the power of *him*?"

"Yes," he said and fell to his knees and lifted his hands in prayer.

Rebecca's eyes narrowed as she focused on him. "Then join the army of God. Do what you were born to do and your path to heaven will be straight and true."

"What about me?" another man asked as he fell to his knees.

"What should I do? What should we *all* do?"

The angel smiled and felt a wave of kindness overwhelm her. Tears flowed down her cheeks as she felt God's presence all around them.

"It's very simple," she answered softly. "You've been told what to do countless times before but I'll say it again. Go out and spread God's love. Be kind to your neighbor and to each other. Treat life….*all* life with respect. Fight against your inner urges to do bad things and you will be rewarded by God."

"It sounds so simple! I don't understand how it'll change things!" a man shouted.

"If you really believe and do as I say then you'll see change like you've never seen before. It will spread like wildfire and sweep the planet. Imagine a world where kindness and love reign supreme free of hate and anger."

"But what about those who don't believe and do bad things?!" another man cried.

"Feel sorry for them," she answered. "They will be lost and pay for their sins. They'll answer to God in the end."

A short man laughed. "Do you love us like God does?!"

She smirked and stared at him. "Don't push it. I'm not God. I'm just an angel."

Men started to laugh in appreciation at her attempt at humor and Rebecca felt herself relax. She raised her arms high and smiled. "Who's with me?! Who wants to join the army of God?!"

"Me!" a man screamed and pushed through so he could stand at the front of the group.

"Me too!" another yelled and he joined the first man.

Men surged from all sides then and joined the first two men. Rebecca saw a few men shake their heads in disbelief. They walked away and she felt sad for them. *Poor lost souls*, she thought.

"When do we begin?" a man asked, his eyes gleaming with hope.

Rebecca gazed down at him and began to walk down the hill towards the group. They moved out of the way and formed a circle around her. She moved among them and touched each one gently on the cheek. A warmth flooded through each of them and they smiled. When she'd touched the last man, she looked up at the sky and softly said, "Dear lord, these men will spread your love. Please protect them and guide them in their path to heaven."

She looked around and her face flushed. "Who's with me?"

"I am!" a man shouted followed by three more men.

"I can't hear you! Who's with me?!" she shouted.

"I am!" more men yelled.

"And what are we?!!" she screamed passionately.

The men surged towards her and Jeff feared for her as he watched from the hill.

"The army of God!!" they yelled.

Rebecca raised her arms to the sky and some men picked her up and lifted her to their shoulders. "The army of God!!" she screamed.

They put her down and she walked back up the hill to join Jeff. He looked down at the smiling men and shouted, "What are we?!"

"The army of God!!!" they screamed in unison and pumped their fists.

"Go forth and spread God's love!" Jeff shouted. "Start right now!"

Rebecca smiled and felt the tears glide down her cheeks again as the men rushed happily out of the yard to spread kindness. The world was about to change. It would take quite a while but in the end it *would* change.

Susanna came and stood by Jeff and he put his arm around her. Rebecca felt Jason's presence then as he took his place by her side. She turned to him and gazed into his eyes. The time was right and she was overcome with emotion.

"Jason…." she whispered.

"What, Rebecca? Is something wrong?" he asked, concerned.

Her eyes were bright and happy. "Come closer," she said softly.

He lowered his head and she put her lips to his ear. "I love you," she whispered.

He stared at her in shock but then slowly smiled.

"Do you mean it?"

She gently touched his cheek.

"With every bit of my heart," she softly said.

CHAPTER THIRTY EIGHT

They held hands as they walked back down the hill to the car, their eyes never leaving one another. Susanna couldn't hear what Rebecca had said to her father but whatever it was had obviously made him very happy. He was smiling like an idiot in love. *Yes*, she thought. *I bet she finally told him she loved him.*

Before they got into the car, she turned to Jeff and said, "I'm very proud of you. Rebecca's right. You're a natural leader."

"Thank you," he said. "I guess I've been silent for way too long."

They drove back to the diner and sat down for another wonderful meal which Jeff cooked up. When it was time for them to leave, his mood turned sad. "I guess I won't be seeing you for a while," he said to Susanna.

She smiled and turned to her father and Rebecca. "I'll be home later this week. Will you come get me on Saturday, dad?"

Jason looked at Jeff and back at her. "Of course. Whatever you want."

Rebecca moved to the big man and said, "You did good today, Jeff. The men are yours to lead now."

He smiled down at her and beamed with pride. "Thank you, Rebecca. I couldn't have done it without you showing the way."

The angel glanced at Susanna and back at him. "Tell her, Jeff. Don't hide your secret. Now's the time to be honest."

He blushed then and looked at her with fear in his eyes. "How do you know?" he gasped.

She smiled. "I know everything about you, Jeff. You have a kind heart and you don't shield your soul."

He nodded and she and Jason walked out to their car. Jeff turned to Susanna and quietly said, "What are you doing? Why aren't you going with them?"

Her eyes were full of kindness as she reached up and gently touched his face.

"Take me home, Jeff," she whispered. "I want to be with you."

CHAPTER THIRTY NINE

Jeff owned a small wood frame house at the edge of town on a quiet street. The view was like something out of a Norman Rockwell painting. They pulled into the garage and he helped her out of his truck. She grunted a little in pain and he remembered she was still recovering from broken ribs. He took out his keys and looked at her before opening the door.

"Are you sure about this?"

"I've never been more sure of anything in my whole life," she answered, smiling.

His hand shook as he put his key in the door. Susanna placed her hand over his and softly said, "Jeff, it's alright. Everything's ok."

He nodded, opened the door and moved aside so she could walk in first. The living room was small but cozy with a fireplace facing the big couch. Jeff locked the door and stepped inside. He stood silently as she walked towards the fireplace. There was a small lamp sitting on an end table by the couch with a picture frame on it. She picked it up and looked at it.

"Jeff, who is this?" she asked as she gazed at the photo showing him when he was younger. He had more hair then and he looked very happy with his arms around the short woman with curly brown hair and a wide smile.

He swallowed hard and came over to her. "She was my wife. Her name was Amy."

Susanna felt a chill creep up her spine and hesitated before asking, "Where is she, Jeff?"

His face turned ashen and he slumped down on the couch. Susanna put the photo down and went to sit next to him. His eyes welled with tears and he looked at her sadly. "She's dead, Susanna. We lived in New York at the time. I owned a small restaurant."

"Oh no," she said and held her hand over her mouth.

"One night when I was at work, three men broke into our apartment. She managed to call me just before they dragged her into the bedroom."

"Oh God, no!" Susanna cried and she gripped his arm tightly.

"Rebecca told me not to hide anything from you and she was right. I'll understand if you want to leave, Susanna."

"I'm not leaving, Jeff. Just tell me the whole story," she said, her heart pounding in her chest.

He began to sob and she moved closer so she could put her arm around his shoulders.

"They took turns raping her, Susanna and when I got there she was still screaming."

He looked at her and she could tell by his eyes that he was still haunted by what had happened.

"I took my time, Susanna," he whispered. "I took my time and enjoyed it."

"What happened, Jeff? What are you saying?"

"I tore them apart with my bare hands. They tried to fight me but they stood no chance even as I was stabbed."

"You killed them?" she asked, her eyes wide.

He looked down at his clenched fists. "No, but when I'd finished with them they probably wished I had. When I knew they couldn't hurt her anymore, I held my wife in my arms as she took her last breath."

"Oh God, Jeff, I'm so sorry," she said, her eyes welling with tears.

"That's when I killed them, Susanna. I don't remember anything except a white light exploding in my head. When I was finished with them they were lying in pieces on the floor. The police said I'd gone too far and I was sent to prison for two years."

"But they killed your wife!"

"It didn't matter. The court said I could have just incapacitated them instead of killing them."

"But that's so wrong, Jeff! Your wife died in your arms! What were you supposed to do? Kiss those men and tell them you were sorry?!"

Jeff looked at her and his eyes were dead. "I thought you should know the truth, Susanna so there would be no secrets between us. I'll understand if you want to leave."

"Oh God no, Jeff! I'm not going anywhere!" she cried and hugged him closer.

His eyes had life in them again and he stood up and held his hand out to her. She got up and followed him to the bedroom. He stopped in the doorway and turned to her. "I know I'm not much to look at, Susanna," he said softly. "But I promise I'll be good to you."

She reached up and put her hand behind his neck and pulled his head down to hers. Her lips were soft and warm and she said, "You're more of a man than you think you are, Jeff. Now please make love to me."

He smiled and she slowly removed her clothes. She wanted him to savor the sight of every inch of her body. When she kicked her panties away, he gasped and she smiled. "Like what you see?" she asked.

He quickly pulled his shirt and pants off and stood in his underwear. Susanna was surprised at how muscular he was. The only thing that seemed out of shape was his stomach. She moved close to him and lightly ran her hand over it. "I'm going to get you into shape, Jeff. Let me be your exercise bike. Ride me."

"I don't have a condom," he said suddenly. "We can't do this!"

"Guess what?" she said, smiling. "I brought one!"

She ran to her purse to retrieve it and came back to him, smiling.

"I'm going to slide this over your cock if you don't mind," she whispered.

Jeff's eyes grew brighter as she squatted and pulled his underwear down to his knees. He had a very large penis but she wasn't frightened. It grew quickly when she took it in her hand. "I think I'm in for one hell of a ride," she said as she stroked him.

When he was hard enough, she opened the packet she'd bought that day when she'd gone shopping with Rebecca and took out the condom. Frowning, she said, "I hope it fits. You're really big."

Very gently, she rolled the condom over his cockhead and smoothed it down his length as far as it would reach.

Jeff picked her up and carried her to the bed. He gently laid her down and got in beside her. She was surprised she was ready and got on top of him.

"I lied," she said, grinning. "I want to ride *you.*"

Looking down into his face, she took hold of his throbbing penis and slipped it inside her. "Oh yes, Jeff. Oh my God, you're so big!" she moaned.

He let her do all the work because he didn't want to hurt her ribs. She closed her eyes and he grabbed her hips to lift her up and down. "Yes....yes...." she groaned. "Let me ride you first."

"Susanna!" he screamed when he came mightily. She lowered herself onto him until her breasts were pressed flat against his chest.

"I'm here, Jeff," she whispered. "I'll always be here."

CHAPTER FORTY

Halfway home, Rebecca turned and looked at Jason. He hadn't said a word for miles and she was worried.

"Jason, are you alright? You're so quiet."

He looked at her and smiled. "I'm fine. I'm just enjoying the quiet company of the woman I care deeply for."

"I'm not a woman, Jason. I'm an angel….*your* angel," she softly said.

"I know that," he quietly said. "I have to tell you though that to me you're both, Rebecca. You're an angel *and* a woman."

"You're so sweet," she said and reached and stroked his cheek.

"When we get home, I want to take my time and love every inch of you," he said. "Will you let me do that?"

"I look forward to it, Jason," she answered and a shiver of pleasure ran up her spine. *Oh God yes*, she thought. *I'm really looking forward to it!*

She settled back in her seat and closed her eyes as they drove on.

The sound of the tires on the highway was very relaxing and she sighed happily.

"What the hell!" Jason suddenly said.

Rebecca opened her eyes and saw he was looking in his rear-view mirror. "That guys fucking crazy!" he said.

She looked in her own mirror and saw a semi truck weaving back and forth behind them.

"What's wrong with him?!"

"He must have fallen asleep!" Jason shouted. "Oh shit! Brace yourself!"

Another car sped around the truck and ended up behind them but was then sideswiped by a van. It spun around and veered off to the right and hit the guardrail.

"Oh no," Jason gasped as he saw the truck bearing down on them. A car suddenly pulled in front of it and the truck slammed into its rear end. Their car jolted forward as they were hit from behind by the car. The semi pushed it forward into them and Jason's eyes widened in fear. "Oh my God!" he cried. "He's not stopping!"

Rebecca grabbed the steering wheel and quickly wrenched it to the left. They veered off and the car that hit them flew ahead with the semi on its tail. They spun around and slammed into the guardrail and bounced off. Rebecca heard a screech behind them and looked in the rear view mirror. Another semi was trying to brake as it bore down on them. "Jason!" she screamed and grabbed his head in her hands. Before he could react, she kissed him and he felt the power surge through his body as they were hit from behind. Rebecca pushed Jason back in his seat as they were smashed forward with intense force.

"Oh fuck!" he screamed.

"Don't worry! I've got you!" the angel yelled as she kept him pressed into the seat. The truck shoved them forward as its brakes screeched. "Fuck!" she yelled. "He's gonna crush us!"

Jason's eyes bugged out in terror and his lower lip quivered.

She flung open her door and screamed, "Unbuckle your seat belt!"

Jason did and she grabbed him by the arm and wrenched him sideways towards her. "Ready?"

He trembled in fear and she dove out of the car with him. Jason thought his head would hit the road but she pulled him close and rolled into a ball. Her wings sprung loose and wrapped around them. He felt the thud as they hit but he wasn't hurt. They rolled to a stop and she stood up to see if he was alright. Jason nodded he was ok and they both turned to see the truck push their car until sparks flew. There was a loud scrunching sound and it suddenly exploded in a huge fireball.

The cab of the truck was engulfed in flames and the driver jumped out. He was on fire and screaming. Rebecca ran to him, flapped her wings quickly and put the flames out. The driver stared at her in amazement and an explosion far down the road lit the sky. She looked at him in horror and asked, "Are you able to help us?"

"Yes," he answered as she retracted her wings.

"Quickly!" Rebecca screamed to Jason. "Let's see if we can help!"

The three of them ran towards the huge pileup.

"Oh my God!" Jason cried when he saw what the first truck had done. A dozen vehicles were in flames and he could hear people screaming as they tried to escape their burning cars. The truck driver ran to the first few cars and started pulling people out of them. Jason stood shaking and didn't seem to know where to go first.

"Quickly! Help them over there!" Rebecca yelled as she pointed to a car that was badly crumpled.

Jason ran to it and saw a young woman slumped against the wheel. He tried to open the door but to his horror realized it was slightly pushed in and wouldn't budge. She slowly raised her head and the look of fear in her eyes filled him with terror. "Shit!" he cried and felt panic surge through him. A whooshing sound caught his ear and he looked quickly to see sparks beneath the back end of the car. A fire started and Jason knew the car would soon be consumed. "Rebecca!" he screamed. "I need help!"

The angel was busy getting two injured men out of a burning van. "I can't! You know what to do, Jason!"

His eyes got wide as he saw the flame expand beneath the car. "God, please give me strength," he whispered and grabbed the edges of the car door. He grunted and pulled with all his might and to his amazement the door tore loose. Shocked at his own strength, he stared at the door in his hands for a moment before tossing it aside. He quickly reached into the car and ripped the seatbelt away from the groaning woman. She cried out in pain as he lifted her from the car and hurriedly stepped back. The car burst into flames then and the intense heat drove him back. He carried her over to a grassy area near the road and carefully laid her down.

"Thank you," she whispered and he nodded.

"Jason! Help me!" Rebecca suddenly screamed.

He looked over and saw the big semi was on its side. Beneath the cab was a crushed car. "I think the driver's still alive!" she shouted.

Jason rushed over and saw a man crumpled sideways in his seat. His head was a bloody mess and he heard a crunch as the weight of the cab slowly crushed the car.

"Oh shit!" he yelled. "We don't have much time!"

Rebecca bent low and grabbed a hold of the cab's frame. She looked at Jason and he did the same. "Together!" she said. "Lift!"

Jason felt his back muscles ripple beneath his shirt as a power he never could have imagined gave him the power he needed. Together, they lifted the cab off of the car and with a powerful thrust of their arms pushed it back. Soon it was clear of the car and crashed to the road. Rebecca reached into the car then and grabbed the lip of the crumpled roof. "Hold the door down while I push up!" she said and Jason grabbed the top of the damaged door and pushed down.

With a grunt, Rebecca pushed upwards and Jason watched in awe as the steel slowly gave way and straightened. "You're doing it!" he yelled. "You're really doing it!"

"Damn right I am," she said proudly as she brushed hair out of her eyes and reached in and pulled the man out of the car. She carried him over and laid him down feet away from the woman Jason had saved. A car suddenly exploded behind her and she heard Jason scream, "No!"

He got there first and she found him staring in horror as three figures twisted and screamed as they burned in the back seat of a small car. Jason made his mind up then and lunged at the car just as Rebecca screamed, "Jason! Don't!"

The explosion threw him backwards into her arms and a fine red mist filled the air. Jason's blood coated her face and she stood frozen in shock.

"Jason!" she cried as he slumped in her arms. She lowered him to the ground and saw a piece of metal sticking out of his neck. "Oh God!" she screamed. "No!"

She pulled it out and a gout of blood shot out. "You're not dying today," she said determinedly. "It's not your time."

She took the jagged piece of metal and quickly sliced a cut into her hand. "Come on, damn you, don't die on me," she hissed as she pressed her hand against his neck wound.

Jason's eyes fluttered open and he looked very bad. Rebecca went against her better judgement and kissed him again. The power rushed through him in a gigantic burst and his muscles tingled. He sat up then and his neck stopped bleeding. "Rebecca, what happened?" he asked, his eyes bright and alert.

"You almost died, Jason. That's what happened."

He glanced around at the chaos that surrounded them. "How many were we able to save?" he asked.

"Just a few," she answered. "We did our best."

He stood up and she followed him as he walked back to the young woman he'd rescued. She smiled when she saw him and he knelt by her side and held her hand in his. "How did you do that?" she asked weakly. "How did you get me out? Are you an angel?"

Jason wanted to laugh but decided against it. "No, I'm not," he answered.

She frowned then and a bubble of blood burst from her mouth. Jason stared at her in alarm and she gasped in pain. "I don't feel well," she whispered. "Is help coming soon?"

He could hear sirens in the distance and said, "Yes, they'll be here soon. Try to hold on."

Her eyes glazed over then and she whispered, "I was saved by an angel."

Jason was about to protest but Rebecca gently touched his shoulder. He looked at her and she whispered, "It's ok."

He knew there wasn't much time left..

"You're right," he said softly to the woman. "I am an angel."

"I knew it," she whispered, her voice getting weaker. A trickle of blood seeped out of her ear then and she asked, "Will you take me to heaven?"

Jason looked frantically at Rebecca but she nodded towards the girl again.

"Yes," he said as his eyes welled with tears.

"I think I'm ready," she whispered and her hand tightened around his. "*Yes*, I'm ready."

She closed her eyes then and Jason fell against her and sobbed. "No! No!!"

Rebecca knelt next to him and stared at the girl. "She's at peace now, Jason. You made her final moments bearable."

He looked at her sharply. "Why?! Why did she have to die?!"

The angel took his head in her hands and kissed his forehead. "We all die in the end, Jason," she whispered. "It's how we live our lives that matters."

The truck driver who'd helped them save lives suddenly appeared by her and asked, "Will he be alright?"

"I hope so," she answered.

"What are you?" the man asked.

"A friend," she said.

A look of pain came over Jason's face then and he turned ashen. Rebecca knew immediately what was wrong and said, "I've got to get you home."

CHAPTER FORTY ONE

Jason collapsed into her arms and she lifted him up.

"Thank you," she said to the truck driver.

"No. Thank *you*," he said and smiled.

"Fuck!" she said when she saw the firetrucks and ambulances in the distance. She jumped high into the air and her great wings opened. Jason's eyes opened when he felt the cool wind on his face and she flew them both towards home.

"I've got you, my love," she said. "We'll be home soon."

She jumped into the air and was amazed at her speed as she flew. Jason fell asleep on the way and soon they were back home. Rebecca carried Jason upstairs and got the keys from his pocket.

"Where are we?" he said groggily as he awoke.

"We're home," she said. "I'm going to get you clean and then put you to bed. You need rest."

He nodded and she quickly removed his clothes and helped him get into the shower. When the water was warm enough she gently wiped the blood and grime from his body until he was clean. He almost fell at one point but she grabbed him before he could. "Almost done," she said.

He managed to stand without assistance as she dried him off with a towel. His body was bruised in spots and had a pasty reddish tint to it. *What's happening to him?* she wondered.

Jason's eyes opened wide halfway to the bedroom and he grunted in pain. "I think I'm gonna be sick," he said weakly.

Rebecca got him to the bed and sat him down. She grabbed the garbage can by his bed and held it as he leaned over and violently threw up.

"My poor Jason," she said as she rubbed the back of his neck. He heaved again and again until he was done.

"I don't think there's any more," he finally said.

Rebecca went to the bathroom and came back with a cup of water for him to drink. He sipped it slowly and when he was finished he lay down and she pulled the covers over him. He started to shake violently and she lay down next to him.

"Rebecca," he whispered. "What's happening to me? Am I dying?"

She wrapped her arm around him.

"No, I don't think you're dying but I have a theory. You keep having delayed bad reactions to my kisses but I think I know how to stop this from happening. We'll talk about it in the morning when you're better."

Jason looked at her and said, "We did our best, didn't we?"

"Yes, Jason. I'm very proud of you."

He closed his eyes then and before he fell asleep he whispered, "We did our best."

CHAPTER FORTY TWO

The crash was all over the morning news and Rebecca sat glued in front of the TV as she watched. There were shots of crumpled cars and bodies covered by sheets as the reporter talked about what witnesses had seen.

"One question authorities have is who are the mystery couple witnesses say saved their lives?"

The camera moved to the truck driver who'd helped them and he said, "I swear to God it was an angel. She had wings."

Rebecca turned off the TV then when she heard rustling in the bedroom. She went inside and Jason looked sick as he lay with his eyes open.

"I feel like I've been kicked by a mule," he said weakly.

"Oh, so you know what it feels like to be kicked by a mule?" she asked, amused.

Jason tried to laugh but grimaced in pain. "No....no....it's just a figure of speech."

She sat down by the edge of the bed and said, "We're on the news."

"We are?!"

"Yes, but they don't know who we are."

"What wrong then?" Jason asked, seeing the worry on her face.

"I don't know, Jason. I really don't know. Usually I keep a very low profile but during my stay with you I've thrown caution to the wind. Now many people have seen me. They know there's an angel among them."

"And that's a bad thing?" he asked as he sat up in bed.

"I don't know," she said quietly. "I hope God's not mad with me."

Jason coughed then and his face turned ashen. Rebecca leaned over him and said, "I think I know how to stop you from getting sick from my kisses."

"How?" he asked weakly.

Her eyes brightened. "You know how they expose people very slowly to bad things to build up their resistance?"

"What are you saying?" Jason asked.

"Well, you keep having bad reactions to my kisses. I don't really know why but my guess is that because I'm an angel they're too pure for a living person to tolerate."

"So?" Jason said, not understanding.

The angel smiled brightly. "So we build up your tolerance until you don't get sick from them!"

Jason slowly smiled. "Seriously?"

"Yes," she said and her eyes suddenly looked different. There was an animal lust in them now.

"When do we start?" Jason asked, swallowing hard.

"Right now," Rebecca whispered. She leaned forward and lightly kissed his lips. Jason felt the rush of energy and she pulled away and looked into his eyes. "Well? How was that?"

He shook his head sadly but cracked a slight smile. "Again," he said.

She smiled and he laid back down. She got on top of him and stared down into his face. "Now just relax, Jason," she said. "I'm going to be your doctor these next few days and take good care of you."

"What's my treatment?" he asked as he reached for her.

She lay down on him and rested her head on his chest. "Lots and lots of kisses," she whispered. "Do you think you're ready for them?"

"Absolutely," he answered and his eyes stared intensely into hers.

"What's wrong?" she asked.

"You have the most beautiful eyes, Rebecca," he said softly. "I could get lost in them forever."

"Oh Jason," she sighed happily and smiled as he bent his head down until their lips met. His tongue pushed between her lips and her eyes got dreamy. Her tongue met his and gently tickled its tip.

"Uuhhmm," she moaned.

Jason wrapped his arms around her and held her tightly against him as their kissing became more frantic. Rebecca had to pull away and her face was flushed when she looked lustily into his eyes. "Oh God," she gasped. "This is just what I needed!"

"It's what I needed too," he said and pulled her head back down. Her long hair tickled his cheeks as their lips mashed against one another and Jason felt waves of power rush through his aching body. Arthritis and muscle pain ebbed away and he smiled because he hadn't felt this good in years. In fact, he'd *never* felt this good.

Rebecca saw how happy he was and asked, "So you like an angel's kisses?"

"You wouldn't believe how much," he whispered and she felt something growing hard between his legs.

She slipped her hand beneath the covers and took hold of his throbbing penis. "What's this?" she asked, a big grin on her face. "Is this my payment for treatment?"

Her fingers lightly moved along his length and he moaned loudly. "What's the matter, baby?" she taunted. "Gonna cum?"

She stroked him faster and he gasped. *He's not going to last long,* she thought.

"Oh no," he suddenly said and he grimaced. "I think I'm gonna be sick again."

Rebecca let go of him and quickly sat up. "How bad are you feeling?" she asked, worried.

"Bad," he said weakly and she reached for the garbage can again.

He lunged for it and she held it under his face. "No," he groaned and then spewed loudly into it.

She rubbed his back as he vomited and said, "I think we're in for a long night, Jason. We're going to keep doing this until you're no longer sick."

He was pasty white when he looked at her. "I'll be ok. Just be patient with me."

She smiled. "Don't worry, darling. My lips are ready whenever yours are."

CHAPTER FORTY THREE

Jason went through the process again and again of being sick and then feeling better after they kissed throughout the night. Rebecca gave him water and food when he felt well enough to eat and held his head when he threw up in the toilet or the garbage can. As the days progressed, he was sick less often and seemed to become stronger. Rebecca couldn't get enough of his tongue and lips and eagerly looked forward to their next session.

After the sixth day, the phone rang and she picked it up. "Rebecca! Is that you?!" Susanna cried. "You guys are all over the news! Jeff and I have been lying low for days and we finally turned the TV on. We knew it was you guys they were talking about!"

"Yes, it was us," the angel answered. "We were in the right place at the right time."

"You're heroes, you know."

"We just did what we needed to do and nothing more," the angel said.

There was silence then but after a moment Susanna said, "You're too humble. I think it's awesome what you both did."

Jason came into the room then and Rebecca handed him the phone and walked away into the living room.

"Hey baby," he said. "How are you and Jeff doing?"

"Dad!" she yelled. "You're a fucking hero! I can't believe some of the things they're saying you two did!"

"Yeah....well, I couldn't have done any of it without Rebecca."

"I know, I know."

"Unfortunately, my cars gone. There's nothing left of it."

"You'll get another one, dad. At least you're alive." She thought his voice sounded tight. "Dad, are you alright? You don't sound alright."

"I'll be ok, Susanna. I haven't been feeling well but Rebecca's taking good care of me."

She snickered. "I'll bet she is."

"How are things there?" he asked.

"Dad, you won't believe this but most of the men are different now. People in town are smiling more and doing things for each other. It's like a switch clicked on in their heads."

"That's fantastic, honey."

"Dad," she said. "I think Jeff's the man I've always looked for. He's so special."

"That's great, Susannah. I'm happy for both of you."

"Are things good between Rebecca and you?" she asked.

"Oh yeah, things are great," he answered as he stepped into the living room. Rebecca was sitting in a chair facing the Christmas tree and she looked so lonely to him.

"Honey, can I call you back?" he asked.

"Sure, dad. Jeff and I are going out but we'll be back tonight."

She hung up the phone and he went to Rebecca. He touched her shoulder and said, "Are you alright?"

She looked at him and seemed so sad. "Can we get a real tree?" she asked.

He was startled by the question. "Sure. But why? Don't you like this one?"

She looked back at the tree. "No reason. I just like real trees."

"Ok, let me get showered and dressed and we'll get one."

She seemed happier then and he walked away to get ready.

Minutes later, he came back fully dressed and his mouth hung open in surprise. Rebecca had found the boxes for the ornaments and the tree and everything had been taken down.

"How did you do that so fast?" he asked. "I wasn't gone that long, was I?"

She laughed. "I surprise myself sometimes. Are you ready to go?"

"Well, I don't have a car yet but I remember there was a lot by the church that sells trees. They should still have some even though it's almost Christmas."

"Let's go," she said, her eyes bright and happy.

He took her hand and off they went.

There were still some nice trees left and Rebecca moved among them until she found the one she wanted. "This one is perfect," she said finally and pointed to a gorgeous tree whose needles still looked fresh.

Jason picked out a tree holder and went to the booth and paid the man plus a little extra for delivery.

"Your tree will be delivered this afternoon," he told Rebecca.

She clapped her hands together like a little girl which made Jason very happy. They stopped at a small café where he had a chicken crepe and some coffee. As he ate, Rebecca gazed at him the entire time with love in her eyes. When he finished, she took his hand in hers. "Thank you, Jason."

"I'd do anything for you. You know that, don't you?"

"I know."

Later that afternoon, Rebecca was anxious as she waited for the tree. To pass the time, Jason sat down at the piano for the first time in weeks and turned on the computer. He went to the music program he used and picked the grand piano instrument. Curious, Rebecca watched him and finally came over to see what he was doing.

"Is this how you compose music?" she asked.

"Yes, I like it better than a real piano because it never goes out of tune."

"I'm sorry I never asked you before about your Youtube channel. Will you show me it before you start?"

"Of course!" he said proudly and went to his channel. Rebecca put on the headphones and closed her eyes while he played her a few of his favorite compositions. A few times she opened her eyes and looked at him in surprise. When the last piece ended, she took the headphones off and said, "Wow, Jason, you're really good. Those are really lovely. What are you going to work on now?"

"A surprise," he answered and smiled. "You'll have to wait and see."

She let him go back to work then and went to rest on the couch for a while. An hour later the tree was delivered and placed in its holder which Jason filled with water. Rebecca leaned in and sniffed the branches. "I love the smell of a real tree, don't you?" she asked.

She sat down on the floor by the boxes of ornaments and looked up at him, hopeful.

"What are you doing?" he asked.

"I'm going to hand them to you just like I did for my father when I was a little girl. Do you mind?"

Jason thought that was very sweet. "Not at all."

There was something very tender about the way the angel handed him each ornament. She'd looked closely at each of them first and he saw the joy in her eyes. It was a slow process but Jason wanted to savor every second of it. Rebecca seemed lost in the past and a tear slid down her cheek when she picked up the last ornament and handed it to him. He strung the lights around the tree then followed by garland and she pulled out the full box of tinsel she'd found at the bottom of one of the boxes. Jason watched as she flung strands of it at the tree as she walked around it. It didn't take long and she backed away to view her handiwork.

"There. That's just the way I like it."

Jason put his arm around her and they sat down on the couch facing the tree. "It's beautiful….just like you are," he said softly.

She gazed into his eyes and smiled. "You know….you're just like him."

"Like who?"

"My father. You're kind and gentle just like he was."

"Tell me about him, Rebecca. Tell me about your life. I really don't know much about you."

"Alright," she said and lay her head against his shoulder. "He was an accountant and worked long hours. My mother did the best she could with me when he was away but she was bored with him. I think she was more of an adventurous type who wanted to travel but he liked to stay at home and sit by the fire. He was very special to me. I remember even when he was tired after work he always had time to read me a story from one of my books. His eyes were a deep brown like yours are. They could see inside of me in a way and it was almost as if he could tell when I was sad. Some nights when I'd wake up frightened of the dark, he'd come in my room and sit by my bed so I'd know he was there. He'd tell me everything would be alright and I believed him. He was such a sweet man, Jason. I loved him so much. I miss him."

"What happened to them, Rebecca?"

The angel's voice got lower. "After I....died, they split up. My dad was lost without me and my mother couldn't stand to be around him anymore. I'd see him sitting in his favorite chair sobbing uncontrollably and I wanted to tell him I was alright but I couldn't, Jason. I didn't become an angel right away so I couldn't go to him like I went to you. I felt helpless and had to watch him wither away until he died alone in a hospital bed with no one by his side. His last words to a nurse a few hours before were "I'm going to see my little girl."

Jason wiped tears from his eyes and asked, "Did you see him after he died?"

"No," she answered sadly. "Being dead is like being in a kind of cocoon. It warms you and makes you feel safe. I never saw him or mom after she died."

"How did you become an angel?"

She snuggled closer to him. "I guess I was a fairly good person and had suffered enough that God took pity on me. Sometime after I passed I was approached by other spirits who he'd sent to observe me. Their eyes gazed into mine and saw how I'd suffered and I remember feeling an intense wave of kindness sweep over me and I turned into an angel. I don't know why some souls become angels and others don't, Jason. For whatever reason, God picked me."

Jason kissed her forehead then and whispered, "He made a great choice, Rebecca."

She lifted her face to his and tears welled in her eyes. "I love you, Jason. I don't know what the future holds but I want you to know that."

He kissed her and she moaned. "Oh God," she whispered. "I can hardly wait until we're together."

"When, Rebecca? When will that be?" he asked, his eyes pleading.

"Soon," she answered, smiling. "Very soon."

CHAPTER FORTY FOUR

The next morning Rebecca woke him and said, "I'm sorry but I'll be gone for a few days. Someone needs me."

"But *I* need you," Jason said, disappointed.

"There are others who need me too, Jason. You'll be fine without me. You're tolerating my kisses far better now. I really have to go."

He grabbed her arm and pulled her to him. She wrapped her arms around him and said, "Jason, I do have to go. I promise I'll be back."

"*Please,*" he said. "Just one more kiss before you go."

She hesitated for a moment but then smiled. An electric shock sparked as their lips touched and Rebecca moaned. It was a gentle kiss and she didn't want to let him go so she hugged him tighter.

"Uunnhh," he groaned and she let him go. His eyes were wide and he gasped for breath. "Sorry," he gasped. "You were crushing me."

"Sorry!" she laughed. "I'll be more careful in the future."

She kissed him again and quickly backed away from the bed before he could grab her.

"Take care, my love," she whispered and his jaw dropped when she disappeared before his eyes.

"I love you," he whispered. "I love you so much."

CHAPTER FORTY FIVE

Jason returned to work and the reception he got was what he expected. No one asked him what had happened to him or if he was alright. It was business as usual until he was called to the director's office later in the day. His supervisor, Peter was also waiting for him when he got there. The director practically sneered at him and said, "Sit down."

He took a seat and waited nervously for her to speak.

"You've missed a lot of time, Jason," she said. "Too much time. Some of it was unexcused."

"I'm very sorry. I was injured. I couldn't help it. I promise I'll be here when I'm supposed to be from now on."

She leaned in close and her eyes were cruel. "And why should I believe you?"

"Because I give you my word."

She chuckled and he felt bile in his throat. "The only reason I haven't fired you is because Peter asked me to give you another chance."

Jason looked at his former assistant and the director said, "I think you should thank him, don't you?"

Jason swallowed hard and said, "Thank you, Peter."

The director grinned then. "And now me. Thank *me*."

Jason stared at her and wondered why she hated him so much that she needed to humiliate him.

"Thank you, Mrs. Walton," he said.

Her eyes narrowed. "I'll be watching you, Jason. Any more absences and I'll be forced to let you go. Do you understand me?"

"Yes," he said quietly.

"By the way, how's your girlfriend?" she snickered.

Jason's eyes narrowed. "My girlfriend?"

"Yes, the girl with the mouth on her. How is she?"

Jason fought the anger rising in him. "She's fine."

The director smiled a fake smile and leaned backward in her seat. "You know she can't protect you, don't you?"

"I never asked her to."

The woman stood up. "I think we're finished now. You may go back to work," she said dismissively.

"Thank you," he said and Peter followed him out the door.

"Hey man, what was that all about back there? I didn't know you had a girlfriend. Boy, Mrs. Walton sure doesn't like her!"

Jason turned to him and said, "I appreciate you fighting to keep me here, Peter. I really do. I won't forget it."

"Hey, I understand why you've been angry. It's the least I could do."

Jason extended his hand and Peter shook it. "So tell me about her, man. You're so damn secretive. What's she like?"

Jason smiled. "She's like no other woman on earth."

CHAPTER FORTY SIX

Over the next few days, Jason went to work and in his free time worked on his music. He thought of how he wanted to convey what he felt in his heart and poured every bit of himself into the song he was writing. The lyrics had to be just right and when he was done with it he smiled.

He went to the fridge and realized he was running low on food. He dreaded riding the bus again and knew it was time to buy a car. The insurance company was still inspecting the crash and hadn't decided yet what it was going to pay. After thinking about it, he decided that one more day without a car wouldn't hurt when he remembered the tiny grocery store on the corner two blocks away from his place. It was owned by a nice Indian couple who were always friendly to him the few times he ever went there for candy or soda. *I'm sure I'll find some things there to eat*, he thought and headed out the door in his winter coat.

The air was brisk and Jason had heard on the news that a massive snowstorm was scheduled to hit around Christmas. *How the hell would they know?* he snickered to himself. *They're always wrong about the weather anyway.*

The store was as small as he remembered but cozy and inviting in a way. Mr. Darshan greeted him with a smile and his wife waved to Jason from the back where she was loading potato chips onto the shelves. He waved back, grabbed a small shopping basket and headed to the refrigerated section. He picked out some packaged ham and swiss chesse. *I think I'll make a panini,* he thought. *I haven't had one in a long time.*

He grabbed an onion from the vegetable isle then and a loaf of sourdough bread. He was starting to get hungry and his stomach gurgled at the thought of the delicious sandwich he was going to make. *Now where's the vinegar*, he wondered as he searched for the last tasty

ingredient he needed.

He didn't hear them come in the store. The three men wore scarves over their faces and their cruel eyes scanned the store. "Hey, man! Hands on the counter!" one yelled at Mr. Darshan.

His eyes grew wide and he did as he was told. He looked nervously over to where his wife was loading shelves and prayed she'd be quiet.

Unfortunately, one of the men heard her and quickly raced over and slammed her headfirst against a metal rack of vegetables. "Hey bitch!" he yelled. "Get over here behind the counter!"

She screamed and he dragged her by the arm to where her husband was. He let her go and she got behind the counter with him.

"Give us the cash," the skinniest one ordered as he pulled a gun from his pants. "Whatever you got! We'll take it all!"

Jason had heard everything and laid low behind the candy shelves watching them. He took a deep breath and slowly stood up.

"What about me?"

The men whirled around and the one with the gun aimed it at him. "Goddamned motherfucker! You scared us! Get the fuck over here!"

The power of Rebecca's kisses had almost completely faded but there was still enough of it left that Jason felt confident he could handle the situation. He moved from behind the candy rack and stood proudly in front of them. "No," he answered calmly. "You come to *me*."

The men's eyes widened in surprise and they looked at each other. "Are you crazy, man?!" the one with the gun asked. "You wanna die?!"

"Do you?" Jason calmly replied and braced himself.

The tallest of the three laughed then and pulled a switchblade from his pocket. He flicked it open and held it in front of him. "I'm gonna cut you up, asshole!" he snarled.

He came in fast and Jason straightened his fingers and thrust them hard into the man's throat. He choked in surprise and fell against a wooden shelf of tomatoes. The knife fell out of his hand and Jason kicked it away. The one with the gun took aim and Jason moved faster than he ever had in his life. He grabbed a tomato and whipped it at the man's forehead where it exploded in a red mist. "Motherfucker!" he screamed and lowered the gun.

Jason dove at him and knocked him back against the counter. Mr. Darshan grabbed a small club he had hidden beneath the cash register and slammed it over his head. His eyes rolled up and he slumped to the floor in a heap and dropped the gun. It went off and a bullet ripped into Jason's leg. He cried out and the two remaining men slowly moved towards him.

Jason held his bleeding leg and looked at them fearfully. They snickered and rushed at him. He was driven backwards into the candy shelves and a fist smashed into his jaw. "Asshole!" one of them screamed.

Jason felt the last of Rebecca's power surge through him and he brushed aside the pain in his leg and jaw. Grabbing each of the men by the throat, he squeezed them tightly with impossible strength. They clawed helplessly at his arms until consciousness fled their bodies. Jason let them go and they fell to the floor in a heap.

"Are you alright?!" Mrs. Darshan cried and rushed to Jason to keep him from falling. He tottered a bit and heard a siren in the distance.

"I have to leave," he gasped.

"You're not going anywhere!" she said. "You're hurt!"

"But….I…."

A haze came over his eyes like blinds then and he fell to the floor, unconscious.

The cops rushed in, guns drawn and saw the men on the floor. "What the hell happened here?" one of them asked.

"They tried to rob us," Mr. Darshan answered.

A big cop pointed to Jason and asked, "What about him? Who is he?"

Mrs. Darshan cradled Jason in her arms and smiled. "He's a hero."

CHAPTER FORTY SEVEN

Jason awakened to the steady beep of the heart monitor by his bed. A nurse was standing over him and smiled.

"You're lucky to be alive, Mr. Wilkes. You lost a lot of blood. The bullet nicked your femoral artery."

"How long have I been here?" Jason asked, his voice weak.

"A few days now."

"What day is it?" he asked.

"It's December 20, five days before Christmas."

"Oh no," he groaned and tried to sit up. "I have to get out of here."

His head was suddenly spinning and he slumped back down onto the pillow. "Oh Jesus," he whispered. "Oh God, I hurt so badly."

Every joint and bone in his body ached and he remembered that this was the way he usually felt unless Rebecca kissed him.

"I'm sorry, sir," the nurse said sympathetically. "I'm giving you as much pain medication as I can."

"Ok, thanks. I know you're trying your best," he said and closed his eyes as he waved her away.

She frowned and left the room. He lay in a sea of pain and didn't know she'd appeared until her soft hand touched his. "Jason," Rebecca whispered.

He opened his eyes and the angel's beautiful face was inches from his. "Rebecca! Oh Rebecca! I've missed you!"

She softly stroked his cheek and said, "I can't leave you alone for a minute, can I? You're always trying to be a hero."

He tried to laugh but winced at the pain throughout his body. Rebecca kissed him then and her power surged through him. His muscles felt alive and the pains he felt ebbed away.

"Your kisses are like a drug to me," he said, smiling. "I could easily overdose on them."

She laughed softly and kissed him again. Her lips were soft and gentle and their tongues met. Rebecca's eyes melted into his and he felt as if he were dying. Rebecca saw the look in his eyes and pulled away from him.

"It's not your time yet," she said, her face flushed. "I won't kill you with my kisses."

"I wouldn't mind if you did," Jason said earnestly. "It would be the perfect way to die."

"Nope," she said and shook her head back and forth. "Not gonna happen."

"Do you know when my time is?" he asked then.

"No, I don't Jason. I only know when it's about to happen and not before."

She sat by the side of his bed and he sat up. "That's a pretty bad leg wound you've got there. I could heal it with my blood but I think you should heal naturally here in the hospital."

"Why? Why don't you heal me now so I can get out of here?"

Her eyes filled with tears. "Because I don't trust that nothing bad will happen to you, Jason. At least here I'll know you're safe and not trying to be a hero."

"But I didn't plan what happened! Those guys came in and tried to rob them!"

"I know, Jason but I'll feel better if you stay here a few more days. Besides, I'm not quite finished helping that other person. I need a few more days."

"And then you'll take me home?" he asked, disappointed. The energy had gone out of his eyes and Rebecca touched his cheek and caressed it.

"Yes, Jason," she whispered. "I'll take you home where you'll be safe in my arms."

CHAPTER FORTY EIGHT

Rebecca did as she promised. After a few days, she reappeared by his bed and woke him.

"Ready to go home, darling?" she asked as she held his hand.

"Yes….please take me home, my angel."

An hour later he was discharged with a fresh pair of crutches and to his surprise Peter was waiting outside to take him and Rebecca home.

"Hey man! You gotta stop hurting yourself! I can't keep making excuses for you at work!"

Jason laughed. "I'm surprised to see you, Pete but thank you. How did you know I was here?"

"Your girlfriend here came in to see me at work a few hours after it happened. You're a hero, man!"

"Am I in trouble at work?" Jason asked, worried.

"Are you kidding? Even Mrs. Walton knows she can't fire a hero! The press would rake her over the coals!"

"I'm sorry for letting you down, Peter. I know you need me at work. I haven't been much help to you lately."

Peter looked at Rebecca in the backseat by Jason and smiled. "Don't worry, buddy. It's my pleasure. You've got quite a woman there. I thought she was gonna break me in half when I said I wasn't sure the director wouldn't fire you or not."

Rebecca laughed. "I was not! I just gave you a look!"

"And what a look it was!" Peter said and laughed.

Thy pulled up to Jason's building and Peter helped get him out of the car. "Well, take care of yourself and come back to work as soon as you can. I can only hold the old battle axe off for so long, you know."

"I will. Thanks, Pete," Jason said and they shook hands.

They watched him drive away and Rebecca pointed to his crutches and said, "Once we get inside you won't be needing those anymore. You have *me* now."

His eyes gazed lovingly into hers. "Sometimes I want to pinch myself to make sure this is really happening. I still can't believe you're here for me."

"Why can't you, Jason?" she asked, smiling. "After all, I *am* your guardian angel, aren't I?"

CHAPTER FORTY NINE

Rebecca had food delivered so the fridge would be well stocked. Christmas was almost here and she wanted Jason to be at his peak so when he was cold at night she wrapped him in her wings and when he had a bad dream she comforted him with soothing words while she held him. She was the perfect angel who showed her love for him in so many wonderful ways that he knew he'd never be able to repay her kindness.

The morning of Christmas Eve, the police came knocking on Jason's door. One of them was a detective and he wore a long overcoat and a hat that made him look like a gangster from the twenties.

"Sorry we weren't able to talk to you at the hospital, Mr. Wilkes but we were still dealing with those bums you disabled. I'm Detective Abrams and these are my men, Joe and Don. I only have one question."

Rebecca sat down by Jason and held his hand. The lead detective stared at her strangely and then back at Jason.

"Why did you do it?" he asked.

"What do you mean?" Jason answered, surprised by the question. "I just did it, that's all."

"But why?" the man asked, staring holes through him with his penetrating eyes.

"I don't understand, detective. Why are you asking me this?"

The man leaned in close and said, "I'm just curious about you. Most people would have hid like cowards but from what I heard you deliberately put yourself in harm's way. It sounded almost as if you knew you wouldn't be hurt."

"But I *was* hurt, detective," Jason said and pointed to his leg. "I got shot, didn't I?"

"I know," the man said and frowned. "But I still think it's odd."

"Am I in trouble? If not, then I think we're done here. I'm kind of tired."

Detective Abrams stood up. "Of course. I'm sorry for bothering you."

He stared at Rebecca and then back at Jason again. "I wish more people were like you two."

"Us two?" Rebecca said, her face flushing.

The man smiled. "Yeah. You're the ones everyone's talking about who saved those people when that truck slammed into those cars, aren't you?"

Jason's face turned red. "How did you know it was us?" he asked quietly, his face grim.

"Don't worry. Your secret's safe with me," the man said and extended his hand.

Jason took it in his and shook it. "Thank you, sir. We're very grateful."

The man looked at Rebecca and quietly said, "People say they saw an angel but I don't think they exist, do you?"

Rebecca smiled. "Oh, I wouldn't say that, detective. They just might."

CHAPTER FIFTY

Susanna called later that evening and she talked to Jason for a long time.

"Do you need me to come see you, Dad? I will if you want me to."

"No, I'll be alright. Rebecca's taking good care of me. I'm healing fast."

"Dad….please stop being a hero," his daughter said. She sounded odd and he knew she was getting emotional.

"Susanna, I can't stop. I *won't* stop."

"But *Dad*," she said, her voice pleading. "One day it won't go well. I can feel it. It's going to kill you."

"I'll be fine, Susannah. Trust me."

"I'll be spending Christmas here with Jeff if that's alright with you," she said then, changing the subject.

Jason looked over at Rebecca who was cooking in the kitchen and smiled. "That's fine, sweetheart. Rebecca and I are going to spend the day quietly here at home. Have a good time and say hi to Jeff for us."

"I will, dad," she said and then quietly added, "Love her, dad. Please love her. She needs you."

"I will, honey. I promise I will," he whispered and hung up the phone.

He went into the kitchen then and wrapped his arms around Rebecca. "I heard you, you know," she said. "What did you promise her?"

"Oh nothing."

She turned and he let go of her. Holding the long spatula in front of his face her voice was stern. "I *can* force you to tell me, you know."

Jason saw the slight smile she cracked and knew she was play acting. "Oh really? How are you going to do that?"

She leaned in close to him and reached behind with the spatula. It tapped his buttocks lightly and she whispered, "I'll take you over my knees and pull your pants down. And *then* I'll pull down your underwear."

His face turned bright red and she smirked. "And then," she said smiling, "I'll spank your bare bottom until you tell me what you promised Susannah."

"I-I- don't…." he stammered.

Her eyes narrowed. "Don't pretend you wouldn't like it, Jason. You really want me to spank you, don't you?"

"I…." he gasped and swallowed hard.

"Relax!" she suddenly said. "I'm only joking!"

He lowered his eyes in shame and she put down the spatula and wrapped her arms around his neck and pulled him to her. "You don't need to feel embarrassed, Jason," she whispered. "I'll spank you anytime you want. I had no idea you were so kinky."

"I'm *not*," he protested but she knew differently when she reached down and felt the bulge between his legs.

She pulled him closer and moved her lips to his ear. "Oh really? Something down here says you are," she whispered. "And guess what? So am I."

He pulled away then and stared at her, shocked.

"What's the matter?" she asked and smiled. "You already know I think kinky thoughts just like you. I've had years to fantasize, Jason. Maybe I want to act them out with you. Would that be so bad?"

"No," he said and blushed. "I just…."

"You just what, Jason?" she asked. "You just thought that because I was an angel I'd be pure and good? Well, I've got news for you. I'm not."

"But…." he said quietly.

"But nothing, Jason. I may be an angel but I'm still a woman and I think of all the sex I've never had over the years and what I've missed. Don't be so surprised."

"I don't want to talk about this anymore," he said then and tried to walk away but she grabbed his arm and pulled him to her.

"Hey," she said, surprised. "Did I shock you? If I did I'm not going to apologize."

"I….I…." he stammered.

Her eyes turned warmer. "Jason, look, I want to do things with you that make both of us happy. Let's just see what happens, alright?"

He nodded and she let go of him and turned back to the stove.

"What are you making?" he asked. "It smells delicious."

She looked back at him and smiled. "Shrimp with onions and garlic in a wine sauce. It won't take long."

He slipped his arms around her and kissed her neck. "Rebecca," he said. "You're so good to me. I wish…."

She took the pan off the fire and turned to face him. Her eyes were sad and she touched his lips with her fingers. "I know, Jason," she whispered. "I wish the same thing."

His lower lip quivered and his eyes were scared then. "When you have to leave me will you say goodbye?"

She pulled him to her and laid her head against his chest. "Wouldn't that make it harder?" she said quietly, trying not to cry. "Wouldn't it be better if you woke up one day and I wasn't here?"

"No," he answered. "I need to say goodbye when the time comes. I don't just want you to not be here one day. Promise me you won't do that to me."

She lifted her head and gazed into his eyes. "I promise, Jason. I promise I'll say goodbye but it'll still hurt. You know that, don't you?"

"Yes, I know."

"Let's not talk about sad things," she said. "Let's talk about what we'd tell the world if they ever find out we're the ones from that crash."

"I already know what I'll say. I thought about it while I was in the hospital."

"Really?" she said, surprised. "You have an explanation about how you ripped car doors away and lifted truck cabs?"

"Of course," he said and smiled. He opened a cabinet and pulled out a big canister of protein powder.

"What's that?" she asked.

"It's what gives me strength. It's Tiger's Milk powder."

Rebecca laughed and put her arms around his waist. "That's what you're going to tell everyone? Really?"

"How else will I explain it? I can't very well tell them the truth now, can I?"

Rebecca smirked. "No, I guess you can't tell them that you get your strength from an angel's kisses. They wouldn't believe you anyway."

She went back to the stove and loaded a plate with the food she'd cooked. Jason poured two glasses of Chardonnay and brought them to the table. He sat down then and picked up a fork. Before he could use it, Rebecca sat next to him and took it from his hand.

"No. *I* want to feed you."

Jason felt like a child as he put his hands in his lap and waited patiently. Rebecca's eyes were full of love as she began to feed him. As she placed the fork to his lips, he gazed into her beautiful eyes which looked back into his with an intensity that made him shiver. He moaned in happiness as the delicious shrimp morsels touched his tongue and she smiled, delighted that he enjoyed her cooking that much.

As he ate, he couldn't help himself and tears formed in his eyes and slowly slid down his face. Rebecca put the fork down and placed her hands over his.

"What's wrong, Jason?" she asked. "Why are you crying?"

"I can't help it. It's just…."

"It's just what?"

"It's just that I can't get over how much you love me. I'm so incredibly lucky."

She picked up the glasses of wine and handed him one. He took it and she clinked hers against his. "To you and I, Jason and the love we're about to share."

His heart beat faster and she smiled and sipped some of the wine. "It's delicious. Have some."

Jason glanced at the clock and back at her. "It's six hours until Christmas."

"Then you should relax a bit and then I'm putting you straight to bed. You don't want to be awake when Santa gets here now, do you?"

He nodded no and had a big gulp of the wine.

Rebecca leaned in close and her eyes narrowed. "Santa might have a gift I think you'll like. It's a very special gift," she whispered.

"Can't I open it now?" he asked as his heart pounded in his chest.

"No, you'll have to wait," she said and took his plate away and went to wash it in the sink.

Jason brought the wine glasses over and was about to help her but she said, "No, I'll do it. Go into the living room and rest now. I need you to be at your strongest later."

He kissed her cheek and left her then. When she was finished, she went to join him in front of the Christmas tree. It smelled wonderful and the scent of pine permeated the room. She sat on the edge of the chair he was in and put her arm around his shoulder. They stared at the tree together for long minutes until she finally stood up and looked down at him. "Time for bed, Jason. Santa will be here soon. I'll let you know when he comes."

He smiled and she took his hand and pulled him slowly to the bedroom where she undressed him and made him lie down in bed. She pulled the covers over him and kissed his forehead.

"Go to sleep now, my darling," she whispered.

He watched her as she got up and closed the door behind her. His mind was filled with excitement he hadn't felt since he was a young boy. *I wonder what Santa's bringing me,* he thought right before he drifted off into a peaceful sleep.

CHAPTER FIFTY ONE

Jason didn't hear his bedroom door open and someone approach the bed. The figure stood silent for a moment and then whispered, "Jason, it's time to wake up. Santa was already here."

"What?" he said groggily and shifted to his side.

A warm hand touched his shoulder. "It's after midnight, Jason. It's Christmas. Don't you want your gift?"

"What?" he mumbled and opened his eyes.

Rebecca was standing in the semi darkness and she was smiling. She was holding his robe in her hands and held it out to him.

Jason felt his heartrate instantly accelerate and asked, "Is it time?"

"Yes, my love. It's finally time," she answered.

He got out of bed and took the robe from her and put it on. She took his hand in hers then and said, "Come."

Rebecca led him into the living room where the tree was. She'd started a fire in the fireplace and turned the tree lights on. The tinsel glittered on the branches and the ornaments shone in the soft glow coming from the fire. She was wearing the light blue dress she'd bought that day with Susannah and Jason gasped. "Oh wow, you're beautiful," he said and she blushed.

"Thank you, Jason. I got it just for you."

He moved closer to reach for her and she said, "Wait. I have something for you."

"Is it my gift from Santa?" he asked.

"No," she answered smiling. "That comes later."

She went to the tree and picked up a small box that was lying underneath it. "This is for you," she said and handed it to him. It was wrapped in purple foil and had a gold ribbon around it. He opened it quickly and looked inside the box. His eyes opened wide and she reached inside and pulled out the small glowing locket. It was attached to a long gold chain. The light inside it was alive and fluid as it

moved around inside the lockets clear case. Jason was utterly fascinated.

"Oh my God," he whispered. "What is it?"

She held it in front of his face and he cried, "It's so beautiful!"

The angel smiled. "It's a part of me, Jason. It's for you to wear close to your heart so you'll always remember me. It will keep you safe when I'm not around."

He lowered his head and she put it around his neck so it hung over his chest. Inside the clear glass locket the glowing blue orb pulsed softly with light. "This is part of you?" he asked as he stared in wonderment at the light.

"Yes, it is. I pulled it out of myself and placed it inside. Do you really like it?"

Jason smiled and pulled her close so her head rested against his chest. Her eyes stared at the bit of herself inside the locket and she whispered, "I'll always be with you now, Jason. Forever and ever."

"I love you," he said softly and kissed the top of her head.

They stood like that for long minutes until he finally pulled away. "I have something for you too," he said. "I finally wrote you that song."

Her eyes brightened. "You did?! You wrote me a song to sing for you?!"

"Yes, would you sing it for me now?"

"I'd love to," she answered and he went to the upright piano that sat in the corner. He opened the bench and pulled some sheet music from it and handed it to her. She glanced at it and said, "These are the lyrics?"

"Yes, it should be fairly easy to follow. I put into words how I feel about our love for each other. I hope you like it. Ready?"

"Yes," she said and stood by the side of the piano.

Jason began to play the intro and when it was time Rebecca began to sing.

"I heard your heart call out to me. I felt your pain course through me. Well, I'm here now to take it all away. I'm here now to take you far away. To a place where there's no longer any pain. To a place where there's no longer any rain. Only sunshine and moonlight to light your day and night. You can count on me to make everything alright. So close your eyes and feel my touch. My darling, I love you so much. Feel my breath upon your face. Feel my warmth when we embrace. You whisper, "I love you" and I know it's true. I've found heaven on earth…yes…I've found heaven on earth…here with you."

The last piano note faded away and Rebecca stood for a moment unmoving. Jason got up and stood by her. She put down the music sheets and looked into his eyes. Her eyes were filled with tears and he said, "I'm sorry I made you cry. Did you like the song?"

Her lower lip quivered and she pulled him to her to hug him gently. She raised up on tiptoes and kissed his cheek and then his ear and whispered, "Its perfect, Jason. It's exactly how I feel about you."

Jason smiled and she whispered, "I *have* found heaven on earth, Jason. Here with *you*."

He shivered then and Rebecca couldn't wait any longer. She pulled her head back and softly asked, "Would you like your gift from Santa now?"

He glanced around the room for it and she gently touched his chin and made him look at her. "It's me, Jason. *I'm* your gift."

He held his breath as his heart beat fast and she let go of him and moved back until she stood by the light of the tree. Very slowly, she peeled the beautiful dress down past her smooth shoulders and watched his face. Her long blonde hair seemed to have a soft glow to it and at that exact moment she was the perfect angel that any man could ever imagine. His eyes went wide then when she pulled the dress down past her bra covered breasts to her hips. Jason thought he was going to have a heart attack when after a moment she pushed it down further until it fell to her knees and her panties were revealed. The dress fell to her feet and she stepped out and kicked it away with her foot. Jason's mouth hung open as he took in the beautiful creature standing in front of him. She stepped forward and he backed away from her which disappointed her. She frowned. "What's wrong, Jason? You act like you're afraid."

"I am," he answered softly. "I'm afraid I won't meet your expectations."

She smiled tenderly and said, "I have no expectations, Jason. I just want you to be who you are. Believe me, I won't be disappointed."

He felt incredibly cold even though he wore the warm robe and the angel knew that she had to show him soon that there was nothing to fear. She reached behind and unhooked her bra and pulled it away from her breasts in one smooth move.

"Oh my God," he whispered at the sight of the angel's lovely breasts. They were small and looked absolutely luscious like two perfectly shaped pears. Standing topless before him she asked, "Do you like what you see, Jason? Was I worth waiting for?"

He gulped hard and she beckoned him with a finger. "Come here," she whispered.

Jason moved slowly towards her as if in a haze and she said, "Take my panties off."

He seemed frozen in place for a moment but then moved closer and slowly sank to his knees in front of her. He looked up at her with adoring eyes. "Why?" he asked. "Why me?"

She moved towards him, her hips swaying sexily and stood above him looking down. "Because I love you, Jason," she answered. "I think I've loved you from the moment I watched over you as a little boy. You're everything in a man I could ever want."

His hands were shaking when he reached up and hooked his fingers inside the hem of her light powder blue panties. Rebecca ran her fingers through his hair and shivered slightly as he slid the panties down past her hips and over her legs. They fell to the floor and she stepped out of them. Jason stared wide eyed at her hairy sex and then her sweet scent hit him. It was slightly musky and he knew she was aroused.

A tear slid down his face and she pulled his head into her stomach. It was soft and smooth and its fine hairs brushed his face. He wrapped his arms around her and began to lightly sob.

"Don't cry, my love," she whispered. "This is our night together. I'm not going anywhere. My body is yours to love."

"Oh God!" he cried. "You're so beautiful! I love you so much! I must be dreaming!"

She pulled him to his feet, took his hands and placed them over her breasts. "Do you really think this is a dream, Jason? Don't these feel real?" she asked, her eyes gazing sexily into his.

He squeezed her breasts gently and she groaned and closed her eyes. "Yes, just like that. Fondle them. Do whatever you want to them. I've waited so long for this."

Jason caressed her breasts and noticed how firm they were. Her nipples hardened and he pinched both of them at the same time. Rebecca gasped and shivered. "Oh God, yes," she whispered.

Jason let go of them and bent low to take a nipple into his mouth. He ran his tongue around the areola and goosebumps appeared on the angel's arms. "Oh *Jason*," she whispered and pulled his head closer. Her fingers ran through his hair and he sucked gently on the tender nub then. "Oh God!" she cried out. "Oh God, yes!"

Jason lightly suckled for a moment and then moved to her other nipple. Rebecca shuddered and felt a warm rush between her legs when his lips closed tightly around it and his teeth bit lightly down.

"Oh God! I think I just came!" she cried and her fingers gripped his hair tightly. "You made me cum, Jason!"

His mouth moved around both breasts then as his wet tongue tasted her smooth skin. Rebecca basked in the feeling and froze when his head moved lower as he squatted before her. His tongue licked down her body and settled over her navel and twirled around. Another warm rush of pleasure ran through her and she shuddered again and felt faint. "Oh….oh…." she moaned.

Jason got on his knees and grabbed her hips then. The angel felt her heart beat fast when she realized what he was about to do. She spread her legs open to provide him access and his lips were suddenly over her mound. "Oh God!" she cried and then his tongue slurped between the lips of her sex. "Oh God, yes!" she screamed, unable to hold back the intensity of feelings she felt.

Jason smiled and inhaled her scent which smelled like musky sweet vanilla. Her sex was moist and he lapped at her nectar and tasted it. It was also sweet and tasted like pure vanilla. He knew then he would drink from this special spot of hers many times in the future.

"Oh please," she moaned. "Please just do it. Do it already."

Jason's lips found her clitoris and it bulged in his mouth as the blood suddenly flowed into it. He sucked on it gently and Rebecca's neck muscles tightened and her eyes closed shut. "Oh fuck! Oh fuck! I'm gonna cum!" she shouted.

Warm liquid gushed onto his face then and Jason was covered in the sweet vanilla scent. It ran down his chin and dripped to the floor as the angel shuddered. He grabbed her buttocks then and pulled her closer. Rebecca trembled with anticipation and his tongue darted inside her. Her moist folds parted and he took his time as he explored her sex. "Oh Jason! Oh fuck! Yes! Yes! Eat me! Eat my pussy!" she screamed.

He looked up at her face as he made love to her with his tongue and she was gazing down at him with hazy eyes. "I love you," she whispered and shuddered again. "Oh God, I *really* love you."

With regret, he pulled his tongue out of her and let go of her buttocks. His face was flushed as he gazed glassy-eyed at her. She looked panicked as he stood up and backed away. "No!"

She swayed unsteadily on her feet and the juice ran down her legs. "No, please don't stop!" she gasped as she held her arms out to him. "Come back. I need you."

Jason smiled and pulled off his robe. He threw it by her dress and walked away to the bathroom to wash his face. Rebecca smiled at him when he came back and moved into her arms. "Thank you for washing me off of you. I know I made a mess," she said.

"Oh, believe me," he laughed. "I plan on going back to the well again later so I can taste your nectar. It's delicious."

She bit his shoulder lightly and said, "Oh Jason, you say the sweetest things to me. I love you so much."

His warmth seeped into her and she trembled in his arms. "My God, Jason, your naked body feels so good close to mine."

She pulled away and looked down. "But why aren't you hard for me?" she asked, disappointed.

He was frustrated. "I knew this would happen. I hate getting old. It just doesn't want to cooperate."

"Don't worry. I know just what to do," she said. She squatted and looked up at his face. "Don't cum yet. I'm just going to make you hard, alright?"

He nodded and she said, "Spread your legs please."

He did as she asked and she reached and cupped his balls with a warm hand. He moaned softly as she rolled them gently between her fingers. "I hope there's a lot of cum in these tonight, Jason," she said. "I plan on draining every drop from you."

His cock twitched and she smiled. "Oh yeah, I know you like it when I talk dirty. This is going to be so much fun."

Her other hand reached out and gently took hold of his penis. She lifted it and inspected it closely. A tiny drop of pre cum oozed out of the hole and her eyes got wide. "I can see you're getting excited, Jason. It wants me. I can tell."

"Ooohhhhh," he moaned when she suddenly leaned in and sucked him into her mouth. He hardened quickly and soon her lips were sliding back and forth over his shaft. Her hand stroked his cock near the base and his balls danced as she tickled them.

"Mmmmmmm," she moaned as she slurped on him.

Jason gripped her long hair with his fingers and moved her head back and forth in a steady rhythm. Rebecca felt his penis suddenly swell and quickly pulled her mouth away. "Not yet, you naughty boy," she said and waved her finger at him. "You're not cumming until I say you can."

"Oh God, please Rebecca," he groaned. "Please finish me."

She stood up and pulled him over to the tree by his penis.

"Here," she said. "Let's make love here on the floor."

She let go of him and spread a blanket down. He watched breathless with anticipation and then she lay down on her back. She spread her legs wide then and lifted her arms out to him. "Come home to me, Jason," she said softly. "This is where you belong."

He cried out and quickly moved his body over hers. She grabbed his penis and held it while gazing into his eyes. "Please be gentle with me, Jason. You're the first and only man I'll ever make love with," she whispered before guiding him into her.

The angel's eyes went wide and Jason thought he had gone to heaven when her silky folds opened up for him. Her hymen resisted for only a moment and she grabbed his buttocks and pulled him deeper. She winced when the barrier tore but then a beautiful smile of satisfaction crossed her face. She was warm and silky smooth inside as her sex sucked him in. "Oh God, Jason, you feel so good inside me," she gasped. "Don't move. Just stay like this for a moment."

He stared into her eyes and smiled. "This can't be happening," he said. "I'm the luckiest man in the world."

"Now," she whispered. "*Now* you can move."

He began to slowly slide back and forth inside her and she shivered beneath him. The intimacy they shared was so great that she began to sob with joy. Pulling him down, she cried against his shoulder and said, "Oh God, Jason! Love me! Love me, my darling!"

He moved gently inside her and her sex gripped him like a warm glove. "Oh Rebecca, Oh God, I'm gonna cum soon," he gasped. "I can't hold out much longer. Please let me cum."

"No," she said and her eyes narrowed in anger. "Not until I tell you to."

She pushed him off of her and his cock slid out with a loud slurping noise. He sat on his haunches and she pushed him onto his back and mounted him. "I want to be on top now," she said, her face flushed.

She found his penis and guided it back to her dripping entrance. Jason sucked in his breath and the swollen lips of her pussy opened for him. She pushed slowly down until her buttocks rested on his thighs and he trembled beneath her. "Now *I'm* going to fuck *you*," she whispered, her eyes full of lust.

He gripped her curved hips and she began to move. She'd pull up and stop right before he could slide out and then push back down until his cockhead rested against her cervix. Her breasts jiggled as her speed increased and she fell atop him and laid her head near his. "Oh God," she moaned as her hips moved faster. "Oh God, yes."

Jason moved his hands lower and grabbed her smooth buttocks. Rebecca's eyes went wide when he suddenly slapped them. "Oh yes!" she cried. "Harder! Spank me harder!"

He slapped her globes harder then as she moved even faster. Her sex gripped him tightly and began to flutter.

"Do you feel it, Jason?" she gasped. "Do you feel my pussy milking your cock?"

"Yes," he grunted. "Stop, please stop. I'm gonna cum."

"You'd better not," she said, her eyes twinkling. "I haven't given you permission yet."

"I can't help it!" he cried and tried to push her off. "Stop! Please stop!"

She grabbed his shoulders hard and lifted her hips up until just the tip of his penis was inside her. Smiling sadistically, she slammed her hips back down and he screamed out at the incredible feeling of her warm pussy engulfing him. "What's wrong, Jason? Is my pussy too much for you?" she taunted.

He began to cry and she suddenly felt bad and whispered, "Hey, it's ok. Cum now. Cum inside me. I want you to."

Her thrusts became slower then and Jason's hands gently caressed her buttocks. Rebecca's eyes gazed into his and she whispered, "My man….oh my sweet man…."

Jason felt the wave off in the distance approaching rapidly. He surrendered to it and let it crash against him.

"Oh my God!!" he cried. He stiffened and his toes curled as his cock exploded inside her.

"Rebecca!!" he screamed. "I'm cumming! Oh God, I'm cumming!"

She clung to him and felt her own wave speeding towards her. "Oh Jason!" she screamed. "It's happening! It's really happening! I'm gonna cum too! Hold me tight!"

He hugged her tightly and felt her shudder against him. Her eyes opened wide with surprise as the massive orgasm rippled through her. The pleasure was incredible and she cried out, "Jason!! Jason!! This is heaven!"

She lifted up slightly but then collapsed onto him, breathing rapidly. His arms wrapped tighter around her and her wings suddenly extended. Jason watched as they slowly came down and wrapped around both of their bodies. Under the warm blanket of her wings, he shivered from the intensity of the love he felt for her. "My angel," he whispered, kissing her forehead. "My sweet angel."

Her eyes were dreamy and unfocused. "Jason," she moaned. "What happened? I've never felt like this before."

"It's called love," he whispered. "I'm in love with you."

She smiled. "As I am with you."

Their lips met then and her tongue lightly caressed his. Her power surged into him and he moaned. She pulled her face away and said, "Feel the power of my kiss, Jason. I got what I could from you without it and you did real well but now I'll help get you through the rest of this night."

His eyes opened wide with alarm and she giggled. "What?" she said. "You thought that was it? Remember I'm an angel. I never get tired. I can go all night. Now I need *you* to."

She kissed him again and he felt his sagging cock harden again inside her. "Yes….yes…."she moaned. "Let's do it again….and again….and again."

CHAPTER FIFTY TWO

Jason lost count of how many times he'd orgasmed inside his beautiful angel but even the power of her kisses couldn't help after the last mind-blowing one which left him tingling all over. Rebecca thrashed above him in the throes of ecstasy until she realized he wasn't moving any longer. She stared down at him and he had a smile on his face and his body shone with sweat. She smiled and gently lay atop him. "You did well, my love," she whispered and touched his cheek with affection. "Rest now."

He slept for a long time and when he finally woke the scent of bacon hit his nostrils. He sat up and for a moment wondered where he was. The fire was still going strong in the fireplace and the heat from it warmed him. "Good, you're finally awake," Rebecca said as she came into the room, completely naked. "Come. I made breakfast for you."

Jason wrapped himself in the blanket and followed her into the kitchen. The table was already set and she motioned for him to sit down. He sat down and waited as she piled bacon and eggs onto his plate and placed a tall glass of orange juice in front of him.

"Thank you," he said and she sat down next to him.

"I thought you'd never wake up," she said, smiling. "Are you alright?"

He shivered beneath the blanket and looked at her shyly. "I thought I'd died and gone to heaven. The last thing I remember was your eyes staring into mine before the world exploded."

Rebecca smirked. "It wasn't the world that exploded, Jason. It was your hard cock. I'm proud of you. You lasted for hours."

"Are you happy?" he asked, hopeful. "Did I satisfy you?"

She picked up a piece of bacon and held it to his lips. Her eyes gazed tenderly into his. "Yes, Jason," she said softly. "You're a fantastic lover."

Satisfied, he smiled and tasted the bacon. "Yummmm," he groaned and she laughed.

"I'd like you to say that when you taste me again. Will you do that for me?"

He nodded and she scooped up some eggs on a fork and slipped it into his mouth. Rebecca saw the intense love in his eyes as she fed him and she blushed when he'd steal glances at her breasts every now and then. When he had finished eating, she stood up and said, "It's time for your shower now. I'm sorry to have to tell you this but you're a little stinky."

He burst out laughing and she turned her back on him and started to head towards the bathroom. Her curved buttocks jiggled slightly as she walked and for a moment Jason thought of a slinking cat. The way she moved was incredibly erotic and made his cock stiffen and caused his breathing to become more rapid. He threw the blanket to the floor and Rebecca glanced back at him and smirked when she saw his erection straining towards her. "Come on, cock man," she said. "I'm going to make sure you're *really* clean for our next session."

When they got to the bathroom, Jason stepped into the shower and she got in behind him and closed the glass door. He turned the water on and she moved against his back until her breasts pressed against him. "Hand me the soap," she said. "I'm going to wash you."

The warm water cascaded over them both and the angel soaped up her hands and ran them gently down his spine until she reached his buttocks.

"Bend over," she whispered.

Wondering what she was up to, he did as she asked and waited. He lurched forward a bit when her hand slapped his left cheek. "Hold still while I spank you," she ordered.

"Why are you spanking me? Have I been bad?" he asked.

"Oh yes," she breathed huskily. "You made me lose control many times last night so now I have to punish you."

Her hand came down on his other cheek and he cried out. His heart jumped in his chest then when her hand suddenly rested between his cleft. He waited breathlessly and felt her finger lightly touch his anus. He held his breath and waited anxiously for what was next. "I've wanted to do this to you for a long time, Jason," she whispered. "Just hold still now."

Her finger pushed into him and he gasped from the sudden pleasure he felt. "Oh," he whispered. "Oh….oh!"

Rebecca slapped his ass hard then and he cried out. "Stand up!" she commanded.

He stood up and her finger thrust upwards and probed deeper. He moaned loudly and she moved close until her hard nipples grazed his back. Her other hand reached around and lightly took hold of his stiff cock. "I'm going to jerk you off now, Jason," she whispered. "I'm going to count down from ten. If you don't cum by the time I'm finished counting then I'm afraid I'll *really* have to punish you. I'll have to take you into the other room and put you over my knees and spank your bare bottom."

"Oh no!" he said, breathlessly. "I promise I'll cum!"

"Good," she said and began to slowly stroke him. "Ten," she whispered and kissed his shoulder.

"Ohhhhh…." he moaned as her finger worked away inside him, pressing on all sides.

"Oh yes," she whispered. "You like an angel's finger in your ass, don't you? Nine."

"Ohhhh…." he groaned and she gripped his cock harder. As the water ran over their bodies, Jason felt his legs begin to shake.

The finger slid out and then pushed back in again and he stood on his tiptoes in an attempt to get away from it.

"Oh no, you don't!" Rebecca laughed as she skewered him like a bug. "You're not getting away from me! Eight!"

Her thumb moved over his bulging cockhead and tickled his peehole. "Oh!" he cried and she laughed.

"Seven, baby!" she cried.

Her finger pressed hard against his special spot then and precum leaked out of the tip of his penis. Rebecca felt the sticky fluid run over her fist and she stroked him faster. "Six," she whispered.

"Oh God, Rebecca!" he groaned as goosebumps appeared on his arms. "I think I'm gonna cum!"

Rebecca masturbated him for another minute as he trembled and clutched at the shower wall with his hands. Her finger worked over his prostate until he thought the sensation would cause his heart to burst out of his chest. "Oh! Oh! My God, Rebecca! I'm gonna cum soon! Keep doing that!"

"Is this what you like, baby?!" she taunted as his spinchter tightened around her probing finger. "Five!"

She twirled her finger around inside him and his cock swelled even bigger which surprised her. "Four!" she cried. "Cum! Cum for me now!"

"Aaarrgghh!" he screamed and succumbed to the pleasure. His cockhead burst open and thick cum shot out and ran down the shower wall.

"Good boy!" Rebecca shouted as she pumped his penis. "More! More!"

Her finger pulled out of his ass and plunged back in and he screamed and pounded the shower wall with his fists as his legs quivered. "That's it, baby! Cum for your angel!" she cried happily.

Another massive blast of cum shot out and he leaned back and sagged against her. She took his weight easily and continued to masturbate him as he moaned. "Yes, Jason, yes," she whispered and kissed his neck. "Submit to me. You're mine....all mine."

When she thought she'd drained him dry, she stopped and held him as he shivered against her. "It's over now, Jason," she whispered. "Now you can rest for a little while."

She let him go when she was sure he could stand and finished her washing of him. Her soapy hands moved lightly over his body and to his shock his cock began to harden again. Rebecca didn't touch it though. She just smiled and teased his nipples with her fingers. "Now it's my turn," she whispered.

They got out of the shower and dried each other off. Rebecca took his hand and led him into the living room. They stood facing each other and she lay her head against his chest. His eyes were full of lust when she looked up at him and asked, "What are you thinking?"

"I'm thinking I want to taste you again," he said quietly.

"My body is yours, Jason. Do as you wish. I won't resist."

He smiled and maneuvered her into position so she was on all fours with her lovely buttocks facing him. She looked back at him and smiled. "Yes….take me from behind."

His hand moved between her legs and his finger ran lightly between the slick lips of her sex. She threw her head back and moaned loudly. He worked the finger up and down and she spread her legs wider to give him complete access to her charms.

"Oooohhhh," she moaned when his warm lips kissed her right buttock. He ran his tongue around it and moved to the other soft globe and she clutched at the floor with her fingers.

"Oh God, Jason….please fuck me," she groaned. "Don't make me wait."

Jason moved behind her and held the tip of his penis between her lips. When the tip lightly touched them she tried to push back on him but he pulled away. "No!" she cried in frustration. "Give me your cock! I need it!"

Jason laughed and leaned in to sniff her sex. "Yummm," he said and his tongue tasted her and made her lurch forward.

"Shit!" she cried. "Oh shit!"

His tongue pushed between her folds and she groaned from the pleasure and feeling of submission. She pushed her bottom back at him to make him go deeper and he slurped up her nectar until she began to shake. "Oh fuck….oh fuck," she moaned.

Jason pulled his tongue out and replaced it with his penis. He inserted it so only the tip was in and she thrust back quickly. His cock sank deep and she cried out. He grabbed her hips and began to thrust in and out and she pushed back harder against him as animal lust filled her. "Yes….yes….fuck me," she groaned.

He surprised her then and touched her anus with a moistened fingertip. "Oh fuck," she moaned. "Oh yes….do it. Put your finger in me."

He pushed his finger in very slowly until his palm rested against her buttocks and she let out a high pitched animal sound. She put her head to the floor and pushed back again as he began to fuck her faster. At the same time his finger moved in and out of her ass and she began to tremble from the intense feeling.

"Oh God, Jason! I'm gonna cum!!" she shrieked suddenly as her anus tightened around his finger. "Don't stop! Oh God, *please* don't stop!!"

But he did stop and to her horror pulled his cock and finger completely out of her. She spun around and angrily cried, "What the hell, Jason! You're not done!"

He gently touched her cheek and she kissed his hand. "I want to look into your eyes when you cum," he said and she smiled and lay on her back. He lowered himself over her and she took hold of his penis and inserted it. Slowly….tenderly….he loved her until she quivered beneath him, her breasts jiggling as she shook in ecstasy.

"Oh God….love me….love me," she moaned and pulled him down so she could wrap her arms around his back. Her hands clawed at him and she began to sob as whatever control she had ebbed away. "Oh! Oh!" she cried and her pussy opened and closed around him and drew out his love.

"Oh Rebecca!" he cried in her ear. "I'm gonna cum!"

"Yes!" she cried and clung tightly to him as her pubis gushed around him. "Oh fuck!!" she wailed and he exploded inside her as her pussy lips milked him. Her fingernails lightly raked down his back and grabbed his buttocks to pull him deeper inside. Jason shuddered as his penis spewed more cum and she whispered, "I can feel it. I can feel the cum spurting from your cock."

"Oh Rebecca!" he cried and kissed her ferociously. Their tongues stabbed at each other and she moaned into her lover's mouth. Jason's hips felt bruised as she banged up into him but he didn't care. He wanted to be one with her and at that delicious moment he was.

"My man….my wonderful man," she whispered when their mouths finally parted to take a breath.

Jason's eyes were glassy and he lay his head against her breasts.

"It's alright, my love," she whispered. "I'm here with you."

They lay like that for long minutes as their heartrate slowed until he finally lifted his head and looked at her.

"Rebecca," he said and his eyes softened. "I need to ask you something."

"What is it?"

"Will I see you again after I die?"

Her mood changed then and she was suddenly very sad. She hugged him tightly to her and his face rested between her breasts. "Please, Jason. Let's not think of that right now. Let's just enjoy each other."

"Alright," he said softly.

She trembled against him and the intense love she felt coursed through her.

"You're everything to me," she whispered. "You're the man I've always dreamed of."

He lifted his face from her breasts and looked into her eyes. "And you're the woman of my dreams. I want to love you forever."

"Oh Jason!" she cried and kissed him. "Hold me and don't ever let me go!"

She began to sob against him and he ran his fingers through her hair.

"I'll never let you go," he whispered. "I may be just a man but you'll forever be my angel."

CHAPTER FIFTY THREE

They lay like that for hours just staring into one another's eyes. Every now and then their lips would meet and their tongues would gently touch. After a while, Rebecca moved her hand between them and held Jason's penis. It began to get hard and she smiled and released him so he could mount her. He slipped inside her sweet depths and she clung to him as he made love to her. Her hands clutched his shoulders tightly as she moaned, "Yes.... oh yes."

Right before he sensed he was about to cum, Jason lifted his head and cried, "Thank you, God!! Thank you for my angel!"

Rebecca smiled up at him and her sex gripped him tightly. "*Now* Jason. Show me again how much you love me."

He cried out and she felt him fill her with his love.

"Yes, my darling," she whispered as she pulled him down and kissed his face. "*Yes....*"

He passed out again and she felt his heart beating rapidly against her chest. Overcome with emotion, she closed her eyes and whispered, "Please lord, let me live again so I can be with this man forever. Show me how."

The answer hit her suddenly and she grew scared. *I don't know if I can do that,* she thought. *Oh please, God. Give me the strength to do it.*

CHAPTER FIFTY FOUR

When Jason woke up she was still holding him. He smiled and said, "Thank you for loving me. I may not have a penis for much longer but thank you anyway."

Rebecca laughed then and suddenly his stomach gurgled.

"I think my man is hungry. Would you like me to make you something?"

His eyes brightened as he thought of something. "I've got a better idea. I know *you* don't need to eat but there's a place not far from here that makes great chocolate crepes. I think they may be open. Would you like to go? I think you'd love them."

She touched his face. "I'll go wherever you want, my darling. I just want to be with you."

They dressed for the weather and went outside into the cold. Snow was falling lightly and they walked arm in arm the few blocks to the quaint bakery. Jason was right. It was open for Christmas to Rebecca's surprise. Glass display cases contained desserts filled with fruit and vanilla crème and chocolate fillings. Jason picked out two crepes filled with Belgian chocolate and after paying for them they sat down at a small table by the window. They looked out at the street and noticed there weren't many people roaming around. It was almost as if the world had stopped moving because it was Christmas. Rebecca glanced around the shop and saw a man sitting at the farthest table behind them. He was eating a cupcake and sat with his back to them with his shoulders slumped.

Jason broke off a piece of the crepe and held it for Rebecca to taste. "Here, try this. It's my favorite thing here."

She took it in her mouth and let it settle on her tongue. It was indeed delicious and she chewed it slowly. "Yummm. This *is* good. You were right."

"I knew you'd like it," he said proudly.

He took a bite of it himself and then handed her the other crepe. Rebecca suddenly had a feeling they were being watched and looked back in the direction of the man at the other table. He had turned around and was staring at them. To Rebecca's horror, he grinned and her face turned pale. The crepe dropped from her hand to the floor and her mouth opened in shock.

"Rebecca, what's wrong?!" Jason whispered.

She sat motionless and seemed paralyzed with fear. Forcing herself to look away, she grabbed Jason's hand and whispered, "Get me out of here! For god's sake, get me out of here!"

Alarmed at her fear, he quickly stood up and looked over at the man. He had turned back around but Rebecca was obviously distressed. They quickly put their coats on and left the shop. As soon as they stepped outside, Rebecca lunged at him and clung to him tightly. She was shaking and Jason couldn't figure out what was wrong.

"Rebecca, talk to me. What happened in there?"

She lifted her eyes to his and he saw the intense fear in them. This was the first time he'd ever seen her like this and it worried him.

"It's him," she whispered. "I *know* it is."

"That man in there?" he asked, not understanding. "Who is he? Do you know him?"

"Jason," she said so quietly he almost didn't hear her. "He's the one. He's the one who took my life away."

His eyes went wide. "What?!"

She gripped his shoulders hard and her lower lip quivered.

"He's the one who killed me!"

CHAPTER FIFTY FIVE

Jason couldn't believe what she was saying and frantically asked, "What the hell are you talking about?! Wouldn't he be dead after all these years?!"

She was terror stricken. "His eyes! It's his eyes! I'd recognize them anywhere! I know it's him!"

Jason felt his heart begin to pound and felt helpless. "What should we do? I don't know what to do!"

"I don't know. Just get me away from here. Please take me back home."

He nodded and led her away. As they slowly walked down the street back to his place, he glanced back at the shop and saw the man standing in the window staring out at them. He was grinning and it sent chills down his spine. *What the hell?* he thought. *That guy would creep anyone out. It's no wonder she's scared.*

They got back to the apartment and after removing their coats, Rebecca lunged into his arms and began to cry.

"Oh Jason! Please hold me!"

He put his arms around her and softly said, "Rebecca, I don't understand what just happened. The man who killed you is long dead by now, isn't he?"

She wiped tears away and nodded.

"Then who was that man and how can he possibly hurt you?" he asked. "You're an angel. You're invincible."

"I know it sounds crazy Jason, but I'm scared. He's come back. I *know* he has."

"Ok, so you're saying he's reincarnated or something?"

She nodded. "Yes, he's started a new life."

"Alright," he said, trying to understand. "But he can't possibly know you. If he 's been reborn he wouldn't remember you, am I right?"

"But he *does* know me. I can tell by the way he looked at me. He *remembers*."

Jason was frustrated. "Ok, but even if he does he can't hurt you again, Rebecca. You're an angel now."

She wasn't really listening to him and her face suddenly turned even paler. "Oh my God," she whispered. "What if he's still bad? What if he's here to kill again?"

"What?!" Jason cried and gripped her shoulders hard. "You're talking crazy! There's no way for you to know that! How would you find out anyway?!"

Her eyes narrowed and she stared intensely at him. "Watch me," she said. Her face was grim and she grabbed her coat. "I'm going back to face him."

"What?!" Jason cried. "Are you nuts?! You can't!"

She pushed him away and snarled, "I'm going and *you* can't stop me."

"Then I'm going with you."

She lifted her hand threateningly and he felt a twinge of fear.

"Just don't get in my way," she said, her voice low.

He gulped hard and she turned her back on him and walked out the door. He grabbed his coat and put it on as he hurried to follow her. She walked at a brisk pace and soon they were back at the shop. They stepped inside and Jason sucked in a breath when he saw the man was still there. He was sitting with his back to them staring off into space.

Rebecca's eyes narrowed in anger and she forced herself to approach the man. His eyes opened wide when she appeared in front of him and pulled a chair out and sat down. Jason sat in the chair next to her and watched the man's reaction. He smiled slightly and asked, "Excuse me, but do I know you? Have we met before?"

The man was dressed in a heavy wool overcoat and Jason could tell that beneath it he was very muscular. He gave off that aura of power that confident men exuded. His thick brown hair drooped slightly over his eyes and he brushed it back. His chiseled face was handsome in a way but the narrow nose had been broken in the past and gave him a cruel look. The scariest thing about him though were his eyes. They were bright blue and seemed almost dead. They stared at Rebecca and waited for her to answer.

"Maybe," she finally responded, her face grim. "But it was a long time ago."

The man licked his lips and settled back in his chair. He seemed strangely relaxed which unnerved Jason. There was something definitely odd about him.

"How long ago?" he asked, his eyes still dead.

Rebecca leaned forward slightly and said, "Many, *many* years. Don't you recognize me?"

The man's eyes brightened a bit and he leaned forward until their faces were inches apart. He studied her eyes and a smirk slowly crossed his face.

"You *do* remember me, don't you?" Rebecca said, fear racing through her as she remembered those eyes staring into hers long ago as he strangled her.

He pulled his head back and let out a loud laugh. Jason felt the urge to run but Rebecca grabbed his arm and kept him still. "You *do* remember me," she whispered.

The man stopped laughing and stared at her intensely. "Maybe," he answered. "But I'm almost certain we've never met. I'm sure of it but yet....I feel like we have."

"Why are you here?" she asked. "How did you find me?"

He smiled a cruel smile. "I have no idea what you're talking about."

"I think that you do," she said grimly and stood up. Jason stood up too and she quietly said, "I'll be watching you."

The man's eyes twinkled with life then. "I'm very honored that you will," he said joyfully.

She looked at Jason then and said, "Let's go."

They were almost at the door when the man yelled, "It's been a pleasure! I hope we meet again!"

Rebecca slowly turned around and to her horror the man held out his hands and pretended he was squeezing something with them. Enraged, Jason was about to launch himself at the man but Rebecca grabbed his arm to stop him. "Later," she whispered.

They stepped outside and Jason said, "You were right, my darling. I'm sorry I didn't believe you."

"I knew it was him," she said grimly. "I just knew it."

"What now? What do we do?"

Her eyes narrowed and he saw the fire in them.

"We wait and watch. He's going to kill again but I'm going to stop him even if it means God gets angry with me."

Jason pulled her close and her anger faded away as she sobbed against him. "Oh Jason!" she cried. "He took my life away! I can't let him kill another woman! I just can't let it happen! Oh, why am I so scared of him?!"

Jason grit his teeth and looked back at the shop. The man was staring out again at them again and smiling.

"Don't worry, Rebecca," he growled. "I promise I won't let him hurt you ever again."

"I don't know why I'm so afraid but I am, Jason. I feel like he could hurt me again."

He sneered back at the grinning man in the window and quietly said, "You came here to save me but now *I'm* going to save you."

She touched his cheek and made him look at her. "You will?" she asked. "You really will?"

His eyes turned soft and he pulled her close and whispered in her ear, "Yes, I promise. Let *me* be your angel now."

CHAPTER FIFTY SIX

Rebecca was very quiet the rest of the day and night and Jason was worried about her. She was obviously deeply troubled by the man they'd seen and he didn't know how to help her.

"Please don't lock me out," he said as they sat in front of the fireplace. "I'm here for you. You know that."

Her eyes were sad. "I know he can't really hurt me again, Jason but when I saw those eyes of his it all came rushing back to me. That evil look of satisfaction in his eyes as my life faded away is something I'll never forget."

"I'm so sorry," he whispered and kissed her cheek as he ran his fingers through her hair.

"How did he find me?" she asked, worried. "Why now? Why today? I wish I knew. It doesn't make sense."

"Please stop worrying," he said. "Remember, you're an angel now. He can't hurt you anymore."

Rebecca looked at him with anguished eyes. "Yes, he can, Jason. By killing more girls he'll be doing it to me all over again. I can't let that happen."

"But how do you know he's a killer again in this life? Maybe he's not."

Her eyes narrowed as she stared into the crackling fire. "His eyes told me. There's that same cruelty there. I know he's the same."

"I don't know what to say about all this, Rebecca," he softly whispered.

He pulled her closer and she let her body meld into his. "This is where I feel the most safe," she whispered. "With you, just like this."

The phone rang then and Jason went to answer it. It was Susanna.

"Merry Christmas, dad!" she cried on the other end. "Jeff and I say hi!"

He smiled. "Merry Christmas, sweetheart."

"Dad? I need to ask you something."

"What?"

"Do you think Rebecca could speak to the men again? They're restless and Jeff seems to be losing them. They're not listening to him as much now. They want *her*."

Jason looked over at Rebecca who was staring at the fire.

"I don't know if she will but I'll ask, alright?"

"Thanks, dad. We could really use her help. Here's the directions to Jeff's place."

He wrote them down as she spoke and said, "Ok, sweetheart, I'll talk to you soon," and hung up the phone.

Rebecca pulled him down to the couch so he could hug her again and asked, "What did Susannah want?"

Jason hesitated and she smiled. "Just tell me, Jason. You know I can get it out of you if I really want to."

He laughed lightly. "She asked us to come back. The men are asking for you."

"What? Why?" she said, surprised. "I said all I could say. Jeff's in charge now."

Jason brushed her cheek lightly with his fingers. "Don't you know, Rebecca? There's no one else like you."

She frowned and he said, "Maybe we should go and see what's going on there. It would help take your mind off of….*him*."

She surprised him when she said, "Maybe you're right."

"When would you like to leave?"

She smiled. "Get your coat and pack a bag with some extra clothes. We'll leave now."

CHAPTER FIFTY SEVEN

When he was dressed for the cold, she took his hand and led him outside. They looked up at the stars and she smiled.

"Would you like to see them up close?"

He nodded and she pulled him close to her body and extended her wings. With a mighty leap, they were in the air in seconds and Jason cried out with joy as his angel's wings beat around them. Rebecca went as high as she could without hurting Jason and he yelled, "I love you!"

She smiled tenderly at him as they flew. "I love you too, my darling."

The wind blew through his hair and he suddenly shivered from the cold but Rebecca pulled him closer and her body warmed him. He felt so incredibly secure and loved and hoped the feeling would stay with him forever.

Hours later, they arrived at Jeff's home and landed. Susanna answered the door when they knocked and her eyes opened wide in surprise. "Oh my God! You're here!" she shouted and threw herself into her father's arms.

He hugged her tightly and she looked at Rebecca.

"Thank you for coming. Thank you so much."

The women hugged then and Jeff appeared from the kitchen. He smiled and came over to shake Jason's hand.

"Hello, my friend," he said and then he saw Rebecca.

"Dear angel," he said softly. "Thank you for coming. We've missed you."

They hugged and he whispered, "Thank God you're here."

They went into the small living room and Jeff and Susanna sat on a small couch by the fireplace while they sat in chairs facing them.

"Tell me what's going on, Jeff," Rebecca said. "Susanna said the men aren't listening to you."

He lowered his head and seemed very tired. "I'm not you, Rebecca."

"What do you mean?"

He stared at her intensely. "I mean *I'm* not you."

He could tell she didn't fully understand and said, "I'm just a man….and they need an angel to lead them."

Rebecca felt very badly and said, "I'm sorry, Jeff but I've done too much here already. I'm sure God will be angry with me if I keep making these unscheduled appearances."

"Just one more time," he asked. "That's all I ask. Please…."

She sighed and quietly said, "When, Jeff?"

"Tomorrow morning. Most of the men will be at work then."

"Alright. Just one more time but that's it," she said firmly.

"Have you eaten?" Susanna asked then.

"We ate before we came but I think your father's tired," Rebecca said. "It was a long journey."

Susanna understood and stood up. "There's an extra bedroom. We can put you in there if you'd like."

"That would be fine," Rebecca said and she and Jason followed his daughter to the bedroom.

"Sleep well," she said and closed the door behind them.

The room was paneled with timber wood and had a log cabin look. A painting of a beautiful sunset hung on the wall and a small lamp sat glowing by the large bed. Rebecca smiled at Jason and whispered, "Let's make love, Jason."

His eyes got big. "We can't. Susanna and Jeff will hear us."

She touched his lips with her fingers and said, "Then we'll just have to be very quiet. Do you think you can do that?"

He nodded and she beamed with pride as he slowly undressed. He blushed from the intimacy he was feeling with her even though they hadn't done anything yet. When he had removed his underwear, her eyes roamed over his naked body with obvious excitement. He stood and waited as she studied him. Her eyes lingered over his flaccid penis for a moment and then she finally pulled off her white dress.

"Jason," she whispered as she moved into his arms. "My Jason…."

Her nipples were hard and pressed against his chest and he shivered at their touch. His hand moved to her mound and felt her there. She was already wet and she put her hand over his and whispered, "Put your finger inside me. I'm ready."

He penetrated her sex then and she lightly bit his shoulder. His finger moved around and she began to moan lightly. "Yes…. yes….just like that."

Jason surprised her then and removed his finger so he could lift her in his arms and lay her on the bed. She pulled the covers back and got underneath them. "Come to bed, my love," she said and he got in beside her. She pulled the covers over them and whispered, "I want your cock in me all night long, Jason."

He smiled and she kissed him so his body would absorb her power. She pulled him close and his cock hardened when it touched her thigh. "Let me put it in," she whispered and guided it between her legs. Jason pushed upwards and his penis sank slowly between the angel's warm folds.

"Oh Rebecca," he whispered. "You feel so good."

She moved slowly with him as they rocked in each other's arms, their bodies pressed tightly together. Jason felt an amazing tingle run up his spine and began to loudly moan. Rebecca placed her hand over his mouth and whispered, "Sshhhhhh."

Jason's eyes grew wide and she knew he was close. "Yes….yes," she whispered. "Cum for me, my love. Cum inside your angel."

"Uugghhh!" he moaned and his cock twitched and burst inside her.

"Yes, fill me with your love," she whispered. "Give me all of you."

Jason felt as if his entire being centered around his penis then and moved faster against her. His cock grew harder and Rebecca felt herself giving in to the pleasure. "Yes," she whispered, her breathing becoming more rapid. "That's it. Fuck me."

Her mouth opened wide in surprise as the wave came out of nowhere and crashed inside her brain. "Oh fuck!" she cried and Jason put his hand over her mouth.

"Ssshhhhh," he whispered and she laughed as the orgasm ripped through her. Her pussy clamped around him and spasmed and if she wasn't already dead then this exquisite moment would have surely killed her.

Afterwards, they lay together and looked into one another's eyes with a love so intense it hurt. Rebecca ran her fingers through Jason's hair and whispered, "You were worth waiting all these years for. There's no other man like you, Jason."

He pulled her close and she rested her head against his chest. "No matter what happens in the future, I'm never going to forget you, Rebecca. You're truly my angel."

She gazed into his eyes and said, "Dream of me while you sleep, Jason and when you wake you'll know I'm here and it wasn't a dream."

He kissed her and closed his eyes. She listened as he began to breathe slower and soon he was fast asleep.

"Can you hear me, Jason?" she asked. "I'm in your dreams now. I'm loving you just as I have when you were awake."

He moaned in his sleep and she whispered, "Yes, my love. I'll *always* be in your dreams."

CHAPTER FIFTY EIGHT

When Jason awoke the next morning, the first thing he saw when he opened his eyes were Rebecca's eyes as she gazed into his. She'd never left him during the night and her body was warm and toasty next to his.

"Am I dreaming about you again?" he whispered, "or are you really here?"

She smiled and reached between their bodies to hold his penis. "Yes, Jason, I'm here and you're not dreaming any longer. My warm hand is holding your cock."

"Oh God, I'm in heaven," he said, his eyes twinkling with love for her.

He began to grow in her hand and she giggled.

"What's so funny?" he asked.

Her eyes teared as she smiled at him. "I was just thinking about breakfast sausage and how I'm holding one in my hand right now."

"You little devil you!" he whispered.

"I hope they don't serve us sausage for breakfast. I don't know if I'll be able to keep a straight face if they do."

"Do you like my sausage, Rebecca?"

"Very much so," she whispered and moved down the length of his body so she could take him into her mouth. Her lips moved up and down his shaft and he clutched the bed with his hands as she pleasured him. "Yummm, you taste kind of smokey," she whispered.

Her tongue swirled around his cockhead and he cried, "Oh God, I'm gonna cum!"

Her hand shot up and covered his mouth as she bobbed up and down. Jason screamed into her hand as her mouth filled with his love. After he'd finished, she held him as he lay panting and covered in sweat.

"Was that good? I know *I* liked it. You've got the best sausage I've ever tasted."

Her fingers traced over his stomach and then to his pubic hair and he moaned as he felt his penis getting hard again. "Oh my," she whispered when she saw it twitch. "Time for an encore."

She ran a finger lightly up and down his length and tickled under the head until it swelled. Jason held his breath and she climbed on top of him and sank down on him. He gasped loudly as her warm bottom rested on his thighs and she smiled down at him. "I want to ride *you* now," she whispered huskily. "You can be my horse."

He grasped her hips and she began to move slowly up and down. Her eyes closed and she began to moan. "*Yes*, Jason.....let me ride you."

He held out for as long as possible and she fell across him and lightly bit his earlobe. "Wait for me, my love," she whispered as her hips moved faster. Her sex gripped him tightly and his toes curled in anticipation. "Now," she finally said and her eyes flicked open wide as she came. "Oh Jason!" she cried. "Oh God! I love you so!"

He began to sob and thrust up into her. His cock exploded and she kissed him so passionately that she bruised his lips.

"Mmmmmm," they moaned together and another orgasm fluttered through their bodies as they trembled with intense pleasure.

Afterwards, they lay in each other's arms and listened to the silence. "You were right, Jason," she said. "This *is* heaven. I've found heaven on earth here with you."

CHAPTER FIFTY NINE

Rebecca lay in bed and stretched her arms as she waited for Jason to finish showering. His penis was bright red and raw looking when he came out and she felt badly.

"Oh my. Did I do that?"

"It's alright," he said.

"Does it hurt a lot?"

"No, it'll be fine soon."

"I hope so," she said, worried. "You know, if you want me to I can make it feel better by kissing it for a while."

Jason laughed and covered his groin with his hands. "No! Stay away from me! It might fall off if you do!"

Rebecca laughed and patted the bed. "Come back to bed, baby," she purred. "I want to wrestle."

Jason felt his mouth go dry and she sat up and spread her legs. "I'm lonely down here, Jason. I need you again."

His sore cock hardened at her words and he moved to the bed so she could cup his balls in her hand. Gazing up at his face, she quietly said, "I promise I'll be gentle, Jason. Do you have more cum in these for me?"

He moaned as she fondled his sac but after a moment reluctantly pulled away. Rebecca pouted and said, "What's wrong, baby? Am I too much of a woman for you?"

"It's not that," he said and looked at the small clock on the nightstand. "We have to get going. I'm sure Susannah and Jeff are waiting for us so we can talk about the meeting later."

"The men?" she said. "Can't they wait? I'm not done with you yet."

He laughed and leaned over her to kiss her. "You're the sexiest woman I've ever known. Did you know that?"

Before she could answer, they heard a loud noise in another room.

"They must be up," Jason said and began to get dressed.

"I think I'll lie here for a while and smell the scent of our love in the air. It's all around us, Jason. Can you smell it?"

"I only smell the wonderful scent of that gorgeous pussy of yours," he said and she smiled happily. He kissed her then and went to open the door. He smiled once more at her and stepped out. She could hear him moving around the house.

"Susannah? Jeff?" he called and she got out of bed. She slipped on her white dress and went to join him in the kitchen. He was holding a piece of paper and looked at her.

"They left us a note. They should be back soon. They went to get groceries."

"Do you think we have time for some more loving? Just a little?" she asked and moved into his arms.

He kissed her and heard a knock at the front door. He was about to go and open it but she said, "No, I'll do it. You still look a little flushed. We don't want Susannah and Jeff to think we were doing anything naughty now, do we?"

Jason laughed and sat down. Rebecca blew him a kiss and walked towards the front door. "I'm coming," she said as she opened it.

The shotgun blast hit her in the chest and she flew backwards against the far wall and slumped to the floor. Jason jumped out of his seat and ran into the room to see Matt standing over Rebecca. A large shotgun was in his good hand. The tip was smoking and he took aim and snarled, "Bitch!"

He shot her again and part of her shoulder was blown away. She moaned in pain and Jason screamed, "No!!!!" and ran at him.

Matt was surprised as Jason's charge drove him away from Rebecca. She tried to move but groaned in agony as her wounds slowly healed.

Jason tried to wrestle the gun out of Matt's hand as they rolled on the floor but he was too strong and drove the butt into his head.

Dazed, Jason saw the hate in the man's eyes and knew he was in a fight for his life.

"Asshole!" Matt yelled. "The angel cunt had it coming! Now you're gonna die too!"

"No!" Jason yelled and punched as hard as he could into Matt's throat. He gagged and stood up on shaky legs. Jason got to his feet but Matt pulled the trigger then and shot him in the chest. The blast knocked him off his feet and drove him to the floor.

Rebecca got to her feet and Matt turned to see she was almost completely healed. There was only a small hole left in her chest and it was closing rapidly. "What the hell?" he whispered, shocked. "How?"

"Asshole," she said and grit her teeth as she prepared to launch herself at him.

He pulled the trigger again and the top part of her skull was blown away. "Oh no," she whispered and held her hand over the massive wound. "Oh God….no."

Jason lay in agony and saw her slump to the floor. Matt laughed and shot her again. Her stomach exploded and a fine mist of blood floated in the air around them. "No…." Jason moaned. "Rebecca…."

Matt kicked her in the face and she fell over sideways and stared at Jason with terrified eyes. He began to crawl towards her and grabbed a hold of Matt's ankle. "Don't….please don't," he begged.

The man turned and sneered at him. "You die first and then that fat pig, Jeff. I'll save Susannah for last. I promise I'll take my time with her."

"No…." Jason moaned.

Matt raised the gun and placed the nozzle against Jason's forehead.

"Say goodbye, asshole," he said and Jason closed his eyes and waited for death.

"No!!!!" Rebecca screamed and drove Matt back with such force that a few of his ribs cracked when she hit him in the chest. He fell to the floor and looked up at her head as it continued to heal.

"What the hell are you?" he asked. "Why won't you die?"

Rebecca sneered down at him. "I'm one of God's angels, asshole."

He smiled grimly then and quickly turned with the gun and aimed it at Jason. Just before his finger could pull the trigger, Rebecca launched herself at him with frightening speed and grabbed his head in her hands. "You'll never hurt anyone ever again," she snarled and twisted his head completely around.

Jason heard the loud crack as his neck broke and stared in horror at Rebecca. She looked down at the dead man and let go of him and slowly stood up. "My God," she whispered. "What have I done?"

She looked at her hands and to his horror Jason saw them begin to fade away. "What have I done?!" she screamed and looked at Jason with wide eyes.

She rushed to him and cried, "I killed him, Jason! I killed him!"

He moaned in pain and she gently touched his face with what remained of her fingers as they disappeared. He was able to see through her as she began to fade away and she cried, "Jason! Please remember me always! Remember that I love you!"

She stood up and looked down at him with great tenderness. "I'll never forget you, Jason," she said, her voice trembling.

He raised his arm to her. "Please, Rebecca! Don't leave me!" but she smiled sadly and was almost gone.

"God's punishing me for taking a life, Jason. I have to go."

"No!!!"

"Keep on being the man I know you are, Jason," she whispered. "You're a hero. Never forget that."

"Please don't go!" he cried and the last thing that was left of her were her sad eyes.

"I love you," she whispered and then was gone.

"Rebecca....my angel," he moaned and then faded into unconsciousness.

CHAPTER SIXTY

Jeff and Susanna found Jason lying unconscious on the floor tightly clutching the locket around his neck. Matt's body lay a few feet away with his eyes open in horror.

"Dad!" Susanna screamed and rushed to him. He moaned and opened his eyes.

"Rebecca….she's gone," he groaned. "She's gone forever."

"What the hell happened here?" Jeff asked when he realized Matt's head was twisted at an odd angle.

"We've got to get dad to the hospital!" Susannah cried then when she saw the bloody wound in his chest.

Jeff saw how bad it looked and said, "I'll drive us there. It'll be faster."

He picked Jason up in his strong arms and carried him out to his truck where they laid him gently in the back seat. Susannah sat in the back with her father and held his head in her lap as Jeff raced to the hospital. "We're almost there, dad," she said. "You're going to be alright."

He could barely keep his eyes open. "Rebecca," he moaned. "My angel…."

Susanna wiped tears from her eyes. "Dad, stay with me. Please don't go to her."

"Rebecca…." he moaned and closed his eyes as he entered a darkness he'd never known before.

He was afraid and stood quietly in the cool air. He could see nothing and felt terribly alone. "Rebecca, where are you?"

A soft hand suddenly touched his face but he wasn't startled. The touch was familiar. It was Rebecca.

"Jason," she whispered. "It's not your time yet. You must go back."

He grabbed her hand tightly and began to cry. "Please don't send me away! I don't want to leave you!"

She pulled her hand from his and it lightly touched his face. "You must, Jason. The world needs you."

"Oh please….no…." he cried.

The hand left his face then and he was suddenly pushed in the chest. He slowly floated backwards and when he looked behind he saw a light in the distance. He held his arms out and screamed, "No!!!! Let me stay with you!"

"I love you," the angel's voice whispered and his eyes popped open.

"Oh dad! I thought you were gone!" Susannah cried happily. "I thought you'd died!"

He began to cry and she softly said, "Rebecca's watching over you, dad and she always will."

They arrived at the hospital and after a minute hospital personnel rushed out and placed him on a gurney. As he was rushed into surgery, he saw the grim look on the nurses faces.

"Don't worry," he said. "An angel's watching over me."

CHAPTER SIXTY ONE

Jason awoke to the sound of beeping. He opened his eyes and saw only darkness for a moment. *Where am I?* he wondered. He looked to his right and saw a machine with a bag of fluid hanging from a hook. A tube ran from it and he followed its length and saw it was inserted into his arm. *I'm in the hospital again,* he thought sadly.

Someone was sitting in the darkness next to his bed and he tried to focus on them. He hoped it was Rebecca but deep down knew it wasn't.

"Dad?" Susanna said and held his hand. "It's ok. I'm here."

"Susannah," he croaked. She held a glass of water to his lips and he took a sip which made his dry throat feel better.

"We've been very worried about you," she said. "You've been unconscious for days."

"Rebecca. I want Rebecca."

"Dad," she said softly. "I'm sorry. I don't know where she is. What happened back at Jeff's house? The police can't figure it out. It makes no sense."

His eyes filled with tears and he whispered, "Matt….he tried to kill us but she stopped him and God took her away from me."

"What?" Susannah said, alarmed. "What do you mean he took her away?"

Jason remembered the anguish he felt as his angel faded away and said, "She faded away right before my eyes, Susannah. God punished her for killing Matt."

"Oh no," she whispered and lowered her head. "Oh no."

"I won't ever see her again!" he cried and pounded the bed with his fist. "Why! Why did this have to happen?! I can't live without her!"

Susannah leaned close to gently touch his cheek.

"Dad," she said softly. "You *must* continue living. Rebecca would want you to. You know that. If you won't do it for her, then do it for me."

"I don't know if I can, Susannah. She was everything to me."

"You can and you will," she said, her voice firm. "Remember, she was only here to show you your purpose in life. Everything else was a bonus. You knew it would end sometime."

Jason was hurt by her bluntness but knew she was right. "I know, Susannah but I miss her terribly. I've never loved another woman like that before."

"Not even mom?"

"No," he quietly answered. "Not even your mother."

Susannah let go of his hand then and stood up. Jason could tell she was angry and said, "I'm sorry. I figured you wanted the truth."

She wiped tears from her eyes with the back of her hand and said, "I know but it still hurts."

He reached his hand out to her but she backed away from the bed. "I'll see you tomorrow, dad. Goodnight," she said and quickly left the room.

Jason lay in the dark and tears rolled down his cheeks. *Oh my sweet angel,* he thought. *I wish you were here.*

He looked at the chair Susanna had been sitting in and thought back to the night he'd woken up in the hospital and Rebecca had first appeared by his side.

"I miss you so much," he whispered. "I'll try to live a good life but I don't think I'll ever love anyone again."

He closed his eyes and hoped she'd appear but only the darkness surrounded him and he cried himself to sleep.

CHAPTER SIXTY TWO

The next morning the surgeon who'd operated on him visited. He stared long and hard at Jason and said, "I've been reading your medical history this past month. How many lives do you have anyway?"

Jason couldn't help but smile at the question and replied, "An angel watches over me."

"I'm sure one does," the surgeon said. "That blast you took sprayed around your heart somehow but didn't touch it. I've never seen anything like it. It should have been shredded and you'd be dead now."

Jason suddenly remembered the locket and touched his neck. It was gone and he screamed, "Oh my God! Where is it?!"

"Relax," the man said. "Your personal items are in the closet here. Your clothes though were thrown out. Unfortunately, they were covered in blood and beyond hope."

"I don't care about them! I need my locket!"

The surgeon stared at him in a curious way and went to the closet to retrieve the box. He brought it over and opened it. "There it is," he said and Jason reached inside and grabbed it.

The man saw how Jason's eyes lit up and he wondered what the big deal was about the object. It was just a plain dull glass locket attached to a chain. There didn't seem to be anything special about it in any way that he could see.

"Thank you," Jason said and seemed to calm down. He held the locket in his hand and the man nodded.

"I'll be in to check on you later. At the rate you're healing I'd say you'll be out of here in a day or two."

Jason waited until the man left the room so he could look at the locket. He frowned when he saw it wasn't glowing and hooked it around his neck. When it touched his upper chest it began to pulsate again with light and he smiled and lifted it to his face.

"My angel," he whispered and kissed it. "My sweet angel."

CHAPTER SIXTY THREE

With the locket around his neck again, Jason healed even more rapidly. Though he was still very sad, he felt Rebecca was with him in a way.

Susanna was cold to him when she arrived a day later to take him back home. "Will you be ok, dad?" she asked, her eyes showing no emotion. "It'll be a long drive."

"Yes, I'll be fine. I need to get back to work. I've been away long enough."

She had brought some clothes for him and stood outside the room while he dressed. When he finished she came back in and he could see the hurt in her eyes. "Susanna, before we go we have to talk."

Her face was set in stone. "We have nothing to talk about, dad."

"*Please,*" he said and took her hand. "Please….just for a minute."

She sighed and sat down on the chair near the bed while he stood and looked down at her. He waited a moment as he tried to collect his thoughts. *Don't fuck this up*, he thought.

"Susannah," he finally said, "I loved your mother very much."

"No, you didn't," she said quickly.

"Why do you say that?" he asked. "How would you know?"

Her eyes glistened with tears and her lower lip quivered. "In all the years I lived with you, you never looked at mom the way you looked at Rebecca. Don't tell me you loved her because you didn't."

Jason looked down at the floor and knew what he was about to say could possibly destroy his relationship with his daughter.

"Susannah," he said, looking again at her, "You're wrong. I *did* love your mother but not like I loved Rebecca. She was different as you know."

Susannah couldn't help but smile slightly at the comment and said, "I know she was different, dad. She was special."

He knelt in front of her and held her hands. "Your mother and I...

you didn't know this but we knew long ago we weren't soulmates."

"So you had a loveless marriage?" Susannah asked, her eyes brimming with pain.

"No," he said gently. "You're not listening. Your mother and I cared deeply for each other but we both realized that we weren't the end all to each other. Even when we were together we knew something was missing between us. We were both lonely in a way. Do you understand what I'm saying?"

"Let me guess," she said bitterly. "You're saying Rebecca was a better fuck than mom, is that it?"

Her words hurt and he winced. "No….I'm not going to talk to you about that. It's none of your business."

She stared at him angrily and stood up. "C'mon, let's go," she said coldly.

Jason clenched his fists and his eyes blazed then as he stood up. "Don't you understand?!" he yelled. "I think Rebecca was my soulmate! I loved her! I need her! She was everything to me!"

He sat on the bed and covered his face with his hands and began to sob. Susannah stared at him for a moment and felt her anger dissipate. She sat down next to him and asked, "What do you mean you *think* she was your soulmate, dad? Didn't she ever tell you that she was?"

He took his hands away and stared with anguished eyes at his daughter. "No, she never did but I feel it somehow. I should have asked."

Susannah reached for his hand and he took it. "I'm sorry, dad," she said. "I'm so very sorry for you."

CHAPTER SIXTY FOUR

They sat and waited for a nurse to bring a wheelchair when three men walked into the room. They looked very serious and the older one stared at Jason and said, "Going somewhere?"

"Why? Who are you?" Jason asked.

The man pulled a badge from his coat and held it up. "Detective Benson. I need to ask you a few questions before you can leave. I need a few things cleared up."

"Alright," Jason said quietly and Susannah held his hand tightly.

"From what your daughter told me, this Matt fellow wasn't a very nice man. I can't honestly say it's bad that he's dead but I need to know exactly what happened."

Jason's mind raced as he contemplated what to say before answering and said, "I was in the bedroom and heard a knock on the door. I went to answer it and he attacked me with the gun. We fought and he shot me. That's when I finally passed out."

The man smiled and knew he had Jason dead in his sights. "Really? Then how was his neck broken? You couldn't have done it while you were passed out. Besides, the coroner said his head had been completely twisted around. It required tremendous strength to do that and I know it wasn't you that did it so why don't you tell me what really happened."

"Maybe he fell after shooting me and broke his neck that way," Jason said, hopeful.

The detective burst out laughing and smiled at his two men. "That's funny! That's real funny!"

Jason looked nervously at Susannah and she knew he couldn't mention Rebecca.

"Wasn't there a woman with you?" Detective Benson asked then, his face serious.

Jason turned pale and asked, "Why would you ask that?"

The man's eyes beamed brightly. "Because I've asked around town and was told a woman accompanies you on your visits to this quiet town. Where is she?"

Jason gulped hard. "I have no idea what you're talking about."

The man leaned down and said, "I heard she's a real fighter."

"Who told you that?"

"Some of the men in town....some of the ones she beat up. It seems she can really handle herself."

Jason looked at Susannah and the detective said, "Your daughter can't help you, Jason. Now tell me where this woman....I think Rebecca is her name....where is she?"

"She isn't here."

"You mean she isn't here now or she wasn't here at all to begin with."

"Both," Jason answered.

The man's shoulders slumped a little and he sighed. "The only reason I'm letting you go is because I know you couldn't have killed Matt but mark my words I'll be searching for that woman friend of yours."

"You won't find her."

"How do you know?"

Jason's eyes were sad and he quietly said, "Because she's gone."

The detective was clearly frustrated and said, "Ok, we're getting nowhere here. Take care of yourself and just know that wherever you are you'll be watched. I want to talk to that woman. I know she's the answer to all this."

"Why are you pushing this? He was a bad man. He deserved to die," Jason said defiantly. "Leave us alone."

Detective Benson stared at Jason for long seconds until finally saying, "We'll see."

He and his men left the room then and Susanna's phone rang. She answered it and looked at Jason as she talked. "Yes, ok....ok....we'll be there," she said finally and hung up. She looked at Jason and said, "We can't go home yet. The men are restless."

CHAPTER SIXTY FIVE

They drove to the lumberyard and Jeff greeted them and shook Jason's hand. "I'm sorry about this but they want Rebecca. Maybe you could talk to them instead," he said.

Jason was visibly annoyed. "I don't understand. You were supposed to be in charge of this. I'm not Rebecca. I don't know what to say."

"Please, Jason," Jeff pleaded. "Please help me out here."

"Fine. Let's get this over with."

He went and stood at the spot where the angel had spoken to the men before. The men were gathered in small clusters in the yard and a few spotted him and shouted, "Where's Rebecca?! We want Rebecca!"

Jason reached under his collar and pulled the locket out. Its pulsing soft glow calmed him and he waved the men closer. Looking down at them, he asked, "Can you all hear me?"

"Yeah, we can hear you!" a man yelled. "Where's the angel? Why isn't she here?"

I don't want to do this, Jason thought but he suddenly pictured Rebecca's face in his mind and smiled. *I can do this. I have to do this for her.*

"I know I'm not who you were expecting," he said.

"Damn right you're not!" a man shouted.

Jason raised his arms and waved them to calm the grumbling that started. "Listen to me! Please just give me a chance to explain."

The men quieted down and Jason suddenly knew exactly what to say. "Rebecca's gone back to heaven. God has an important job for her. I don't know what it is but she asked me to tell you that you should continue spreading his love. Be kind to one another and the world will slowly become a better place."

A man sneered and yelled, "How do we know she said that?! Who the hell are you?"

Jason felt tears in his eyes then and answered, "Who am I? I'm the man she chose to love."

He lowered his head and quietly said, "I'm the luckiest man in the world. You can believe what I'm telling you."

The yard was completely silent then until a man yelled, "Will she be back?!"

Jason raised his head and tears rolled down his cheeks. "I don't think so," he answered. His face flushed then as the locket suddenly glowed brighter around his neck and flooded his body with her power. He raised his fist in the air and shouted, "But why should that stop us! Who are we?!"

The men smiled and surged towards him. "The army of God!" they screamed in unison.

Jason put a hand to his ear and screamed, "I can't hear you! Who are we?!"

The men raised their arms and screamed louder. "The army of God!!!"

The light from the locket suddenly exploded outward and sprayed over the entire yard so quickly the men didn't even have a chance to blink. It was over so fast they stood in shock and Jason smiled and watched as the locket went back to its original state.

Stunned, the men looked at each other and began to smile. They patted each other on the shoulders and looked up at Jason with an intensity in their eyes that made him shudder. He smiled and whispered, "Who are we? What are we? What will the world become?"

The power of the angel was in the men now and they'd never look back. They raised their arms together and shouted, "The army of God!"

"Yes!" Jason screamed joyfully. "We!.... are!.... the army of God!"

Susannah and Jeff went to stand by him and she asked, "What the hell just happened?"

Jason looked at her, smiled brightly and said, "Rebecca spoke to them. She spoke to them through me."

CHAPTER SIXTY SIX

Jason felt exhausted then and said, "Please take me home."

It was a long drive and Jason slept most of the way. His stomach wound had almost fully healed but it still ached a little. When they hit a bump in the road, he'd groan in pain. Susannah kept glancing over at him to make sure he was alright and every now and then he moaned and mumbled, "No….no….don't go."

Susannah grew worried and finally shook his shoulder. "Dad….wake up. You're having a bad dream."

His eyes shot open and she asked, "You were dreaming about her, weren't you?"

He didn't answer but stared at the road ahead and she said, "Dad, she's gone. She may never come back."

He looked at her and whispered, "I know."

Susannah kissed him on the cheek when they arrived at his place "Will you be alright?"

"Yes," he replied. "Thanks for bringing me home. I love you, Susanna."

"I love you too, dad. Please stay safe."

He nodded and she got in her car and left for home.

Jason stood outside his building and looked up at the stars in the sky. One small dot of light twinkled and he whispered, "I wish I was that star, Rebecca so I could be closer to you."

He went inside then and when he was inside his apartment the silence hit him immediately. It was the kind of silence one felt after a beloved pet died. The emptiness in the air was cruel and final and hurt badly.

Jason took his coat off and started a fire in the fireplace. He sat down in front of it then and stared into the flickering flames. The logs began to crackle and he felt a tear slip down his face.

"Why God?" he asked. "Why did you take her away from me? She was good and pure. I love her so much."

He sat for hours until the fire began to die out. His eyes began to get tired and just as he felt himself drifting off a strand of smoke stretched out of the fire in front of him and came closer. He watched as it moved around as if blown by the wind and it became larger. His eyes grew bigger as it began to take the shape of a dim figure. "Rebecca?" he asked, hopeful. "Is that you?"

The figure became more detailed and soon a tall woman stood in front of him. Her white dress looked just like the one Rebecca had worn and her long black hair covered her bare shoulders. She was very beautiful and her eyes were kind as she looked at him.

"You must be Jason," her sweet voice said.

"Who are you?" he asked, bewildered by her presence.

She moved closer and said, "Rebecca sent me."

"She sent you?!" he cried. "Oh God, I miss her so much! Where is she?!"

The angel's face turned sad. "God is very angry with her. She's being punished."

"But why?" he asked. "She only killed to save me."

She stared at him and slowly knelt in front of him. "That's what puzzles us. You must be very special for her to have crossed that line we never cross."

"I'm not special. I'm just a man," he said and lowered his head.

Her soft fingers touched his chin and pushed up to make him look at her. She gazed into his eyes and seemed to be exploring them. He felt a soft probing sensation in his head then and she smiled. "I see now what she sees in you. You *are* special."

Jason's lower lip trembled and he whispered, "I miss her so much. Will she ever come back to me?"

The angel stood up and nodded sadly. "No, Jason, she may never come back. She asked me to check on you to make sure you're alright."

"Tell her I'm not alright. I'm not."

The angel stared hard at him and pursed her lips. "Jason, you must go on without her."

"But I miss her….so much," he whispered.

The angel could hear the ache in his voice and said, "Rebecca loves you with all of her heart, Jason. Always remember that."

He nodded and she slowly faded away. The loneliness in his heart overwhelmed him then and he hugged himself tightly. "Please God," he whispered. "Don't be angry with her. She did it for me. I'm to blame. Only me."

God didn't answer and Jason lay his head back and fell into a deep sleep. The locket began to glow around his neck then and his heart suddenly felt less lonely. "I'm here with you," Rebecca whispered as he lay dreaming. "I'll *always* be with you."

CHAPTER SIXTY SEVEN

The library was as uninviting as ever the next morning when he walked in. No one asked how he was except Peter who looked very solemn. "Welcome back, man. We need to talk."

They went to the basement and Margo, the department head who'd ignored him for months was waiting there for them. Peter looked very nervous and the woman said, "We have a new job for you. You'll be in charge of cleaning our media."

"What?" Jason said and she led him to a corner closet where a large machine stood. He had heard they were getting a very expensive piece of equipment that would grind scratches from DVD's and CD's.

"Here's the manual," she said and handed him a small booklet. "You'll be doing this every day each morning. I want a report at the end of each week telling me your progress. Start with the action films and go from there."

Jason felt the rage growing in him. "I was a supervisor for over thirty years. This is really what you want me to do?"

"Sorry," she said and he knew she genuinely meant it. She didn't wait for his reaction and headed into the elevator.

Jason turned to Peter who looked ashamed. "Sorry, man," his old assistant said and he turned and went to join her.

Jason stood stunned and felt the tears in his eyes. He knew in his heart that they were trying everything possible to make him leave. His humiliation was complete and through tear blurred eyes he read the small booklet so he could learn the machine. After a few minutes of inspecting a few parts he'd have to clean after a certain number of uses, he headed upstairs and grabbed a book cart. Everyone in the department turned and looked at him and his shame was complete. He didn't look at them and went out to the shelves to retrieve the first batch of DVD's.

As he began to remove the movies from the shelves, a man who was known as a trouble patron moved close to him and got in the way. He looked at Jason and smiled as he farted.

"You're disgusting," Jason whispered.

A woman across the aisle made a face. "You're sick! What's wrong with you, dude?!"

She looked angrily at Jason. "You work here. Why don't you do something?!"

The man grunted and farted again. Jason gagged and stumbled away. He could hear the woman screaming at the jerk so he went to the security office and found Alan, the head of maintenance who also ran security for the library. The man was lazy and overweight and Jason wondered how he'd ever gotten the job.

"Alan, you know that creep that harasses the girls at the front desk? He just farted near me and a woman. She's really pissed."

Alan got that patronizing look on his face like he always did and settled back in his chair. He looked way too comfortable and smugly said, "Now Jason, I can't stop people from farting. I'm sorry the woman was offended but there's really nothing I can do."

Jason wanted to scream, "You're useless!" but he just nodded his head and walked away. He suddenly heard yelling in the distance and ran to where it was coming from.

"I swear I'll break this chair over your head!" a man's voice yelled.

A chill ran down Jason's spine as he recognized the voice. It was the big man who didn't like noise. He was the black sheep from some super rich family. His name was Art Ponce and had a reputation of threatening patrons in the past who made noise near him. Staff were absolutely terrified of him and the library had already met with him in the hopes he'd calm down after discussing the issue but it didn't do any good. The man was a raving nut job and Jason was sick and tired of the way the library allowed people like him to get away with disturbing everyone else.

"I said shut the fuck up!" Art screamed and Jason found him in the history section between some shelving units holding a chair above his head. A shelver he knew named Jim had been shifting books and now cowered in the corner on the floor staring up at the crazed man. He looked absolutely terrified. Jason slowly came up behind the lunatic and said, "Art, put the chair down."

The man whirled around and Jason knew he wasn't all there. His enraged eyes looked madly at Jason through his dirty glasses. "Who the fuck are you?!" he shouted.

Jason raised his hands slowly. "Hey, calm down. You're disturbing everyone."

"I don't give a shit!" he screamed, spittle flying from his mouth. "This asshole won't be quiet! I warned him!"

Jason fought back his anger and quietly said, "Art, listen to me. You need to calm down *now*."

"Or what?!" the man yelled. "Who's gonna make me?! You?!"

He laughed and Jason looked over his six foot five frame. He wasn't particularly muscular looking but Jason knew that a whack job like this possessed crazy strength.

The man broke into an evil grin then and moved towards Jason with the chair. "Stop, Art," Jason said quietly. "Don't make me hurt you."

The man's eyes opened wide in anger and he raised the chair higher to strike Jason. "Watch out!" Jim cried but Jason had already moved out of the way. The chair crashed against the floor and Jason swung from his hips. The punch hit the creep flush in the jaw and his head snapped back. His eyes rolled back in his head and he began to fall but Jason caught him in his arms and gently lowered him to the floor.

"Get security," he told Jim who watched, amazed.

Minutes later, Alan came rushing over and his jaw dropped when he saw Jason standing over the big man everyone had been afraid of.

"Holy shit," he whispered. "It's Art Ponce. What the hell happened?"

"He was threatening to break a chair over Jim's head here so I asked him to put it down. He was going to attack me then so I hit him."

"With what? A crowbar?" he asked, amazed. He bent down and touched the unconscious man's neck. "He's breathing," he said.

He stood up and called the police and then an ambulance.

Art Ponce began to moan and was partially awake when they arrived. After hearing Jason's story the police escorted the ambulance to the hospital. Peter came over and said, "Mrs. Walton wants to talk to you."

Jason sighed and Peter said, "She doesn't sound very happy. Be nice and get out of there as fast as you can."

Jason started to walk away and Peter suddenly said, "Hey! I forgot to ask how your girlfriend is!"

Jason felt the sadness deep inside and quietly answered, "We broke up, Pete. We're not together anymore."

"Oh, I'm sorry. She seemed so nice."

"She was, Pete. She was an angel."

He headed upstairs and the frail secretary led him to the director's office.

Mrs. Walton told him to close the door and motioned for him to have a seat. He picked the one that was farthest from her. They sat staring at one another for a long minute which Jason found nerve wracking.

"What the hell do you think you're doing?" the woman finally asked.

"What do you mean?" Jason asked, not understanding.

She leaned forward in her chair and her cruel eyes blazed into his. "I *mean*….you hit a patron, Jason."

"He was threatening one of our shelvers and when I told him to stop he attacked me. I had no choice but to stop him."

"I've been hearing quite a bit about you lately, Jason. You seem to be quite the hero in fact."

She laughed then and said, "But here you're nothing."

Jason's face turned ashen and he felt as if his heart had been stabbed. "What did you say?" he whispered.

She smiled cruelly. "How do you like your new job, Jason?"

His face flushed and he'd never felt smaller in his entire life.

"Why?" he asked quietly. "You're the director. Why are you treating me like this?"

The woman's smile lingered a moment longer and she looked away. "I don't care if you're a hero or not. To me, Jason, you're just a man who's outlived his usefulness."

She'd brushed him aside as if he were nothing and he stood up, clenching his fists. "You can't talk to me like this," he said as he tried in vain to control his heartrate. "I'm *not* a nobody. I have a purpose in life. I *mean* something."

She laughed and brushed back her hair. "You mean nothing, Jason and if you tell anyone what I said I'll just deny I said it. You can go now."

He stood trembling in humiliation and felt the tears dripping down his cheeks. She wouldn't look at him and had turned her back to resume typing on her computer. Jason turned and headed to the door and just before he opened it, she turned and said, "By the way, how's that girlfriend of yours?"

Jason felt empty inside and looked back at her. She was grinning and he knew she was enjoying his suffering. "We're not together anymore," he answered.

She stifled a laugh. "I'm not surprised. Why would any girl want to be with a man whose job is cleaning DVD's?"

Her cruelty struck him like a hammer and his eyes blurred with tears. He turned and headed back downstairs to resume his duties.

Pete came over and asked him how everything went but Jason didn't answer him. He kept quietly to himself for the rest of the day and worked like a robot. When it was time to leave, he punched out and didn't say goodbye to anyone.

The apartment was cold when he got home and he called the landlord to tell him the heat was out. He kept his coat on and fell asleep in his favorite recliner. His joints ached and he felt very old and weary. He didn't know how long he'd been asleep but a knock on his door woke him up. He opened it and was surprised to see Jim, the shelver standing in the hallway.

"Jim! What are you doing here?"

"Mr. Wilkes, I just wanted to come in person and say thanks for what you did for me."

The boy was about sixteen or so and had started at the library only a few months before. He reminded Jason of himself when he'd started there all those years ago.

"You don't have to thank me, Jim," he said. "I did what should have been done a long time ago. The library's been way too lenient with troublemakers in my opinion."

"I know what you mean!" the teen laughed. "They don't seem to care about the people who matter."

"I know….I know," Jason agreed.

"Well, I guess that's it," Jim said. "See you tomorrow at work."

"Goodnight, Jim and thanks for stopping by."

Jason was about to close the door but something about the way the boy was looking at him told him not to. "Jim, would you like to come in? Do you want to talk?"

The teen's eyes lit up. "Oh, that would be great! Thanks, Mr Wilkes!"

"Call me Jason, alright?"

"Ok, Jason," Jim said and stepped inside.

Jason saw the boy shiver. "The damn heat's out. Would you like to wear one of my coats while you're here?"

"Yes please."

Jason went and got a coat for him and they sat down in front of
the fireplace. Jason slapped his head in frustration then and began to
make a fire. "Man, I'm such an idiot," he said. "Why was I sitting in
the cold when there's this?!"

They sat in silence in front of the fire and after a while the room
felt warm enough that they could remove their coats.

"Mr. Wilkes….I mean Jason….can I ask you something?" the teen
said, breaking the silence.

"Sure, Jim. Ask me anything."

The boy stared at the floor. "Do you have a girlfriend?" he asked
shyly.

Jason smiled and realized where the conversation was probably
heading. "Why do you want to know, Jim?"

"Oh, I was just wondering," the boy said.

Jason was quiet for a moment but then said, "I did have one, Jim
but now she's gone."

"I'm sorry. Was she nice?"

"She was the nicest girl I've ever known. I miss her terribly," Jason
answered.

"Can I ask you something about her?"

"Sure, Jim. What do you want to know?"

"How did you ask her out? I mean what did you say to get her to
like you?"

Jason thought of all the reasons that he and Rebecca had been
attracted to one another and said, "I didn't say anything to get her to
like me, Jim. She just accepted me for who I was and I accepted her
for who she was."

Jason could sense the angst in the teen. "Who is she, Jim?"

He blushed and said, "Its Jill, Jill Monroe. You know, the shelver
from work."

Jason remembered the shy girl from the library. She was tall and had long brown hair and pretty eyes. "Oh yes, I know her. She's very nice."

Jim smiled. "Yes, she is. She's shy but the way she looks at me makes me…."

Jason nodded knowingly. "Let me guess. When she looks at you it's as if her eyes are looking inside of you. Am I right?"

"How did you know that?" the boy asked, surprised.

"Because that's how my….because that's how my angel looked at me, Jim."

The teen lowered his head and quietly said, "When I'm around her, I feel powerless sometimes."

Jim chuckled and said, "You know what, Jim? The feeling you're describing is called "love." If she looks at you like that then it means something. Just surrender to it, Jim. Don't fight it."

"But I'm afraid," Jim said. "A guy's not supposed to feel "weak."

"You're not weak, Jim. When a woman picks you just thank your lucky stars that you've been chosen."

"You make it sound so nice, Jason. I really like her and I know we're both just sixteen but I….I feel like she might be the one. Does that sound stupid?"

Jason stood up and smiled down at the teen. "Jim, it doesn't sound stupid at all. Get to know Jill and after a while you'll both know if you're meant for each other."

The boy stood up and shook Jason's hand. "Thanks, Jason," he said. "I'm glad I came here. I wish I could talk to my dad about these things but he drinks and doesn't have time for me."

"I'm sorry to hear that. You're welcome anytime, Jim. I'll be here whenever you need to talk."

Jason yawned then and said, "I'm sorry but I need to hit the sack. It's been a long day."

Jim nodded and Jason saw him out. He closed the door and went into the kitchen to get a bite to eat. He made himself a sandwich and ate it quickly. Afterwards, he turned the TV on but didn't really pay attention to what was on and turned it off. The silence was deafening and combined with the lack of heat his apartment felt like he imagined a crypt would feel. He headed to the bedroom and took off his clothes and stood naked looking at himself in the dresser mirror. He was still muscular from years of physical work at the library but the wear and tear of the job had taken a toll on his joints and they ached terribly. The hair on his chest and in his beard was beginning to turn gray and some specks of silver were in his thick dark brown hair. *I'm getting old*, he thought. *I feel old. Maybe I'll get lucky and freeze to death tonight.*

He shivered from the cold and got into bed. The covers were freezing but he pulled them up over his body anyway. Closing his eyes, he fell into a restless sleep. He began to moan from the cold and that's when the locket began to glow and emit warmth. It entered his chest first and he stopped shivering as the soothing heat slowly spread throughout his body. He suddenly woke up and smiled. "Rebecca," he whispered. "You're here with me."

The locket glowed brighter and he closed his eyes again and drifted off into a peaceful slumber. He would sleep well this night. His angel was with him.

CHAPTER SIXTY EIGHT

The phone rang before he woke up and he groaned and reached for it.

"Dad!" Susannah yelled into his ear. "Did you see the email I sent you?!"

"No," he said and rubbed his eyes. "I didn't. I was asleep."

"Oh….sorry I woke you. Look at the email. Dad….it's spreading. It's started."

Jason had no idea what she was talking about and said, "Ok….ok….I'll look at it now."

She said goodbye and hung up. He got out of bed and took a shower. Then he put on some clothes and made himself a bowl of oatmeal and sat down at the computer. Susanna's email was titled "LOOK AT THIS!!"

He opened it and clicked on the attachment. It was on the front page of her town's newspaper. The bold letters of the headline blared out at him and he smiled. "IS THIS THE WOMAN WHO LEADS THE ARMY OF GOD?" it read. The article was accompanied by a photo of Rebecca with her arms raised above her head. On her face was an ecstatic look of joy as she chanted "Who are we?!" to the men.

"Well, I'll be," Jason said and read further. The piece mentioned the subtle changes taking over the town since Rebecca had spoken to them. People were looking out for each other now and there were less arguments and old enemies made peace and families came closer together. It seemed kindness had spread and the author of the article asked, "Who is this mystery woman and what does she want?" Jason laughed when the piece talked about the difference between this movement and others. There was no asking for money, no church to go to and seemingly no hidden agenda. Something seemed too right about it and apparently the surrounding churches were beginning to grumble about the threat they perceived from the new startup. "Is it a cult?" the reporter asked. Jason burst out laughing then and turned off the computer. He was surprised that there was no mention of himself in the article about the time he told the men Rebecca wasn't coming back.

His thoughts turned to work then and he knew there was at least one person he looked forward to seeing there.

When he arrived at work, Jim greeted him warmly and Jason realized how different the boy was from everyone else with their fake smiles. He worked all morning cleaning more DVD's and was left alone. He sat quietly and did the work and counted each minute as they slowly ticked by.

Late in the afternoon, the director called for him and a feeling of dread filled him. She didn't look happy when he knocked on her door.

"You broke Art Ponce's jaw," she said, staring at him strangely. "He's suing the library and you but we'll handle it."

"Oh," Jason said. "I'm sorry."

The woman sighed and shrugged her shoulders. "I suppose he got what was coming to him. What I want to know is how did you do it, Jason? Do you take Karate lessons in your spare time? You've worked here for many years doing capable work and only recently you've turned into some kind of.....*Superman*. How?"

Jason allowed himself to smile at the rare compliment she'd given him and answered, "No, I don't know Karate. I guess I've just found my purpose in life."

Her eyes changed then. They were no longer cold and she quietly asked again, "How?"

He smiled then. "My girlfriend showed me the way."

Mrs. Walton rubbed her chin and contemplated what he'd said. "I see," she said and sat down. "Thank you. You may go now."

Jason left her office and went to work by the sorting machine for the rest of the day. By the time it was time for him to leave, he was aching all over. He took the bus home again and knew he'd have to buy a car soon because it was tiring waiting at the bus stop in the cold.

The apartment was as quiet as ever and he sat down with a heated bowl of pasta with shrimp. The locket sat lifeless around his neck and he frowned. It had begun to glow less and less the past few hours and Jason wondered why. *Please don't leave me*, he thought.

It pulsed once and he smiled happily. He turned on the TV and saw he'd made the national news. A reporter was talking about what witnesses said he and Rebecca had done at the crash site. He laughed lightly when the reporter suggested things they thought they saw might have been exaggerated in the heat of the moment. The feats of superhuman strength they'd seen couldn't possibly have happened, he said. It was physically impossible. Jason smirked but a chill ran through him when a blurry photo of him suddenly appeared on the screen. "Who is this man and why hasn't he come forward to talk about what happened?" a voice asked.

Jason turned off the TV, undressed and went to bed. He stared up at the ceiling and whispered, "I'm not a nobody."

He closed his eyes and the locket glowed brightly around his neck. Taking hold of it in his hand, he knew he wasn't alone. "Goodnight, my sweet angel," he whispered.

CHAPTER SIXTY NINE

Jim didn't seem to be his normal happy self the next afternoon at work. Jason waited until breaktime and pulled the boy aside.

"Hey Jim, you alright? Everything ok between Jill and you?"

"Yes, we're good, Jason. I asked her out yesterday and her parents are taking us to a movie this weekend."

"Then why do you look worried? What's wrong?"

The teen stared at him. "I am worried. A man was watching her outside her window."

"What?" Jason said.

"She said she got a weird feeling and looked out her bedroom window. There was a man standing in the snow looking up at her."

"Oh no. That *is* weird."

"What's creepy is how he stared at her. She said his eyes looked odd."

A chill raced up Jason's spine and he whispered, "His eyes?"

"Yes," Jim said. "She said they looked dead to her."

Jason's heart began to race. "I need to talk to her. When does she work?"

"She works tonight. Why do you need to talk to her? I already told her to call the police the next time she sees him."

"Were her parents home when this happened, Jim?"

"No, they go out a lot. She was alone."

Jason fought the rising fear in his head and grabbed Jim's arm. "Thanks, Jim. I'll talk to her tonight."

"But why? What can *you* do?" the boy asked, wondering why Jason was so concerned.

"I'll tell you later, Jim. In the meantime, don't worry. Have confidence in me."

The day went by quicker for some reason and Jason waited impatiently for Jill to arrive to work. At six o'clock she walked in and he approached her. "Jill, may I talk to you for a moment?" he asked.

"Sure, Mr. Wilkes," she said shyly. "Am I in trouble?"

"No….no, I just need to ask you something about that man you saw last night."

"Jimmy told you about him?" she said, surprised.

"Yes, he did. Let's go talk away from here."

She followed him out of the circulation room and he walked to the small snack area reserved for patrons. There was no one there and he said, "Jim told me you said there was something strange about the man's eyes. Can you describe them in detail for me?"

"Well, he was standing by the side of the house and I'm up on the second floor but I could still see his face clearly."

"Ok, what did he look like?"

She described the man in detail and Jason felt the fear seep into his aching bones. She saved the description of his eyes for last. "They looked lifeless to me. Not cruel or happy….just lifeless. They creeped me out, Mr. Wilkes."

Jason sucked in a deep breath and Jill grabbed his arm. "Am I in danger?" she asked, suddenly panicked. "Do you know who he is?!"

"No….no…." he reassured her. "Just call the police the next time you see him, ok?"

"Ok," she said and took a deep breath. "You had me worried by the look on your face when I described him."

"No, everything's fine, Jill. I'm sorry I frightened you."

"Ok, Mr. Wilkes," she said, staring at him curiously as she backed away. "I need to get to work now."

"Have a good night," he said and watched her walk away.

It was cold outside, colder than it had been in weeks and Jason felt very alone as he stood at the bus stop.

It's him, he thought. *I know it's him. Why is he watching Jill?*

A large crow suddenly dove at him out of nowhere and he ducked before it could hit him. "Shit!" he yelled and stood shaking, his heart beating wildly.

The crow settled on the lightpole across the street from him and seemed to be staring at him. A thought crept into his head then and he smiled. *I know I've watched too many monster movies in my life*, he thought.

The crow raised its head and let out a bloodcurdling shriek. Jason laughed loudly and yelled, "Yep, you said it, buddy! The devil's in town!"

CHAPTER SEVENTY

For the next two weeks each night after work, Jason waited patiently in the darkness outside Jill's house for any sign of the man. He made sure to stay far away from the street lights so he wouldn't be seen. He didn't need the neighbors calling the police on him so he'd wait close by a large tree across the street. It sat to the right of a corner house and was the perfect hiding place.

Finally late one night as he shivered in the cold, he thought he spotted a dark figure by the side of Jill's house. Her parents had pulled out of the garage and as they turned onto the street their headlights caught the shape for a split second. *There you are....*Jason thought.

He waited by the tree and watched closely. A light came on in an upstairs bedroom and he guessed that Jill had waited for her parents to leave before turning it on. A car came down the street and its headlights shone in the same spot where the figure had stood but this time there was nothing there. Jason frowned and stepped away from the tree. Jill suddenly appeared in the window and was staring down at something by the side of the house. A minute later, she stepped out of sight and the light went out. Jason looked around to make sure no one was watching and crept silently across the street to the house. He walked slowly around its perimeter and saw footprints. *Oh my God*, he thought. *There was someone here.*

He followed the footprints until they stopped by the corner of the front of the house. The footprints seemed different from that point on as if the person had walked on the tips of their shoes. He followed the smaller prints and his blood ran cold when they stopped by one of the windows by the porch. It had been jimmied open. "Shit!" Jason whispered.

He heard a muffled cry from inside and quickly pushed through the open window. "No! Please no!" he heard Jill scream and he followed her cry to the front stairway. She screamed again and he raced up the stairs to where he guessed her bedroom was. The door was closed and when he tried to open it he groaned. It was locked from the inside. He could hear the man talking.

"Bitch….slut," he said cruelly. "You pure bitches think you're so much better than me. Well, you're not. Yeah….that's right. Keep looking at me. I wanna see the light fade from your eyes as you die."

Jason looked down at the locket around his neck and whispered, "Rebecca, please give me strength. I need you."

It glowed brightly and he reared back then and rammed his shoulder against the door. It splintered inward as he burst through. He quickly found the light switch and flicked it on. Jill was lying on the bed and Jason was shocked to see the man had tied her hands and feet to the bedposts and was straddling her. Her pajama top had been unbuttoned and her small breasts were exposed. There were bite marks on them and Jason felt rage whip through his mind. Jill looked at him and her eyes silently begged for help as the man's hands tightened around her neck. Jason yelled, "No!" and the man glanced angrily at him.

"*You*," the attacker whispered. "I remember you. You were with that cunt at the bakery."

"Get off of her," Jason said grimly as he clenched his fists.

The man smiled and Jason shuddered because he was really quite handsome except for his eyes which were lifeless and cold.

"Would you like to share her?" he asked as he pulled his hands away from Jill's neck. He moved them to her breasts and squeezed them gently. "Her tits taste delicious."

Jill groaned in terror and he pinched her nipples cruelly which made her wince in pain. She didn't cry out though and instead bit her lip and drew blood.

"I said to get away from her," Jason said, his eyes blazing.

The man laughed and bent down to take a nipple in his mouth.

Jason knew he was going to bite Jill again and charged at him and hit him in the side of the face with his fist. Surprised, he was knocked off of Jill by the force of Jason's blow and fell to the floor by the side of the bed. Jason leaped on top of him and began pounding his fists into the attackers face.

"Who are you?!" he screamed.

Jason felt intensely cold then as the man's eyes suddenly seemed bright and alive. He grabbed Jason by the throat and pulled him down until his mouth was by his ear. His strength was incredible and no matter how hard Jason punched his stomach and ribs he wouldn't let go. He gasped for breath and the cruel man whispered, "I wanted to fuck her, you know but I was interrupted so I ended it quick. You should have seen the light go out of her eyes. She was so frightened. It was delicious."

Jason knew he was talking about Rebecca and screamed, "No!!"

"Oh yes," the man whispered. "I *was* able to enjoy her titties though. They were some of the ripest I've ever tasted….almost like sweet apples."

Jason grunted and grabbed the man's wrists, trying to pry his hands off his throat. "She was so pure," the man whispered. "Poor pathetic virgin."

Jason felt bile in his throat and drove his knee into the man's groin. His eyes shot open in shock and his hands loosened from around Jason's neck.

"You son of a bitch!" Jason growled. "You killed her! She didn't deserve to die!"

The man pushed Jason away then with such force that he flew over the bed and landed heavily against the wall at the opposite side of the room. Jason gasped in pain and watched in horror as Jill screamed, "He's coming! Oh God, save me!"

The man rose from the floor and stared at Jill. "When I'm done with him, I'm going to taste your pussy next before I watch your eyes as you die."

"Leave her alone!" Jason shouted. "She doesn't deserve to die!"

The man looked at Jason and his handsome face turned red with rage. "They *all* deserve to die! They think they're so pure but they're nothing but whores! Sluts!"

He lowered his head then and a cruel smile came across his face. Jason shivered in horror when those evil eyes stared deeper into his. The life had gone out of them again and he knew he was about to die. He clutched the locket around his neck and whispered, "Please, Rebecca, I need you."

He took his hand away and just as the man was about to advance on him, a brilliant blue light shot out of the locket and bathed him from head to toe. He began to scream and swiped at the light with his hands but it moved around him and clung to him like a living thing.

"It burns!" he shrieked. "Get it away!"

Jason stood up and sneered. "Get out."

The man's eyes brightened again and he whispered, "You may have stopped me now but I won't be denied. The pure ones *must* die."

Before Jason could ask him what he meant, the man barreled past him and ran into the hallway and down the stairs. Jason tried to follow but the fiend's speed was amazing. He jumped out the open window and disappeared into the night.

Jill was lightly crying when he came back to her. She looked away from him when he covered her breasts with her top and then he untied her wrists and hands. When she was free, she flung herself at him and hugged him tightly. "Oh thank you, Mr. Wilkes! I thought I was going to die!"

She quickly got dressed and called her parents while he called the police. When they got to the house, they interrogated Jill first alone.

She told them everything but left out the locket and her bite wounds because she was so embarrassed by where they were. When they brought her back to her parents, Jason quietly told her she needed to go to the hospital and she refused at first but finally agreed when she saw the caring look in his eyes. Then they spent a long time with Jason. They were very suspicious of his answers and found it hard to believe that he'd just happened to be strolling down the street at that particular time and heard Jill's screams.

"I don't care if you believe me or not," he said. "I'm telling you the truth."

The head detective smiled and almost laughed. "Let's see if I understand correctly. You live miles from here. I still don't get what you were doing around here. Maybe you're the guy's partner."

Jill became indignant then and shouted, "He saved me! I don't know why he was around but I'm glad he was! I'd be dead now if it wasn't for him!"

Another detective came closer and stared intensely at Jason before going back to whisper something to his boss. The man's eyebrows lifted and he smiled at Jason. "Wait a minute….you're that hero everyone's been looking for, aren't you?"

Jason's face flushed and nodded his head. "Yes."

"Well, I'll be," the man said and looked at his men. "This guy's a fucking hero. He's all over the news. He makes a habit out of rescuing people."

Jason squirmed uncomfortably and Jill's parents walked in the door. They were dressed in expensive clothes and had a snooty air about them. They stared at him with hate in their eyes and he glared back at them.

"Why is *he* still here?" her father asked.

The detective answered, "He's still here because we've been questioning him. He saved your daughter's life."

The man snorted. "Yeah, right! He's probably a fucking pervert who was waiting outside until he had his chance to get to our daughter."

Jason had heard enough and sneered at Jill's father. "Maybe if you didn't leave your daughter alone all the time this wouldn't have happened."

Jill's mother screeched, "You have no right to tell us what to do! Jill does just fine by herself!"

The detective couldn't resist and said, "Yeah, just like tonight."

The couple were silent then and stared at Jason with sullen eyes.

"May I leave now?" he asked. "Or do you have any more questions for me?"

"Yeah, you can go. I guess we're done here."

Before he could leave, Jill raced over and gripped him tightly around the waist. "Thank you so much, Mr. Wilkes," she whispered. "You're my hero."

Jason glanced at her parents glowering faces and the curious stares of the police and thought, *If I'm such a hero, why don't I feel like one?*

The detective offered to drive Jason home and he gratefully accepted. Before he got out of the car, the man asked, "Who is he?"

"What are you talking about?" Jason asked.

The man sighed. "Look, the girl told us you and he seemed to know each other so I'll ask again. Who is he?"

Jason clenched his jaws tightly and stared straight ahead. "I don't know for sure," he whispered. "But I promise you I'm going to find out."

CHAPTER SEVENTY ONE

A woman died that same night. A man broke into her house a few miles from where Jill lived and strangled her slowly after sexually torturing her. Jason saw it on the news the next morning and knew what he had to do. "Concord," he whispered. "Rebecca said she went to Concord."

During breaktime at work, Jason got on one of the patron computers and went to the internet. The first thing he typed was "Concord School." There was nothing for that so next he typed "Concord School For Women."

His eyes lit up when a listing came up that read "St. Francis School buys Concord School For Women." Jason clicked on it and a page from an old newspaper popped up from 1973. It didn't say much other than St. Francis College had purchased the Concord School For Women located in Waltham, Vermont which had closed the year before. Jason printed the clipping and smiled. He was amazed how easy it had been to find the information he needed. He went back to the first page and scanned down until he came across a listing that read in bold type: YOUNG WOMAN MURDERED AT CONCORD. The page was a photo of a newspaper clipping from 1962. He clicked on it in a flash and to his disappointment saw there was only a short paragraph that read: The Concord School For Women mourns the death of Rebecca Monroe. She has been a student at Concord for two years and was studying to be a professional singer and actress. We will never forget her kind nature and wonderful talent. Police are investigating.

Jason held his breath and tried to calm his heartrate. *I found you*, he thought. *Now I know who you are.*

He went back to the original listing and searched more extensively until he found only one other headline which read: Police have no leads in Concord School murder. Due to the lack of witnesses, they remain frustrated and say it's highly unlikely the crime will ever be solved.

Oh my sweet Rebecca, Jason thought. *I'm so sorry they never caught him.*

He sat for a few minutes and stared at the computer screen as he gathered his thoughts. Pete suddenly appeared and said, "I hate to interrupt you, Jason but you've been up here for a while. People are noticing you've gone past your break."

Jason stood up. "By how long?"

Pete swallowed hard and looked ashamed. "Five minutes."

Jason fought the anger back and grit his teeth. "I've seen staff take an extra fifteen minutes and I'm being talked to about five lousy minutes?"

"I'm sorry, Jason," Pete said quietly. "You know they're watching you. You have to be more careful."

Jason closed his eyes for a moment in an effort to shut off the world and when he reopened them Pete was still there. "Fine," he said. "It won't happen again."

Pete walked away without saying another word and Jason followed him back to the department to resume his time beside the hated sorting machine.

At the end of his workday, Jim approached him and shook his hand. "I don't know how to thank you, sir," he said. "Jill told me what you did. She'd be dead now if it wasn't for you."

Jason smiled. "I'm glad she's ok, Jim. She's a special young lady. You're very lucky."

Jim stared intensely into Jason's eyes and said, "I hope I end up being half the man you are."

Jason was surprised and said, "No, Jim. You don't want to end up like me. What do I have to show for my life? The library has erased everything good I've ever done. It's as if I never existed."

Jim shook his head back and forth and said, "I've heard gossip about how you were demoted and how they've treated you here but you have to remember your legacy, Jason."

"What legacy, Jim?"

The teen smiled. "You really don't know, do you? Think of all the people you've worked with over the years. For some of them, you were their first boss. From what I've heard from the few that are left, they love and respect you for your decency and kindness towards them. Don't you see that means something?"

Jason swallowed hard and his eyes blurred with tears. "Jim," he said quietly. "How did you get so wise? You don't talk like a lot of teenagers talk. Thank you for your kind words. I never thought of myself in the way you say."

"You're a good man, sir," the boy said. "I wish my father was more like you."

Jason was genuinely touched by the teen's words. "Thank you," was all he could say. He retrieved his coat then and headed outside. Jill was just about to enter the library and when she saw him she smiled brightly. "Mr. Wilkes! I'm so glad to see you!" she cried happily.

"Jill! I'm surprised you're here. Should you be back to work so soon?"

"I'm ok, really I am. Besides, I don't feel like staying at home and brooding about what happened."

"You teenagers," he said, smiling. "You bounce back from things a lot faster than us older people do."

"You're not old, Mr. Wilkes," she said and touched his shoulder. Jason suddenly thought of Rebecca and resisted the urge to hug Jill. He knew it would look bad and people might accuse him of something inappropriate so he just said, "Thanks, Jill, but believe me, I may not look like it but I'm old inside."

The girl's pretty eyes grew brighter and she gazed at him with affection. "Thank you again for saving me. I'll never forget what you did."

He nodded and she pulled her hand back. "Jill," he said, "Thanks for not telling the police what really happened last night."

Her eyes twinkled and again he was reminded of Rebecca. "That locket," she said softly. "What *did* happen?"

He lowered his voice. "It's special, Jill. It was given to me by a special woman. It protects me in a way."

"It also protected me. I don't understand what happened and I won't question it. I'm grateful to her whoever she is."

"She's an angel, Jill….just like you," Jason answered. He sucked in his breath then and was worried he'd gone too far with his compliment to the girl.

She smiled shyly and blushed. "Thank you, Mr. Wilkes. You're so kind."

"Well, I'll be seeing you," he said, relieved and walked away to the bus stop.

Jill watched him for a minute and felt very bad for him. He was limping slightly and his shoulders were slumped. He seemed defeated in a way. It was as if the life had gone out of him.

When he got home, Jason quickly made plane reservations for the weekend. He also made some phone calls and to his surprise he was able to reach people who could help him. When the last phone call proved successful, he smiled to himself and thought, *"I'll find the truth, Rebecca. You can count on me."*

CHAPTER SEVENTY TWO

He had a suitcase packed and ready to go early Saturday morning when the Uber driver picked him up to take him to the airport. The flight itself was a little over two hours and it arrived on time.

He took a taxi to the college and watched as the scenery flew by. It was a beautiful area and he imagined how lush and green it must be in the Spring and Summer. For now, everything was under a layer of glistening snow and looked very pretty.

The driver dropped him off near the main building which was surrounded by a number of smaller ones. Jason looked at his notepad and glanced around. He'd been told to go to the small building which taught music. It was the farthest from the main one.

He opened the big wooden door and imagined Rebecca walking through it years before. The office he'd been told to go to was directly to his left. The woman he'd talked to on the phone was waiting for him. She smiled when he entered the room and stood up to shake his hand.

"Mr. Wilkes, it's so nice to meet you. Please have a seat."

Jason sat down in the big leather chair facing her desk and noted the silver streaks in her hair which still retained some of its original black. For a woman in her sixties, she didn't look her age at all. Her eyes were bright and she seemed filled with an energy he wished he'd had.

"It's so nice of you to meet me on such short notice, Mrs. Dunham," he said and settled in the chair.

"I trust you had a good flight. It can be quite bumpy up there sometimes, you know."

"I know!" he laughed.

She grabbed the book sitting on the desk in front of her and he noticed she had the page marked. "Here's what you asked to see. I must say though that I'm very curious. Why are you asking about Rebecca Monroe? She's been dead for years and you look too young to have known her."

Jason had his lie ready. "My parents knew her and I promised them I'd look into her murder someday."

The woman frowned. "Well, I don't know what you can do after all these years. The police hit a brick wall, you know. They never did find her killer."

"I guess I'm just curious," Jason said. "My mother used to talk about how beautiful Rebecca's voice was when she sang and how kind she was."

"Well, that yearbook you're holding was hard to find. I had to do a lot of digging in the basement of the main building. When St. Francis took over, they packed up a lot of Concord's history there."

"Thank you so much, Mrs. Dunham. You don't know how much this means to me."

She eyed him suspiciously and said, "Unfortunately, I can't let you take that with you so I'll just leave you alone for a short time with it. I'll be in a room down the hall. Just yell for me when you're finished with it."

"Thank you again," Jason said and waited until she left before opening it to the earmarked page. He scanned it quickly and held his breath when he saw her photo at the bottom of the page which also listed her name and interests. Rebecca Monroe, it read. Interests are singing, acting and dancing. Member of the girls swimming club and musical theater group.

Jason was surprised at the mention of her interest in swimming and then looked at her photo. It was definitely her. Her beautiful eyes stared back at him and though the photo was in black and white it was obvious her hair was the golden blonde he knew so well. He touched the photo with his fingertips and felt tears form in his eyes. "Rebecca," he whispered. "It's you."

She was smiling shyly in the photo and Jason smiled back at her.

He brushed away his tears and went to the Yearbook's index and found one more listing for her. He went to the page and immediately spotted her in the group of women gathered on a stage. She wore a flowery dress and wasn't smiling. Her eyes gazed out from the page at him and he felt like he was being sucked in by them. "Oh God," he moaned. "I miss you so much."

He quickly took photos of the images with his cell phone and closed the book. He put it back on the desk and sat quietly for a moment. Mrs. Dunham came back into the room then and said, "I hope I'm not disturbing you. I finished what I needed to do. Take more time if you need it."

Jason stood up and wiped his eyes again. "No, thank you. I saw what I needed to see."

She came close and stared up at his face. "You've been crying. Why?"

"I don't know. I guess I just got emotional."

She looked at him strangely and said, "Why do I get the feeling you're not telling me everything?"

Jason wanted to tell her the truth about Rebecca but knew he couldn't. She'd think he was crazy and he didn't want that.

"No….no, really I'm not hiding anything. It's just so sad that she died at such a young age."

Jason could tell she didn't believe him and she stood silent for a moment before saying, "I asked around and there's someone who works here that knew her. Would you like to speak to her?"

"Oh yes! Please, yes!"

His answer was so enthusiastic that she grew more suspicious and her eyes narrowed. "You're a strange man. It's almost as if you knew her which I know is impossible."

"I'm sorry. My mother talked about her so much that I feel like I *did* know her, that's all."

"Alright," she said. "Her name is Cathy Grodin. She's right down the hall in the main auditorium. Go ahead and I'll call her to tell her you're on your way to see her."

"I can't thank you enough, Mrs. Dunham. "I'll never forget your kindness."

"Anytime," she said and shook his hand. "I hope you find what you're looking for."

Jason wiped his eyes again and composed himself before entering the auditorium. It was the largest room in the building and could seat around two hundred people. There was an old woman standing on the stage and she waved to him. He made his way there and climbed the steps to get to her.

"Hello," she said. "I'm Cathy. I understand you have a few questions about Rebecca."

Her hair was completely white and she still had the same figure she had from when she was a professional dancer.

Jason smiled and said, "I know this sounds strange but would you tell me about her?"

"Well," the woman said quietly. "Rebecca was the best singer in our group back then. In fact, she had the loveliest voice I've ever heard. Even now, I can still remember the emotional way she'd perform songs. She made them her own in a way and touched the hearts of everyone who heard her sing. She was very special."

That's my Rebecca, Jason thought happily.

Cathy's eyes grew sad then and she softly said, "I think of her every day and miss her terribly. She was the kindest person I've ever known. She didn't deserve to die that way."

Jason fought the urge to cry. "I know it must be difficult for you but can you tell me about the day she died?"

"I was the one who found her," she answered. "She was murdered the night before. Oh, it was horrible the things that beast did to her. Her poor breasts had deep bite marks all over them and her eyes, oh

God, her eyes! They were open and looked so sad. I could sense she was crying out to live by the look in them. I closed them before the police arrived and I covered up her breasts. It was the least I could do. I didn't want them seeing her that way."

Jason felt the anger boil up inside of him and felt helpless. *That bastard!* he thought. *That fucking cruel bastard!*

"Why didn't they find out who did it?" he asked then. "Weren't there any leads? Didn't the police find out anything at all?"

She glowered and waved her hand away as if to dismiss them. "Oh, they were useless! Absolutely useless! I told them to check on that school for boys because one of them was always hanging around outside the campus. They didn't do a damn thing as far as I know."

Jason felt a chill race down his spine. "You say a boy was hanging around campus. Do you remember what he looked like?"

Her eyes narrowed and she shivered. "Oh, he was creepy, that one. He had the strangest eyes. They seemed dead even when he smiled. We all stayed away from him and reported him. I don't know if he was talked to or not but one day he stopped hanging around. Rebecca was murdered three days later. The main door had been left unlocked and he came right in. I was lucky. I was only three doors down from her. It could have been any one of us but for some reason he picked her."

"Oh my God," Jason whispered.

"The strangest thing is we never heard a sound," she said. "You would think that what he did to her breasts would make her cry out but she never made a sound. Poor Rebecca, oh how she must have suffered!"

Jason shuddered and wiped the tears away that finally dripped from his eyes. Mrs. Grodin looked at him strangely and lightly touched his arm. "Are you alright, Mr. Wilkes?"

"Yes, yes, I'm fine. I'll be fine. Can you tell me anything else about her? Anything at all?"

Her eyes turned sad again and she softly said, "Not really but I'll tell you one last thing. Rebecca was so pure that I'll bet she's an angel in heaven now."

The comment made Jason freeze and he had to sit down. He sat on the edge of the stage and she sat down beside him. "Who are you?" she asked. "Why all these questions about my friend?"

Jason looked at her and she saw something in his eyes that made her say, "If you see her, tell her I miss her."

Jason's eyes opened wide in surprise and she smiled knowingly. "I knew it," she whispered. "Rebecca used to talk about a kind man she'd dream of. A man that would love her unconditionally with all of his heart. She used to fantasize about him all the time. Are you that man, Jason?"

The tears rolled down his cheeks and she pulled him close and put her arm around his shoulders. "I believe in the hereafter, Jason. I know Rebecca's not really dead. She was too pure."

There was that word again. *Pure.*

"Yes," Jason said quietly. "She is pure….and good….and kind."

"How did you find her? Was it a séance? I believe in those things, you know. Or was it through a psychic?"

Jason stared intensely into the old woman's eyes and she smiled when he said, "She heard my heart call out to her. She's my guardian angel."

CHAPTER SEVENTY THREE

Mrs. Grodin and he talked for a long time and she told him how Rebecca would help all the other students with their studies or lend them money when they needed it. She was indeed kind but also fun loving as she loved to swim in the small lake behind the school. "We'd go skinny dipping there," she said, her eyes suddenly bright as she remembered those fun days. "Rebecca wasn't like the rest of us and had no shame. I really believe she would have walked around naked all the time if she could."

Jason laughed at the thought but then turned serious. "Do you know where she's buried?"

Mrs. Grodin smiled tenderly at him and quietly said, "I was waiting for you to ask me that. Her parents knew she loved this school very much so they had her buried in the small cemetery on the grounds. I visit her at least once a week. Most of the professors from back then are buried there too. Would you like me to take you there?"

"Please. I'd like that very much."

The cemetery was only a few hundred feet behind the building they were in. It covered about an acre and a half and she led him straight to Rebecca's grave. She stared down at the old worn headstone and said, "Rebecca, someone's here to see you, dear."

Jason ignored the snow covered ground and knelt in front of the headstone. He brushed some snow away from the front of it with his hand and read the inscription. It read: Rebecca Monroe, Beloved daughter, Rest in peace in God's arms. 1939-1962.

Jason looked up at Cathy and said, "She was only twenty three. My God, she never got to live life."

She placed her hand on his shoulder and said, "I know. She was taken away from us much too soon."

Jason touched the headstone and closed his eyes as he pictured her beautiful face in his mind. After a minute, he stood up and asked,

"Do you know where this school for boys was?"

Mrs. Grodin nodded. "It's still there but I wish it wasn't. It's a dark place and I always get a bed feeling when I drive by it every day. It's down the street about two miles from here. I can drive you there if you'd like."

She was right. As they pulled into the parking lot, Jason felt a sense of foreboding as the large dark brick building came into view. The first thing that popped into his mind were photos he'd once seen of long closed mental asylums. This building looked very similar to them.

"Would you like me to wait for you?" she asked.

"You've done more than enough for me," he answered. "I can see why Rebecca was friends with you. You're very kind. I need to go on alone now."

Before he left, Jason gave Mrs. Grodin his phone number in case she remembered anything else. She was deep in thought and touched his arm. "Take care of yourself, Jason," she said. "Remember, Rebecca's watching over you."

CHAPTER SEVENTY FOUR

The director was far less accommodating than Mrs. Dunham had been back at the girl's school. "You could have called, you know," the middle aged man gruffly said. "We need advance notice for those types of requests."

Jason fidgeted with his hands as the man leaned forward in his big chair and said, "Why do you want to see those old yearbooks anyway? No one's asked about them in years. Did a relative of yours go to this school?"

"No," Jason answered truthfully. "I'm looking for a relative of a friend of mine."

Then he lied, "He said his uncle went here."

The man had big lips and his beady eyes narrowed. "Forget it then. If you're not related to anyone who attended here, then I'm not helping you."

Jason felt desperate and pulled out his wallet. He picked out a few twenty dollar bills and handed them to the man. "Please," he said as humbly as he could. "I really need your help here."

The man's eyes lit up at the sight of the cash but they narrowed again and he said, "More."

Jason opened his wallet again and pulled out another twenty. He handed it over and lied, "It's all I have."

The man took it and his narrow face turned red with the excitement of his good fortune. "I think I can help you," he said. "Give me a few minutes. We keep the old yearbooks in the storage room down the hall."

The man walked off and Jason sat and stared down at his hands. He noticed his skin was beginning to wrinkle and knew that old age was taking over. "How many years do I have left?" he whispered sadly. "I'm beginning to look old."

The man came back a few minutes later and handed him a few leather covered books. "These are the years you asked for. I have work to do so I hope you don't mind if I sit here while you look through those."

"No, not at all," Jason said. "Thank you."

It was a time consuming process as Jason had to look at every page. The first volume didn't have what he was looking for as he carefully studied each student's face and eyes in the old photographs. He opened the second of three books and there on page sixty eight was who he'd been looking for. The young man in the photo stared back at him with those cold emotionless eyes and he knew immediately it was him. *Oh my God!* Jason thought. *I've found him!*

The text below the photo read: Austin Phillips. Interests are hiking, boxing and theater. Member of the performing arts club and boxing team.

Jason noticed the man had a slight smirk on his face and he muttered, "You smug bastard."

The director heard him and looked up from his desk. "What did you say? Are you talking to me?"

"No, sorry," Jason said and shifted uncomfortably in his seat. "I was just thinking of someone I met once."

"Oh," the man said and looked back at his notes. Jason quickly pulled out his phone and took a picture of the photo and then looked to see if there were more of Austin which there were. He found him in photos of the boxing club, theater performers and an odd one with him presenting a flower to a naked female mannequin.

"That's strange, don't you think?" he said and showed the director the creepy photo. "I'm surprised they allowed this to be printed."

The man's eyebrows raised in surprise and he looked at Jason. "Yes, you're right. That is strange and just a bit unsettling."

Jason let him take the book and he stared intensely at the photo. "Oh yes," he said quietly. "I remember hearing about this boy. Very disturbing."

"Please tell me about him," Jason said, trying to hide his excitement.

The man studied the photo again and his eyes opened wider as he remembered the story he'd been told.

"This young man was expelled. Normally I can't discuss personal information but it happened so long ago I don't really see the harm in telling you."

"Why was he expelled? Do you know?"

The director shuddered as he recalled what he'd been told. "He was caught in bed with this mannequin."

Jason shuddered. "Eewwww, that's creepy."

"But that's not all," the man continued. "He'd carved a hole between its legs in an apparent attempt to have sex with it. We have no idea if he was successful or not and frankly I wouldn't want to know if he had."

"Ok, this is seriously creeping me out. What else did you hear?"

The man leaned across the desk and whispered, "I also heard he'd bitten the mannequin's breasts."

"What?!" Jason cried. "How do you know that?!"

"Because there were bite marks on them. Would you like to see the thing?"

Jason felt cold seep through his body and his throat felt suddenly dry. "You kept it?! You have it here?"

"It's in an old storage closet. We should have thrown it out years ago but those things are expensive. The theater kids sometimes use it as a prop in their shows. Of course, it's fully dressed now. Not like it is in that photo."

"Please show it to me," Jason said grimly.

"I guess I'm earning that money you gave me!" the man laughed and led Jason out of the office to the back of the building. He pulled a set of keys from his pocket and unlocked the door. He motioned into the dark room. "It's in there. I don't want to see it. It scares me."

Jason gulped hard and said, "Thanks" and went inside. There was a cord hanging from the ceiling and he pulled on it. A yellowed lightbulb came on and Jason wondered why the director had called it a closet. It was a very large room and contained many chairs, old broken tables and battered file cabinets. He looked around the dimly lit room and shivered when he saw the mannequin against the far wall looking back at him, its painted eyes emotionless. He gathered what courage he had and forced himself to walk slowly towards it. A few old wooden chairs were in the way and he picked them up and set them to the side. The mannequin's arms were outstretched and seemed to reach for him. He forced himself closer and soon stood eye to eye with the thing. A pretty frilly blue dress covered its plaster body and he felt dirty when he pulled the dress down past its shoulders. The director had been right. There were bite marks on the plaster breasts. In fact, there were many. They were all around the mannequin's nipples and went lower towards the stomach. Jason pulled the dress down further and frowned when he saw the word "slut" painted on its stomach. *Nice kids*, he thought grimly. *No wonder that murdering son of a bitch went to this school.*

He saw something he couldn't believe then and pulled the dress down to the mannequin's ankles. Gasping in horror, he backed away when he saw the plunger rammed into the hole between its legs. The name "Rebecca" was scrawled in red above its pubis.

Jason felt his face go white with rage and he yelled, "Motherfuckers!"

The director came rushing in. "What's wrong?!"

Jason pointed to the plunger sticking out of the mannequin and screamed, "Is this what you teach your students to do? On top of it you named this thing "Rebecca?!"

The man frowned and came closer. "Ok, I see I'll have to look into the plunger thing. It's totally unacceptable and some kids are going to be awfully sorry if I find out who did this but…."

"But what?!" Jason yelled. "Making excuses for them already?!"

The man's face turned pale when he quietly said, "The name was already on it. Austin put it there."

CHAPTER SEVENTY FIVE

Jason felt as if the world was closing in on him and whispered, "He named this thing "Rebecca?""

"Apparently so. But I have no idea why. I only arrived here twenty-five years ago. The people who ran this place back then are all gone now."

Jason had a thought. "Did he have any friends here? Anyone who might still be alive?"

The man laughed. "How would I know if they're alive or not? I did hear that he had a friend though. He was expelled with him. Let me see if I can find out who he was."

They left the room and went back to the office where Jason waited patiently as the man went immediately to the photo of the boxing club. "Here he is," he said and pointed to a muscular boy who towered above the rest of the boxers. "I remember being told they were almost like brothers. His name was Arlen Downing. That's all I know."

Jason took the book back and looked up the boy's main photo. It read: Arlen Downing. Interests are hiking, boxing and theater. Member of the performing arts club and boxing team. Jason looked up and said, "Oh my God. They had the same interests."

"About that boy named Austin," the man said. "It seemed to upset you."

Jason grimaced. "Yes….it upset me greatly."

He called a taxi then and thanked the director for his help. Like he had done with Mrs. Grodin, Jason gave the man his phone number in case there was anything else discovered. While waiting for his ride, he went to a website that contained people's personal information and looked up the name of the boy who'd been close friends with Austin. He found three. One of them lived in Colorado but was only twenty years old while the second was forty nine and lived in Arizona. But the third was eighty five years old and lived right there in town. *Jackpot!* he thought excitedly and quickly dialed the number before he could change his mind.

After the second ring a frail voice answered the phone. The man said, "Who is this?"

"Hi! My name is Jason Wilkes! I work for Best Places magazine and was wondering if you had time for me to interview you?"

"What for?" the man asked, suspicious, his voice stronger.

"I randomly picked your name out of the phone book, sir and wanted to ask you some questions about what it's like to live in this beautiful state. I can pay you forty dollars for your time."

The man's voice got higher then and he said, "Sure! Sure! I could use the money! When do you want to meet?"

"How about today? Is there a good time for you? I know this is very short notice."

"How about in half an hour?"

"Fine," Jason said. "I'll be there."

The man hung up and Jason marveled at how easily he'd made up the lie he'd told. He didn't feel guilty about it though. *I need answers,* he thought. *Maybe the police didn't dig far enough but I will. For Rebecca's sake, I will.*

CHAPTER SEVENTY SIX

Arlen Downing lived just at the edge of town in a small green vinyl paneled house. Jason took a deep breath and knocked on the door.

A giant answered and Jason gaped in awe at the man's size. No wonder he'd looked so tall next to the other boxers in the photo. He had to be close to seven feet tall. "Mr. Downing?" he said warily. "Hi. I'm Jason Wilkes."

The giant stared down at him and nodded. "Come on in," he said in a deep voice.

Jason opened the screen door and the man moved aside to let him walk in. He closed the door behind him and pointed to a far chair by a small television that sat by the wall. "Have a seat," he said. "Coffee?"

"No thanks," Jason answered and realized his palms were sweating. The room he sat in was bare of objects beyond what was necessary to watch TV. There was no china cabinet or paintings on the walls. It seemed sadly lifeless.

The man sat down in a big chair across from him that creaked under his weight and Jason wondered to himself if the giant had ever lost a boxing match. His arms were very long which meant he could have kept any man who fought him at bay with a good left jab. Even though he was in his eighties, he looked more than formidable. He was dressed in overalls which made him look like a farmer. Trying to hide his disgust, Jason saw food particles hanging from Arlen's stubbly gray beard and his face was weathered and pockmarked. The man looked as if he'd had a rough life just by the tired look of his gray green eyes alone.

"So....Mr. reporter, what do you want to know about life around here?"

Jason didn't like the way Arlen Downing was looking at him and tried his best to hide his nervousness. "Well, Mr. Downing, is life more relaxed in this part of the country?"

"Compared to where?" he asked.

"Oh say, New York or California?"

The giant's eyes flickered and he half smiled. "I wouldn't know. I haven't been to those places."

"Oh," Jason said.

"Aren't you gonna write that down?" Arlen asked, his eyes narrowing.

"Oh yes, of course," Jason said and quickly pulled a pen from his pocket with the notepad he'd brought in. "How stupid of me."

The man stared at him and licked his lips. "What magazine did you say you was from?"

"Best Places," Jason answered. "So tell me, do you like having the wide open spaces around here compared to more crowded places?"

"Like where?"

Jason realized he should have had better questions ready to ask and said, "Like Burlington for instance."

Arlen shifted forward in his chair and stared at Jason. "Don't know. Haven't been there either. I haven't been much anywhere except this part of the state."

Oh Christ, this isn't going the way I'd planned, Jason thought.

The man stood up and Jason again marveled at his size. He must have weighed three hundred pounds at least. Arlen walked to the front door and locked it before glancing back at Jason with a strange smile on his face.

"What are you doing, Mr. Downing?" Jason asked, his voice coming out weaker than he wished.

The man sat back down and grinned. "You're not a writer at all, are you?"

"Why yes, of course I am," Jason said as he wiped a bead of sweat from his forehead.

The giant leaned forward in his chair and his eyes narrowed. "I'm not as dumb as you think I am. I've got a computer in my bedroom. I checked and there's no magazine called "Best Place."

Jason gulped hard and felt his face flush. "Ok, ok, you got me. I lied."

"Who are you and what do you want?" Austin asked, his voice way too calm.

Jason sucked in a deep breath and said, "I wanted to talk to you about Austin Philips."

Arlen's eyes flickered slightly and one of his eyelids began to twitch. "Who?" he said, his voice low.

"Austin Phillips. I'm trying to find information about him."

"What makes you think I know him?"

Jason figured he should just tell the truth and said, "I visited the school you both went to. I was told you were good friends."

"So you're some kind of spy checking up on me, huh?" the man said and clenched his fists.

"No! No! You've got it all wrong! I'm investigating the death of a friend of mine!"

Jason realized immediately that he'd made a mistake by saying that because the giant's eyes opened wide in surprise. "I should have known," he said and a sadness seemed to overtake him and his massive shoulders sagged. He stared at his hands and quietly said, "You're wrong about Austin and I. We weren't just good friends. We were *best* friends."

"Oh," Jason said.

Arlen looked at him sharply then. "You want to know about the girls, don't you?"

"Girls?" Jason said, surprised. "I'm just here about one."

The man's eyes turned lifeless then. "There were many," he said.

"Oh shit," Jason whispered.

"Who are you asking about?"

"Her name was Rebecca Monroe."

Arlen Downing appeared to shrink slightly and his eyes seemed sadder than before. "Ah yes, poor sweet Rebecca. She was the final straw."

Jason squirmed nervously in his seat. "Look, I don't know what you're talking about. What do you mean she was the final straw?"

"I loved her," Arlen replied, his eyes moist. "She never knew it but I loved everything about her. Unfortunately, so did Austin….in his own way."

Jason kept silent and the man continued. "We'd heard about her beautiful voice and went to see her perform a few times at the women's school. She never knew we were in the audience but we fell in love with her grace and beauty and the well….she kind of put a spell on you with that magnificent voice she had."

Jason nodded. "Go on."

"Unfortunately, Austin ended up hating her like all the rest he picked."

"Picked? What are you saying?" Jason asked as terror raced through him.

"There were others from other towns. Quiet girls. *Pure* girls as Austin liked to call them."

That word again. *Pure.*

"How many more were there?" Jason asked, trying to keep himself from shaking.

Arlen laughed then. "Quite a few. People still think most of them ran away but they didn't."

He leaned forward until his face was inches from Jason's. "I know where they are," he whispered and sank back into his own chair.

A chill ran up Jason's spine and he felt a strange calm come over him. "How do you know, Arlen?"

"Because I helped him get rid of them."

Jason tried to calm his heartrate and asked, "Did you help kill them too?"

"Nah," the man said, waving his hand at Jason as if to dismiss him. "I just had my fun with them and he finished up."

"Oh my God, why?! Why?!"

The man smiled. "Because we wanted to, that's why. We were best friends. We did everything together including hunting women. Austin would stalk the pure ones and I loved how shy they were when he held them down so I could finger them. That's all I did mind you and they seemed to like it but then Austin took over. It was always the same. He'd start out all friendly like and then I'd see the rage build in him. By that time it was too late and he took it out on their tits. He'd rip them up and bite them. Man, let me tell you it was hard to watch. They'd squirm and squeal and I couldn't bear to watch so I'd leave him alone with them. When he was done, I'd help him dump the bodies."

"How many were there, Arlen?" Jason asked as he felt adrenaline begin to course through him.

"Maybe eight, maybe ten, I don't remember exactly."

"Oh my God," Jason whispered.

"Hey," Arlen said then and reached out with a massive hand. It thumped on Jason's shoulder and Arlen stared intensely at him. "I'm not a bad man if that's what you're thinking. I didn't kill them girls."

"But you didn't stop it," Jason said quietly.

"No, I didn't," Arlen said regretfully. "Looking back, I wish I had. I see their faces in my nightmares. They're always there."

"Where are they?" Jason asked. "Where are they buried, Arlen?"

The giant's eyes glistened with tears. "They're in the lake behind the women's school. I threw them in there with weights around their feet. They've been there ever since."

"Oh Jesus!" Jason cried, aghast at the horrifying confession.

The giant removed his hand then from Jason's shoulder and mumbled, "Poor Rebecca."

"Tell me, Arlen. What happened to her?"

The man's eyes were full of pain. "I could see Austin wanted to do to her what he'd done to the others but I warned him to stay away from her. I was getting up the nerve to ask her out and he must have sensed it because he found a mannequin and named it after her as a joke."

"I know. I saw it."

"They still have it? Yeah, pretty sick, huh?" Arlen said and smiled. "Austin would take the damn thing to bed with him and try to fuck it. I kept quiet about it until we were both called into the dean's office one day. Austin had told him that I was the one who thought the idea up and we were both expelled. Man, I was so pissed at him for doin' that and my pop wasn't happy but I was too big to fight so he let me stay in the house. *This* house as a matter of fact. You're in the house I grew up in."

"What happened next?"

"Austin wanted to play with Rebecca and kill her too but I told him not to touch her. He got real pissed and stalked off. We didn't see each other after that and a few days later she was dead."

His eyes turned mean then and he growled, "I found him after I heard what happened to her."

His eyes blazed into Jason's. "I killed the sick motherfucker. I did it for *her.*"

"You did? Where is he now?"

"He's buried in the backyard. Want to see him?" Arlen asked, smiling.

Jason shook his head no and felt the scream building deep in his throat. He stared with dread at the man.

Arlen's eyes glistened and he quietly said, "You know I can't let you leave, don't you?"

Jason stood up. "C'mon man, you don't have to do this. I won't tell anyone. I promise."

The giant stood and towered over him. "You're a liar. I like my quiet life here. I know I've only got a few years left and I won't let you ruin it for me."

"Please, Arlen, let me go. I love Rebecca like you did."

The man grew enraged and grabbed Jason by the shoulders. "What do you mean?! She's dead!"

Jason made his move then and punched the giant in the stomach. He laughed and said, "You think you can hurt me?"

"Shit!" Jason cried as he was lifted up by the shoulders and carried over to the far wall. The man's strength was enormous and Jason knew he was about to die unless he did something fast.

"Little man, I like you but you gotta die," Arlen said and he slammed him against the wall. Jason felt something snap in his back and he cried out in pain. He kicked out with his foot and hit the man in the groin. The grip loosened on his shoulders then and he kicked out again, this time hitting the giant in the stomach.

"Fucker!" Arlen gasped and dropped him to the floor. Jason tried to get to the front door but a big hand pulled him back.

"You're not going anywhere," Arlen growled and threw him easily to the floor.

Before Jason could rise, the giant jumped on him and held his arms down by the wrists.

"Let me go!" Jason screamed. "Get off of me!"

The man straddled him and soon all his weight pressed down on Jason. *This is it*, he thought. *I'm going to die.*

Arlen smiled down at him and a bit of drool dripped down onto Jason's cheek.

"Say goodbye, little man," he said and moved one of his hands to Jason's throat.

Jason punched Arlen in the face over and over again with his free hand but saw it wasn't having any effect. Soon he weakened and dropped his arm to the floor in defeat. The giant began to squeeze Jason's neck and the locket suddenly began to glow brightly.

"What the fuck?! What is that?" Arlen yelled as he stared at the locket.

Jason gasped for breath and whispered, "It's Rebecca."

"What?!" Arlen cried. He let go of Jason and got off of him.

Jason got to his feet and faced the man. "It's true, Arlen. She's here with me because she loves me."

"You're crazy!" the big man screamed and waved his arms back and forth as if he could make Jason disappear. He backed up until he was against the wall and Jason sneered at him.

"You're a pathetic man," he said. "You let those girls die *and* my sweet Rebecca. She never got to live life because of you and your sick friend. When you're rotting in your jail cell for the last years of your life, I hope you realize that the fires of hell await you. Just think. You and Austin will be together again. Forever."

Arlen clamped his big hands over his ears and screamed, "No!!!"

Jason pulled his phone from his pocket and called the police. Arlen made a move forward to stop him but the locket glowed brighter and a wave of blue light pushed him back and held him pinned. The man started babbling nonsense and his terrified eyes pleaded to Jason for help. He found no help there though and Jason stood there and waited until the police arrived. He let them in and while Arlen was being handcuffed, he told them about what Austin and Arlen had done many years before. He also told them to check the bottom of the small lake behind the women's school for the missing girl's bodies and to check the backyard for Austin's body. Their eyes opened wider and wider as he revealed more and more of the gruesome story. Before leaving the house, he looked directly at Arlen and said, "Rot in hell and say hi to Austin for me."

CHAPTER SEVENTY SEVEN

Before he took a flight home, Jason went back again to visit Rebecca's grave. He knelt in the snow by her headstone and said, "I found out what happened to you and why, my darling. I wish I could have been there to stop him. At least I know who you are now, Miss Rebecca Monroe. I'll always love you, you know."

The locket glowed brightly around his neck and he lunged at the stone and grabbed it tightly. "I love you! I love you!" he sobbed and all the emotional tension of the day poured out of him. "I love you," he whispered.

He was exhausted for the rest of the weekend and mentally drained. He watched TV all day while sitting quietly eating left overs. It didn't take long and the story was all over the national news as reporters descended on the college. The authorities worked fast and found the girl's bodies at the bottom of the lake and stunned family members looked into cameras and said "thank you" to Jason for finding out the truth.

Austin's body was indeed in Arlen's backyard and the skeleton was dug up and taken away. The only question left was why the investigation into Rebecca's death had gone nowhere all those years ago. An old man who lived near the school finally confessed to what he knew. He'd been on the police force at that time and it turned out that Austin's father was the chief of police. He knew his son was sick but covered up his crimes anyway. Unfortunately, he'd died years before so he wouldn't be paying for what he did.

Jason had had enough and switched off the TV and went to bed. Loneliness was his companion that night and he cried "I'm sorry! I'm so sorry!" as he thought of Rebecca's horrifying last moments on earth.

The locket glowed softly and seemed to sob with him. Jason held it in his hand and when he finally fell asleep he dreamed of her.

"Jason," she whispered as she gently touched his cheek. "Thank you for caring. Thank you for finding out the truth. Live your life now. You've done what you can for me. Let me go."

"No," he moaned in his sleep as he clutched the bedsheets. "I can't."

Her beautiful eyes faded away as she whispered, "You must."

CHAPTER SEVENTY EIGHT

Over the next few years, Jason turned down all interview requests and eventually reporters moved on to other news and he was forgotten. The library left him alone and he continued to do what he wasn't meant to do. They didn't care and hoped he'd leave but he was stubborn and wouldn't let them win.

Jason felt helpless as more women died over the years. Each one had died by strangulation and had the same cruel marks on their breasts. Jason knew it was the same man but couldn't figure out how to track him as he moved all over the country to claim his victims. They were of course all *pure* women. The authorities were frustrated as the serial killer continued his death spree.

Jill and Jim were officially a couple now and held hands whenever they could. The love in their eyes for each other was genuine and Jason smiled every time he saw them together because it reminded him of the way he had been with Rebecca.

Susanna and Jeff were very happy together and had created "Army Of God" chapters across the United States. The movement of kindness and love was spreading despite organized religion's fear of it.

Jason would visit them whenever he could for Easter and Thanksgiving. Christmas was the one holiday though when they'd take a cruise somewhere or visit one of the army's many chapters. Jason would buy a bottle of eggnog blended with brandy and finished the whole bottle while sitting in front of the fireplace. He'd also buy a real tree because he knew how much Rebecca loved them and smiling, he'd make a toast to her before going to bed. He'd pull the covers up to his neck and whisper, "Goodnight, my love," before closing his eyes.

As always, the locket would glow and keep him warm.

More years passed and Jason became depressed because he hadn't had any opportunities to rescue anyone in a long time. He felt as if he didn't have a purpose anymore and the drudgery of each passing day took a toll on him as he grew older.

The library went through many changes and after a few renovations it looked nothing like the place he'd started at years before. He knew the end was approaching when he began to feel like a stranger.

One late April day, he stepped into the director's office and handed in his resignation.

"This should make you very happy," he said as she read it.

She was older now too and her cruel eyes looked tired as she looked up at him when she was finished reading.

"I have to give you credit," she said. "You lasted a lot longer than I thought you would."

He smiled at the thought of his small victory over her and went back to work. Late in the afternoon, Pete raced up to him and said, "Hey man, come outside. Everyone's looking at the sky. I've never seen anything like it."

Jason stretched his aching arms and followed Pete outside. Jim and Jill were there and they looked scared. The sky was a strange darkish green and there was no wind.

"Get everyone inside!" he yelled when the sirens suddenly blared.

The wind suddenly picked up and trees began to bend. Patrons and staff raced inside the building and the director, Mrs. Walton appeared in the lobby. She waved her hands and screamed, "Everyone stay right here! This is where we need to be!"

Jason had always disagreed with the library's emergency manual instructions which instructed people to stay in this spot. He knew that the only reason they picked this area was because it could hold the largest number of people. He stepped forward and said, "No, not here. The basement's safer."

Mrs. Walton's eyes narrowed in anger and she stared intensely at Jason, "Are you contradicting me?"

"Yes, because you're *wrong*."

Before she could respond, a patron pointed out one of the surrounding windows and screamed, "A tornado! It's coming right at us!"

Jason ran to the window and saw leaves blowing around as dark greenish clouds swirled in the angry looking air. A gigantic tornado was bearing down on them from across the street and would hit them in seconds. He knew there was no time to get to the basement and screamed, "Everyone! Get down!"

Patrons and staff dove to the floor and covered their heads with their hands. One man however stood stupidly by the window and stared in horror at what was coming. Jason screamed, "Get the hell away from there, you fool! You're too close to the glass!"

It was too late and suddenly the window imploded inward and a large shard of glass sliced through the man's neck. His head rolled and stopped directly in front of the terrified director who stared in shock at the man's still blinking eyes.

"Eeeeeee!!!" she screamed and the tornado hit the building. There were creaks and groans everywhere and that's when Jason saw the crack in the ceiling above them. One of the foundation pillars suddenly buckled and the ceiling began to droop directly above where Pete lay. Jason ran over and stood above him and waited. He looked around the large lobby and felt a tear run down his cheek because he knew he couldn't save everyone. Another large window exploded and pieces of glass shredded the bodies of people who lay too close. The director crawled over to where Pete was and looked up at Jason with terrified eyes. "We're all gonna die," she whispered.

The ceiling began to collapse and Jason grabbed the locket and kissed it. "Rebecca, give me strength," he whispered and let go of it and raised his hands high.

The locket glowed brightly then and bathed Jason in its light. He felt the power surge through him just as the ceiling caved in. He pushed up against it and felt the enormous weight press down on him. His wrist broke and he cried out in pain and pushed back harder. "I can't do it," he grunted as he looked down at Pete and Mrs. Walton's frightened eyes.

He felt his wrist heal and pushed harder against the sagging ceiling.

"You're doing it!" the director screamed triumphantly. "You're really doing it!"

Sweat poured down Jason's face and his muscles felt engorged with a strength he knew he'd never feel again. He pushed up with all of his strength and the ceiling crunched as it moved upwards. Pete's jaw dropped as he watched what Jason was doing and an idea hit him. He stood up and yelled to a group of patrons, "Quickly! Follow me! I know what to do!"

They followed him to a storage room in the small hallway close to the lobby and minutes later came back carrying large end panels and T bars made of steel which were used for shelving units. Jason felt a crunch in his right forearm then and he screamed in agony. His strength began to ebb and the ceiling sagged. Chunks of it caved down around him and he heard screams as people were crushed. "Please don't let me die!" Mrs. Walton cried. "Please, Jason. You can do it."

He stared down at the woman who'd treated him so cruelly over the years and nodded. "Don't worry, I won't let you die," he grunted.

Pete directed everyone to prop up the ceiling with the T bars and end units and Jason felt the weight slowly decrease. "We did it," Pete said finally. "You can stop now."

Jason felt dizzy then and sagged to the floor. Pete grabbed him halfway down and gently lay him down to rest. "You did it, man," he said. "Somehow you did it. You're a hero."

Jason closed his eyes then before consciousness left him and Rebecca was there in his mind. "You're alright, Jason," she whispered. "Everything's alright now."

CHAPTER SEVENTY NINE

The hospital bed was as uncomfortable as he'd remembered. He woke and heard the familiar beeping from the machine that monitored his vitals. Looking down, he saw his broken forearm was heavily bandaged but other than that he seemed fine though thoroughly exhausted.

Mrs. Walton was sitting by his bed and she smiled when she saw he was finally awake.

"Why are *you* here?" Jason asked.

The woman's once cruel eyes were tender now. "You saved me, Jason. I don't know how you did what you did and I don't care. What I do want to know is why? After all the years I've been so cruel to you I don't understand why you did it."

Jason licked his lips and she knew his mouth was dry so she held a cup of water to his lips. He sipped a bit and she took it away.

"It's what she'd want me to do," he answered.

"Who?" she asked.

"Rebecca."

"That girl you knew?"

"Yes, she'd have wanted me to save as many lives as I could including yours. I guess I failed."

She actually reached for his hand and to his surprise held it tightly.

"You didn't fail, Jason. Don't you know how many you saved?"

"No," he answered.

Her face was sad and she said, "It's true many died but because of you, Pete and I plus twelve other patrons and staff survived."

Jason swallowed hard. "Jill and Jim….are they alright?"

Mrs. Walton's eyes filled with tears and Jason began to sob. "No!!! No!!!" he screamed as he pounded the bed with his fists. "Why, God?! Why?!"

Mrs. Walton squeezed his hand tighter. "You did what you could,

Jason. It wasn't your fault."

He was quiet after that and didn't say another word. She kissed his cheek then and quietly left the room. He lay there thinking of how Jim and Jill loved each other and felt empty inside. *What a loss*, he thought. *They were pure and good.*

Over the next few days, his arm healed rapidly and was soon as good as new. The doctors were amazed and told him they'd release him the next day. The survivors he'd saved came and visited him to thank him for what he'd done. He was grateful they didn't ask *how* he'd done it. They just accepted it as the will of God. It was a miracle to all of them but Pete knew the truth. When they were alone, he quietly said, "She helped you, didn't she?"

"Yes," Jason answered and smiled. "She's my guardian angel."

CHAPTER EIGHTY

Jason got out of the hospital in time to attend Jill and Jim's funerals. Jill's parents scowled when he showed up but he ignored them and knelt in front of the casket. It was closed and he placed his hand on the lid and whispered, "Rest in peace, sweet girl. I hope you and Jim are together in heaven."

At Jim's funeral the day after, the boy's father approached him and shook his hand. His eyes looked sad and tired and Jason could tell by his red cheeks that he was a drinker as Jim had said.

"Thank you for being a friend to my boy," he said. "Jim talked very highly of you."

"He was a special boy with a bright future. I'll miss him always," Jason said and the man broke down in tears and sagged into a chair.

"Do you think there's a heaven? Is Jim there?" he asked as he wiped his tears away.

Jason wrapped his arm around the man's shoulders and quietly said, "Yes, there *is* a heaven. An angel told me so."

The man's face brightened and he looked into Jason's eyes. "I believe you."

"Be strong for your son," Jason said and went to stand over the casket.

"You would have been a great man, Jim," he whispered. "I don't know why God took you away and I'm sorry. I hope you're holding hands with Jill in heaven now. Rest in peace, my friend."

He turned away then and went home to cry.

A week later, the library threw him a big retirement party at a nearby hotel and the director said a lot of nice things about him. He was genuinely grateful but the whole event seemed very empty because of the people who weren't there like Jim and Jill. Mrs. Walton asked him to stay on a little while longer and he accepted because she finally treated him with respect and asked him to supervise shelvers during the hours Pete wasn't there.

The damage to the library was slowly repaired and the director announced her retirement upon its completion. Jason was invited to her party and she greeted him warmly. When he said goodbye and good luck to her, she knew she'd never see him again and pulled him close and whispered, "I'm glad you were in my life, Jason. I'm sorry for everything I've done."

They parted and he shook her hand and left.

I'm free, he thought as he stood in the night air. *I'm finally free of that place but now what? What do I do now?*

When he got home, the day got worse. There was a call on his answering machine from Jeff. He asked Jason to come right away because Susannah had been diagnosed with cancer.

Jason sank to the floor after listening to the message again and began to sob. "My little girl!" he cried. "Oh God, my little girl!"

CHAPTER EIGHTY ONE

"What's the prognosis?" he asked Jeff when he arrived at the hospital. The big man's face was pale and he pulled Jason to him.

"It's not good. The doctor said it was too advanced. She has two weeks maybe."

"Oh God no," Jason whispered and shoved his fist against his mouth. "How did this happen?"

Jeff shook his head sadly. "I don't know. She didn't have any pain until a few days ago and there were no clues. It evidently started slowly deep inside her and remained hidden until now. There's nothing they can do."

Jason went to her room and sat beside her bed. She looked very tired and after a few minutes she opened her eyes and saw him. "Dad?" she whispered. "You're here."

"Of course I am," he said and knelt by the bed and gently held her hands. "I wouldn't want to be anywhere else."

"I'm dying," she said.

He'd thought long and hard about it and knew what he would do by the time the plane had landed.

"Susanna," he whispered. "I want to give you something. It'll stop the cancer."

He pulled the locket from around his neck and was about to place it over hers but she grabbed his wrist to stop him.

"No, dad," she said weakly. "Rebecca gave that to *you*. *You* need it."

He felt helpless and said, "Please Susanna, I want you to have it. I don't want to lose you. I *can't* lose you."

She looked at him with those pretty eyes of hers and he saw the little girl he once knew in them. "No, dad," she whispered. "I've had a good life. I want to go to mom now. I miss her."

"Please no!" he cried and she drew him close and he lay his head against her shoulder and sobbed.

"Don't cry, dad," she whispered. "I'll tell Rebecca you said "hi.""

CHAPTER EIGHTY TWO

Susanna didn't last two weeks. She died in Jeff's arms three days later and Jason stepped out into the hallway and collapsed to the floor. He began to sob uncontrollably and two nurses came rushing over. They were crying too. He asked where the chapel was and they led him there. He asked to be alone and he knelt in the small pew in front of the altar and stared intensely at the large cross on the wall.

"I hate you," he said quietly. "I hate you for taking Rebecca and Susanna away from me. I also hate you for taking Jim and Jill from this life."

He stood up then and pounded his fists into his face and screamed, "I hate you! Oh God, I hate you!"

At the funeral, Jason placed a rose on Susanna's coffin and whispered, "I love you, Susannah. You'll always be my little girl. Say hi to your mother for me….and Rebecca."

He shook Jeff's hand then and saw the man was crushed by his loss. He'd loved Susannah very much but Jason knew he was strong and would continue doing all the good things they'd started.

When it was time to go back home, Jason hugged him and said, "Call me anytime, Jeff. Day or night I'm there if you need me. Alright?"

"Yes," Jeff said but he wasn't as strong as Jason thought he was because four days later he sat on his couch and put a gun in his mouth.

"I'm coming, Susannah," he whispered and pulled the trigger.

CHAPTER EIGHTY THREE

Jason heard about Jeff's death days later when a news story asked, "Who will lead the "Army Of God" organization now?"

To his dismay, Jeff had already been buried and Jason felt bad that he'd missed the funeral. He sat stunned for hours until he finally got up to go for a walk. *I have to find a purpose*, he thought.

He *did* find a purpose by volunteering at homeless shelters and helping veterans with their bills by giving his savings away to those who really needed it.

The years went by until one day when he was lifting something heavy at the shelter and something snapped in his back. He looked down at the locket around his neck for help but knew there wouldn't be any. It had glowed less and less the past few months. *I'm old now*, he realized. *It's time to be a realist. I can't do this anymore.*

He went to the head of the shelter, said his goodbyes and headed home. It was Christmas Eve and he started a fire in the fireplace. He used a heating pad for his aching back but eventually turned it off in disgust when he realized it wasn't helping. Sitting down, he stared at the fresh tree he'd bought and smiled at the glistening tinsel and the glowing lights.

After a while, he drifted off to sleep but didn't dream. He woke up a few hours later and saw the clock. It was almost midnight and the fire in the fireplace was almost out. A chill settled in his bones and he began to cry as he thought of all the people he'd loved in his life who were gone now. It was just him now and he was all alone.

"I've had a good life, God," he whispered. "But I'm tired now. Please take me home. I want to die."

He closed his eyes and thought of going into the kitchen for a knife to end his suffering.

"Don't do it, Jason," a voice suddenly whispered. "You're not finished with this life yet."

The locket began to glow, slowly at first but after a few seconds it pulsed rapidly with energy. He felt its warmth, slowly stood up and turned around.

"Rebecca!" he cried when he saw her standing only feet away from him. "Am I dreaming? Is it really you?!"

She looked gorgeous in her simple white dress and looked as young as the last time he'd seen her years before. She came closer to him and smiled. "No Jason, you're not dreaming. I'm here. I've come back to you."

"Oh my God!" he cried and she went to him as he fell to his knees. He wrapped his arms around her legs and pressed his head against her stomach "Oh God, I've missed you! I've missed you so much!!"

He sobbed harder and she smoothed his gray hair back with her hand. "Don't cry, my love," she whispered. "I'm here now and I'm not leaving you again."

He gazed up at her beautiful face and said, "But I'm old now. There's nothing left of me to love."

She smiled tenderly at him. "Let *me* be the judge of that, Jason. You may be older but you're still handsome to me."

"But I'm dead inside. I hurt all over and nothing works anymore."

He looked down at his groin and then back at her, ashamed.

She made him rise and looked deeply into his eyes. "I've never stopped loving you, Jason. Don't you now that by now? I'll take you any way I can get you. You're everything to me."

His eyes glistened when he realized how intensely she loved him. "My angel," he cried. "My sweet angel."

She held him for long minutes and finally he pulled away and asked, "How did you come back to me? I thought God was angry with you."

She smiled and answered, "He's a forgiving God, Jason. Over time he realized I had no choice in what I did. I had to save your life. He knows that now."

Jason gently took her hands in his and said, "I have something to tell you."

She touched his lips with her finger to silence him. "I don't want to talk now, Jason."

Her eyes stared into his and he knew what she wanted. "I can't, Rebecca. I told you. I'm an old man now."

"You'll be fine. Trust me," she whispered and backed away from him. He watched as she slowly reached down and took hold of her dress. She lifted it up and he saw she wore nothing underneath. In one smooth motion she pulled it over her head and tossed it aside. She stood there for a moment to let him admire her.

"My God," he whispered. "You're so beautiful. You're the most beautiful woman I've ever known," he said.

Her eyes seemed to twinkle at him and the smooth skin he remembered so well had that same light sheen to it. She motioned to him and said, "Now you."

He took his time and saved his underwear for last. When he finally pulled them down, it was her turn to admire him. Her eyes roamed over his body and she smiled. "My handsome man," she said. "You haven't changed a bit."

Jason's eyes opened wide as she slinked towards him, hips swaying sexily. "Do you want me like I want you?" she asked in a husky voice.

He touched her breasts and brushed his fingers over her nipples. She moaned and closed her eyes. "Yes, oh yes, I've missed your touch," she whispered.

Jason bent low and took a nipple into his mouth and sucked lightly on it. Rebecca grabbed his head and pulled him into her. "Yes, just like that," she moaned.

He pulled his mouth away and her hand moved down and touched his stomach. It lingered there and the feeling of her fingers so close to his groin was so sensual that he gasped in anticipation. She smiled and reached lower then. The warmth of her hand shocked him and he shivered as it gently cupped his balls.

"While I was away I realized I never really got to play with these," she said. Jason seemed frozen in place and she purred sexily. "I'm going to drain these dry," she said and squatted down until she was staring directly at his groin. She looked up at him and said, "Just stay like this and enjoy what I'm going to do to you."

Jason put his hands behind his back and she said, "Yes, stay just like that. Surrender to my touch."

She leaned in and took one of his testicles into her mouth. She rolled it around with her tongue and looked up at him to see his reaction. He stared down at her with glazed eyes and she knew she was making him happy. "Mmmmmm," she purred around his ball and as she suckled him his penis began to twitch. She moved to the other ball and gently sucked it into her mouth. Her warm lips closed tighter around it and his penis filled with blood. She took her mouth away and smiled up at him. "I knew that would get a rise out of you," she said, proud of herself.

Jason began to breathe heavier and she licked her lips as she stared at the precum dripping from the tip of his penis. She stuck her tongue out and tasted him and he moaned and closed his eyes. "Poor little peehole," she whispered. "Did you miss me?"

Jason cried out then when her mouth suddenly engulfed him. "Oh God!" he cried and she began to bob back and forth on his stiff cock.

He grabbed her hair and pushed her head back until his cockhead popped out of her mouth with a loud slurping noise. Surprised, she looked up at him and asked, "Don't you want to cum in my mouth?"

"No," he answered in a husky voice. "I want to lose myself inside of you."

She stood up and kissed him. It felt like his brain exploded and splattered against his skull and Jason swooned. Rebecca grabbed hold of his shoulders and kept him from falling as her tongue gently moved over his in a sensual mating. Jason was able to pull away and lay his head against her shoulder and began to cry.

"What's wrong, my love?" Rebecca asked as she stroked the back of his head. "Why do you cry?"

He sobbed harder and she kissed the top of his head. "I know you missed me, Jason," she whispered. "I promise you I'll never leave you again. I'm yours to love tonight. Please don't be sad. This is a happy time for us."

He raised his head and looked at her. She brushed his tears away with her hand and whispered, "Make love to me, Jason. Make me scream your name."

He suddenly scooped her up in his arms. "What are you doing?!" she giggled and wrapped her arms around his neck.

"I'm going to carry you over the threshold," he said tenderly and carried her to the front door. She laughed happily and opened it. He stepped out into the hallway and she lay her head against his chest.

"Jason, we can't stay out here too long," she whispered. "We're both naked. What if someone see us?"

He ignored her and spun around. She laughed and he stepped back inside. Rebecca closed the door behind them and locked it. He looked at her with more tenderness in his eyes than she'd ever seen before.

"Now you're my wife," he whispered and her eyes opened wide. "I just carried you over the threshold."

Tears formed in her eyes. "Oh Jason! You're so romantic! I love you so!"

He kissed her then and she felt as if she was melting in his arms. Pulling her lips away from his, she huskily said, "Take me to bed now and make love to me. I can't wait any longer."

Jason carried her into the bedroom and lay her down on the bed He stepped back to gaze at her beauty and she raised her arms out to him. "Come to bed, my love."

He climbed into bed and she moaned when his body pressed against her. His penis bobbed between her legs and she reached for it.

"Not yet," he whispered and moved down so his head was between her legs. He took hold of her thighs and she waited breathlessly.

"Oh Jason, yes!" she groaned. He moved his mouth to her sex and over the next few minutes she writhed in pleasure and clutched the bedsheets with her hands as he tasted her nectar.

"My God, stop!" she finally cried and grabbed him by the hair to pull him away. "I can't wait any longer! I need you inside me!"

He moved up her body with his tongue and by the time his lips were over hers again she was panting. "Mmmmm," she moaned and his penis strained against her belly. He pushed himself up on his arms and she reached and gently grabbed his cock to guide him in. She was slick and he entered easily. "Oh God! I've missed you!" she moaned and pulled him down to lightly bite his shoulder. Her hips began to grind against his and he gently pumped his throbbing cock in and out of her. "Oh Jason!" she cried out suddenly. "I'm gonna cum! Oh God, I'm gonna cum!"

He pulled almost completely out then and she froze. Looking into her eyes, Jason whispered, "I love you so much, my angel."

She gripped his shoulders tightly and he sank slowly back inside of her, deeper this time until the knob of his penis touched something that caused her to scream.

"Oh fuck! That's it! That's it! Jason! Jason!" she shrieked and a tremor raced through her body as the massive orgasm rippled through her. Jason moved slowly inside her and she screamed his name many times as smaller orgasms tore through her quivering body.

"Oh, my love!" she cried as she felt her pussy grip him tightly. "Fill me with your love! Cum for me! Cum for your angel!"

Jason had held out for a long time and was very proud of himself but now the feel of Theresa's sex milking him was the last straw. He grit his teeth and an animal sound burst from his lips.

"Yes….yes…." she moaned as she watched his face. "Cum, baby. Cum for me."

Her pussy fluttered around his cock and he screamed, "Rebecca! Oh God, Rebecca!"

His penis exploded then and he thought the world had ended. The pleasure in his groin spread throughout his body and she held him close as he shuddered against her. "Yes….give me all of you," she whispered in his ear. "I'm here for you. Just you, Jason and no one else."

Her words drove him over the edge again and his penis blew up inside her as he let out a high keening sound of exquisite pleasure.

Her sex gripped him tightly as the last of his cum seeped out and he felt himself succumb to the sweet warmth of her body as it melted against his. Rebecca held him tightly and didn't want to ever let him go and whispered, "This is what I've dreamed of all the years I was away."

He lifted his head and his eyes were glazed. She laughed when she saw the drool at the corner of his mouth and asked, "Are you alright?"

He nodded and wiped the drool away and lay his head back against her. "It's alright if you can't speak," she said. "I'm going to hold you like this all night long."

He began to sob against her then and she whispered, "There's no need to cry. Your angel's here."

CHAPTER EIGHTY FOUR

Jason thought he'd died and gone to heaven because when he woke the next morning he was still lying in his beautiful angels arms.

"You're here," he whispered. "It wasn't a dream."

"No, Jason," she said. "It really happened. We made love."

He lay his head back down and felt her heart gently beating against his ear. "No other man has ever experienced what I just did," he whispered. "To be loved by an angel is a wonderful thing. I'm so incredibly lucky."

She rubbed his head. "I'm the lucky one, Jason. You're the man I always dreamed of."

Being mortal had its disadvantages and Jason groaned unhappily when his stomach suddenly growled. Rebecca laughed and said, "It sounds like somebody's hungry!"

He looked at her. "I don't want to let go of you. I want to hold you forever."

Her eyes twinkled at him and she smiled. "I'm sorry, Jason but you have to eat. I don't want to lie here holding a corpse because you'll be dead soon by the sound of your stomach!"

He laughed and was about to push off of her and was stunned when he realized his penis was still inside her. "Yes," she said happily. "You stayed hard all night long for me. You never went soft."

He blushed and she laughed. "You're so cute when your face turns red. I love it."

He pulled out of her then and she moaned in pleasure as the tip of him rubbed over her clit. She grabbed him and lunged up at his face and grabbed his lower lip in her teeth. Jason's eyes opened wide in fright and she let go of him and smiled. Her eyes blazed with intensity.

"I'm sorry. I guess I got carried away a little."

He backed slowly away off the bed and felt as if she were about to eat him.

"Jason," she asked, her eyes narrowing. "Would you like to get kinky with me?"

He stared at her in disbelief. What had gotten into her?

"I'm asking because *I'd* like to get kinky with *you*. Do you remember that fantasy of mine?"

He didn't know where this was going and warily nodded yes. That made her happy and she smiled.

"After I'm done feeding you," she said, "I'm going to spank you and then I'm going to tie you to the bed and go for a ride. Would you like that?"

Jason's face turned redder and she laughed harder this time. "Oh yeah, I think we're going to have a lot of fun together."

She sat up and pulled him to her until her mouth was by his ear.

"I'm going to make you my love slave," she whispered and lightly bit his earlobe.

Jason groaned and Rebecca giggled happily. "Oh yeah, I like the sound of that, don't you?"

He stared into her eyes and softly said, "I'll do anything you want. I surrender myself to you, mind, body and soul."

Her eyes squinted in delight but she said, "I just need your mind and body, Jason. Your soul is for God."

She made him breakfast and fed him like she had done years before. They gazed into each other's eyes with a love that had no boundaries and were happy beyond belief. When he was done eating, Rebecca led him back to the bedroom, took him over her knees and spanked him lightly until his bottom was a bright red. When she'd finished, Jason stared at the floor breathing heavily and Rebecca's face flushed from the excitement of what she'd done. She gazed down at his reddened globes and caressed them.

"Thank you for letting me do that to you," she said. "That was kinky as hell."

He wasn't surprised when she gently pushed him off of her and made him lie down on the bed. She tied his arms and legs to the bedposts with twine she'd found in the kitchen drawer. Then she used one of her feathers to torture him with like he remembered from her fantasy. It moved lightly over his entire body until he was writhing with pleasure and begging her to make love to him. Finally, when she sensed he'd had enough she caressed his cheek and straddled him. Grasping his penis, she stroked it for a moment before placing it lightly at her entrance. Staring down into his face, she bit her lower lip and sank down onto him. Her warm pussy lips encircled his shaft and his cockhead swelled as she began to move her hips.

"Now I'm fucking *you*," she whispered as she gazed into his eyes. "You're my love slave," she said. "You'll do anything I ask, won't you?"

He shook his head yes and she laughed and closed her eyes. Her breasts jiggled up and down as she moved faster. "Yes....oh yes," she moaned. The small orgasm hit her fast and her sex gripped him tightly as she came. "Oh Jason!" she cried as she rode him. Jason grit his teeth to keep from cumming and she slowed down after a minute. Afterwards, she lay atop him breathing heavily before pulling herself off of his cock and untying him.

He watched as she got off the bed and lay on the floor. She held her arms out to him and said, "You fuck *me* now."

Jason gazed at her with a crazy animal lust and he shivered mightily when he slid his cock into her. She pulled him close and kissed his neck and shoulder as he fucked her. "Yes, yes, my love slave," she moaned. "*You* can cum now."

Jason screamed and shuddered as he came on command. "Oh Rebecca!" he yelled and she bucked up against him. Her nipples rubbed against his chest and stiffened as she followed him into an earth shattering orgasm.

"Jason! Oh dear God! Jason!" she screamed.

They clung to each other like two survivors in a lifeboat and cried and laughed as their orgasms went on and on until he lay exhausted and couldn't go on.

"Wow, that was fucking amazing," Rebecca whispered. "You let me spank you and tie you to the bed and fuck you. I love you so much. Thank you."

Jason's face flushed then and she smiled. "I'm sorry I got so kinky. I just knew it would turn both of us on."

"I don't mind," he said. "I already told you I'd do anything for you."

"I know," she whispered and kissed him. Her power surged through him again and he moaned happily.

After a few minutes, she pulled her lips away and Jason saw that her face was flushed and there was a strange look in her eyes.

"What's wrong?" Jason asked, worried.

"Nothing's wrong," she answered, smiling shyly. "But don't you think it's time you spanked *me* now?"

CHAPTER EIGHTY FIVE

By the time he was finished, Rebecca's bottom was red and tingly and she was dripping wet with arousal. She looked over her shoulder at him and said, "Now I want to make love again."

She was insatiable and Jason lasted as long as he could but in the end his mortal body finally succumbed to exhaustion again. Rebecca patiently waited for him to recover and he sighed happily against her as his strength slowly came back. When he finally opened his eyes again a thought hit him and he grew worried. Rebecca could see it in his eyes and asked, "What's wrong?"

He stared at her for a moment before saying, "You're going to leave me again, aren't you?"

"What?! Don't be silly! Of course I'm not leaving you! Why would you say that?!"

His eyes looked sad then. "Because it just hit me that you're acting out all the fantasies you've ever thought of and it feels rushed. Why?"

Rebecca's heart sank but she couldn't tell him the truth. She'd come back to him because she finally could but also because she had a premonition that something very bad was looming closer every second and she didn't know what it was.

"Jason, I'm acting like this because I missed you terribly these past years," she lied. "I'm just making up for lost time. Aren't you happy?"

"Of course I am," he said but his eyes said different. She felt badly about not telling him the truth but she didn't want to scare him with the warning signs going off in her head. Great danger was coming and she didn't want to tell him that.

She changed the subject then and said, "You were going to tell me everything that happened while I was away. I'm ready to listen now. Besides, I think you need a break," she said, giggling.

Jason hesitated for a moment and said, "Please don't be mad at me but I did a little digging. I know who killed you and why."

"What?!" she cried and she gripped his shoulders hard with her hands and rolled over on top of him. He tried to rise but she pushed him down hard and he cried out in pain. "You did what?!!" she screamed.

"Please, Rebecca! You're hurting me!" he shouted. She let up a little but still held his shoulders down.

"Tell me what you did!" she hissed. "Tell me everything!"

Over the next half hour, Jason slowly told Rebecca how Jill had been stalked by the reincarnated Austin and how he'd prevented her from being killed. Then he told her about what he'd found on the internet and how he'd visited the colleges. She listened carefully to every word and frowned when he told her about Austin and his friend, Arlen. She cringed and shivered when he told her about the mannequin with her name on it. She bit her lower lip when he told her of his fight with the giant and about all the women who had been murdered and where their bodies were found. He finally finished with all the serial killings which had occurred over the years she'd been gone.

She stared at him for a long time and he held his breath and waited.

"You fool," she said finally. "You stupid wonderful fool. You could have gotten yourself killed. Why did you do all that, Jason?"

"I did it for you, Rebecca Monroe. I needed to find out why you died. Please don't be angry with me. The locket protected me."

"Oh you sweet fool," she whispered and kissed him. "I love you so much. Thank you for getting me answers."

"There's more," he said dreading what he was about to tell her.

The look on his face said it all and she knew it wasn't good. "Just tell me," she said. "Just get it over with."

"Let me up first."

She let him sit up and he took her hands in his and said, "It's bad. It's about Susannah and Jeff."

She didn't say anything and tears rolled down her cheeks as he told her what had happened. "Oh God!" she cried and sobbed against his shoulder. "Oh my God!"

Jason let her cry and she sniffled and asked, "Did Susanna suffer?"

"No," he answered. "She died peacefully in Jeff's arms."

"Oh Jason! I'm so sorry! I'm sorry for both of us!"

"I am too."

Rebecca got very quiet then and said, "I was going to make love to you again but now I'm not in the mood. I'm sorry."

She stood up and went to retrieve her white dress. Jason watched as she slipped it on. "I need to be alone for a while," she said and walked out of the room. She went into the living room and sat staring at the Christmas tree.

Jason gave her the space she needed, put on some clothes and waited patiently for her to process everything he'd told her. An hour later she appeared in the bedroom again and sat down on the bed across from him. He'd fallen asleep in the desk chair and she lightly touched his face. Jason opened his eyes and she patted the bed. "Sit by me," she said.

He sat next to her and she held his hand. Her eyes were moist as they looked into his. "I'm so sorry you had to go through all this alone, Jason," she said softly. "I know I wasn't here for you all those years."

Her eyes grew more intense and she said, "I know you love me very much. Not many men would have done what you did. I think you're a little bit crazy to do it but I love you for it."

He raised her hand to his face and kissed it. "I had to get answers," he said. "For both of us."

"You did…except for one."

His eyebrows raised in surprise. "What do you mean?"

Her face turned grim and she said, "The unanswered question is why has he come back to do it all again? It doesn't make sense. If a soul begins a new life they become a better person than the one they were before."

"Maybe he sold his soul to the devil," Jason blurted out without thinking.

Rebecca's eyes opened wide in terror then and she stared intensely at him. Jason could tell she was very frightened.

"That's the answer, Jason! He sold his soul to the devil himself! He's come here straight from hell!"

CHAPTER EIGHTY SIX

"So what can we do?" Jason asked. "The authorities can't find him and neither can I."

Rebecca didn't answer him right away and sat in silence. Her brow was furrowed and Jason could tell she was deep in thought. She finally turned to him and said, "I know what to do."

"What?!" he asked excitedly.

"We lure him out. We make him come to *us.*"

"How?" Jason asked.

Rebecca smiled. "We let him know I'm here again. It'll drive him crazy. I just know it."

Jason frowned. "I don't understand. So what if he finds out you're here? What difference does that make?"

"It makes all the difference in the world, Jason. Don't you remember the bakery and how we first saw him there?"

"Yes, but so what?"

She touched his forehead. "C'mon….think. That wasn't a coincidence. It couldn't have been. He was waiting for me. It was deliberate."

Jason still didn't understand. "Ok, but why?"

She stopped smiling. "That I don't know."

"This is silly. Why would he care if you're here or not?"

A shudder went through the angel and she knew the answer then. "Because he has unfinished business, Jason. He's not done with me. He killed me once but he's not happy because I'm an angel now. He wants to finish the job he started."

"What?!" Jason said and laughed. "That's crazy! You're an angel! How could he hurt you again?!"

"I don't know," she answered. "I just know we have to stop him from killing again."

Jason was silent then and Rebecca pulled him close. "Jason, will you stand against him with me? I don't know if I can do this alone."

He gazed lovingly into her eyes. "You know I will. I'll never let him hurt you again."

She rested her head against his shoulder and whispered, "I hope so. Oh god, I hope so."

Jason jumped when his phone rang but ignored it. Rebecca had a premonition something was wrong and said, "You better see who that was."

Jason's face turned ashen as he listened to the message the caller had left and Rebecca felt a chill run up her spine. She didn't like the look he gave her and asked, "Jason, what's wrong?"

His eyes were frightened and he whispered, "That was the director at the men's college. The mannequin's been stolen."

Rebecca hugged herself and bit her lower lip. "Oh no."

Jason went to her and gently held her. "I told you I won't let him hurt you again."

Rebecca looked up into his eyes. "I'm afraid, Jason. He won't stop until he kills me again."

Jason closed his eyes and whispered, "Over my dead body he will."

Rebecca's eyes flooded with tears and she pulled him closer. "I may be an angel," she whispered. "But you're my hero."

CHAPTER EIGHTY SEVEN

They talked about what to do and Jason went out and bought a police scanner. Within hours, he and the angel were able to hear calls for help.

"We only answer the ones where women are in trouble," she said. "*Young* women."

"But why no others?" Jason asked.

"Because we can't be everywhere, Jason. People die every day."

"Ok, but why just young women?"

"Because those are the ones he likes to kill. The innocent ones. The *pure* ones."

They waited patiently and two weeks later were finally rewarded when a call came over the radio about a young woman in her twenties reporting that someone was in her house. It was only two blocks away and Rebecca kissed Jason so he'd keep up with her. They raced to the scene and got there before the cops did. They walked around the house and saw the broken window. Jason was the first inside and he could hear cries on the second floor. Rebecca followed behind and they ran up the stairs.

"Please no!" a woman's voice screamed. "Oh God! It hurts!"

The bedroom door was locked and Jason didn't waste time. He barreled his way through it and it blew apart into splinters. His eyes quickly adjusted to the dark and he saw a figure lying on the woman in the semi darkness. She was tied to the bed and her mouth was open in a silent scream of agony. Jason heard the slurping sounds and ran at the figure. "Get away from her!" he shouted and the figure bolted upright to take Jason's charge head on.

"You!" the man yelled in surprise as their chests butted together. They grappled and Jason felt himself being pushed backwards. Rebecca lunged from the side but the man punched out at her and her cheek exploded in pain. She fell onto the bed atop the tied woman and tried to shake the stars away.

Jason was surprised by how much stronger the attacker was than the last time they met and the way the man's eyes blazed into his seemed totally unnatural. "I'm going to kill you," the killer grunted and Jason kneed him in the groin which made him fall to his knees.

"Please don't let him hurt me again!" the woman on the bed shouted and Rebecca lunged again at the attacker.

He was very fast and his hand shot out and gripped her neck. Rising from the floor, he swept a leg out and knocked Jason down. Rebecca felt herself being lifted into the air. The man's eyes burned into hers and he smiled. "We meet again, Rebecca," he said soothingly.

Her body stiffened in terror and in that moment she remembered how helpless she'd felt all those years before when the cruel monster had strangled the life from her.

Jason rose from the floor and the man flung Rebecca at him. They crashed into the wall and spittle flew from the monster's mouth as he screamed, "You can't stop me! She dies today!"

They rose as one and faced him.

"Not today," the angel said determinedly. "You won't kill today."

The man saw the look in their eyes and then looked back at the nude woman on the bed. He was clearly anguished and began to back slowly away towards the doorway. "You may have won today but I grow stronger every day. We'll meet again, Rebecca and when we do I'll make you suffer all over again."

His eyes gazed into hers tenderly then and she shuddered from the intimate connection they shared at that horrifying moment. He'd seen and felt her terror and she hated him for it. It was as if he'd raped her very soul.

"You bastard!" she screamed and clenched her fists. "I won't let you hurt me again!"

Tears poured down her cheeks and she advanced on him. Snarling, he turned to flee.

"Get him!" she screamed at Jason. "We have to stop him!"

They ran as fast as they could behind him but couldn't catch up as he ran down the stairs and out the front door. When they emerged outside the house, they looked around but there was no sign of him. Rebecca felt defeated and sagged into Jason's chest.

"We lost him," she said quietly. "He grows stronger every day and we lost him."

"What is he?" Jason asked, incredulous.

Rebecca shivered and he pulled her closer. "He's a monster," she whispered. "A monster from hell."

CHAPTER EIGHTY EIGHT

They went back into the house and untied the crying woman. Her poor breasts had been savagely bitten and she whimpered as Jason covered her with a blanket.

"We have to leave now," Rebecca said as she gently touched the woman's face. "The police will be here soon. They'll take you to the hospital."

"Thank you," she said and looked at Jason. "Thank you both."

They got out of the house just in time. The police were a block away and they watched from behind a tree as they ran into the house. Rebecca looked at Jason and said, "We're done for tonight. Let's go home."

He killed again three days later far from town but they couldn't do anything to stop it because it wasn't called in. Rebecca cried for the poor woman's soul when her horrifying injuries were reported. They'd been inflicted on her before she died and Rebecca shook with rage.

"He's so cruel!" she cried. "Why does he have to be so cruel?!"

Jason pulled her close and quietly asked, "Why is he getting stronger? He's just a man. I don't understand it."

"I need to talk to the others," Rebecca said. "I'll be back later."

Before he could react, she disappeared. Jason went into the bedroom to lie down and felt a growing horror as he stared up at the ceiling. *What are we dealing with?* he thought. *Why is this happening?*

He closed his eyes and drifted off into a deep sleep. He began to dream and Rebecca was gliding towards him. She was smiling and her eyes glowed brightly with her love for him. A dark swirling cloud suddenly appeared behind her and his eyes opened wide with horror as a monstrous demon emerged from its center. The creature's great reddish wings flapped as it flew towards her. Jason tried to scream to warn her but his lips had been sewn shut. Horrified, he groaned as the thing moved closer to his unsuspecting angel. Its clawed hand reached out and grabbed her ankle. She looked back and her eyes were filled with terror. The monster pulled her back to face him and held her arms tightly to her side. It smiled at her and opened its mouth wide. A long black leathery tongue slurped out of its mouth and gently licked her cheeks. She didn't make a sound and seemed frozen with indescribable fear. Jason gagged and the thing looked at him. Its blazing orange eyes squinted with delight.

"She's *mine*, you know," the demon said in a raspy voice that hurt his ears. "She'll *always* be mine."

Jason darted awake and sat sweating in the bed. The darkness caressed him and he began to cry. "Please God!" he wept. "Please don't let him take Rebecca from me! Don't let him kill her again!"

CHAPTER EIGHTY NINE

A day later, Rebecca came back to him. She noticed he looked pale and wasted and grew worried.

"Jason," she said and touched his face. "What's wrong? Did something happen while I was gone?"

He fell to his knees and wrapped his arms around her. She held his head to her stomach and he whispered, "I can't lose you again, Rebecca. I'll die if you go."

She made him rise and kissed him. Her eyes were soft as they gazed into his and she said, "I talked with the other angels. They can't help us. We're on our own here."

"But why?! Why won't they help us?!"

Her soft hand touched his cheek and she said, "Because each of us has our own storyline, Jason. I have to finish mine *alone.*"

"Without me?!" he cried, aghast.

"Yes," she said sadly. "He wants me and *only* me. I won't let you die because of me."

"But I *want* to protect you!" he cried. "I *have* to protect you!"

She lay her head against his chest and said, "I know you do, darling but this is the way it has to be."

He trembled and she knew the inevitable was rushing towards her at lightning speed. They didn't have much time left.

At that moment another young woman was savagely murdered but they didn't know it. Rebecca looked into Jason's eyes and he could sense the end was near.

"No," he whispered. "Oh God….no."

She took his hand and led him into the bedroom where they both undressed. "Please make love to me," she said and he took her gently in his arms. Her warm soft body pressed against his and he shivered at its touch. He had never felt as close to her than at that exact moment and the intimacy between them made his heart beat faster against her hand when she pressed it against his chest. They stood like that for long minutes gazing into each other's eyes. Finally, she lay her head against his shoulder and whispered, "I have something to show you."

He pulled away and asked, "What?"

She went back to her dress which lay on the floor and retrieved the photo she'd rescued from Susannah's house in the fire years before. Holding it close to her breasts, she went back and showed it to him. "I carry it with me always," she said. "This is the little boy I fell in love with who's now a man."

Jason's eyes filled with tears. "You saved this?" he said, amazed.

"Yes. I wanted you close to me always."

"Oh Rebecca!" he cried and pulled her to him.

She dropped the photo to the floor and whispered in his ear, "I don't need it now though. You're right here in front of me."

Jason scooped her up in his arms and she kissed his neck as he laid her on the bed. He trembled at the sight of her beautiful body and took it all in as if it was the last time he'd ever see her again. *I must remember*, he thought. *I must never forget.*

She practically read his mind because as he lay on top of her she touched his lips with her fingers before he could say anything. "Shhhh," she whispered. "I want to remember this night. I want to remember the softness of your lips and the tenderness in your eyes and the strength of your arms about me."

She pulled his head to her breasts and began to cry. "I know you have the locket but tell me you'll remember me too, Jason. Oh please, don't ever forget me!"

He kissed her gently, his lips brushing against hers like a soft feather. Wiping away her tears with his fingers, he softly said, "I promise I'll never forget you, Rebecca. No matter what happens or where we are, I'll always remember you even if it's in another life."

Her eyes opened wide when she realized what he'd said. "In another life?" she whispered. "You'll remember?"

"Yes," he answered. "Nothing on this earth or beyond will stop me. I'm yours forever."

She pulled him down for a kiss and her eyes closed as tears ran down her face. "Oh Jason," she whispered. "My lover....my *man*."

They made tender love throughout the night and cried out with pleasure many times. After they were finally satisfied, Rebecca lay against his chest and looked into his eyes. "I love you, dear mortal," she whispered.

His eyes stared back into hers and she felt incredibly loved. "And I love *you*, sweet angel," he replied softly.

They felt their hearts beating as one against each other's chests and smiled. They were truly unified in love, their minds and bodies completely in tune with one another.

"I don't think I'll ever feel as close to you as I feel right now," Jason softly said.

"Nor will I," Rebecca whispered.

They closed their eyes then and for the first time in a long while Rebecca allowed herself to sleep so she could share his dreams. They floated on clouds together and their love for each other was stronger than any evil could ever defeat. They were truly one and would be forever.

CHAPTER NINETY

The next day, Rebecca made Jason breakfast and insisted on feeding him again. He watched her eyes the entire time and said, "Thank you," when she'd put the last piece of bacon between his lips. Before she could pull her hand away, he grabbed it gently and pressed it against his lips. He kissed it and tears ran down her cheeks as his eyes looked tenderly into hers. She touched his cheek with her other hand and whispered, *"My love."*

They could both feel the electric tension in the air so Rebecca lay with him in bed as they listened to the police scanner. Holding her close, Jason felt her beating heart against his chest and felt himself begin to relax. She watched him closely and their hearts suddenly beat as one. He closed his eyes and drifted off into a peaceful sleep.

As Rebecca listened to him breathing, a low voice came from the scanner. *"Rebecca,"* it whispered.

She sat up in bed and her heart froze as she suddenly felt a chill race through her.

"Rebecca," the voice whispered again. "Come to me….I'm waiting."

She looked at Jason and smoothed the hair away from his eyes and whispered, "Goodbye, my love. I go to finish my story now."

It was late afternoon and the sky looked angry when she stepped outside into the chilly air. She looked back at the apartment and whispered, "Please God, watch over him now."

The voice was suddenly in her head again and whispered, "Yes….yes….come to me."

"Where are you?" she asked and looked in all directions for a sign.

"Follow your heart and you'll find me, pure one," the voice answered.

Rebecca closed her eyes and began to walk down the sidewalk.

Something told her he wasn't far. One block, then two and nothing. Frowning, she whispered, "Please lord, guide me."

Her feet moved then and she let them lead her away. Her jaw clenched tightly and she growled, "I'm coming….I'm coming for you."

CHAPTER NINETY ONE

Jason woke up groggily and looked around in a panic when he realized Rebecca wasn't in bed with him. "No!" he cried and he got up and walked around looking for a clue to where she'd gone. A sharp pain ripped through his head then and the locket pulsed weakly.

"Oh God, you're in trouble," he whispered and ran out of the apartment. He stood in the cold night air and looked frantically around. The locket pulsed brighter and he held it in his hand and whispered, "Guide me. Lead me to her."

He held it above his head like a beacon and turned in different directions until it grew brighter still. *This is the way*, he thought and headed to where the locket glowed brightest.

It took only minutes and soon he stood in front of a huge abandoned warehouse. He circled the building until he found the cracked open door. It was partially off its hinges and creaked sharply as he slowly opened it. Stepping inside, he smelled something putrid and knew something dead was close by. He squinted in the half light and saw the decomposing corpse of a dog lying near some broken wooden pallets. Moving as quietly as possible, he walked past the remains and looked around. There was a stairway leading to a second floor far off in the corner. Broken wooden crates and pallets lay scattered around the massive room and he crept slowly towards the stairs. There was someone standing by them facing the wall and he smiled. "Rebecca!" he whispered and ran towards the figure.

He touched its shoulder and it spun around to face him.

It was the mannequin from the men's college. Its painted eyes stared into his and he screamed and moved backwards. He tripped over a piece of wood and fell sideways. A large rat ran by his face and he screamed again. He stared back in horror at the mannequin and saw again the name "Rebecca" scrawled above its pubis. The plunger still stuck out from between the thing's legs and he gagged.

"I see you found it," a voice suddenly said and hands pulled him to his feet.

It was Rebecca and she wasn't happy. "Why did you follow me here, Jason?" she asked angrily. "I told you I needed to do this alone."

He felt like grabbing her hand to pull her away from the place but she read his mind and said, "No, he's here and I'm not leaving."

Jason brushed the dirt from his pants and quietly said, "How do you know? It's so quiet in here."

She glanced around nervously. "He called me here. That's all I know. I've been standing here in the darkness waiting."

Jason nodded and looked at the stairs. "Have you been up there yet?" he asked.

"No," she answered. "I haven't been here very long. I stood outside for quite a while trying to get my nerve up before I finally came inside."

Jason looked around again and said, "Ok, so we're *both* here now. Where is he?"

Rebecca listened to the silence and said, "I wish I knew. I don't like this. It's too quiet."

Jason felt the hairs on the back of his neck standing up because of being so close to the mannequin and said, "Let's check the upstairs. I have to get away from that thing."

Rebecca nodded in agreement and whispered, "Stay behind me at all times."

Jason gently grabbed her arm. "The hell I will."

She was about to scold him when they heard the faint sound upstairs. It sounded like the soft cry of a small bird in the distance and Rebecca's face turned pale. "Stay close to me," she said.

The stairs were old and rusty and flakes of steel fell from them as they slowly crept upstairs. Compared to the first floor, this one was almost completely barren with only a few wooden pallets lying about.

Rebecca frowned. "Something's not right. Where the hell is he?"

Jason's eyes adjusted to the semi darkness and he saw something off in the distance by the far wall. "Look! More mannequins," he whispered.

Rebecca put her finger to her lips as a signal to be quiet and they slowly walked to the figures standing side by side. As they got closer, Jason saw that there were three of them. "Let's get out of here," he said, suddenly stopping. "I really don't like mannequins."

Rebecca sniffed the air and her lower lip quivered. Her eyes opened wide with fright as she looked at Jason. He felt his heart begin to race and whispered, "What's wrong?"

"I smell blood," she said and walked ahead towards the mannequins.

Jason reluctantly followed and when they were two feet from the mannequins his eyes opened wide in horror.

They weren't mannequins at all. They were the naked bodies of three women. Their breasts had been horribly mutilated and Jason saw that the murderer hadn't stopped there. Blood dripped to the floor from between their legs and he knew they'd also been raped.

"Oh my God!" he shouted and fell to his knees when he saw that one of the poor women was still alive. He threw up and gagged on the bile in his throat and rocked himself with his arms.

Rebecca lightly touched the woman's face and her frightened eyes locked onto hers. "Please kill me," she whispered. "I'm in so much pain. I can't stand it."

Rebecca looked closer and saw that the women's wrists were tied together with barbed wire which was attached to iron spikes jammed into the wall behind them which held them upright.

Jason began to cry. "Do something for her!" he whispered. "You have to help her!"

Rebecca looked sadly at him and shook her head because she knew there was nothing she could do. The dying woman suddenly gurgled and her head fell forward until her chin touched her chest.

"Go home to God now. He's waiting for you," Rebecca whispered and lightly stroked the woman's cheek. She turned to Jason and sadly said, "She's dead."

Jason managed to get to his feet and avoided looking at the poor women's faces. He bent low and saw the name "Rebecca" scrawled in blood on each of their bellies. He glanced up at the angel and said, "He really hates you. Why would he do this to them?"

"I have no idea," she said. "I really wish I knew though."

Jason spit bile from his mouth onto the floor and rubbed his stomach. It hurt and he felt like throwing up again.

Rebecca walked around the floor and said, "Why did he call me here? To taunt me?"

Jason went to one of the broken windows and looked out into the night. He saw something and his face quivered. Rebecca moved to where he was and looked out the window. An apartment building off in the distance was on fire and black smoke billowed upwards into the glowing sky. It moved around in slow sensuous movements and to their horror began to form letters. "Oh my God," Jason whispered.

"It's time," Rebecca said. She was strangely calm and Jason felt like she had somehow resigned herself to the inevitable.

She turned away from the window and headed downstairs. He took one last look at the letters in the sky before he followed her.

"*Rebecca,*" they spelled.

CHAPTER NINETY TWO

They ran to the building as fast as they could. When they arrived the firemen were already there and screaming at each other. They could see people's frightened faces in the windows above and seemed powerless to help them.

"What's wrong?!" Jason yelled, out of breath.

"We can't get in!" a fireman yelled back. "I've never seen anything like it! The doors and windows won't break!"

Rebecca pulled Jason aside and said, "Are you ready, Jason? Will you help me finish my story?"

He smiled. "You're asking me? You'll really let me help you?"

"Yes, but on one condition. You get those people out that are trapped inside. Let me deal with him alone. Understand?"

"Ok, let's go," he said and to the astonished eyes of the firemen, the angel scooped Jason up in her arms and extended her beautiful white wings. She squatted and with a powerful thrust of her legs flew high into the air. Looking down at the burning building, she yelled, "Brace yourself! We're going in hard!"

Jason screamed as she flew downwards at top speed towards the roof. Right before they were about to hit headfirst, she retracted her wings and flipped around so her feet would hit first. There was a slight resistance but the roof gave way and they crashed through it and landed in a smoky hallway. Rebecca put Jason down and he picked pieces of the ceiling out of his hair. "Wow, that was something," he said.

The angel heard screams in the distance and shouted, "This way!"

They found a stairway which led down to the next floor and there were people crowding the hallway. They were terrified and pounding on the exit doors. Rebecca pushed them back and yelled, "Stay back!"

She lashed out with her leg and the first door burst free from its hinges. "Run!" she yelled.

The crowd ran down the stairs to the next level and she moved to the next exit door and did the same thing. "Jason!" she screamed. "Get them out!"

He grabbed her and cried, "I need a kiss first!"

"Of course!" she said and kissed him. Her tongue drove deep into his mouth and wrapped around his in a loving embrace. Jason's eyes went wide as her power raced into his muscles. Rebecca's eyes closed for a moment and when they reopened he saw the love in them. Her tongue released his then and she said, "Remember, Jason. Get them out of here. Don't come back inside."

He nodded and looked at the crowd. "Come on!" he yelled. "Follow me!"

He raced down the stairs with men, women and children not far behind. The next floor was filled with smoke and the exit doors were locked again. Jason screamed and pounded at them with his fists until they burst open. Floor by floor, the crowd watched in amazement as he smashed past every obstacle. When they finally got to the bottom level, Jason found the doors curiously unlocked. He hurried the tenants out and waved at the firemen to come inside. They rushed to the open doors but couldn't step through.

"What the hell?!" the captain yelled. "Something's stopping us!"

Jason stuck his hand through the door and grabbed onto a fireman's arm. He tried to pull him through the door but had no success. Something unknown was keeping anyone outside from coming in. He heard a scream somewhere above him and looked helplessly at the captain.

"There are more in there!" the man shouted. "Get them out!"

He nodded and the locket suddenly glowed brightly. *Rebecca needs me*, he thought.

"I'm coming, my love," he whispered and grabbed the locket in his hand. Raw energy flowed through him and he smiled.

Just then, a small piece of ceiling fell a few feet away and he knew he had to get to the angel soon. Something deep inside his mind told him the battle was about to begin. It was time to fight.

CHAPTER NINETY THREE

As he raced towards the screams, Jason worried about Rebecca. Where was she? Was she alright?

Rebecca found a few doors that were on fire and extinguished the flames with her wings long enough to get the people out that were trapped inside. "Head downstairs as fast as you can!" she shouted. They did as she said and she stood in the hallway listening for more screams.

"*Rebecca….*" a low voice spoke from somewhere in the distance. The voice was almost sensuous in a way and Rebecca felt herself drawn to it.

"Where are you?" she asked and the voice whispered, "*Here….I'm here….Come closer….You're almost there.*"

She turned and saw a closed door at the end of the hallway. The fire which surrounded it was acting oddly. It seemed to dance around the edges of the doorframe. *He's there*, she thought. *He's waiting inside for me.*

Jason heard terrified cries coming from behind the last door on the floor he was on. It was closed and he saw gray smoke billowing out from underneath it. He put his hand against it and felt the intense heat from the other side. "Is anybody in there?!"

"Help us!" a woman's voice screamed in response. "We can't get out! There's too much fire!"

Jason stepped away from the door a foot and then exploded into it. He burst through the shattered wood and saw flames all around. "Over here!" the woman screamed from behind a couch in the corner of the room.

Jason ran to her and could barely make her out through the smoke.

"Come on! Let's get out of here!" he shouted.

She didn't move and he reached out to grab her. He froze when he touched her arm. It was hard to the touch. *What the hell?*, he thought.

He pulled on her arm and it came off her body. He cried out and quickly pulled her body to him.

The female mannequins eyes opened wide and she smiled at him.

"Thank you for rescuing me, Jason," she said seductively. "Wanna fuck?"

He screamed and dropped the horrifying thing. Standing up on shaky legs, he stared down in horror at it and it began to laugh maniacally. He backed slowly out of the room and the mannequin shrieked, "You can't save her, Jason!"

"No!!" he screamed and backed slowly out of the room. The thing began to laugh again and he felt pure terror grip his heart. His love was in trouble.

"Rebecca," he whispered. "Where are you?"

Rebecca stood in front of the closed door and the surrounding flames flicked out at her as if they were inspecting her to see who she was. She grabbed the doorknob and slowly turned it. The door creaked open and she stepped inside.

He was standing by the window in the darkness.

"I've been waiting for you, Rebecca," his voice said in a slithery whisper. "You and I have unfinished business."

The angel heard a moan and saw a naked young woman tied to a chair in the corner of the room. Her hands were tied behind her back and she struggled to free them when she saw Rebecca.

"Help my daughter! Please don't let him hurt her!"

Rebecca looked closer and saw the little girl huddled in fear behind the chair. She gripped the legs tightly and stared with terrified eyes at Rebecca.

Rebecca turned back towards the dark figure. "Let them go. It's me you want."

"No. I *need* them."

"Why? Why did you come back?"

"Because I wasn't finished eliminating the *pure* ones."

"Why do you hate us so much?" she asked.

He stepped out of the shadows into the light of the fire coming from the doorway and smiled. Rebecca noticed there was no other fire in the room other than around the doorway and thought it was strange.

"You did this," she said. "You started the fire and you're controlling it. How?"

"You asked why I hate you and your kind," he said, ignoring her question. "You're wrong there. I don't *hate* you. In fact, I love all of you for what you've given me up to now."

"What do you mean?" she asked as he stepped forward to meet her. "I've given you nothing!"

When he was about a foot away, he stopped and she could feel his warm breath on her face. His eyes weren't dead anymore. Instead, they were alive with joy.

"Oh, but you have and you will again. Your purity is what I need in order to gain strength so I can serve him," he answered.

"Him?" she said calmly.

A small trickle of blood escaped from the corner of his mouth and dripped down his chin. "My master," he answered softly. "You have yours and I have mine. You and I aren't much different from one another, you know."

"You're wrong! I'm an angel!" she said angrily, "and you're nothing but a perverted murdering monster!"

His hand reached out and she didn't flinch when he lightly touched her cheek. "Poor Rebecca, you don't see it, do you? You and I are the same."

"Stop saying that! We're *not* the same!" she spat back at him.

He chuckled in response and she stared into his eyes and felt the same level of fear she'd known the moment he'd strangled her all those years before.

"*Yes*, I can see you remember," he quietly said. "I took everything from you that night or so I thought."

Tears formed in her eyes then and her lower lip quivered. "Why?!" she cried. "I was a good girl! I never hurt anyone! Why did you kill me?!"

A small dark spot appeared on the floor behind him and began to expand. Rebecca's eyes opened wide with fear and he smiled and gently wiped away a tear which ran down her cheek with a finger.

"I already told you. You were kind and good and loving, that's why," he answered. "I had to take you to satisfy my king. Now that you're an angel you'll be my supreme gift to him."

"No!" she yelled and shoved him backwards with her hands and moved back towards the doorway. He laughed and pointed to the tied woman and her daughter.

"Your life for theirs!" he shouted. "That's the deal!"

Rebecca looked over at the terrified woman and her daughter and said, "No deal. You can't have any of us."

He was faster than she'd expected and within a blink of the eye he was standing by the helpless woman. His hands roughly fondled her breasts and she groaned in pain.

"Get away from her," Rebecca growled.

"Come with me or she dies right now," he said as he gripped her breasts tightly. The woman cried out and Rebecca knew she had no choice.

"Stop....just stop," she said. "What happens if I go with you?"

He licked his lips and leered at her. "I take home the ultimate prize....you. My king will put me in charge of his army then."

"You?!" she laughed. "You're nothing but scum!"

He glowered at her and she saw his forehead bulge slightly outwards. His eyes turned a strange shade of black and he calmly said, "Just think about the fun we'll have together in hell. Whenever I want, I'll play with those lovely tits of yours and your cunt. You're going to scream until you can't scream any longer but I'll never stop hurting you. I'll feed off your power like a leech."

Rebecca shrank back from his cruel words and shuddered at the thought of being perpetually tortured by the madman. He waited a moment and then bent low to take one of the woman's nipples into his mouth. Rebecca knew what he was about to do and shouted, "No!"

He raised his head and smiled. "You'll go with me then? Willingly?"

Her head lowered in defeat. "Yes," she whispered.

"No, you won't," came a voice from the doorway behind her.

She whipped around and saw Jason standing there.

"Well, well!" the murderer laughed. "Come on in and join the party, old man!"

Jason stepped into the room and Rebecca's murderer glared at him. "So we meet again. That damn locket won't help you now. I'm much stronger than the last time we met."

Jason sneered at him. "We'll see, Austin," he said in a low determined voice.

The monster looked at Rebecca and snickered. "Why don't you tell this idiot what I am?!"

Rebecca felt the chill race down her spine but bravely said, "Tell him what? That you're a perverted scum who preys on helpless women?"

The man's eyes narrowed. "I guess I'll just have to show you what I am."

Jason and Rebecca watched as he stepped away from the tied woman. He began to groan and looked as if he was in intense pain. His shirt and pants tore in spots as his muscles expanded and he cried out as his bones cracked to accommodate the new muscle mass.

Blood seeped from two spots on his forehead and he grimaced as two small horns emerged. His face became fuller and his teeth grew longer until they were sharp and pointed. Jason gasped at the horrifying transformation and the monster's flesh turned a sapphire blue. His clothes finally tore completely away and his large penis was exposed. The tied woman screamed in terror at the sight of it and then blood colored wings sprouted from his back. A long tail emerged from his backside and the transformation was complete. He stood looking at them and smiled. Though he was pure evil, he was magnificent in a way.

"What is he?" Jason gasped.

Rebecca swallowed hard and whispered, "He's an angel….an angel of death."

The monster extended his clawed hand and whispered seductively, "Come with me now, Rebecca or I kill the girl and her mother."

Rebecca's eyes narrowed and she whispered, "No."

Before anyone could react, she launched herself at the demon. Her wings blew out from her back and she screamed, "You can't have any of us! I'll kill you first!"

The monster laughed and dealt a savage blow to her face. Rebecca shook it off and clawed at his thick neck with her hands as she attempted to strangle him but it was so muscular that she couldn't get a good grip and he shoved her backwards. She landed sideways and he stood over her, holding his erect penis in his hand. He stroked it and cruelly said, "After I win, I'm going to strip you and shove this deep inside your cunt. Just think about it. Satan's angel is going to fuck you."

Blood seeped from its tip and dark blue veins ran the length of its blood red shaft and Rebecca felt complete and utter horror at the thought of the monster raping her. Rage filled her and she sneered bravely at him.

"You're not an angel," she said. "In fact, you're nothing at all.

What is your purpose? To hurt? To kill? That's not a purpose that God would be proud of."

The monster snarled and Jason moved towards him. Rebecca yelled, "Jason, no! Stay back!"

The little girl suddenly ran from behind the chair and began to hit the demon in the back with her tiny fists. His tail whipped out and hit her in the chest. Something snapped in it and she collapsed to the floor.

"No!!" her mother shrieked.

Rebecca tried to rise but the demon grabbed her around the neck and lifted her up. She kicked out and he grunted from the powerful blow to his stomach and dropped her. She rubbed her neck and inhaled deeply before charging at him. He was unprepared for her savagery and her blows drove him backwards towards the far wall. His hideous face exploded in blood each time she hit him and she looked quickly back at Jason and screamed, "Get them out of here!"

Jason was only able to take one step before the demon's tail lashed out and wrapped around his leg. It pulled violently then and he fell heavily to the floor.

The demon was weakening as a result of Rebecca's powerful blows. He groaned and finally his eyes closed as he slumped to the floor. The small hole in the middle of the floor had expanded and was now two feet in circumference. Jason crawled over and gasped when he looked down into it. There was fire spewing from the steaming rocks surrounding its sides and the screams of the damned rose upwards towards him. Heat poured from the hole and Jason whispered, "Oh my God."

Rebecca slammed her fist into the monster's face one last time and stepped over to where Jason was. Looking down into the hole, she said, "It's the entrance to hell. I beat him so why doesn't it close?"

They didn't hear the demon rise behind them until he cackled fiendishly.

"Oh my God," Rebecca gasped. She quickly kissed Jason and he felt strong again. The demon laughed and said, "You're lovers? I should have known!"

He grabbed Rebecca before she could react and flung her towards the wall. She hit hard and slumped to the floor. Jason jumped to his feet and punched the monster in the jaw. The blow surprisingly drove him backwards and he smiled.

"Jason, no!" Rebecca shouted. "You can't fight him! He's too strong for you!"

He ignored her and the locket glowed brightly and he staggered the creature with a punch to his cheek. The thing grabbed its face in pain and lashed out with its claws. Jason's chest ripped open and blood spurted from the wound. He screamed and looked down to see a rib was exposed. The monster laughed and grabbed Jason by the throat and lifted him high into the air.

"Pathetic useless mortal," it hissed. "You're *nothing*. You've *always* been nothing. *You* serve no purpose."

Tears welled in Jason's eyes and he gurgled, "You're wrong! I do have a purpose!"

The creature smirked and threw him violently to the floor. Jason felt his shoulder dislocate and he screamed in agony. The demon quickly pulled the locket from around his neck and threw it to the side.

"Now you can die," he said.

Rebecca drove into the monster with her shoulder and he flew sideways. Before he could hit the floor, she punched him relentlessly over and over again but he shrugged off the blows and drove a crushing uppercut into her jaw. Her neck cracked and she started to fall but he caught her and lowered her slowly to the floor. He wiped blood from his face with the back of his hand and looked at her with admiration.

"A valiant effort but I've won. I'm taking you home now, my lovely angel so I can ravage you for all eternity."

"No!" she cried weakly and he smiled. Her body ached horribly and she knew she'd lost. The demon grabbed her by the feet and began to drag her towards the expanding hole.

"No! Please don't!" she cried in a terrified panic. "I don't want to suffer!"

The monster laughed and said, "Yes, you *will* suffer and I'll become stronger from every scream that comes from your mouth."

The demon climbed into the hole and Rebecca clawed at the floor as he began to drag her towards it. Jason lay moaning and holding his shoulder and she called out to him.

"Jason! I need you! Please don't let him take me!"

He groaned and saw her lower legs had already disappeared into the hole. "No," he whispered and prepared himself. He screamed and slammed his shoulder into the floor to reset it. The pain was tremendous and tears rolled down his cheeks as he sat groaning.

"Jason! Jason!" she screamed.

"Rebecca," he moaned when he felt the last remnant of strength from her kiss fade away. He slumped in defeat and her eyes became hard.

"Jason! What are we?!" she yelled.

He groaned in pain, his entire body weak and hurting more than it ever had in his life. "What?" he moaned.

"What are we?!" she yelled again. Her stomach scraped against the edges of the hole and she clawed desperately to avoid being dragged further. There was a sick giggle below her and she cried out as the demon ran his clawed hand up between her legs to grip her there.

"The army of God," Jason whispered, his eyes closing.

"Yes, Jason! We're the army of God! I need you to fight for me! I know you can do it!"

"I can't," he moaned. "I hurt so badly."

"You can!" she screamed and shuddered when the demon's fingers slipped inside her. Rebecca knew she'd be helpless soon and he'd have her.

Jason got to his feet and stumbled towards her. She stretched her arm out to him and cried, "Yes, Jason! Be my hero! Save me!"

"Rebecca," he moaned again but the crippling pain he felt made him wince and fall. Why was his body failing him at the moment he needed it most?

Rebecca's eyes pleaded with him and he began to crawl towards her.

"Yes, Jason! Come to me! You can do it!" she shouted.

He crawled faster and she cried out in joy when his fingers touched hers.

"I've got you," he said and began to pull her towards him. He reached down with his other hand and grabbed the demon's wrist. "Let go of her," he growled. His grip tightened and the monster's fingers slipped out of her but grabbed onto her ankle.

Tears rolled down Rebecca's cheeks and she cried out, "Jason! You're my hero!"

Her words encouraged him and Jason was filled with impossible strength. He got to his feet and pulled upwards and she slowly emerged from the fiery hole.

"You're doing it!" she cried and the demon raged behind her as he was also pulled out of the hole.

Jason kicked the monster's hand loose from her and it rose to its full height. Before Rebecca could get out of the way, it slammed into her with all its strength and she slumped unconscious to the floor. Then it turned to Jason and smiled.

"Now, mortal. I'm going to make *you* suffer," it snickered.

Jason lifted his arms and whispered, "Please, lord. I love Rebecca with all of my heart. Please help me protect her. Let me join your army."

A blast of light suddenly shot through the ceiling and showered

Jason with its brilliant glow. It wasn't strength he felt though. It was God's intense love for him.

The demon had to shield its face from the light and Jason advanced on it.

The wound in his chest sealed and the demon squinted back at him.

"You can't win!" it shouted. "I have Satan on my side!"

Rebecca moaned and opened her eyes. She saw the brilliant glow surrounding Jason and smiled.

"My love," she whispered. "God's answered your call."

Jason looked back at her and smiled.

"What are we?" she asked weakly.

Jason's face was grim and determined. "The army of God," he said as he moved closer to the monster.

The angel gathered as much strength as she could then and screamed, "What are we?!!"

"The army of God!!" he shouted and rushed at the demon. The monster met him halfway and reached out with its claws to grab his hands. They stood locked in a standstill and their foreheads butted together. Jason stared into the cruelest eyes he'd ever known and knew no living man had ever faced evil such as this before.

Their muscles tore and healed and the process repeated as they remained locked in their struggle to see who was the strongest. Sweat poured from Jason's body and he felt himself begin to weaken.

"No...." he whispered as the monster slowly pushed him back.

The creature laughed a hideous laugh and whispered, "Just think, Jason. She'll be my pet every second, every minute and every hour of her angelic life in hell. I'll take her over and over again and she'll wish to die."

"No!" Jason yelled and called upon every bit of strength he had. The demon felt the man's power coming back and screamed in frustration.

Jason grit his teeth and pushed the demon closer to the hole. In desperation, the monster roared and bit into Jason's neck. He tore a chunk of flesh away and Jason howled in agony and lay down to die.

The demon turned away and walked towards Rebecca. She tried to rise but he grabbed her by the face and slammed her head against the wall. Her eyes rolled in her head and she lashed out weakly with her fists but he avoided them easily.

"Now you come with *me*," he sneered.

She gurgled helplessly and he pulled her towards him so her face was against his.

"You're going to enjoy hell," he whispered and she moaned when he licked her ear.

"Oh God, Jason! Help me! Help me please!" she cried pitifully as the demon dragged her again towards the fiery entrance to hell.

Jason sat up and looked down at the floor at the spreading pool of blood spouting from his neck and grimaced. *It can't end this way*, he thought. *My angel needs me.*

He got to his feet and with a surge of strength powered by God's love he charged at the monster.

The demon's eyes opened wide in surprise as Jason's hands wrapped around his neck.

"Let go of her!" the man screamed. "You can't have her!"

The monster stared in shock and saw the fury in Jason's eyes. *Where was the man getting his power from? He should be dead by now*, he thought.

Jason was actually hurting him and he released Rebecca. She slumped to the floor and looked up at Jason. "Do it, Jason. I know you can," she said.

The monster tried to pry Jason's hands away but couldn't. In desperation, he clawed strips of flesh from his arms but still Jason wouldn't let go.

Jason wrestled the monster over to the hole. "Go back to hell, you bastard!" he snarled and threw him down into it.

An immense feeling of relief ran through him and he turned back to Rebecca and smiled. "I did it," he said.

Her eyes opened wide when she saw the clawed hand emerge from the hole. "Jason, watch out!" she screamed.

The demon climbed out and stood at its full height. It cackled and Jason turned to face it again. "Your woman is *mine*," the monster whispered.

"No!!" Jason screamed and threw himself at him, driving them both into the hole.

"Jason!!" Rebecca screamed when she saw them disappear into hell.

She crawled over to the hole and looked down into it. Screams of agony bellowed from its depths and she ignored the intense heat and again screamed, "Jason!"

There was no answer for a long time and she moved away from the pit and rocked herself in her arms and sobbed. The unnatural fire the demon had created around the doorway began to spread then and she looked through the open door to see it racing down the length of the hallway. She didn't hear the scraping noise coming from the pit and suddenly something touched her leg.

"Rebecca," the raspy voice weakly said.

She quickly turned and saw Jason crawling from the pit. He was horribly burned and she gently pulled him out. The hole slowly closed then until there was no trace of it. She found the locket on the floor and put it back around his neck. He began to slowly heal and pointed to the tied woman.

"Help her," he weakly said.

Rebecca untied the woman and she rushed over to her daughter. She picked her up and the girl was limp in her arms.

"Oh my God!" she screamed. "She's dying! Oh God! She's dying!"

Jason staggered over and went to his knees in front of the girl. He knew what he had to do. Looking at Rebecca, his eyes asked for permission and she nodded. He removed the locket from his bleeding neck and placed it around the little girls. Her color improved immediately and she moaned in pain.

"She'll be alright now," Jason rasped. "Have her wear this always."

"Oh, she will! Oh God! Thank you so much!" the mother cried and gently touched his scorched cheek. "You're a good man."

"Go," he said.

She nodded and scooped her daughter up. She looked back at him before leaving and said, "God bless you."

He watched her go and felt a massive wave of pain sweep over him. He slumped over and Rebecca grabbed him.

"Oh Jason!" she cried and opened her wings to protect him from the suddenly expanding flames that came closer to them. She held him in her arms and he shuddered from the pain.

"I killed him," he gasped weakly.

"You saved me, Jason," she whispered as tears fell from her eyes. "You're *my* guardian angel."

Rebecca wiped the tears away and looked over his body. His neck wound pulsed blood and he was bleeding from many wounds. From the way his breathing sounded, she knew he'd also inhaled fire.

"Rebecca," he asked in a voice so quiet she could barely hear him.

She pulled him closer and said, "Yes, Jason. I'm here."

His pain filled eyes gazed into hers and she could tell he was frightened.

"Am I dying?" he asked.

Her lower lip trembled as she looked into the eyes of the man she loved with all of her heart.

"Yes, Jason, you are. It's your time. Your story has come to an end."

"I'm afraid," he whispered.

"I know you are," she said and kissed him.

This time her kiss gave him no power and she saw the light begin to fade in his eyes. She held him closer and he reached up to touch her face with his charred fingers. "Rebecca, are you my soulmate?" he asked.

The angel's eyes flooded with tears again and they slid down her cheeks. "*Yes*, Jason, I'm your soulmate," she answered.

He smiled and caressed her cheek with his fingers. "I love you," he whispered.

"Oh God, Jason!" she cried. "I love you too! I love you so much!"

He smiled again and whispered, "My angel."

His eyes closed then as his hand slowly fell back to his chest and she knew he was gone.

"Jason! Oh God! Jason!!" she screamed and pulled him tightly against her and rocked him in her arms.

The fire suddenly raced through the open doorway and crept up the walls and licked the floorboards as it came closer. She knew she had to make a decision. *I can't let it end this way*, she thought. "I'll love you forever," she whispered and kissed the man's lips. She retracted her wings then and let the fire consume her. There was no pain and she only felt a slight tingling in her muscles. She felt a moment of fear but then looked again into the face of the man she loved and smiled. *I'll remember,* she thought.

Her consciousness faded away as their souls floated together to the place where people are reborn. It was a place where they went for a second chance at life. It was a place where souls went for a second chance at love.

CHAPTER NINETY FOUR
TWENTY FIVE YEARS LATER

He'd come here many times before because something drew him to the old apartment building he'd seen in his dreams. Something had happened here many years before but he wasn't sure what. He only knew that he found comfort here by being so close to the building.

He stared up at the window on the second floor which had a sign in it. It read APARTMENT FOR RENT and there was a phone number to call. The window seemed so familiar to him and he shivered as he felt the cool breeze tickle his neck.

He knew she'd be here soon. She usually came after he left. The last few times he'd stayed and hid behind a tree and watched her as she stood where he stood now, staring up at the same window.

This time however, she arrived while he was still there. He turned and saw her standing at the corner. Today she was wearing the blue beret he liked. There was a slight chill in the air and she hugged herself for a moment. He watched her pull her coat tighter around her body and then she saw him. Her arms dropped to the sides. He held his breath as she slowly walked towards him. When she was only feet away, she stopped and looked at him strangely.

"You're here again," she said.

"What do you mean?" he asked, surprised. She had a British accent which he immediately liked.

"You come here every Saturday just like I do. Usually you watch me from behind that tree over there."

She pointed at the tree and his face turned red.

"I'm sorry. Please believe me. I wasn't stalking you."

"Why are *you* here?" she asked and came closer. He was a handsome man with long wavy brown hair which blew gently in the wind.

Up close, Anthony saw how beautiful the woman was. She was shorter than he was and her long hair was the color of light gold and her lovely face was kind and welcoming.

"I'm not sure," he answered. "But I feel at home here. Something draws me here that I can't explain."

She nodded and looked up at the second floor window. "That's strange. I feel the same way. I dream of this place, you know."

His eyes opened wide in surprise. "Oh my God! So do I!"

She looked at him more intensely and extended her hand. "My name's Melissa."

Anthony felt a lump in his throat and quietly said, "I'm Anthony." He took her hand in his and there was a small electric shock when their fingers touched and they both laughed.

"I wonder what that means," she said.

"Maybe it's telling us something," he softly said.

Her eyes gazed into his and he felt himself falling into them. They seemed so incredibly familiar. She pulled her hand away.

"Have we met before?" he asked. "I feel like I know you from somewhere."

Her full lips parted and he wondered how they'd taste.

"I'm pretty sure we haven't but I feel the same way."

There was something about his eyes that struck her suddenly. They were warm and tender and she knew she'd seen them before which was impossible.

She tore her eyes away from his then and looked over at the sign a few feet away from the apartment building. It was stuck in the grass close to the sidewalk and read: JOIN THE ARMY OF GOD….MEETING AT ST. JOSEPH'S CHURCH TONIGHT 7PM.

Anthony looked over at the sign and said, "It seems to be spreading. I haven't joined yet. Have you?"

"No, I haven't but I've thought about it," she answered.

"I don't want to seem creepy but would you like to go to the meeting with me? The church isn't far from here." he asked, hopeful.

She smiled for the first time then and he felt a tremendous ache in his heart. *Oh God*, he thought. *I just want to hold you!*

"I'd love to," she said and moved a little closer to him. There was something about him that made her feel safe. *Who are you?* she thought. *I know you somehow.*

She came closer until their bodies were almost touching and looked up at his face. "I *do* know you," she whispered. "But I don't know from where."

Anthony tried to hold himself back but couldn't resist the urge and touched her cheek with his hand. He suddenly realized what he'd done and was about to pull away but she put her hand over his to keep it there.

"It's alright," she whispered. "I don't mind."

His eyes welled with tears then and he wanted so much to pull this beautiful woman who he'd never met before into his arms and kiss her and hug her and love her. Something deep in those beautiful eyes of hers was calling him and a tear slipped down his cheek.

"Don't cry," she softly said. "You're safe with me."

She moved closer and lay her head against his shoulder and they both turned to look up at the second floor window again.

"It says it's for rent," she said.

They looked at each other then and suddenly knew. The apartment held the answers to their questions. They looked up at the window again and moved as one and went into the building. Once inside the small lobby near the stairs leading up to the apartment, the feeling of familiarity grew stronger and Melissa looked into Anthony's eyes and he didn't resist their pull. He leaned over and kissed her. Her eyes opened wide and she returned his kiss. It was intimate and as gentle as a feather. He pulled back in surprise. *I know this kiss!* his shocked mind screamed at him. Melissa watched him carefully and her eyes twinkled. Anthony felt a soothing wave of warmth rush through him then as she raised up on tiptoes and put her lips by his ear.

"I *remember*," she whispered.

Please visit the Youtube channel: Hal Dickens Songwriter and go to the Jason And The Angel - novel playlist for added emotional impact to this story. The track that should be played at this moment is the song sung by Bunny Lo called "I Remember."
You will also find more music and songs written specifically for certain scenes from this book.

Novels by Hal Dickens coming in 2019:

Jason And The Angel (Soulmates)

Jessica , The Demon And The Torturer